UNDER A BLOOD MOON

JOHN DEAL

DARK LAKE
PRESS

UNDER A BLOOD MOON
ISBN-13: 978-1-7375382-2-6 (paperback)
ISBN-13: 978-1-7375382-3-3 (ebook)

Cover design by Danna Mathias Steele, Dearly Creative

Dedicated to the wonderful people of the Lowcountry, a place with beaches, marshes, lots of water, a diverse culture, and a long history, and the two littlest men in my life.

On December 21, 2010, something occurred that hadn't happened in nearly four hundred years. The winter solstice, a lunar eclipse, and a full moon all coincided. The winter solstice marked the longest night of the year, fourteen hours of darkness, and when the eclipse reached its peak in the early morning hours, the moon turned dark red . . . the color of blood.

Elias's frail eight-year-old body was snug in the dark little crevice. His pale ice-blue eyes were riveted to the old Black man in the dim light. He was invisible, and he liked it that way. It was safer.

The old man mumbled words he didn't understand. His hands flew, and items appeared from a wooden box one by one. Crude items made of stone and bone, then short white candles, which he put on the floor. Over each, he spoke, more strange words.

The old man held up something white and tan, then he crushed it into powder using his tools. Over and over, the old man repeated the process, mixing the powders and pouring them into a small bag—then more mumbling. Once filled, the bag was placed in the ring of brightly burning candles.

Elias's breath caught when the old man's milky eyes shifted. "I know you're there."

Elias squeezed his eyes shut tight. *No, no, no.*

"Don't be shy. Come out."

Is this a trick? How does he know I'm here?

A hand extended. "Come on now. I won't hurt you like he does. I'll teach you to be powerful so no one can hurt you. I'll show you how to stop the pain."

The boy stood and joined the old man.

—

Elias worked his way through bushes and crossed the yard under the moon's glow. He tried to be quiet as he crawled through his tiny bedroom window. As his second foot touched the ground, brightness engulfed him. Terror swallowed him when he saw the glossy, bloodshot eyes swaying in front of him.

Whiskey-laced breath hissed before the back of the old man's hand landed. "You ain't nothing but a worthless little freak. I hate you, and I hate my son for fathering you." Stars swirled before Elias's world went black.

Ten Years Later
Harleston Village, Charleston, South Carolina

The evening sky was angry, and it fueled Elias. Flashes crisscrossed the black clouds; rumbles followed, causing the shutters to rattle. He stood under the overhang and let the mist from the sheets of rain caress his face. He peered at the dates circled on the calendar he'd pulled from his pocket. This was a critical night. If the heavens gave him the go-ahead, his plan would at long last proceed. Deep, long inhale.

He forced the back door of the vacant house open with his shoulder and entered the darkness. A beam of light led him to a spot near the ash-covered hearth of a fireplace. Carefully, he removed a small wooden box from his bag. His fingers brushed against the emblem adorning the lid— it was his most precious possession. He opened the box.

Squatting, he used chalk to mark the floor. He shut his eyes and tried to remember how the white candles should be arranged. He needed to focus on the vision from his childhood.

Removing dried herbs from a burlap bag, he cut them into small pieces, then ground them into dust. He mixed the piles of dust together in a bowl and carefully poured the mixture into a small red cloth bag, pulled the drawstrings tight, and dropped it in his backpack. He double-checked the pack—rope, roll of tape, and knives. When the sign came, he had to be ready.

At long last, the rain moved out, and the dark clouds split. Elias peered through the window, and his breathing stopped when he saw the brilliant orb. His pulse increased, and goose bumps covered his arms. He had hoped for the sign, but now that it had come, he was almost overwhelmed.

He grabbed the backpack, yanked the black hood over his head, and crept through the backyards, careful to stay close to the dense boxwood hedges and overhanging jasmine vines. He knew where he was going—he had planned it all for so long.

———

Naomi stood in her knee-length white nightgown, staring into the mirror, brushing her long brown hair as she got ready for bed. Elias's eyes flared as he watched her from under the limbs of a magnolia tree. The low hum of crickets drowned out his shallow breath.

Thirty minutes after the lights went dark, he removed the screen and crawled through the window. Then, silently, he slipped down the hall and into her bedroom. He stood at the foot of her bed, watching her chest rise and fall.

Her eyes went wide when his hands pressed the pillow over her face and the weight of his body pinned her down. She never had a chance to scream. Then, as the darkness came and her breath escaped, he whispered a word she didn't understand: "*H'aa't.*"

It had begun.

HUNTER'S MOON

The full moon at the time of year when the leaves are falling and the game is fat and ready to hunt. Also known as the travel moon.

Monday, October 25
The Business District, Charleston, South Carolina

I can't believe he's already done it again.

Charleston detective CJ O'Hara brushed her shoulder-length auburn hair back and lifted the sheet with her gloved hand. There were no signs of fluids on the mattress or linens. She scanned the bedroom floor—no used condom or wrapper. Again, nothing appeared out of place; it was just the unmade bed of a young woman who'd reported to the emergency room.

She leaned close, and her bright emerald-green eyes peered at the windowsill. Faint scratch marks scarred the mustard-yellow paint. *So that's how he got in.*

"CJ?" a familiar voice called to her.

"Back here."

Crime Scene Investigator Eddie Rodriquez appeared in the doorway. His tan khakis and a navy blue polo over his slim five-eight build offset his short brown hair. CJ loved working with Eddie due to his warm and friendly personality. His attention to detail and ability to remain positive no matter the situation made him an excellent CSI.

"Sorry, it took me a while. I had to swap out some equipment in the van."

She smiled. "No worries. Our week is off to a shitty start."

He sighed. "Yeah, just once, I'd like to finish a cup of coffee before these assholes disrupt things. So, what do we have?" he asked.

She looked at her notes. "A twenty-two-year-old woman named Cindy Evans came into the Roper emergency room at four this morning and reported a rape. She's still there getting her kit completed."

"Was she assaulted beyond the rape?"

She held up a Polaroid. "Yeah, he punched her in the left eye. She said the blow felt like her head exploded. She'll have a black-and-blue face for a while and a scar. The doc's gonna put in a few stitches, but there were no broken bones."

"Did she see him?"

"No. She told me he wore a mask, but she saw enough to know he was White. She said he was a younger guy and tall, but she couldn't give me anything else. Maybe she'll have more once she collects herself. I'll go back and check on her once we finish here."

Eddie had pulled on his latex gloves and scanned the room with a black light while she spoke. He frowned. "The UV's not showing any fluids. I'll have the crew collect the sheets and take the mattress back to the lab and double-check."

She pulled off her gloves and rubbed her eyes. *Damn it!* This was the fourth rape she'd worked in the last two months. The victims described the rapist as a tall, young White man with dark hair and light brown eyes. *Do we have a serial rapist running around Charleston?*

As Eddie dusted the window for fingerprints, she held her breath.

"Nothing." He shook his head. "He must have worn gloves."

CJ rubbed at the knot in her neck. She couldn't confirm with evidence, but her gut told her the same person had committed the last four rapes on file. "We need a break. My guess is it's the same assailant, and he'll eventually kill a victim once he gets bored with just raping them."

It was only midmorning, but Charleston was already a blast furnace. The temperature pushed toward ninety degrees, and the sun had baked the sidewalks and roadways. Humidity hung in the air; it was the kind of day where sweating in the shade was easy. CJ squinted against the glare off the black hood of her Ford Explorer.

She took a right off Calhoun Street onto Jonathan Lucas Street and turned into the Roper Lucas parking garage. She found a spot, parked, and briskly made her way to the emergency room. A Black nurse with a soft face and kind eyes took her back to Cindy Evans's bed.

Cindy sat on the edge of the bed and stared into space. Her long sandy-blond hair fell across her back, and her deep-blue eyes were swollen, red, and wet. A bandage covered the stitches under her left eye, and the bruising had become more pronounced. She nervously shifted her slender five-foot-six body when she saw the detective.

"Cindy, how are you feeling?" CJ quietly asked.

The young woman fought not to cry. "I'm okay, I guess. The doctor said she was almost finished, then I can go home."

CJ smiled at her and placed a hand on her arm. "Can I take you home, or do you have someone here?"

"My mom and dad are in the waiting room. They'll take me home with them to Moncks Corner. They live on Lake Moultrie." Cindy sniffed. "I don't want to be alone, and my boyfriend doesn't want to . . ." She crumpled and cried on CJ's shoulder.

The two women sat for several minutes—Cindy's sobs were the only noise that broke the silence. CJ waited until Cindy regained her composure and got dressed, and then they went to the lobby to meet her parents.

Simon and Nancy Evans were in their early fifties and badly shaken by the incident. Simon, six feet tall and husky, had his arm around his wife. Paint stains dotted his blue khaki shorts and yellow T-shirt. Nancy's wrinkled floral sundress swallowed her five-foot-six frame. Her light brown hair was a mess, and her deep-blue eyes, matching Cindy's, were puffy and glazed.

CJ knew neither had planned to come into the city today nor were prepared for this. *"Is any parent?"*

She provided an update on the case and outlined the next steps. She gave them her card and told them she'd keep them in the loop as the case progressed. They thanked her and escorted their daughter through the double entry doors. It was nearing noon as CJ turned and headed back to the emergency room.

———

Dr. Emerson flipped through the chart as CJ waited. She was midthirties with dark, almost black hair and serious, russet-brown eyes hidden behind wire-rimmed glasses. She finally glanced up. "There were no obvious signs of semen, but we ran the kit for the lab so we can check more closely."

CJ scribbled a note. "Let's hope the lab can find something that can help us. How about the physical damage?"

The doctor cleared her throat. "The patient had bruising consistent with forced intercourse. I doubt it will be an issue, but we collected a specimen to test for STDs just in case. We also put five stitches under her left eye. She should recover physically without issue—mental recovery is another story. It's gonna take the poor girl a long time."

CJ took a copy of the records and walked through the wall of heat to her truck. Her gray blouse stuck to her. The cool blast from the air-conditioning vents refreshed her. Dropping her forehead on the steering wheel, she rubbed again at the permanent vise on her neck.

———

At 1:10 p.m., CJ slid the key card and unlocked the door of the Chief John Conroy Law Enforcement Center, fondly known as the LEC. As she strode down the hallway, the pit was buzzing with officers talking to each other or on the phone. A light layer of condensation had settled on the windows, thanks to the battle between the outside and inside temperatures.

Investigator Ben Parrish stood at the end of the hallway in jeans, a white button-down, and a pair of cowboy boots. He was six feet four, and at thirty-one, he was still well built. His amber eyes contrasted with his dark brown hair.

She eyed him as she approached. *He is a handsome man.*

They had partnered on the Lowcountry Killer case. A case where ultimately it had turned out that Ben's twin brother, Bryan, had abducted, raped, and murdered eight women and his mother. Once it was closed, she had stayed with the Central Investigations Division, and he had returned to the Homicide Investigation Unit.

"Hey, Ben. What brings you by?" she asked.

He smiled at her. "Just wanted to stop by and see how you were doing. Dad and I had a great fishing trip in the Keys. He says hello."

"Glad you guys had a good trip. Tell your dad hello for me." She exhaled. "I'm still chasing whoever has committed four rapes. I just left the fourth victim, who checked herself into Roper this morning."

He shook his head. "Hope you get a break soon."

"Let's grab a drink in the next couple of days." She touched his arm. "I need to run and see Paul."

He nodded and hustled off, and she watched him walk away. The tension between them lingered in the air, and she jumped when her cell phone rang. *Area code 907 . . . Where is that?*

TWO

Monday, October 25
Downtown Charleston, South Carolina

CJ punched the green circle on her cell phone as she moved to a quiet corner of the LEC hallway. "Detective O'Hara."

"Hello, Detective. This is FBI special agent Wally Gauge. I'm in the FBI field office in Juneau, Alaska, and Special Agent Robert Patterson told me to call you."

She smiled. "How is Robert?"

"He's fine," he replied. "He's busy as hell chasing some guy in Virginia who likes middle-aged women. The bastard has managed to kill four so far. The press is calling him the Roanoke Strangler. He takes the victim's right hand as a souvenir."

"Jeez, sounds like a lovely fellow." There was silence. "Wally, is there something I can do for you?"

Papers rustled at the end of the line. "I hope so. The monster you caught in May, Bryan Parrish, lived in Sitka until he returned to Charleston. We have three rapes and murders here that may be his work before his killing spree there. I'm hoping you'll agree to review the files and give me your opinion. Robert told me you were a bright detective with damn good instincts. He gave me his opinion but told me I need yours as well."

She was honored by the compliment but wasn't sure how it worked for a detective in a small department to assist the FBI in a jurisdiction thousands of miles away. "Wally, I'd be happy to look at the files. I'll talk to my lieutenant about it, so he's in the loop."

"That would be great. I'd appreciate any help you can give me."

"No problem. You said there are three cases, right?" she asked.

"Yes. There were two in Sitka and one in Ketchikan. All with the same MO. He raped them, sliced their throats and midsections, and dumped them near the water. The three women were White and twenty-two to twenty-five years old, with light brown or blond hair and blue eyes. They were gorgeous.

"The FBI's Juneau office supports all of southeast Alaska on cases like this one. The police departments in Sitka and Ketchikan are small, with no more than thirty people in each."

She gave him her email address, and he agreed to email her the most critical files—police reports and crime scene photos. He let her know that there was no forensic evidence.

From his grave, where CJ had put him, the Lowcountry Killer's weight pressed down on her. The vise moved from her shoulders to her chest, and her pulse ramped up. Not a day had passed when she didn't relive a part of the case. The faces of his eight victims haunted her dreams, and every day the scar from the wound he had given her reminded her how close she had come to losing her life.

At 1:45 p.m., Lieutenant Paul Grimes motioned CJ in as he talked on the phone. Paul was Black, forty, and a narrow six feet tall. His close-clipped black hair was receding, and his hooded dark brown eyes focused on her. She had grown quite fond of him since transferring to Charleston from Boston in April.

Her cell phone buzzed, and she opened an email from Special Agent Wally Gauge. *That was quick.*

Paul hung up and asked, "How's the girl?"

"She's doing as well as can be expected," she replied. "Her parents have taken her back with them to Moncks Corner."

Nodding, he said, "Good. She needs support, and there's nothing like Mom and Dad to give it." He stood and looked out the window. "Alaska."

She was stunned. "You've heard?"

He chuckled. "Yes. That was the chief when you came in. Robert called him asking for support in having you review the case." He turned and stared at her. "I'm fine if you review some files here, but I'm not ready to agree that you should fly to Alaska as Robert requested. That'd be a long trip and take several days. I'm worried about these rapes and don't want you to take your eye off the ball. We're shorthanded. Understand?"

"Yes, sir. I'll review the files around my workload and give them my thoughts. It won't interfere."

As he settled back into his chair, he replied, "Fair enough." Then he leaned forward and pointed at CJ. "You're not putting it off any longer. Keep your appointment with the doc."

Her throat tightened, and she slowly nodded. "Yes, sir. I'll meet you and Cap in the conference room at three o'clock."

———

CJ stared at the evidence board in the conference room as she prepared for the meeting—four young women with bright smiles. Nothing like what she'd seen when she met with them at the hospital. The trauma of being raped had replaced their happy expressions with pain etched deep.

"Ready?" a voice asked from behind her.

She looked up at Paul's dark brown eyes. "Yes, sir. Hey, Cap."

He dropped into a chair, and Captain Stan Meyers did the same. Stan was slightly taller and older than Paul, six feet one, early forties, with dark brown hair and penetrating brown eyes.

She handed each of the men a summary of the four rape cases. She wished the small conference room had more air—it was stale, hot, and humid. Her arms stuck to the table. *We need a damn fan in here.* She took a deep breath and stood. "Okay, let's go over what we know so far."

For the next forty-five minutes, she covered the key points of each of the four cases—backgrounds on the victims, where they were raped, and what they remembered about their attacker.

As she passed photos across the table, she continued. "So far, our perp has been consistent and not crossed racial lines—they are all White women. All have been attractive, but age, hair, and eye colors have varied. There's nothing consistent about height or weight."

Stan picked up a photo. "Anything consistent with their backgrounds, place of work, anything like that?"

"No," she replied. "A waitress, a hotel clerk, an elementary school teacher, and a grad student. They don't know each other or run in the same circles."

"Any evidence?" Stan asked.

"Not yet. Forensics found no fingerprints or DNA at any of the scenes. Clearly, the rapist wore gloves, and he knows enough not to leave any of himself behind.

"Two women said it was too dark and they couldn't tell what race the man was or anything about his height or weight. Our third woman told me she believes he is White but wasn't sure of his physical attributes. Our latest victim says he was White and tall. Two women said he had dark hair and light brown eyes. Unfortunately, he wore a mask."

Stan stood and walked to the board. He looked at the map marked with the locations where the women were raped. "You said 'rapist'—singular. Do you think we have one guy or multiple?"

She shifted her weight. "My gut tells me it's the same guy for all four."

"Even with nothing on the first two?" Stan turned and stared at her.

A lump rose in her throat. "Yes. I believe it's the same guy. The MO matches in all four cases. He slips into the victim's home at night, attacks them while they sleep, and leaves nothing behind. He's calculating and a planner."

Stan's brown eyes remained fixed on her. "Okay, let's stay on it. Let me know what you need to get this guy off the street." He headed for the door, followed by Paul, and the room fell silent.

Does he agree with me?

CJ's cell phone broke the silence, and she glanced at the number before she answered. "Hey, Eddie. What's up?"

"I wanted to let you know we found a dark yellow fiber on the bedding from the Evans bedroom. I'd call it mustard. We'll run it to see if it might give us DNA. I expect we won't get results for several days, but let's hope we have a break."

"Thanks, Eddie. DNA would really help us chase this guy down."

"If there's no DNA, maybe we can narrow down something with the fiber," he added. "It looks like a thread or string under the microscope. Could be from a piece of clothing. We'll get it to SLED's fiber expert in Columbia. Not great, but it's a start." *SLED* was short for "State Law Enforcement Division."

"Absolutely," she replied. "Thanks for the update. Keep me posted."

"Will do. I'm gonna go back over and double-check if there's anything in the room that might match the fiber. Based on the video, there doesn't appear to be anything dark yellow in the room, but I want to recheck the closets."

It was almost four thirty when CJ closed the conference room door and walked past the buzzing bullpen to her desk. She logged on to her computer and popped open the first file from Alaska. A young woman, her eyes the color of the ocean on a sunny day under flowing blond hair, stared at her. Her smile was magnetic, and her skin was blemish free. She flipped to the next photo—*Oh my God.*

THREE

Monday, October 25
Harleston Village, Charleston

"Detective!"

CJ was lost in the crime scene photos she'd received from Alaska but snapped to attention.

Helen, from dispatch, stood in the doorway, her forest-green eyes wide under her curly reddish-blond hair. "I'm so sorry. I didn't mean to startle you. We have a body over in lower Harleston Village, and Paul said to send you to the scene. I've already sent Investigator Parrish, and officers are on site. It sounds really bad."

CJ closed the file she'd opened. As she stood, she glanced at the clock on the wall—5:14 p.m. "Let Paul know I'm on my way. Is the Crime Scene Unit en route?"

"Uh . . . not yet."

"Let's get them there," CJ curtly replied.

"Will do." Helen hustled off.

———

Officer Johnny Jones had just celebrated his fifth year with the force. Johnny had never seen anything as gruesome as this crime scene. He had to get out of the room and away from the rotten odor. Hands on knees, he struggled to regain his composure on the back porch of the Harleston Village home. *Deep, slow breaths. You gotta stay calm, man. Do your job.*

When Ben Parrish arrived, he leaned down to catch Johnny's eye. "You okay, Officer?"

Johnny stood. The young Black officer was almost as tall as Ben, six feet two, with jet-black hair and dark brown eyes. Embarrassed, Johnny did his best to get it together. "Yes, sir. I needed some air. Sorry, Investigator Parrish."

Ben still couldn't get accustomed to everyone's knowing who he was because of the Lowcountry Killer case. First, he had been a vital part of the investigation, then a suspect under arrest, and then he'd been back in everyone's good graces. "Not a problem. Some cases can hit you hard." He caught sight of Johnny's badge as he patted the officer on the shoulder. "Tell you what, Officer Jones, how 'bout you wait here while I take a look?"

"Ben?"

Ben turned to find CJ stepping onto the porch. "Hey, CJ."

"Paul sent me."

"I just got here and haven't gone in yet," he replied. "I'm working with Detective Jackson on one of his cases, and we were up in North Charleston." He turned back to Johnny. "Where's the body?"

"Bedroom on the first floor, past the den on the left." He motioned to the house. "The house also has a second bedroom upstairs, but it's used as a gym. The smell is wicked."

"Do we know who lives here?" CJ asked.

Johnny checked his notes. "Jeff and Naomi Sims."

CJ and Ben slipped on foot covers. When they were ready, he motioned to her. "After you."

"Oh gee, thanks."

The house was small, less than two thousand square feet. The kitchen, immediately inside the back door, was well kept. CJ checked the sink—it was clean, with no signs of blood. The trash can was empty. *Wonder when the trash is picked up?*

Ben squatted. "Place is spotless." He pointed at the floor. "The linoleum may give us something."

"Maybe." She bent over, hands on knees. "I don't see signs of footprints, but we'll have the CSU guys check it out."

The den area was separated by a partial wall, and like the kitchen, it was pristine. It held a small couch, a coffee table, a side chair, and a television. Not fancy, but very cozy. She pointed to a photo on the mantel above the gas fireplace. A man in a navy uniform was standing with a woman in a wedding dress. Both were smiling brightly. "Beautiful couple."

The odor of death increased as they moved down the short hallway—the smell of rotting garbage. When she entered the bedroom, the scent made her eyes water. Then she saw the reason for the stench. "Oh, Jesus." She stepped backward, slamming into Ben, who grabbed her by the waist. Her lunch rose in her throat. *Damn it, CJ, don't puke on the crime scene.*

CJ swallowed hard. "Let's get gowned and gloved up before we go in. We can't contaminate the scene."

"Okay. I'll go grab some stuff out of the car." Ben retraced his steps and left her standing alone in the doorway.

CJ stood staring at the nude body of a woman who looked about her age. Someone had cut her midsection open, and her mind flashed back to the victims of the Lowcountry Killer. The bed and surrounding carpet were bloodstained. In addition, there was blood spray visible on the wall behind the iron spindle headboard.

Rustling noises approached her. CJ turned to find Ben wearing a white gown. "Here you go. Might be a little big. CSU is pulling up, and I saw Eddie."

She simply nodded, stepped into the gown, and pulled on her latex gloves.

"Let's do this." She stepped across the threshold into the twelve-by-twelve bedroom—it was hot, humid, and stale. "Do you think we can pull back the curtains and get more light in here without letting onlookers see?"

He glanced at the sheer curtains and dimming early evening light. "I'm not sure how it will help with it getting dark, and there're people milling out front. I'm sure Eddie's crew will set up lights."

She stood as close to the bed as she could without stepping in the blood on the floor. The victim's mouth had been taped shut. Her glassy eyes stared blankly at the ceiling. Her midsection lay open, with two long flaps of skin folded outward, exposing her reddish-purple insides. A pillow, stained with blood, lay above her head. *Did she fight?*

"Hey, guys. This is a nasty mess," said a voice behind them.

They both glanced back at Eddie. Neither responded.

"The guys are bringing in portable lights, and we'll get to work," Eddie added.

CJ pointed toward the kitchen. "Can we have the kitchen floor dusted for prints before too much more traffic?"

"Sure thing. We'll do that before covering the room."

Ben held up his Maglite. "Let's use this. See if we find anything."

He joined her near the bed, and the beam moved from the foot of the bed to the head. There were no apparent signs of foreign substances. The light hit the pillow, and he pointed the beam at the bloodstains. "You think this is transfer, or did he have the pillow over her face?"

She leaned close, fighting the urge to gag from the coppery scent of blood. She gently pushed the pillow against the headboard. "My guess is the latter. I think he put the pillow over her face. Maybe he smothered her with it before taping her mouth."

He sighed. "It would explain how he killed her and kept her from screaming. We'll need to check again with the neighbors, but no one reported hearing anything."

The two worked their way around the room. There were no signs of forced entry. Other than the bed area, nothing looked unusual.

Eddie appeared in the doorway. "Okay, guys. We're ready to process the room. We've dusted the kitchen floor for prints. Nothing useful. There are some smudged footprints but not enough to give us size or pattern."

"Okay, we'll let you have the room," CJ said. "Ben and I will take a closer look around the house and interview any witnesses."

Eddie waved two of his crew into the room. "Let's set the lights up and work out to in. Be careful of the blood."

Johnny greeted them on the back porch as they came out and removed their gear. "The scene is secured," he advised. "I have officers on the perimeter, and I told them to keep any press on the street. We have two witnesses. The woman's coworker is in the back of my squad car, and a neighbor is on her porch. Both are shaken up, but the coworker is, well . . . hysterical. I asked one of our female officers to stay with her.

"I haven't taken the witness statements yet, only got some preliminary info. The coworker came to check on the vic, saw the back door ajar, went in, and found the body.

She screamed, and the neighbor came over. Both said they only went as far as the doorway of the bedroom."

CJ appreciated his thoroughness. "Thanks, Officer. There's no point of entry in the bedroom. You find one?"

He leaned in the door and pointed. "He came in through the window in the den. We found the screen leaning against the outside wall. I made sure it wasn't touched, and a tech dusted for prints on the window and screen."

"Did you find any pry marks on the windowsill?" CJ asked.

"No," he replied. "The window was either unlocked or up. It's been warm, so the vic may have left the window open to catch the breeze."

She rubbed her forehead. "Oh, jeez. Not a good idea. Ben, how 'bout you interview the neighbor, and I'll handle the coworker?"

He turned and headed next door. "You got it."

———

CJ tapped on the patrol car window. A female officer climbed out. "Hey, Detective. I assume you want to interview her?" the officer asked.

CJ leaned down to see a woman sitting in the back seat with her head buried in her hands. "Yeah. You think she's up to it?"

"Not sure." The officer shrugged. "She's better but still pretty upset. Her name is Mindy Walsh, and she worked with the victim."

She wrote down the name. "Okay, let me see what I can do." She opened the door and gently sat. "Mindy? Do you feel up to talking?"

Mindy peered up at her with puffy, sky-blue eyes. She wiped her nose with the back of her hand. "I, I . . . I'm not sure. Naomi was the sweetest person and my friend . . ." She started sobbing again.

CJ eased her arm around her and let her cry. "Take your time. We can do this later if you'd rather."

Mindy took a big sniff. "No. If I can help you catch whoever killed Naomi, I want to talk now."

"Okay, tell me what you know."

Mindy ran her hands through her short blond hair. "Naomi and I work together over at Lowcountry Titles processing applications. We met five years ago and have become terrific friends . . ."

"It's okay. Take your time."

"She didn't show up for work this morning, and she never misses work or is ever late." She sucked in a deep breath. "I called and called, but she didn't answer. I kept getting her stupid voicemail. I was worried, so I came to check on her after work.

"I knocked on the front door—no answer. So, I went around to the back, and the door was cracked open. I knocked and yelled to her. When she didn't answer, I went in. I looked around and then went to her bedroom and, and— screamed."

She broke down in tears again, her face back in her hands and in her lap.

This was the part of her job CJ hated the most. Watching people suffer over the loss of someone never got any easier, no matter how much experience one had. She let Mindy cry as she caressed her back. "I'm so sorry, Mindy."

Once the woman composed herself, CJ learned she hadn't entered the room. The neighbor, who'd heard her scream, came over, and called 911. Mindy had no idea who would do such an awful thing. Everyone loved Naomi and her husband, Jeff.

CJ stepped out of the car and asked officers to help the woman get home safe. Ben joined her, and they compared notes from the witness statements. Not much to go on.

Buzzing, and she looked down at her cell phone. *Uncle Harry. Crap, I forgot to call him and it's after seven.* She answered. "Hey, Unc."

"Are you lost?" Harry asked.

"Sorry, I forgot to call you. I need a rain check on dinner. I'm on a case that just popped up and will be here for a while."

"Bad one?"

"Yes," she replied. "A young woman was butchered in her bed in Harleston Village. CSU is here processing the scene, and I'll need to stay until we clear everything."

"I'm sorry. Your uncle Craig and I will miss you. If you're up for it, how about brunch tomorrow at Poogan's?"

"Sounds good, depending on when I get home."

"No problem. Call me in the morning when you wake up and let me know." She ended the call, and a voice behind her drew her attention.

"Detective?"

She turned to a smiling CSU tech who looked like he was still in high school.

"CSI Rodriquez told me to tell you he and Medical Examiner Whitehall should be ready to give you a prelim in thirty minutes. We're about to load the body for transport."

As the tech hurried away, he said, "You won't believe what this guy took as a trophy."

FOUR

Monday, October 25
Harleston Village

A little before ten, the long faces of Eddie and ME Thomas Whitehall rounded the corner of the house and approached CJ and Ben on the front sidewalk. Behind them was the gurney carrying the body of Naomi Sims.

Thomas, sixty years old, was one of CJ's favorite people. He reminded her of Uncle Harry. She wondered how long this slim, silver-gray-haired man with kind bluish-gray eyes would serve as the Charleston County ME. *Your job sucks, but I need you.*

"I didn't see you arrive," CJ said.

"Yeah, you were interviewing a witness, and I didn't want to disturb you."

"What did you find?" she asked anxiously. "The tech mentioned something the murderer took with him."

Eddie and Thomas looked at each other.

The CSI cleared his throat. "Okay. I'll cover what we found and collected and let Thomas handle the rest." He glanced at his pad. "First, the point of entry. It appears our guy came in through the den window, which isn't very visible from the street. It's also further hidden by two large inkberry holly bushes, one on each side of the window. He removed the screen, and it was easy to crawl into the house."

She made a note and looked back at him. "Did you see signs of the window being forced open?"

Eddie shook his head. "No. I think she had the window up. The two windows in the bedroom were up as well. I assume she wanted the fresh air. I'm sure he picked the window in the den because it was so hidden, and he could sneak in without letting anyone know he was in the house."

He checked his notes. "We dusted the window and screen for prints. None. He must have worn gloves. We found a partial footprint under the window. The ground is soft from someone watering the bushes. We measured and molded it and will see if we can determine anything."

Pointing toward the kitchen, he added, "We dusted for fingerprints in the kitchen and collected a few. They seem small, so they may be the woman's. The linoleum floor didn't show footprints. This appears to be the way he exited, but we had no luck finding anything helpful."

Clearing his throat again, he glanced back at his notes. "Now for the bedroom. Like the kitchen, we found a few fingerprints—on the dresser, nightstand, and lamp. They also appear small, so again, probably the woman's. We're taking the carpet with us to check it at the lab.

"There were no signs of fluids, and Thomas can cover the details, but we found no evidence she was sexually assaulted. We collected lots of blood samples from the bedding, headboard, and floor and will run them for DNA. We may get lucky and the guy cut himself.

"We'll see if there is anything unusual about the tape on her mouth, but it appears to be a standard duct tape you can buy in any hardware store. There were no fingerprints on it."

He flipped through his notes. "Oh. One last thing. We found a dark brown substance on the vic's forehead. It's not a fluid, really more like a powder."

Ben's brow wrinkled. "Could it be makeup?"

The CSI nibbled at his thumb. "I don't think that's what it is, but we'll run some tests and figure it out. We collected all of her makeup for comparison."

CJ stared at the bullet points she'd jotted down. "So, we have a shoe impression, fingerprints, blood, and a mystery substance to analyze."

Eddie ran his finger down the page. "Yep. That sums it up from my end." He motioned to the ME.

Thomas opened a small brown leather folio. "Based on the body temp and state of rigor, I estimate she was killed around midnight Friday, very early Saturday morning. She's been dead for sixty to seventy-two hours."

"That appears to match with what her neighbor told me," Ben said. "She told me she spoke to Naomi on the phone around nine o'clock Friday night."

Thomas continued. "I'll confirm it during the autopsy, but I believe the cause of death was asphyxiation."

CJ looked up from her notes. "He choked her to death?"

"I don't think so," he replied. "I think he smothered her with a pillow."

Ben spoke up. "We thought that was a possibility, but then why did he tape her mouth? She wouldn't be able to scream."

"True. I think he smothered her until she was unconscious but not dead, so he taped her mouth. He wanted to make sure she couldn't come to and scream or fight. I have no clue why he didn't smother her until she was dead."

Thomas cleared his throat. "Once she was subdued, he lacerated her midsection. I'll need to take a closer look at how, but it appears he stuck the knife in her and sliced down and then up." He demonstrated the movements and added, "There are no signs of sexual assault, which brings me to why he may have done it. He removed her heart and took it with him."

CJ stared at Thomas in shock. "He took her heart? Why in the hell would he do that?"

"I'm not sure why. Maybe it's a trophy for him."

She whispered, "Oh, Jesus."

When the CSU and ME had left, CJ and Ben double-checked their notes. There was one more item . . . notifying Naomi's husband, Jeff Sims, of her death. The neighbor had provided them with an emergency contact number. Jeff was a petty officer currently working in Norfolk, Virginia, helping get the *USS George H. W. Bush* ready for its maiden deployment.

"Ben, let's make the call and break the news," CJ said.

"Okay. I can do it if you want."

"No. I'll do it. How about you double-check to make sure the house is all buttoned up?"

As she went to her truck, reporters from News 2, News 4, Live 5 News, and Fox 24 screamed questions at her. She held up a hand to signal "no comment." She knew they'd only yell louder, but she wasn't up to answering questions with the case so fresh. *Hmm, where's my nemesis, Wendy Watts?*

CJ sat in her truck, staring at the number. She despised this part of her job. It was hard enough to tell a spouse they had lost the most important person in their life face-to-face, but doing it over the phone was worse. *I hope someone is there to support him.*

She dialed the number the neighbor had provided, and a formal voice greeted her. She gave the name of who she was trying to reach, and they let her know they'd get a message to him to call her.

Within minutes, her cell buzzed—Norfolk, area code 757. She blew out a breath and answered. "Detective O'Hara."

"This is Commander Matthew Jenkins," a deep voice announced. "How can I help you?"

"Hello, Commander. I appreciate the quick return call. Sorry it's so late. I'm a detective here in Charleston, trying to reach Jeff Sims. Unfortunately, I have terrible news about his wife. She's been murdered."

The man groaned and then CJ provided the details they knew thus far. "That's awful news. I think it's best I convey it to him personally. I'll have one of our chaplains attend with me. Any ideas on who killed her?"

"No, sir. We haven't caught who did this yet, but we will."

He was quiet before responding, "Okay. I'm sorry about this."

"Thank you, sir. I'm sorry too. Please let Jeff know he can call me anytime and I'll keep him updated on our investigation."

CJ sat numbly in her truck. She wiped tears as Ben looked in her window. She motioned for him to join her, and he slid into the passenger seat.

"Did you reach him?" he asked.

"I talked to his commander. He's going to tell Jeff. He thinks this is best, but I feel like I'm not doing my job by not telling him myself."

"Think about it, CJ. His commander is there and will ensure he has support when he's hit with the news. They'll probably have a chaplain there as well."

"Yeah," she replied. "You're probably right. He did mention a chaplain."

Ben stared at the front of the house with the mint-green paint and rust-brown shutters, and they sat silently. A dog barked in the distance.

He turned to her. "You wanna go grab a drink and something to eat? Been a long night."

"Yeah. I'm beat. I'm not sure I can eat, but I could use a drink," CJ said.

"Henry's isn't far. It'll be hopping, but we can find a spot."

She pinched her blouse and held it to her nose. "You know what, Ben? I'm not sure we wanna go around anyone. The coveralls didn't help much. I stink."

He lifted his arm and smelled his shirt. "Yeah. You're right. Let's swing through a drive-thru, grab a burger, and pick up a six-pack. We can sit at the Battery—watch the moon on the water and listen to some waves. I'll follow you, and you can drop your truck at your place and ride with me."

She wasn't sure she was up for it, but she needed to unwind after her long day—a rape victim before dawn and a murder victim at night. "Sounds fine."

The moon sent a white strip edged by a yellowish tint across the harbor. The breeze coming in from the Atlantic kicked up foam against the seawall and pushed the salty odor into Charleston. It was clear, warm, and perfect for those walking the Battery, although, at nearly midnight, the crowd was gone.

CJ and Ben found an unoccupied bench on the side of White Point Garden overlooking the harbor. The pink pampas grass provided a sharp contrast to a towering magnolia with its fingers reaching out over the bench. Luckily, the spot gave them a view of the harbor but was far enough away from the walkway to provide privacy.

Ben dug into the Wendy's bag and handed her a burger and a small container of fries. "Burger with lettuce, tomato, and mustard for you—pretty plain. I always add some pickles, onion, and ketchup to mine. I got two cups so we can pour our beer in them, and no one will be the wiser."

An elderly woman with a miniature collie passed them. CJ's eyes followed, and she fought the worry that someone might suddenly appear out of nowhere and grab her. Charleston was a safe place, undoubtedly beautiful, but she saw its underbelly. It stained everything around her.

Chewing a bite of burger, Ben asked, "You okay?"

She realized he was watching her. "Yeah, I guess I'm just, well . . . drained."

"Hard not to be some days. We started our day on shitty cases, and it only got worse."

Although she had difficulty choking down her food, the two sat and ate. The food was tasty, and she should have been starved, but her senses were spent. It hit her that their conversations had changed. Now all they had was a lot of general chitchat. She couldn't put her finger on it, but there was none of the closeness she had felt when they talked before Ben's arrest in the incident with the Lowcountry Killer case. *Let's talk about the weather next.*

Between bites, she asked, "How are things between you and your dad?"

Ben pushed sand into a small pile with his foot. Without looking at her, he said, "Better. It's taken some work by both of us."

He stopped playing with the sand and stared out across the harbor. "First, I find out my twin brother is alive and a serial killer, then that my dad didn't get him mental help but instead sent him away. I always believed the lie my dad told me, that Bryan drowned. I guess it makes more sense now why my mom left."

She reached out and touched his arm. "I can't imagine dealing with it, but I do know your father loves you. I guess he was doing what he thought was best."

"Yeah. I guess." He shrugged. "Dad told me Bryan scared him. Even when he was small, he started hurting animals and doing weird shit, but when he hurt the little girl—it was too much. He said sending him to live with an old friend in Alaska was part of what kept the girl's father from pressing charges." He rubbed at the back of his neck. "I actually wish charges had been pressed. Then Bryan would have got the help he needed."

"Maybe so, but twenty years ago, I'm not sure how well we handled mental health issues."

They sat silently for several minutes, until CJ broke the silence. "How's your brother handling things?"

Ben shrugged. "I guess Will's doing okay. He doesn't seem to want to talk about Bryan, and nothing's different between him and my dad. Will leaves the past in the past."

"Since he's older, do you think he noticed anything strange about Bryan?"

He shrugged. "I don't know. From what little he's said, I don't think so."

Back to silence. She sat thinking about how different Ben and Will were and wondered what he really knew. She had more questions but kept them to herself.

Ben was stuffing the wrappers and leftovers into the white paper bag. He sat within a couple of feet of her but seemed a million miles away.

"Can I ask you something and get an honest answer?"

He stopped his cleanup project. "Yeah, sure."

"I can't exactly describe it, but there's a wall between us that wasn't there before all that went down with Bryan's case. Does that make any sense?"

For a moment, his eyes remained fixed on the water as he sipped his beer. Finally, he exhaled. "It does. I don't know how to describe it either."

She wiped at her eyes. "I'm not looking for love. I'm still new here, and we've only known each other for six months, but I miss that feeling I had. We had a natural closeness, a connection, and it was genuine. Maybe we were just close friends, and I'm fine with that, but now we only talk about cases or superficial bullshit."

He sat with his eyes locked on the water. She wondered what he was thinking, and she just wished he'd spill it.

"CJ, when you arrested me, my head knew you were only doing your job and following the evidence at the time." His voice dropped to a whisper. "But my heart was broken that you didn't know I could never do those awful things."

She wiped away a tear that ran down her right cheek. "I understand."

He leaned over and hugged her. "Let's just give it some time. I, too, miss that feeling. How 'bout I get you home? I'm sure Jake's wondering where I am and where his dinner is. That dog expects to eat promptly at six."

They walked to the truck—only feet from each other but miles apart.

FIVE

Tuesday, October 26
Downtown Charleston

CJ squirmed in her bed. Since getting home at close to two o'clock in the morning, she hadn't slept—catnapped at best. After Ben had dropped her off, she showered, hoping to remove the smell of death, and dropped her clothes in a plastic bag until she could wash them.

She looked at the digits on the clock—5:14 a.m. Too early to get up, but sleep eluded her. *I may as well go for a ride on the punisher.* She climbed on her stationary bike, and her legs churned.

It was a few minutes before ten when CJ arrived at Poogan's Porch and dropped into a wicker chair with a floral cushion on the front veranda. She loved the hanging baskets at the famous Charleston eatery, which were filled with pots of multicolored flowers and ferns. The overhead straw fans kept the area comfortable. The whole place felt like home, and she needed some home right now. She was patting the head of the small white statue of the dog Poogan when she heard her uncle's voice and looked up to see his smile.

"Uncle Harry. It's so good to see you!"

Harry O'Hara gave her a big hug. "Great to see you too, young lady. Sorry I kept you waiting. I was looking for a place to park."

"No worries. I was enjoying the porch. Plus, it gave me a chance to pet my friend here."

Harry chuckled as they looked at the dog who had inspired the restaurant's name. The place was more like an antebellum home than a restaurant—two stories, bright yellow paint, white shutters, and a wrought-iron railing.

Harry gave her a last squeeze. "Not sure about you, but I'm ready for some food. I was up early sitting on my back deck watching your pelican, and I'm starved."

She pointed to the door. "Thanks for waiting for me for brunch. Let's eat."

The stocky hostess with brown hair in a tight bun seated them at a table by the window, and they had a perfect view of the hustle and bustle of Queen Street. They both studied the brunch menu, and Harry announced it was time she tried chicken and waffles. "You'll love them," he said.

"Okay. I trust you, but I have to admit, I never thought of having fried chicken and waffles together. I'd love to have a mimosa, but I'll have to pass since it's a workday."

"Poogan's Bloody Mary for me. The pickled okra they put in that thing makes it extra tasty."

While they waited for their food, he caught her up on his latest fishing exploits. He was happy that his brother Craig had joined him on several occasions.

"It's been wonderful to get to spend more time with my brother, and I'm so happy he finally agreed to meet you. He said to tell you hello. He wanted to come today, but he's off on a charter trip."

"Yeah. I was sorry to miss last night. Dinner with you two would have been much better than how I spent my time." Her heart rate increased, and a bead of sweat ran down the back of her neck.

He watched her and then spoke in a hushed tone. "Not to ruin a nice morning, and you can keep it bottled up if you want, but I'm happy to chat."

The waitress placed their food on the table and CJ immediately cut a bite of chicken and waffle and shoved it in her mouth. They both ate without a word for several minutes. Her meal was excellent, but she only picked at it. Finally, the busboy cleared their plates, and coffee was dropped off.

"Uncle Harry, I'll never understand how someone could be so evil. So evil, for no reason. I've got one case where four women have been raped in their homes, and last night, I found a woman murdered in her bed. Home should be a safe place."

"There's no rhyme or reason to it," he replied. "I worked cases for more than thirty years and never made sense of it. The only way to keep your sanity is to focus on the positive things you're doing and the people you help."

He reached and took her hand.

CJ stared out the window. "I know. It's so damn hard, though.

"This murder. Why do you think the perp did it . . . sexual assault?" he asked.

"No. I'm not sure why he did it. I'm assuming it's a he. There was no apparent sexual component, no robbery, only something bizarre."

He took a sip of coffee and asked, "What's that?"

"Whoever killed the woman took her heart."

Harry's hazel eyes, greener than brown, stared at her. "Her heart?"

"Yes. I know some perps take souvenirs, but a heart is a strange thing to take."

He frowned and shifted. "Let's hope this is just an isolated case of some deranged mind. Could be drug related." She read his face and knew he didn't believe this. She knew from all his years with the Boston Bureau of Investigative Services that his alarm bells were sounding.

Slowly, she nodded. "I hope so. We just need to catch whoever did this and make sure it doesn't happen again. Eddie and his crew gathered some possible evidence, and I'm heading over later to see what Thomas found."

"Both are excellent at their jobs, so they'll come through for you. Anyone else helping you?"

"I need to talk to Paul to confirm, but perhaps Ben and I will work it. He was there last night as well."

"He's good at his job too," he said. "You ready to partner with him again?"

She knew that look. He was asking about more than the case. "Yeah. Ben and I work well together, and we'd be fine to team up. Unfortunately, we're still shorthanded, so no one in the CID is available."

"Well, I'm happy to help if you need me," he stated.

She knew he would, but she didn't want to go there. He'd helped her on the Lowcountry Killer case, and he wouldn't admit it, but it had been hard on him. At sixty, he'd served his time and earned his retirement. "I'll be fine." She grinned. "You need to improve your fishing."

"Hey now," he exclaimed. "Let's not forget who caught the most last time."

"I was only being nice." She laughed. "Next time, it's no holds barred. I'll get tips from Uncle Craig."

"Oh, that's right. Bring in a pro." He ran his hands through his salt-and-pepper hair and stood. "Let's let them have this table. The lunch crowd is hovering."

They hugged goodbye on the porch and agreed to get dinner on the schedule soon.

CJ arrived at the morgue around one o'clock. She expected Thomas would be winding up his autopsy, and she was anxious to see what he'd found. She decided that she'd do what she could to protect her jeans and T-shirt and gowned up before knocking on the door to the autopsy room.

"Thomas?"

"Come in, come in. Perfect timing. I'm just finishing up."

"Thanks for jumping on top of this one," she said. "I know we all had a late night."

"No problem. For these types of cases, I like to expedite things. If there's evidence, we need it ASAP. I'll get the full report typed up for you, but it'll probably be tomorrow. I've made a copy of my notes and key findings. You can take that with you."

As she approached the table, a tightness gripped her chest. Her mind flashed back to the night before, when she first saw Naomi Sims. The bright lights made the victim's skin even paler, and her midsection seemed more purple.

Thomas motioned her closer, and she realized she had stopped several feet away from the cold metal table. "Let's start so we can get out of here," he said.

"Okay," she squeaked. *Get it together, CJ.*

"My external exam . . ."

She stared at his lips as they moved, but there was no volume. Her world had gone silent, and she had lost her ability to focus. She blinked her eyes, trying to regain herself, and struggled to breathe.

Thomas touched her arm, shocking her back from her daze. "CJ, are you okay? You look— kinda out of it."

She cleared her throat and gave him a feeble smile. "Yeah. I'm fine. I guess my mind wandered a bit. Sorry. Please keep going."

He stared at her for a moment, pursed his lips, and continued. He pointed to the woman's midsection. "Based on my internal exam, I believe the attacker inserted the knife here in the epigastric region and sliced down about six inches to her navel. Then he sliced upward from where he started to the bottom of her sternum.

"At this point, I believe he forced the cavity open enough to allow him to reach her heart." He added, "It was crudely done, but he sliced the arteries and surrounding tissues and pulled the heart out. All lacerations were done with an uneven, somewhat dull blade."

Pulled her heart out . . . She felt dizzy. Her vision blurred, and her head went light as the volume of his voice dropped again. She grabbed at the edge of the table as her world spun and dimmed. Thomas quickly grabbed her arm and guided her to the floor. "Easy, CJ. Let's sit down right here while I get you a chair."

Thomas gently lifted CJ up and onto a chair. "Try to relax. You'll be fine. Do you want some water?"

She tried to shake her head. "I, I need to . . ." Her stomach turned upside down, and she fought not to vomit.

"Okay, don't talk now. Just relax. I'll hang on to you. We don't want you to leave the chair."

A tech appeared, and the last thing she remembered was being lifted.

Her face was wet. CJ almost panicked until she saw the tech sitting beside her applying a damp cloth to her face. He was a Black man, she guessed twenty-five, and he whispered to her, "Take it easy, miss. I got you. You're okay."

After several minutes, she'd gathered herself and managed to sit up on the side of the gurney. Thomas and the tech stood beside her. "Jeez, I'm so sorry," she mumbled. "I'm really embarrassed."

The ME smiled at her. "Don't be. It was my fault for being, well, let's say, 'direct' in my descriptions."

She knew that wasn't it. She'd seen and heard much worse. "I didn't puke, did I?"

Thomas laughed. "Nope. No puke. Is your stomach better now?"

"Yes. I feel much better. I'll be fine in a few more minutes."

He patted her on the arm. "Okay. Once I'm sure you're fine, I'll let you leave. Have you been feeling okay?"

She shrugged. "Yes. I've felt fine. A little beat from all the long hours."

"Are you eating and drinking lots of water?" he asked.

"Yeah. Well, I miss lunch a lot or grab something small. I guess I don't drink much water." She wasn't being truthful.

His sharp eyes scanned her cautiously. "A syncope could be nothing, or it could mean there's an underlying issue."

"What's a syncope?"

"Sorry." He smiled. "That's the medical term for fainting or passing out."

"I didn't really pass out. I—"

His palm went up. "Let's not argue. I know what I saw. You could be dehydrated since it's been pretty warm and you're not drinking enough liquids. If you're not getting the nutrients you need, you could be anemic, although passing out isn't that great of an indicator. On the other hand, it could be more serious." Leaning down, he asked, "Do you have panic attacks or anxiety?"

"Uh, I don't think so. But the damn job is stressful."

"Fair enough. When was your last physical?"

"Last year in Boston," she said.

Thomas patted her shoulder. "I'll give you the name of a doctor friend. Call her and set up a physical. You'll like her, and she's excellent. Stay sitting here, and I'll get a copy of my notes for you to take and will shoot the final report over once it's ready." He pointed to the tech. "By the way, meet Byron. He just came on board and is already a tremendous help."

Byron smiled at her. "I'll stay until I have the final report ready for you today, miss."

"Thank you. I appreciate it." She rubbed at the back of her neck.

Pulled her heart out—

Wednesday, October 27
Downtown Charleston

CJ stretched her arms above her head, her pulse picked up. She suddenly dreaded her morning appointment, which she had postponed during the Lowcountry Killer case. The clock had run out, though, and she had to go.

She forced herself out of bed, exchanged her T-shirt for workout clothes, and laced up her shoes. As she passed the kitchen, she grabbed a bottle of water and climbed on the punisher in front of the picture window overlooking the Charleston harbor. The city was just beginning to wake up, and daylight peeked over the horizon.

Her favorite paperboy worked his way down State Street. He couldn't have been more than fourteen or fifteen and was carrying a canvas bag full of newspapers. As he made his way toward her, he dropped copies of *The Post and Courier* along the way. Then, as he often did as she rode, he stopped in front of her apartment and looked up. He smiled and gave her a little wave. She returned the gestures as she continued to pedal.

He turned back for his route—then suddenly he stopped. He glanced back up and then sheepishly blew her a kiss. She laughed and produced a big kiss back with both hands. His face turned the same red shade as his hair. Then, quick as a cat, he resumed his work.

Showered, dressed in tan pants and a green blouse, she headed to her favorite coffee shop, Sal's Coffee. The temperature was already climbing, but she threw on a light jacket to conceal her creds and Glock. No need to freak out any passersby as she walked.

She saw the pale robin's-egg blue storefront and the butterscotch sign on the front door. Bells rang as she pushed the door open, and the smile that always made her happy flashed. Sal, the shop owner, was a tall and gangly man in his midfifties. He had black curly hair and a bushy mustache, and his nose was thin and pointed.

"Good morning, CJ. You're exceptionally lovely today. Your blouse matches your eyes. Wowza!"

Her face turned pink. "Thanks, Sal. You're such a flirt."

He spread his arms and grinned. "Only calling it as I see it. Do you want your usual drink? How about a fresh apple Danish?"

"Yes. I'll take both, please. I had forty-five minutes on the bike this morning, so I can afford a little treat."

He handed her a large black coffee and a small bag, and she went outside to a wrought-iron table overhung by a tree with pale pink flowers. Two pigeons waddled over and cooed at her feet, hoping for a snack. Their bluish-gray heads glistened under the morning sun.

"Okay, guys, be patient."

A small boy, maybe four, approached hand in hand with a young woman. CJ smiled at him, which caused him to stop to show her his new toy truck—fire-engine red with chrome wheels. Try as she did to move him along, the woman had no choice but to stop while the boy flipped the truck bed up and down for CJ. The woman mouthed, "Sorry."

His presentation completed, CJ got a quick hug, and the boy was off, stopping along the route to proudly display his new prize to everyone. *I wonder what it would be like to be a mom.*

Her phone buzzed, breaking the calm, and CJ realized her quiet time was over—she had to head to her appointment. The pigeons got their wish and gobbled up the remaining pieces of her breakfast. "Enjoy, guys."

An hour later, CJ stood outside a door that read *Charles Greedsy, PhD*. She exhaled and knocked, hoping the doctor had forgotten their appointment. No luck. The door opened.

"Good morning. Cassandra Jane O'Hara, I presume."

She stood looking down at a man she guessed was in his midsixties. He had salt-and-pepper hair, chocolate-brown eyes, and wire-rimmed glasses too small for his face. He was going bald, and his exposed scalp was bright pink.

"Hey, Doc. Yes, it's me, although I just go by CJ."

"Perfect. Short and sweet. I like it." He waved her into his office. "Come on in and have a seat."

Steeling herself, she dropped into a dark brown leather recliner opposite a massive mahogany desk. The strategic positioning of the chairs put their eyes at the same level. *So much for my four-inch height advantage.*

She sat quietly as the doctor cleaned his glasses, then dug through a stack of files. Finally, he seemed to find what he was after, and his eyes fixed on her.

"Okay, CJ. How about we get started? By the way, please call me Charles. No need to stand on ceremony."

She squirmed to get comfortable.

"I'm glad we're finally able to meet," he continued. "That nasty mess with the Lowcountry Killer ruined our timing."

She quietly nodded. *Yes, it ruined lots of things.*

"So, while we want to follow up on the shooting incident in Boston, we will also cover the latest incident. Fair enough?"

The vise tightened on her neck. *So you mean we'll talk about the two men I've now killed in the last six months, and whether I'm gonna lose it.* "Sure, whatever you want."

"Dr. Matthews was kind enough to send me his files from Boston. Thanks for signing the release, as this is quite helpful. I'll do my best not to rehash every detail."

"You're welcome." She shifted. *Yeah, you two can gang up on my mental state.*

"First, let's talk about Boston. I understand you shot and killed a suspect during an alleged robbery. Correct?"

"Yes, but it wasn't an 'alleged' robbery. It was a robbery. We caught the two men in the act, and I had no choice but to shoot."

"Okay. As I understand it, one of the suspects was killed, and one was wounded. Why did you have no choice?"

She tamped down her irritation. "One man had a gun to my partner's head and was counting down, and the other attacked me with a knife. I'm not happy about it, but I had no choice. If I didn't shoot, my partner, and perhaps myself, would be dead."

"Do you feel guilty about it?"

She wasn't sure how she wanted to answer this. *Hell yeah, I feel guilty about killing a man.* "If I'm honest, I do feel some guilt, I guess, but mostly regret."

"Regret?"

"Yes. I regret I was given no choice but to shoot. I wish the guy had surrendered, but it was his decision in the end."

The doctor sat and stared at her. "It's hard to understand your dilemma as a civilian, but it's clear from the police report and Dr. Matthews's notes that you were justified in your actions." He leaned forward. "It's healthy that you feel regret. All law enforcement officers should, and some feel a bit of guilt. But my take is that you should only feel regret and leave the guilt out of it."

She rubbed her eyes. *You're right, but I still took someone's life, and I'll always feel some guilt.* "Okay, understood."

"How about the Lowcountry Killer?"

"Bryan Parrish."

His brow furrowed. "Excuse me?"

"That was his name. Bryan Parrish," she replied. "A.k.a. the Lowcountry Killer."

"Oh. I see. How do you feel about shooting him?"

Her heart rate escalated as she remembered looking into Bryan's cold, dead eyes as he sneered at her. He was pure evil, regardless of what he thought had driven him to murder eight women and his own mother. "I feel different about him."

"Different? In what way?"

"Sometimes people commit crimes, and they're not necessarily evil. It doesn't make them any less of a criminal, but it's more about a wrong choice. I think this was the case in Boston. The two men never intended to kill anyone. It was a robbery gone sideways and a stupid choice not to surrender."

She cleared her throat. "Other times, people are evil, doing the vilest things they can imagine. It's a part of who they are. Bryan Parrish was pure evil. While I'd have rather arrested him, I'm not sure I regret killing him. My only guilt in his case is because I didn't catch the bastard earlier and save several innocent women from being brutally raped, tortured, and murdered."

She was breathing hard and a little shocked by her response. Dr. Greedsy sat rubbing his chin, studying her closely. "I think I understand why you feel differently. Based on what I've read about the two cases, you're right that the actions of the two men you killed were very different." He leaned back in his chair but held her gaze. "My grandmother always said that some people are born bad. Called it 'bad wiring.' I hate to say it, but in my opinion, Parrish may well have gotten what he deserved. He intended to kill you."

Spreading his hands, he continued. "Professionally, of course, I have to say it's not healthy for you to not regret it." He folded his hands. "So, I have to ask you: if you could have apprehended him without killing him, would you have done it?"

She slowly nodded. "Yes. I'm sworn to uphold the law, and no matter how I feel, that's what I aim to do. If I could have, I would have taken him alive and let justice be served by the courts."

He pursed his lips. "Fair enough."

She struggled to calm herself. Her hands shook as she sipped her now-cold coffee, and she hoped he didn't notice. *Fat chance of that. The guy's got eyes like a hawk.*

"We have about twenty minutes left today, so let's talk about your parents."

She bit her bottom lip. *Jeez. What's there to talk about?* "A drunk driver killed my parents and older sister when I was eleven. Not much else to say."

He tapped the folder. "That's what the file says. The file also says that you feel guilty about it. So let's talk about how you handle that."

I do feel guilty. It was my fault my family was out that night, but I've never said that aloud. "I'm not sure what I told the doctor in Boston, so I'm not sure why it says that in the file."

"Don't try to fool me, young lady." He pointed at her. "You may not have told Dr. Matthews directly, but that's the way he read it. How about we don't rehash why you feel guilty but focus on how you deal with it?"

Wetness ran down her cheeks. "I miss them every day."

"Do you still use alcohol to help with the guilt and their absence?"

Damn it! Does the file say I'm a raging alcoholic too? "I drink socially. I keep it to a couple of beers." *Except when I drink a bottle by myself in my apartment—excess to escape.* She waited for him to push it.

"How well do you sleep?"

She was surprised he'd moved on and shifted again. Her chair was uncomfortable no matter how much she adjusted herself. "Okay, I guess. The cases I work on can keep you awake."

"Do you ever see the faces of the victims?"

Hell yeah. Every damn night! Dead eyes stare up at me. "Sometimes. It's difficult not to recall the victims."

He took off his glasses, cleaned them with a handkerchief, and squeezed them back on his face. "So, you sometimes drink too much and have bad sleep habits. How about eating?"

She rubbed her ear. "I eat okay, I guess. Work is hectic, so I don't cook that much."

He leaned forward. "How about sex?"

What the hell! "Uh . . . what do you mean? If you mean do I have a boyfriend, the answer is no."

"How about casual sex?"

Holy shit! "You mean like one-night stands?"

"That's exactly what I mean."

She squirmed. "No." *I'm not telling you about my sex life.*

Again, he didn't push her. "Last question for today. Does alcohol or your restless sleep habits impair you, keep you from doing your job?"

There it is. I'm an alcoholic who has nightmares and can't sleep. "No. Alcohol is not a problem. I've never had a drink on the job, nor would I. Some nights I sleep better than others, but it doesn't affect my ability to do my job."

He sat staring at her, then scribbled in his notebook. "Okay, we'll leave it there for today."

She knew he wasn't convinced she had it all together. Maybe she wasn't either.

SEVEN

Wednesday, October 27
Harleston Village

Ricky pedaled hard, rounding the corner of a house in Harleston Village before he locked up his brakes. He loved to make his bike skid, and since no one lived here now, he didn't worry about getting scolded. Wesley flashed by him before hitting his brakes.

"Damn, you smoked me that run," Wesley yelled.

Ricky hopped off his Huffy. "Yeah, I got you good. Old lady Paulson was pissed when I cut the corner and almost got her roses."

Wesley laughed. "She'll live. She sure loves those stupid flowers." He pointed to the back door. "Hey, look. The door is cracked open. Wanna check it out? Maybe we can find something we can sell."

Ricky was already halfway to the door. "Yeah. Since it's open, we can't be accused of breaking in."

The two twelve-year-olds stood at the edge of the partially open door, peering into the house. "Whaddya think, Wesley? Still wanna go in? It's kinda dark."

Wesley punched the other boy in the shoulder. "Hell yeah. Don't be chicken." He pushed the door—it didn't budge. "Let's lean into it."

With both pushing hard, the door broke free and slammed open. Ricky slipped and fell into the doorframe. "Shit! Make more noise, dumbass," Wesley said.

Ricky had his head inside. "Chill. No one's around. We're all good."

The boys crept into the structure. There was no power, which meant no lights. Spiderwebs hung in every corner, and trash littered the floor. Both of them jumped when a furry creature ran between them. Room by room, they searched for anything valuable, but all they found was more trash and lots of grime until they reached the living room.

"What the hell is that?" Wesley pointed to something near the fireplace hearth.

Ricky pulled the dirty drapes back to let in more late afternoon light. "Hell if I know. Check it out."

"Me?" Wesley asked. "You do it. It's nasty."

"Who's the chicken now? Hold the curtain open, wuss."

Dropping to a knee, Ricky bent down. "What the hell is that? It looks like a piece of meat."

"You think somebody's been cooking?" Wesley asked.

"Don't look like it. Be hard to cook with just candles." His face closed the gap. "Oh, man. I think it's a heart."

"What?! You're crazy."

Ricky poked at the reddish-black object and popped up. "Aw shit! It is a heart. Let's get the hell out of here."

Both boys raced out of the back door and almost crashed into the pear-shaped Clarice Paulson, who was coming onto the porch.

"What are you two little shits up to? Come back here!"

Clarice muttered until she got home and dialed 911 from her kitchen. "Nobody controls their damn kids anymore. Hellions, I tell you. Let's see how they do when the cops get here."

At 4:10 p.m., CJ rounded the corner of the house to see an officer waiting for her. "Officer Jones. We meet again."

"Yes, ma'am."

"Whatcha got?"

He pointed at the back door. "I think it's a heart. Guessing it belongs to that woman we found the other night."

She pulled on her shoe covers and asked, "How'd we find it?"

"Neighbor called in some boys messing around in the house. I answered the call and went in."

"Okay, I see you've already stretched the tape, so how 'bout you hang here, and I'll check it out?"

"It's in the living room, in the opposite right-hand corner, by the fireplace."

———

CJ exited through the back door.

"Well, Detective. Do you think it's connected to our other case?" Johnny asked.

CJ exhaled. "Yes. We've found our missing heart."

She punched at the numbers of her cell phone, called dispatch, and asked for the CSU to be sent as soon as possible. She sat on the edge of the porch as she hung up. "Officer Jones, how about you go round up those boys, and I'll wait for the CSU."

"Yes, ma'am. You want me to bring them here or just get their statement?"

Her lips curled. "Bring them here. I want to talk to them."

As he turned, he chuckled. "That'll scare the shit out of 'em. They probably won't go in any vacant buildings again."

CJ dialed another number on her cell phone and pinched the bridge of her nose as she heard Ben's voicemail message. She said, "I think we found Naomi Sims's heart."

She left the address and sat staring at the pinkish-yellow sky, where a lone seagull rode the breeze.

Johnny rounded the corner with Ricky and Wesley in his grasp. Both were pale, with tears streaming down their cheeks. "Detective, here are the two boys who entered the house. Meet Ricky and Wesley. Say hello, boys."

Their heads stayed bowed, and with barely a whisper they said, "Hello."

She bent over until she was eye-to-eye with them. "Nice to meet you, boys. How about you look at me and tell me what happened? If you lie to me, I'll know it. You first, Ricky."

His amber eyes caught hers, then quickly darted back to the ground. "We, we . . . were riding our bikes and went in the house."

"Is this your house?"

"No, ma'am. We didn't mean no harm, just a little curious."

"Did you steal anything?"

His head shook furiously. "No, ma'am. We didn't take nothing. It's empty 'cept for the stuff by the fireplace, and I . . . I poked the heart-looking thing. We didn't touch nothing else, promise."

She bit back a smile. "Look at me, Ricky, so I can see if you're telling me the truth."

His head slowly rose. A soft sob escaped. "Promise you, ma'am, I'm telling you the God's honest truth."

She had to give him credit. He squirmed and sobbed, but he held her gaze. She turned to the other boy. "Okay, Wesley. You have anything to add?"

"No, ma'am. Ricky's right. We went in and looked around but didn't take or touch nothing. Well . . . we both touched the drape on the window, but only to hold it open so we could see better." He had looked at her but dropped his head after he spoke.

She looked at Johnny and the boys' dads, who stood in the background. She winked. It was time for a lesson. "Officer Jones. Do you think we should arrest these boys?"

Their tears came faster and sobs grew louder.

"Hmm . . . I can't decide. Maybe we only give the boys a warning. I think their pops can handle the rest."

She hid her smile. "Okay, boys. Here's the deal. No going onto others' property without permission, and that includes entering anyone's home without being invited. You got it?"

Both boys nodded aggressively. "No, ma'am, we won't. Ever."

"Okay, you're free to go."

She watched them leave. Johnny's grasp was replaced by their fathers', and she was sure more discomfort was to come at home.

"Think you scared them pretty good, Detective. Their dads will be happy about that. They told me I should take them down to the station, put them in a cell, and scare the hell out of 'em, but that's a bit over the top."

CJ's cell phone buzzed. *Ben.*

Johnny waved. "I'll leave you to it, Detective. I'll head round to double-check with the guys whether there's anything else."

She answered her cell phone. "Hey, Ben."

"Hey. Listen, I'm up in North Charleston on a case. It's tough for me to leave."

"That's fine," she replied. "We've been here about an hour and are finishing up. Eddie and his crew are about to leave."

"Is it a heart?" Ben asked.

"Yes. I'm sure it's the heart of our victim. Whoever left it placed it in the center of some weird-looking chalk-marked circle on the floor and white candles. I have no idea why."

"That's sick." She heard him sigh.

"Yep. Very sick. Let's dig into it tomorrow."

―――

Eddie patted the cooler as he left the house with the CSU. "We collected what was left of the heart. It's been exposed for several days, so it's not in great condition. The flies and maggots got to it, but we'll see what Thomas can find. We took lots of photos and video. The place is full of dust, so anywhere it looked disturbed, we checked for prints. Didn't find any. We collected the candles, so maybe we'll find prints on them at the lab."

CJ jotted a note about the candles. "Anything else?"

Eddie passed the cooler to one of the techs and pulled out his pad. "Only other thing we found is the same powdery substance we found on the vic's forehead. The lab will run it and see if they can identify it. Maybe it matches what we found on our victim's body."

"Could it be drugs?"

He rubbed his chin. "Could be. It would explain a lot."

Johnny walked up. "Excuse me, Detective."

"What's up, Officer?" CJ asked.

Johnny motioned to the edge of the porch. "One of the guys found a footprint near the porch overhang. Not sure it means anything, but I think you should check it out."

"Sure." She turned to the CSI. "Eddie, let's take a look. We'll snap some photos and take measurements."

Eddie followed her and added, "We may want to cast it."

EIGHT

Friday, October 29
Downtown Charleston

CJ's head was wet, and her pillow was soaked. *What the hell?* She sat up in her bed and pulled at her damp, tangled hair. She glanced over at the clock—4:37 a.m. She unwrapped the sheets and went to the bathroom. After a quick shower, she got dressed and headed down the steps to her truck.

She pulled off Lockwood Drive into the LEC parking lot and raced up the steps. After three tries and a few choice words, she got the lock to buzz and entered the hallway. The station was quiet this early as the night and day shifts exchanged.

She punched in the code to the conference room door, entered, and flipped on the lights. The room was a sterile chamber under the fluorescent glare. A chill went through her, and the back of her neck tingled. She paused before dropping into a black high-back mesh chair at the honey-colored table. Bryan Parrish haunted this space.

CJ started the coffee, opened the first rape case file, and made a few notes as she read. Then, one by one, she covered the following three files and sat staring at the scribbles she'd made on her pad. *There has to be more than that.* She repeated the file review process with no changes in the scribbles. *Shit!*

CJ was adding bullets of the critical aspects of the rape cases to the evidence board as Paul entered the conference room at eight thirty.

"Will Stan be joining us?" she asked.

"I doubt it," Paul replied. "He's due in Columbia for a meeting, so I expect he's left. I'll brief him."

She heard knocking and opened the door to the towering figure of Police Chief Walter Williams—an unexpected guest. He was Black and stood six feet six, was balding, and had dark brown eyes. A scar ran down his right cheek, and his ordinarily friendly expression was gone.

"Hey, guys. I have a few minutes after having my ass handed to me by the mayor. Mind if I join you?"

Paul was filling his cup with coffee. "No, sir. We were just about to get started." He held up the pot. "Coffee's fresh."

Walter moved to the small corner table. "Coffee would be good."

CJ politely smiled. The temperature in the room seemed to jump. "Good to see you, sir." She stood patiently as he dumped sugar in a brown cardboard cup. She swore he had grown taller, his bald head shinier and eyes more strained.

The chief remained standing as he turned to her. "Okay. Tell me what you have."

After one unsuccessful attempt, she finally cleared her throat. She covered the pertinent details of the first rape and had moved to the second when the chief cut her off.

"How 'bout we skip what happened and get to the part where you tell me how you're going to arrest whoever raped the women? Are we putting one or four in jail?"

Paul flinched. It wasn't just her who was struck by the abruptness of their normally cordial leader. Her face flushed.

"I believe one person is responsible for all four rapes," she replied. "We have a consistent MO, witnesses with similar descriptions, and the guy is intelligent and hasn't left any of himself behind. The only real forensics we have so far is a fiber. The lab said the fiber is some type of thread." She sucked in a deep breath, held his gaze, and continued. "But, as all criminals do, he'll make a mistake, and we will catch him."

The chief pursed his lips, and she waited for the storm. He turned and asked, "Paul, you agree it's one guy?"

Her lieutenant's eyes locked with hers. "If CJ says we have a serial rapist, we have one. She's got damn good instincts."

Walter approached the board, eyes scanning the marked locations of the rapes. "What do you need, CJ?"

"Three things. First, I need a fire lit in Columbia to have SLED's fiber expert give me his findings. I've been told it will be more than a month for results, and we can't wait that long." She paused. There was no response. "Second, we need to increase patrols in the city. Finally, we need to go door-to-door and interview those in the areas where the rapes occurred. Sometimes people don't realize they have important information."

Walter nodded. "Paul?"

Paul leaned forward, causing his chair to squeak. "Sounds right to me, Chief. Let's give CJ what she needs. She can't be everywhere, and she can't interview all the people we need to cover. As for the fire, well, Walter, I've seen you raise hell when hell needs to be raised."

Paul stood and headed back to the coffee. "One more thing. Let's reassign Sam Ravenel back to the CID. Have her report to CJ and coordinate things, chase down information . . . girl's a hell of a resource and knows lots of the SLED folks. Plus, we have a situation beyond this case where her local knowledge will be useful."

The chief's head snapped to CJ. "What situation?"

"I assume Paul is referring to the Harleston Village murder, sir," she said.

He raised his palms. "All right. Before we pile on, let's button up the rapes. As soon as I leave here, I'll raise hell with Columbia. If needed, I'll have the mayor call the damn governor. Paul, you work with the Patrol Division and get the officers increased, then sit down and sort out how to get the interviews done. We're shorthanded, and I'll remind the mayor her downward pressure on our budget and hiring has consequences."

"Thanks, Chief," Paul said.

CJ spoke up. "If possible, I'd like to have Officer Johnny Jones help with the interviews. He's impressive and has an easy way with people. Harleston Village is his zone. They'd be open to him." She thought she saw a fragment of a smile on the chief's face.

"Fine by me. Work it out with Patrol." He added, "By the way, speaking of shorthanded, I agreed the FBI could ask you about their unsolved cases in Alaska, but it can't interfere with your work. They need to solve their own damn cases."

She nodded. "Yes, sir. Paul's been crystal clear it can't interfere with what's on my plate."

Paul spoke up. "CJ, let's go over the details of Harleston Village."

Walter interjected as he landed hard in a chair, "Murdered young woman with mutilation. What am I missing?"

Paul motioned to CJ, and she opened the file.

"That's true," CJ said. "Naomi Sims was murdered in her bed late Friday night, early Saturday morning. She was smothered with a pillow until unconscious, then her heart was removed."

Walter's eyes went wide. "He took her damn heart?"

"Yes, sir. We found the heart in a vacant home on Wednesday afternoon. Thomas has confirmed it's Naomi's.

We had shoe impressions at both crime scenes, and the lab confirmed they're the same. Same size, pattern, and indentation on the outer right sole. The perp must have damaged the shoe somehow."

Paul pointed to the file. "Show the chief the photo from the location where the heart was found."

She thumbed through the file and handed an eight-by-ten photo to the chief.

Walter's eyes went wide, and he exhaled. "Oh, shit." His eyes went to her, then to Paul as he pointed at him. "You need to personally be involved in this, Paul. You know who to take her to see, right?"

Paul slowly nodded. "Yes, sir. I do."

NINE

Saturday, October 30
Wando, South Carolina

"Holy smokes! Look at all the cars," CJ exclaimed as she pulled off the gravel and onto the grass at Harry's home on the tidal creek. He'd said oyster roasts were popular in the Lowcountry, but she had underestimated what that meant. *"Come over. Join a few friends and me." A few?*

She found Harry scurrying back and forth in the kitchen. "Hey, Unc! I thought you told me a few people!"

He laughed. "It is a few, sweetheart. At least as far as oyster roasts go."

"Sorry I'm late," she said. "What can I do to help?"

"You're not late. Folks were excited and came early. Not to worry. We're in great shape. You can help me bring out the food in about an hour. I figure we'll eat around six thirty, so we give folks time to get here."

"How many people are coming?" she asked.

"Well—I'm not exactly sure."

"How many did you invite?"

He laughed again. "The way it works here is you strategically invite a dozen or so, and lots more will show up. My guess is we'll have about a hundred. I got twelve bushels of oysters, so we're prepared. Let's go out and get a beer." He grabbed her hand and led her through the back door onto the deck. She jumped when a group of people yelled, "Surprise!"

She suddenly realized the surprise was for her. She stood on the back deck with her jaw dropped. Harry chuckled as he hugged her. "Gotcha! Happy birthday, sweetheart. A little early, but I knew that was the only way to pull this off."

"Thank you, Uncle Harry. I'm not sure what to say."

Someone yelled, "Speech!"

CJ laughed as she gazed at new and old faces. "No speeches except to say thank you to everyone. This is quite a shock. My dear uncle here has outdone himself." She patted him on the back. "Please enjoy yourself and, again, thank you so much."

Ben bolted up the steps and took her hand. "Come on, old lady, let's get you a beer."

"Oh yeah, I'm way older than you."

They made their way through the crowd, and she was hugged all the way to the coolers.

"Ben, I suppose you were in on this?" she asked.

"I helped a little, but the credit goes to Harry and Craig." He pointed over her shoulder. "Look behind you."

She turned to face a man with dark brown hair and the same chiseled features as her father. She grabbed him. "Uncle Craig!"

"Happy birthday!" He kissed her on the cheek. "I told Harry a sharp detective like you would be onto us, but this proves he's still the sneakiest one in the family."

She leaned back. "Hey, wait a minute. He said you were away on a fishing trip."

He released her, and his arms spread. "A big fat lie, my dear. Now, if I can borrow Ben here, we'll get the grate out of my truck so we can roast some oysters. Won't be long and the coals will be ready."

A tap on her shoulder caused her to turn. "Bill!"

Bill Parrish hugged her, followed by Will, Ben's older brother. Both men resembled Ben—well over six feet, lean, dark brown hair, and amber eyes.

"Happy birthday, CJ! How are you?" Bill asked.

"I'm doing great, Bill. Been staying busy with work. There are lots of crazies out there. How are you feeling?"

"Actually, I feel terrific." He patted his side where his son had stabbed him when he saved her. "My wounds are all healed up, and I've been getting a lot of fishing in. I'm sure Ben told you, but he, Will, and I just got back from the Keys. We caught lots of fish."

"Ben did tell me that. The trip sounded fun. I've never been there." She pointed to the coolers. "Can I get you two a beer?"

Bill clapped his hands. "Yeah, I'd love a beer, but the birthday girl isn't supposed to work at her own party." He punched Will on the shoulder. "That's why I let Will come."

Will smiled at her. "Pop's right. Enjoy the party. I can always find the beer."

She spent the next thirty minutes talking to everyone she knew in Charleston. Sal was there with his wife, as were her landlord, George Watkins, and his wife. Thomas and Eddie showed up, and she was surprised that the chief, captain, and lieutenant came. Mayor Margie Sellers's smiling face shocked her the most. True to form, the mayor worked her way through the crowd, shaking everyone's hand.

When the chief motioned to her later, she joined him away from the crowd. *Oh jeez.*

"Happy birthday. When is the official day?"

"Wednesday, sir."

He smiled. "Listen, I'm sorry I was a bit terse yesterday. I had a bad start to the day and took it out on you."

"No problem. We're all feeling the strain right now."

He nodded, and she found herself fixated on the scar on his right cheek. *Wonder how he got that.*

"I spoke to SLED and have a commitment to have the results for the fiber and substance from the Harleston murder within three weeks," he said. "Seems there are several high-profile murder cases in the queue ahead of ours. I may have another, much faster option."

She tilted her head. "Okay, what would that be?"

He exhaled. "We trade a trip to Alaska for the FBI's help. Robert called me last night pushing me, and after some discussion, we came up with you going north for three days, and him getting us at the top of the heap for our stuff. Robert wanted you on the ground for three days, which is a nonstarter, but he's offered a private jet to fly you there and back. So you'd be gone a total of three days."

She nibbled at her lip. "How long does it take to get there?"

"Jet could have you there in about seven to eight hours. With the four-hour time difference, you'd hit Sitka before noon if you left here by eight o'clock. You'd have the rest of that day, plus all the next day, before heading home."

"What do Stan and Paul think?" she asked.

"They're not thrilled about it, but they agreed it's your call." His eyes narrowed. "You can't let your cases slip, which means getting certain items handled before you leave."

More weight pressed down on her. "When would I leave?"

"The jet would pick you up at the Charleston Executive Airport on Wednesday morning at eight o'clock."

Happy thirty-third birthday to me. "Well, sir, I think I should go. We need the FBI's help and probably still owe them for the Parrish case. Robert pulled out all the stops for us. I can work the next three days to cover the most critical items and set it up so things move while I'm away."

He slowly nodded. "Okay. I'll be sure that you get the resources you asked for yesterday."

"Officer Jones and Sam?"

"Yes. They'll both be informed by morning."

"Thank you, sir. Can I ask you something else? You appeared to smile a bit yesterday when I mentioned Officer Jones, or did I read you wrong?"

Walter smiled. "Very perceptive, Detective. Johnny is my nephew."

"I see." She slowly nodded. "Makes sense now."

He patted her shoulder. "Enough about work. Get back to your party. I'll call Robert and let him know we have a deal. Happy birthday again."

CJ watched him walk over and whisper to Stan and Paul and disappear around the corner.

The roar of the party was at full volume when a petite woman exited the back door, followed by Harry, her arms loaded with a large box and bags hanging from both hands. Her baby-blue eyes met CJ's, and a big grin spread across her face.

CJ made her way forward and exclaimed, "Sam Ravenel! What are you doing here? I thought when I asked you about having dinner, you said you had a date."

Sam tossed her head toward Harry. "I do. Meet my date." Both women laughed.

CJ reached for the bags. "Can I help you?"

The younger woman shook her head. "No way. It's your party, so go mingle. I got this. Come on, Harry. Back to work, you slacker."

Harry winked at his niece. "She's the best-looking date I've had in years."

CJ saw Craig and Ben struggling with a large piece of metal. Will appeared out of nowhere to help them get the grate positioned on cinder blocks over the bed of coals. She circled around the noisy crowd. "You guys know what you're doing?"

"Yes, ma'am," said Craig. "We have the grate ready and are about to put on our first batch of oysters. They'll be roasted and ready to eat in less than ten minutes."

Wet burlap bags of oysters were dropped on the grate, and a mixture of steam and smoke filled the air. "How do you know how long to cook 'em?" she asked.

"Some of them will start to pop open," Ben said. "Plus, we'll do some tasting. Do you like oysters?"

She shrugged. "I think so. It's my first oyster roast, so we'll find out."

Craig pulled an oyster out of one of the bags with a gloved hand and popped it open with a flick of a small blunt knife. He dropped the oyster in his mouth. "I'll try one just in case. I like 'em naked." He chewed and smiled. "Oh, yeah. The first batch is ready. Okay, folks, take your positions!"

Ben grabbed her hand. "Come on, your spot is at the head table. I'll show you how it's done."

Steaming oysters were poured onto the centers of tables made from sawhorses and plywood. People gathered around, carrying plates that held potato salad, corn on the cob, and corn bread muffins. Some simply stood with a glove on one hand and an oyster knife in the other. Harry said a quick prayer and announced, "Dig in!"

Ben showed her how to shuck an oyster and let her know she could eat them naked, as Craig called it, or add a little cocktail sauce, hot sauce, or lemon juice. "I like a dab of hot sauce on mine. Help yourself to a saltine if you want."

She slid an oyster into her mouth. "Wow. These are good. I think I like them best with a little cocktail sauce and a bit of cracker."

Ben hustled off to help with more oysters, and Harry dropped into his spot.

She nudged him. "Thanks for this, Uncle Harry."

"You're welcome. Just happy our surprise worked."

She laughed. "Where'd your date go?"

He gazed around the yard. "She's off bringing in more food. She's been a big help, and she sure thinks a lot of you. But, of course, if I was thirty years younger, it'd be a real date."

"Yeah. Sam's become a close friend." She opened another oyster, placed it on a saltine, and added a dab of cocktail sauce. "By the way, it looks like she may be coming back to the CID to help me with my cases."

"That would help, but no shop talk during the party. Only happy talk."

Ben was showing some young woman in skimpy white shorts and a pale blue blouse how to shuck oysters at another table. CJ knew it was a ploy. The damn girl had already eaten a dozen and was a pro at shucking them.

"Who's Ben talking to?" she asked her uncle.

Harry looked back. "Oh, that's Kelsey. She's the daughter of one of my neighbors. Just graduated with her master's from Clemson. She and a couple of girlfriends came. Pretty little thing, isn't she?"

Long blond hair made of silk, sparkling ocean-blue eyes, and a body that hits the gym every day. "Yeah. She's okay."

Harry's smile was sly. "Honey, have your eyes gotten greener?"

"Stop it, Uncle Harry."

Three more gorgeous twentysomethings joined Ben and Kelsey.

Jeez, girls, you'll paw the poor man to death.

From his perch on a chair, Harry yelled, "Peach cobbler and vanilla ice cream for dessert!" He jumped down and headed to the kitchen with Sam trailing after him.

CJ and Harry sat alone on the back deck after everyone had left, both staring skyward. The sky was unblemished, and the heavenly bodies were brighter than usual. She loved how dark the night was away from the city lights.

"Thanks again for the party, Uncle Harry."

"You're welcome. I still can't believe we surprised you. I guess all your work distractions paid off—at least for the party."

"About that. Now that the party's over, I have a question. What do you think about my latest murder case?" She could sense his uneasiness.

"The missing heart? I still lean toward someone on drugs in some dazed state."

Staring upward, she leaned back again. "I don't think that's what it is. Whoever did it was cold and calculating. Someone on drugs would have made mistakes and left something behind. Why else would someone remove a heart and take it with them?"

He cleared his throat. "Only two reasons I can think of. He's either a sadistic psychopath, which means this may not be the first or the last time, or it's some kind of ritual."

"Ritual? You mean like a cult or witchcraft?"

"Yeah. Maybe. Could be someone who thinks a heart was needed to perform some type of ceremony."

"You mean like placing the heart in a circle of candles?"

His eyes locked on her. "Yes. If so, let's hope that the ceremony sufficed and there won't be more."

They sat silent for several minutes before he spoke. "So you're going to Alaska? You think there's a connection to Parrish?"

She shrugged. "I can't be sure until I look."

He stood and stretched. "Enough of this. Let's have a little more cobbler and ice cream, then call it a night. We need something pleasant to dream about."

You mean not the faces of dead women or missing body parts.

TEN

Sunday, October 31
St. Helena Island, South Carolina

CJ smiled from Harry's front steps as Paul pulled up the next morning. It was too early on a Sunday to get coffee, so she'd filled a thermos and brought to-go cups. St. Helena Island, where they were headed, was two hours away, and they had to arrive before church started at ten.

"Morning, Paul. I brought some coffee if you want some."

"Love some. I'm still a bit foggy this morning. It was a fun party last night."

"It was. I can't believe so many people came."

He chuckled. "We had good reasons. An oyster roast and your birthday."

The sun peeked over the horizon as they crossed the Ashley River Memorial Bridge. Seagulls stretched their wings as they soared over the glistening water. CJ remembered her first trip out Highway 17 with Ben and how he'd described the numerous rivers crisscrossing the marshes on their way to the Atlantic Ocean. She cracked the window, and the salty odor rose.

"How about I tell you why we're going to St. Helena?" he asked.

"Sure. The suspense has been killing me."

His eyes never left the road. "How familiar are you with the Gullah people?"

"Uh, not really. Ben told me the beautiful sweetgrass baskets in the market are made by the Gullah. I watched a lady sit on the corner and finish one. It was so amazing how much skill she used."

He smiled. "Yes. That's what most people know about. There's a lot more to know, and today you'll find out why it's important. But first, I'll give you a quick crash course."

For the next hour and a half, Paul provided her with highlights. He told her the Gullah were slaves brought to the area from the west coast of Africa to work with live-stock and in agriculture. They were predominantly located on the sea islands along the South Carolina and Georgia coasts.

Since the Gullah were composed of a mixture of people from different countries and tribal groups, they'd created a blended language. As a result, the language, which was still spoken, had pieces of both African and English dialects.

As they neared the island, Paul finished his summary. "After slavery was abolished and the plantation economy collapsed, the Black population migrated to find work elsewhere. As the sea islands became less isolated from the mainland, the migration increased. There are many famous people who trace their roots back to the Gullah. For example, Clarence Thomas, Michael Jordan, Jim Brown, Joe Frazier, and Michelle Obama."

"Wow!" she exclaimed. "I never knew that."

"St. Helena Island is important as it's at the center of the Gullah culture. I was born there. It was also the home of Dr. Buzzard, a well-known root doctor. In hoodoo, a root doctor is a conjurer who knows how to make charms and potions from herbs and roots and perform rituals. Some people even add clairvoyance to the list."

"Wait. Hoodoo? Do you mean voodoo?" she asked.

He shook his head. "No. Hoodoo is correct. It's what the Gullah practice. Hoodoo is a blend of Christianity, herbalism, and folk magic, and is mostly positive, although there are some darker sides.

"Most think of voodoo as more of a religion. Both use charms, spells, rituals, roots, and herbs to reach the desired outcome. Both hoodoo and voodoo can involve conjuring, which is black magic, so I guess both can be dangerous if misused."

The sign for the Woods Memorial Bridge, which connected St. Helena Island to Beaufort, crept into view. CJ rubbed her chin. "Do you think hoodoo has something to do with the Harleston case?"

"I'm not sure." He frowned. "I know a lot about hoodoo, but I'm no expert. But you're about to meet someone who can tell us, if she will. Everyone calls her Grannie, not because she's their grandmother, but because she's a community healer."

"A healer?"

"Yes," he replied. "She uses herbal medicines for remedies."

"You said 'if she will.' Do you know her?"

"I do, and most importantly, there's a connection. I'm a descendant of the Gullah people. My ancestors were brought here as slaves. So were Walter's."

They rode in silence until they turned onto Dr. Martin Luther King Junior Drive, a main road on St. Helena Island. Paul glanced at her. "We're meeting Grannie at the Brick Baptist Church. It's an old church built by slaves in 1855. Grannie insisted we attend the ten o'clock service, and afterward, she'll meet with us. We'll see if she will talk. Let me clarify that. She'll talk to us, but in the Gullah language. I'll understand it, but you'll only catch certain words."

"Does she speak English?"

"She does. Very well, in fact. But she will read you and only speak English if she trusts you."

She narrowed her eyes. "Read me?"

Paul smiled. "Sorta like you and your instincts. So just smile, be respectful, and listen."

A shiver crossed her. *This will be a new experience, and on Halloween at that.* "Is there anything else you can tell me about Grannie?" CJ asked.

"Well, she was born on St. Helena and has lived there her whole life. I'm not sure she's ever set foot off the island. Reportedly, she's nearly one hundred years old. Her grandfather was brought to South Carolina from West Africa to work the rice fields. He became a free man in 1861, not long after arriving."

"How's her health?"

He smiled. "Probably better than ours. Grannie doesn't get around like she did, but since she's a healer, she knows how to care for herself." Paul pulled into the parking lot and put the truck in park. "She can be mysterious, but I've known her all my life, and she's the kindest person you'll ever meet. Don't be thrown off when you meet her. She's wary of strangers."

Two stories of brown brick and white-framed windows stood on the rise in front of them. More than one hundred fifty years old, the church was pristine and beautiful. The simple yet elegant structure oozed history. Dr. Martin Luther King had worshipped there when in the area and penned part of his famous "I Have a Dream" speech in a small cottage on the island.

Paul led her up the short steps and into the building. Along the way, he smiled and greeted numerous other churchgoers as he introduced her. Everyone treated her warmly, and she was the only White person in attendance. She loved the service, especially when the voices of the choir rose. Being Catholic, she had heard some excellent choirs, but she hadn't felt this sensation before. The pastor's sermon about loving each other resonated and was met with continuous amens.

———

After the service, CJ stood under the moss hanging from a massive oak near a cemetery filled with various markers of all shapes and sizes. She was reading the monument for the Penn School, the first school for Black students in the South, when Paul approached with an elderly woman on his arm.

Grannie was no more than five feet two, was stocky, and wore a red-and-white checkered dress. A matching red hat sat atop her gray hair, and her white pearl earrings complemented her necklace. However, it was her eyes that stuck out—the odd green eyes of a cat.

"Grannie, this is CJ. She's my friend."

The old woman's lips produced a small smile, followed by a slight bow of her head.

CJ returned the smile. "It's an honor to meet you, Grannie. I absolutely loved the service. Thank you for inviting us."

Paul helped Grannie into a folding chair in the shade. The old woman sat, quietly fanning herself, while he delivered two more folding chairs. He positioned his chair in front of Grannie while CJ sat a few feet away, slightly to his right. Close enough to listen, but far enough away not to intrude.

She had never heard the Gullah language. Most of the words were foreign, but there was something about the cadence that she found soothing. As Paul had described, she was able to pick out some words, and Grannie's eyes never left her. *She's reading me.*

After several minutes, Paul turned. "CJ, do you have the photo of our victim?"

CJ opened a yellow folder and handed him the eight-by-ten. Paul placed the photo in Grannie's hands as if handling an egg. The old woman's eyes left CJ and went downward. She squinted and shook her head, first slowly, then faster. Her lids squeezed shut. *"Daa'k dainjus oagly chil'."*

Grannie's eyes popped open and focused on CJ. *"Twis' med'sin."*

She waved them away with her hand. "Go. No more talking today. Bye, CJ. Be careful on your trip."

What? CJ struggled not to question her. Grannie knew more, but she stood silent as the pastor approached from the church steps, took the old woman's arm, and led her away.

CJ followed Paul back to his truck. As she dropped into the truck seat she turned to Paul. "So, what did she say?"

"'Dark, dangerous, ugly child,' and 'Twisted medicine.'"

"What does that mean?"

Paul turned the key. "Hell if I know, but it's not good. I know it doesn't seem like much information, but Grannie confirmed my fear. Whoever killed our victim was practicing some form of ritual. It wasn't just some crazy."

"Do you think we can talk to her again?"

"We can try. We need Grannie to trust you, so she'll speak English and maybe look at more of what we have. I think we know what our guy is doing or trying to do, but not why. We need the latter to find him."

She jotted down the words *dark, dangerous, ugly child* and *twisted medicine* on her notepad. *What the hell does that mean? And how did Grannie know about my trip?*

The talk was sporadic on their return journey. Both were lost in thought. Paul dropped her back off at Harry's to get her truck, and they agreed to meet the following morning.

CJ spent the rest of the day organizing her trip to Alaska. She had a long list of things to do before she left, and she still had to pack. *So how cold is Alaska this time of year? I'll need to dig my Boston winter gear out of the storage room.*

ELEVEN

Sunday, October 31
St. Helena Island

Elias's eyes were fixed on a Hobie Cat struggling against the rough waves. The red-and-yellow sail battled to stay upright. Two boys, younger than him, worked feverishly to gain control. Despite how it looked to many, he was sure these boys were having the time of their life. He couldn't remember ever being happy.

He lay back and stared upward. A lone white seagull floated above him against the background of a clear, darkening blue sky. Like him, the bird was alone. *Is he happy that way?*

The truth was, he wasn't alone but wished he was. His father had blamed him for his mother's death at his birth and had never cared for him. Instead, he was either on the road driving long-haul trucks or, when home, ignoring him. He could not have cared less about whether Elias had anything to eat or about anything he did at all, for that matter.

The only person he could remember ever giving him the time of day was his grandmother. She was no saint, but she at least made sure he got fed once a day. She also protected him from his grandfather. Unfortunately, her death when he was seven had meant he had no more protection. No protection meant constant physical and verbal abuse. When there was a lot of alcohol involved, the physical abuse had turned sexual.

He'd always been powerless. But meeting the old man had given him hope, and through his training, he would soon have the power he needed to control his own fate. Assuming, of course, that his training had been sufficient. If only the old man hadn't died. Having his mentor now would have ensured his success.

—

Elias crawled through the small window. The house was silent. He quickly went to the kitchen and rummaged through the cabinets to find what food he could. He tossed it in a plastic bag and ran out the back door. He knew where his grandfather had been all day and that he'd come home drunk.

—

Elias squeezed into the tight little corner as the sun hid for the night. He lit a small candle and opened a can of sardines with his knife. Then, one by one, he laid sardines on crackers and shoved them in his mouth. Not a big supper, but better than most.

He glimpsed at himself in a grimy piece of sheet metal. Elias didn't look any different or feel any more powerful. He was the same ugly-looking freak as before. Had he properly followed the steps? *Maybe the power only comes after I complete them all.* The sardines rose in his throat. He wiped his eyes on his sleeve. Perhaps the old man had been wrong and it wouldn't work.

TWELVE

Tuesday, November 2
Downtown Charleston

The sky was dim—predawn. It was too early to grab a coffee. Hell, it was too early to do a lot of things. CJ climbed into her truck, and after the short drive, she pulled off Lockwood, entering the LEC minutes later. She tipped her head to a couple of officers loitering by an empty coffeepot. *Guess I'll make the next pot, guys.*

"Excuse me." She bent down to grab what she needed from the bottom shelf.

"Here you go, Detective. Take mine. I haven't touched it. I'll get a new pot going." One of the officers smiled and handed her a brown paper cup. "It's not too old, and if you want a Danish, there's a couple left."

She returned the smile. "Thank you so much. Coffee works. I'll grab something to eat later." She turned and headed to her desk in the corner of the bullpen.

Flipping to the front page of each of the rape victims' reports, she groaned. *I'm missing something.* She laid the sheets side by side and stared at them. *The trick is, what am I not seeing?* Four victims with nothing in common except they were raped in their beds. *Damn it!*

CJ grabbed the files and walked down the hall. She punched in the code to the conference room, flipped the light switch, and dropped the files on the table. She dismantled the reports and pinned them to the evidence board. *This room creeps me out.* She scanned the pages, searching for some connection. *How do I find one?*

All the women lived within the city limits, but none claimed to know each other, not through work, school, church, or places they frequented. *We need to talk to neighbors again. Maybe we missed something.* She scribbled a reminder.

Her cell phone rang, and she answered the 843 number. "Detective O'Hara."

"Hello, Detective. This is Dr. Emerson over at Roper. Do you have a minute?"

"Sure. What can I do for you, Doctor?"

"I was going through my notes and files on Saturday, and I noticed a couple of things I didn't point out when you were here last Monday. First, our third rape victim, Marcy Willis, and our fourth victim, Cindy Evans, had almost identical physical damage from their rapes. This probably isn't a colossal finding, but I wanted to point it out.

"Something more relevant is I noted in Marcy's file that she said she scratched the guy who raped her. She thinks her nails caught him on the side of his neck. I guess I didn't really think it was important since we didn't find anything under her fingernails. I wanted to make sure you knew, though."

CJ added notes to her pad. "Thanks, Doctor. Everything helps." *Shit! Too bad we didn't get the asshole's skin or blood under her nails, but at least she wounded him.*

CJ was staring at the stack of files again when the latch to the door clicked. She glanced at the clock—7:35 a.m. *Who is . . .* Sam entered the conference room. "Good morning, CJ."

"Hey! How'd you find me?"

Sam's baby-blue eyes sparkled. "One of the guys said you came in here." She smiled. "I've been reassigned back to the CID."

CJ nodded. "Yes. I hope this is okay."

"Better than okay. I don't mind organizing patrol files all day, but it's freaking boring, and I miss working with you." The younger woman dropped her purse and a plastic bag on the table. "I've got a couple of desks coming, and we'll set the war room back up. This will be our home again. At least for now."

"Really? When did that happen?" CJ asked.

"Yesterday. Paul called me about the change, and I suggested he assign us this room, and he agreed. Officer Jones will be here soon too. The three of us can share it. Oh!" Sam pulled a foil wrapper from the plastic bag. "I brought you breakfast. Hope you like sausage-and-egg burritos. They should still be hot. I just made them."

Same old Sam. "Thanks. I'd love one. Sal wasn't open yet, and I need to go to the Piggly Wiggly and stock up on food."

Until the spicy sausage, scrambled egg, and melted cheddar cheese hit CJ's tongue, she hadn't realized how hungry she was. Sam's eyes stayed fixed on her. "Are you feeling okay?"

CJ gulped her bite down. "Sure. Why?"

"You look thinner." She shrugged. "Like you've lost weight."

Her mouth stopped, and her eyes connected with Sam's. "I don't think so. What am I missing?"

"Well . . . Thomas mentioned he was worried about you."

Damn it! Pass out, and I'm national news. "Did he say why?"

"No, not really, but he pulled me aside at the party and said he was worried about you. He wouldn't give me any reason except that he thought you looked run down."

CJ flipped her hand. "I'm fine. I've just been busy."

Thankfully, a knock at the door distracted Sam. She went over and opened it to two men in blue coveralls with a desk on a dolly. She pointed. "Thanks, guys. Let's put them over here on this back wall. I want a computer station set up on each. There should also be another mobile evidence board in the storage room. If one of you could be a sweetheart and bring that in, I'd appreciate it."

CJ chuckled softly. *Yep, same old Sam. Charming while bossing her way to what she wants.* Neither of the men seemed to mind; they were eager to make Sam happy.

"You guys need any help?" The smiling Officer Johnny Jones entered.

"Hello, Officer Jones," CJ said, and motioned to Sam. "Not sure you know her, but this is Sam."

"Hello, Sam. You can call me Johnny. You too, Detective."

After the desks were set up, the three of them spent the next two hours going over the details of each case. CJ leaned back in her chair and pointed to the evidence board. "Okay, let's cover what's next. We have two cases we need to solve. First, I believe we have one person who has committed four rapes in the last two months. Second, we have a woman murdered in Harleston Village a week ago. For each case, I've come up with a list of initial work for you.

"Johnny, the key for you is helping me determine what, if any, connection there is between our four rape victims. You'll see from the files none is apparent, so I need you to interview the neighbors again."

He nodded. "Yes, ma'am."

Her eyes went to Sam. "It's a bit unusual, but I need you to do background checks and research on each young woman. If there's anything that connects them, find it. Also, the FBI is running an analysis on a fiber found at one of the scenes. Stay on them and get their report."

Sam took the FBI contact information. "I'll get right on it. I love to research."

CJ cleared her throat. "For the murder case, it's early on. The FBI is analyzing a substance on our victim's forehead and near the heart we found on Wednesday. They'll also examine the shoe impressions. Same drill, Sam. Stay on them.

"Johnny, I need you to expand the interviews in the neighborhood. We need to know if anyone saw anything. A lone person walking, recent visitors, a strange car, heard a noise, whatever."

He made a note. "Sure. By the way, did CSU find any fingerprints on the candles?"

"No. Eddie said the candles were clean," CJ said. "He also told me so far, the blood found at the murder scene is all the same type and the DNA all matches Naomi."

Sam stood and grabbed the files. "I'll make copies of each of these for you and keep the originals here. That way, you'll have everything with you." She hesitated. "How about Alaska?"

How does she know about that? CJ leaned forward. "At this point, that's not a case for us. I've only been asked to look at the FBI's file on three murders in Alaska and give my opinion. I'll take a trip there tomorrow but be back late Friday night. It's a favor, and we get priority at the FBI's lab in Quantico in return."

She stood and walked to the board. "Let's focus on what we have here?" She pointed to a circled area on a map of Charleston. "Johnny, how about you and I interview some of the neighbors in Harleston today? Then, tomorrow, you can continue and start on the neighbors of our rape victims. I'd also like to talk to you about the Gullah culture, assuming you know about it."

His cognac-brown eyes flashed. "I do."

Sam's head snapped around. "Gullah?"

CJ nodded. "There may be a connection in our murder case. Someone could be trying their hand at conjuring."

The younger woman exhaled. "Oh, jeez. Let me know if I need to research anything."

CJ looked down when her phone buzzed and read the text. "Chief needs to see me. I'll be back as soon as I can."

Johnny stood. "I'll get on those interviews unless you need me to wait on you."

"No. Go ahead," CJ replied.

CJ opened the door to Chief Williams's office. He stood staring out the window. "Hey, sir. I understand you wanted to see me?"

"Yes. Yes, I do. Grab a seat." He turned but remained on his feet.

She settled in the uncomfortable chair across from his desk—his eyes looked down on her. She felt a sudden smallness.

He cleared his throat. "I'm troubled."

"Sir?"

"Well, let me say it another way. I'm having, uh, let's say buyer's remorse."

She wasn't sure what the hell he was talking about. "I'm sorry, sir. I don't follow."

A low grunt. "I just had my ass chewed out by the mayor. I made the mistake of mentioning the Alaska case, and she went ballistic. She wants to know why in the hell I would be so stupid as to let you go to Alaska when we have four unsolved rapes and now a fresh murder."

She squirmed in the chair.

His face closed the gap as he leaned toward her and put his palms on the desk. His dark brown eyes bored into her. "It got me thinking. Am I making a mistake letting you go? Seems to me you're not close to solving either of your cases and here you are trotting off to help a department three thousand miles away."

What am I supposed to say? "Uh, sir . . . I'm not sure what to say. I've been working my ass—"

He slapped his hands down on the desk. "Save it! We don't get points for trying. We have to show results."

Her tension skyrocketed, and her pulse escalated. *Maybe he's right . . . I'm lost.* She bit her bottom lip and tried to remain composed.

He rubbed his bald head, dropped into his chair, and leaned back. She sat, waiting.

He blew out a long breath. "Okay, I'll tell you what. You can go on the trip, but you better not lose a step on solving whoever's raping women in Charleston and who butchered that poor girl in Harleston Village. Are we fuck-ing clear?"

She croaked, "Yes, sir. We're clear." He spun his chair around and returned to staring out the window. *Guess I'm excused.* She quietly closed the door as she left.

CJ made her way back to the conference room and packed up copies of the files. Sam must have sensed she was in no mood to chat and silently helped her. In addition to the armload of files for Alaska, she grabbed part of the files for her two Charleston cases.

"Okay, Sam. I think I have what I need." CJ picked up the large file case and checked the round clock on the wall—2:47 p.m. *A little early, but to hell with it.* "I'm going home to pack some clothes."

"Feel free to call me anytime. Okay? I'll make sure the items you assigned Johnny and me get done while you're gone."

"Thanks, Sam," CJ whispered. She headed to the door, a weight crushing her.

PART TWO

BEAVER MOON

The full moon at the time of year to set beaver traps before the swamps and rivers freeze. Also known as the frosty moon.

THIRTEEN

Wednesday, November 3
Sitka, Alaska

At just before noon local time, CJ stepped out of the door of the Cessna CitationJet and made her way down the stairs to the tarmac of Sitka Rocky Gutierrez Airport. A light mist floated in the air and spritzed her face. Sitka wasn't as cold as she'd expected but still only half as warm as Charleston. A slight chill made its way down her back.

"Detective, please follow the marked walkway into the terminal, and I'll bring your bag," the co-pilot said. She smiled and thanked him.

A short, stocky man in his midforties approached her. "Welcome to Alaska, Detective. I'm Special Agent Wally Gauge. Call me Wally."

She took his hand. "Nice to meet you."

"How was your flight?"

"Not bad. I must admit, flying on a private jet was a luxury. First time for me."

Wally chuckled. "Yeah, it's the only way to go, but it's infrequent for us. Robert pulled some serious strings. Let's get you inside. This rain isn't bad, but it'll slowly soak you. I've got a rain jacket with a hood for you in my truck."

"Thanks. This jacket is warm enough but not waterproof."

He took the black file case from her. "Did you have a chance to review what I sent?"

"I did. The plane had a foldout table and plenty of room to work. Thanks for getting me some information ahead of time."

"Thanks for helping us. Robert speaks highly of you, and I understand you're in great demand from your chief. I hope you can help me close our three murders and give the families some peace. The Sitka and Ketchikan communities are still freaked out, wondering if the murderer is still on the loose. Do you want to go check into your hotel or head straight to the station?"

"Let's grab my bag and go to the station. I can check in later."

As they drove, he gave her an overview of Sitka. The city of fewer than ten thousand people was located on Baranof Island's west coast in southeast Alaska. Sitka had a significant fishing industry but also lots of tourism. As with most places in Alaska, outdoor recreation was the most popular pastime.

"While the city itself is small, the city and borough of Sitka is the largest incorporated area in the US, totaling almost five thousand square miles," he finished as they neared the station.

She stared at the snowcapped peaks in the Tongass National Forest looming in the background. "It sure makes it a massive area to cover."

Wally sighed. "It does. Well, here we are."

The Sitka police station was a white one-story building with a rust-colored fascia along its upper portion. The two entered through the small door and were met by a husky man she guessed was ten years older than her. Wally smiled. "Chief Richardson, meet Detective CJ O'Hara from Charleston."

"Hello, Detective. Call me Freddie. Thank you so much for coming all this way. I hope you can help us bring this mess to a close." He motioned down the narrow hallway. "I've got a spot for you in our conference room, so you have a place to work while you're here. Let's get you settled in. We've got plenty of coffee, sodas, and water, but I thought we'd go out to grab a bite and chat."

He opened the door to the twelve-by-twelve room, which held a chalkboard, computer, and speakerphone. CJ smiled. "This is perfect."

The small diner was buzzing. The intoxicating aroma made CJ's stomach rumble. A skinny black-haired woman in jeans and a long-sleeved, light blue T-shirt waved them to a table in the far corner. "Back here, Chief. I saved the quietest spot we have for you and your guests." She dropped menus on the table and added three glasses of water. "Today's special is fish and chips—lightly breaded fried halibut, fries, and coleslaw. Made the slaw myself, and it's yummy."

Freddie looked at CJ and Wally. "Sound good?"

Both nodded.

"Please bring us three specials, Kira."

The chief gave CJ an overview of the department, which consisted of thirty-two people. While their jurisdiction extended over the entire massive area, over 90 percent of the residents were concentrated on the island's west side in the city. The department was split into two divisions. The Patrol Division provided twenty-four-hour coverage with a dozen officers and two detectives. The Service Division covered the jail and dispatch and had one evidence technician.

"Most of our crimes here involve traffic mishaps, drunk and disorderly, minor assault, petty theft, drugs, and an occasional wild animal that wanders into town. We don't have many major crimes like rape or murder. Unfortunately, we're not equipped to fully investigate these, so we rely on the FBI to help us," the chief explained.

"How about your two detectives?" CJ asked.

"One deals with drug cases, the other handles everything else, and we're not equipped to process any complicated evidence."

She raised her eyebrows. *One detective to cover five thousand square miles.*

Their orders arrived, and CJ did her best not to gobble the tasty food down. Kira was right. The coleslaw was yummy. *I swear I taste brown sugar.*

The chief provided more details on the department and their work on the two murders the prior year. He also described how he had coordinated with Ketchikan PD on their murder there. He agreed with Wally that all three seemed connected.

Later, at the station, CJ stood in front of the chalkboard in her temporary office. Wally and Freddie sat staring at her.

"Based on my review of the files, here's the way I'd summarize all three cases." She wrote the bullet points on the board.

- *White women*
- *Twenty-two to twenty-six*
- *Blond hair, blue eyes*
- *Naturally beautiful, little use of makeup*
- *Abducted, raped, and murdered elsewhere*
- *Lacerations to throat and midsection*
- *Bodies dumped near the water*
- *No forensic evidence left behind*

"Does this sound accurate?" she asked them.

Both men nodded.

"So, the next question is, how do these compare to what we had in Charleston? I'd say other than the locations, the crimes are identical."

Freddie asked, "Does that mean Bryan Parrish was the guy who killed our girls?"

She dropped into a chair. "It's a possibility based on the MO, but I can't say for sure, not yet. I'd like to spend the next day and a half digging further to see if we can answer that question. I want to see the crime scenes and how they compare, and I believe you had a witness?"

The chief exhaled. "We have a witness, but I'm not too sure he's helpful. Seth's a drunk notorious for telling whoppers. So who knows what he saw, if anything?"

She politely smiled. "Fair enough. I'd still like to talk to him."

Freddie held up his hands. "Whatever you need, I'll make it happen. Let's go to the crime scenes, and I'll have one of my officers find Seth."

They pulled off Lincoln Street near a marina that held around forty boats at 3:05 p.m. Freddie pointed down the shoreline. "We'll need to walk to the spot where one of the boat owners found our first victim."

The shore was a mixture of coarse sand and small rocks. Debris had washed up with the tide—wood scraps, plastic bottles, and kelp. CJ opened the file and pulled out the crime scene photos to orient herself. She pointed down the shoreline. "Based on the photos, she was found just below where those rocks jut out."

Freddie glanced at the photo. "Yeah. That's correct. We put the measurements on the diagram on the back of the photo." He flipped the image over. "Our notes say she was about eight feet from that rocky point and about four feet from the water's edge. The tide's coming in, so the exact spot is underwater now."

She squatted at the water's edge and looked in all directions. "It's hard to see this spot except from where the boats are docked. He knew she'd be found, but not easily. And, as we found at most of the scenes in Charleston, he used the tides to help cover his tracks."

The second crime scene was on the outskirts of town off Sawmill Creek Road. There was a small dock nearby, but it only held six boats. Like the first location, it was impossible to see from the road. Only a boat owner would have been able to see the body. CJ stared at the spot. "He dropped the second body by boat."

Wally spoke up. "How do you know?"

She pointed toward where they'd parked. "No way he would carry a body from where he could park to this spot. It'd be too easy to be seen and take him too long to get back to his vehicle. Chief?"

Freddie's eyes went from the spot to where they'd parked. "I think you're right. Too risky by car. He must own a boat."

She pointed at the dock. "Can you find out the name of everyone who has used those slips over the last year?"

"We can try. I'll get in touch with the owner, and hopefully, we can get some records."

She furrowed her brow. "Where did our witness say he saw a man?"

"At the first scene," Freddie replied.

CJ paced. "The witness stated he saw a man bent down, and then the man walked away. Correct?"

"Yes. That's right."

She closed her eyes. *Something's missing.* "According to the notes, the witness said the man walked away, but there's nothing about where he went."

"I'd need to check, but I think that's right," Freddie said.

She scribbled on her pad. "Okay, let's go back to the station. I wanna talk to the witness. Did your officers find him?"

Freddie pulled out his cell phone and made a call. He hung up and said, "We've found him, but he's dead drunk. My officer says he's in no shape to talk to us."

CJ sighed heavily. "Tell your officer to arrest him. Let's stick him in a jail cell overnight and see if we can sober him up."

The chief slowly shook his head. "I'm not sure we have a legit reason to arrest him. He's sitting in the Caribou Bar, not bothering anyone. I mean, I guess—"

She cut him off. "Public drunkenness."

Wally laughed. "Sounds like a good reason to me. Let him walk out of the bar, and as soon as he's on the sidewalk, it's perfectly legal."

Freddie grabbed his cell phone and called his officer. "Yep, that's what I said." He hit the end button. "I hope we don't get sued for this. We don't arrest drunks unless they're driving, and Seth doesn't own a car. He walks everywhere he goes."

"I'll make nice with him tomorrow when we chat," CJ said, smiling. "I also want to meet with the officer who responded for the first victim and took the witness statement."

The sky was dimming, so Wally suggested they call it a day and get CJ checked into her hotel. The group agreed and headed back to the station.

Wally pulled into the parking lot of a pale yellow building with a maroon roof, the Totem Square Hotel & Marina. The grounds were well kept, and the views of the mountains across the water were spectacular. A tall totem pole stood in the grassy area in front of the hotel.

"This is where I usually stay when I come to town from Juneau. The place is nice and close to everything. I made sure they had a room with a king-size bed and a view. How about we get you in your room, grab a drink, and have an early dinner? I'm sure you're beat."

CJ nodded. "That'll work. The trip's catching up with me. The four-hour time difference is a bitch."

CJ got her key and made her way to the room. She dropped her bag on the bed. The bedding had the same maroon color as the exterior. She opened the curtains to the sky, now turning a dark orange with streaks of yellow. A lone eagle sat atop a post on the pier at the marina. In the distance, a hint of snow was visible on a 3,200-foot dormant volcano, Mount Edgecumbe. She threw some water on her face and headed to the bar to meet Wally.

Wally smiled as CJ approached. "I grabbed us a table here by the window."

A woman with cropped black hair, freckled cheeks, and a nose ring approached. "Hey, I'm Cheyenne. I'll be taking care of you folks. What can I get you?"

They ordered a beer, a local Alaskan brew, and dinner when their drinks arrived. Even though CJ was tired, she enjoyed the baked lingcod and wild rice. They talked about Wally's twenty years with the FBI and her ten years in Boston and now Charleston. The small talk was fine with her after the long day.

"How about we call it a night?" Wally asked. "Let you get some rest."

CJ stretched her arms over her head. "That would be great."

She looked at her cell phone when it chimed. "Chief says Seth is safe and sound in a cell. Hopefully, he'll sleep it off and be coherent tomorrow."

As they walked to their rooms, Wally asked her what she thought about the case so far.

"I can't put my finger on it yet, but something's missing."

FOURTEEN

Thursday, November 4
Sitka

"More coffee?"

CJ smiled at the waitress in the hotel restaurant. "Yes. Thank you, Cheyenne."

"Would you like to order some breakfast?"

"I'll wait until my friend gets here. He shouldn't be too much longer."

CJ's eyes returned to the section of the aerial photograph of Lincoln Street where the first body had been found. The photos had been taken at a different time of day than when she'd visited the site, but the area appeared the same as when she'd seen it yesterday. There wasn't a scale, but she could estimate that the distance between the parking area and the bus stop where the possible suspect was seen wasn't far. Anyone could see one spot from the other, wherever they were standing.

She closed the file and gazed out the window. The sun was waking up, and the water sparkled. *Something is out there.* She leaned toward the window and mumbled, "What the heck is that?" She motioned to Cheyenne and told her she'd be back, then went through the glass door leading onto the deck. Crossing the grass past the totem pole, she made her way to the wooden dock walkway.

What is that?

"See something?" Startled, she turned to the weathered face of an old man with sharp eyes the color of a clear blue sky. He had to be at least eighty and wore bright yellow fishing waders over a long-sleeve camo shirt. His salt-stained floppy hat matched his shirt.

"I'm not sure." She pointed out to the horizon. "I was sitting in the restaurant and kept seeing something dark way out in the water." He leaned closer and stared down her arm. "There! There it is," she said excitedly.

He chuckled. "That's a whale playing around."

Her eyes went wide. "A whale?"

"Yep. They love to roll along the top of the water." Something black jutted up. "There's his tail."

"Wow. It's amazing. I wish I was closer."

The two stood, eyes fixed—waiting. For the next several minutes, she squealed every time the whale surfaced.

CJ eased to the edge of the dock, and something else popped up in the water right at her feet. She jumped back, and the old man caught her before she hit the ground. "Shit!"

The old man roared with laughter. "Don't worry. That's Ollie."

She peered over the edge. A dark gray furry creature with whiskers rolled over and returned to floating on its back. There was a loud crunching sound as its jaws worked. "Who's Ollie?" she asked.

"She's an otter. We named her Ollie when we thought she was a him, then she showed up with a pup, and it was too late to change the name. It had already stuck."

CJ bent down. "What's she eating?"

"Oysters," he replied. "Loves 'em. She'll swim, roll, and eat all day long." He patted CJ on the arm. "Well, I gotta go. Hope you enjoy your visit. Make sure you get someone to take you out in a boat. A pretty lady like you should enjoy herself."

She watched him shuffle down the walkway. *If only I had time.* She waved to Ollie and went back to her table as the rain started.

"Good morning, early bird."

She looked up at Wally's chestnut-brown eyes when he joined her just before eight o'clock. "Good morning. I guess with the time change, I was up super early. I think I've had a pot of coffee by myself, and I got to see a whale, an otter, and an eagle."

He poured himself a cup of coffee. "Whatcha got there?"

"I'm not sure yet. I'm just trying to think through things. So, for today, we'll talk with the responding officer, the witness, and the Ketchikan PD on a conference call."

"Yep. If we need to travel to Ketchikan, we could do it before you have to leave. It's only about an hour by air."

She thought for a moment. "Let's see how the call goes. Then, if needed, we could swing through Ketchikan tomorrow before I leave for Charleston."

Officer Travis Walker joined CJ, Wally, and the chief in the small conference room at nine. He was CJ's height and rail thin. His curly, sandy-blond hair was unkempt, and his cheeks were stained reddish from the sun and wind.

CJ gave him a warm smile. "Thanks for joining us, Officer Walker. I wanted to put some color on your report about the crime scenes for the two murders from last year. It always helps me understand the picture."

"No problem. Happy to help."

For the next hour, she went over the two reports. Throughout, Travis referred to his handwritten notes and answered her questions. It all seemed straightforward, and nothing unusual came out. The only thing that stuck with her was the officer had the same dismissive attitude about the witness. "He's not very reliable," he said.

After their discussions, CJ decided to revisit the crime scenes. She wanted the officer to walk her through everything again. "Let's start at the beginning, and I'd like you to go over every detail as you remember it." So she, Freddie, and Wally followed the officer's truck and they drove back to the scenes. He walked the group through what he'd found—again, nothing new.

On the way back to the station, CJ had another request. "Chief, I'd like to talk to the victim's parents if you could arrange it."

Freddie squirmed. Clearly, he was losing his patience. "Not sure that'll help. All I feel like you're doing is second-guessing what's in the files."

"That's not my intent at all. I'm trying to be thorough and bring fresh eyes."

He grunted. "I'll see what I can do. But I have to tell you, I hate making the parents go through their nightmare all over again."

"Understood. If it wasn't important to me, I wouldn't ask."

An hour later, CJ sat across from the parents of the first victim. They both looked drained, as if they hadn't slept. Neither could suggest anyone who would hurt their daughter. "Everybody loved her. She was a good girl, and there's no one here in Sitka who would harm her." The same scenario repeated itself with the parents of the second victim.

CJ and Wally went to lunch after the second interview. Freddie begged off, saying he needed to handle a couple of things. The rain had moved on, and the temperature had risen to an unusually high fifty degrees. The two decided to sit on the deck at the hotel for lunch. CJ was lost in thought and watched the eagle spreading his wings to dry in the sun.

Wally broke her trance. "Well, we still have our witness to talk to and our call with Ketchikan. What are your thoughts so far?"

She turned to him. "Nothing proves it, but it has to be a local. There's no way someone unfamiliar with the area would find those drop spots."

"Bryan Parrish was a local."

"He was," she replied. "What happened to the man he lived with?"

Wally shrugged. "I'm not sure. He died is all I know."

CJ jotted down a note. "Let's go by where he lived after lunch and see if we can find out how he died. If he died of unnatural or suspicious causes, it might make more sense for Parrish to be our guy for these murders."

He nodded. "What time do you want to talk to the witness? Freddie says Seth's bitching about wanting out, and he doesn't want to hold him for more than twenty-four hours."

She nibbled at her thumb. "I tell you what. Let's tell Freddie I'll talk to Seth at five. Just me."

Wally pursed his lips. "You don't want me there?"

"No. I want to talk to him alone. He may be more comfortable if it's only one person."

He simply stared at her. She knew he was wondering what she was thinking.

Wally steered onto Sawmill Creek Road. "Anything jump out at you from the discussions with Ketchikan?"

CJ shook her head. "No. Everything we covered was in the file. I'll go over it all again tonight, but I'm afraid there's nothing new." She checked the time on her cell phone—1:05 p.m. "How far is it to Bryan's old home?"

"Uh, I'd guess about twenty minutes past the second crime scene we visited yesterday. Popov lived outside of town."

"Who are we meeting?"

"Mikhail, Popov's nephew. He was surprised his uncle left the property to him in his will. I take it they weren't close."

"Is he operating the business?"

"Naw. Mikhail plans on selling the property and whatever equipment has value. Since the old man died, the place has been empty. Not many folks are interested in it, I guess."

The dirt road through the trees led to a crumbling white sign with faded red letters reading *Popov's Seafood*.

"It's no wonder this place has been tough to sell. It's way off the beaten path."

Wally snorted a laugh. "I'll say. I'm glad I got decent directions, or we'd have never found it."

A husky man with long black hair waved to them. His face was weathered, and CJ noticed a jagged scar on the right side of his face. His smile revealed a missing front tooth. "Jeez, this guy looks a little rough."

They climbed out of the truck and shook the man's hand. Mikhail Popov stood staring at CJ before speaking with a heavy Russian accent. "Miss, you may be the prettiest woman I've ever seen."

She ignored his compliment as she cleared her throat. "Thanks so much for meeting with us on short notice. Hopefully, we won't need much of your time. I'm sure you're busy."

"I've got all day for you." His gap-toothed smile got bigger. "Anything you need, I'm happy to provide."

Wally trapped a laugh. He gave CJ an *It's all yours* wink.

She opened her notebook. "Okay, Mr. Popov—"

"Mikhail."

"Okay, Mikhail. I'd like to sketch out the buildings and make a few notes if you could show us around. Would that be okay?"

"Sure," he replied. "Right this way."

For the next hour, CJ and Wally were led around the property. Wally hung back and let CJ lead since Mikhail was eager to please her. He recorded video of the buildings as they went with a small handheld camera.

Ivan Popov had lived in a small house, more like a shack. He had three small outbuildings filled with various pieces of equipment and junk. A dock in dire need of repair was home to a forty-seven-foot wooden trawler.

CJ pointed to the water's edge. "What's the small building way over there?"

Mikhail rubbed his chin. "I think that Parrish dude lived there. He was one weird guy. Only met him a time or two. He gave me the willies, but Uncle Ivan said he was a good worker."

She turned to Wally. "Doesn't the file say Bryan lived in the house with Ivan?"

He thumbed through the folder. "Yep. That's what it says."

Mikhail spoke up. "He did live in the house most of his life, but Uncle Ivan made him move into the shed a few years back."

"Do you know why your uncle made him move?" CJ asked.

"Nope. All I know is he moved out of the house."

She scribbled and then asked Mikhail, "Was he your uncle's only employee?"

"Yeah, except for a part-timer who helped some during peak season."

"Oh. Do you know his name and how to reach him?"

"Her."

"Excuse me?"

"It's a her," he said. "Her name's Sasha. I have her number somewhere in my truck. I'll find it for you when we go back up."

"Okay, thanks. Can we look inside the building where Bryan lived?"

She watched as he flipped through a set of keys. "I don't have a key," he huffed. "I have keys for everything else."

CJ walked to the small building. Like every other building, it was in bad shape. The dark red paint was peeling, the wood siding was cracked, and the shingles were covered in moss. A dingy curtain kept her from seeing through the lone window. "I sure wish I could see inside."

"Hold on." Mikhail scurried off and returned with a sledgehammer. "I can help you get inside." The padlock burst open with his overhead swing, and a quick kick slammed the door inward. "There you go."

"Wally, do we have a flashlight in the truck?" CJ asked.

Mikhail was already on the move. "I have one. I'll run and get it."

Wally chuckled. "Damn, CJ. This guy's gonna hurt himself trying to help you."

Within minutes, Mikhail had handed CJ a large flashlight. "How 'bout you guys wait here while I take a look?" she asked. The two men nodded.

CJ stepped over the threshold into the tiny interior. There were only two rooms. A small counter in the front room served as a makeshift kitchen, and there was a two-person table and a dark brown fake-leather couch on the back wall. There was no television or radio.

The back room had a twin bed and a four-drawer chest. A cracked mirror hung crookedly on the wall. A clothes rack held a few hanging shirts.

She backed up and looked more closely at the bed. There were no visible signs of blood or fluids, even though it was hard to tell with the filthy sheets. She worked her way back into the front room. The beam hit the couch, and she leaned in close, pulling a pair of latex gloves from her pocket. *What is that?* She carefully flipped the cushion upward before recoiling and smashing her knee into the edge of the table leg. "Oh, shit!"

"You okay?" Wally stepped into the doorway.

"Back up." CJ pushed him out the door. "We need forensics in here. Unless I'm way off, we have blood on the couch."

Mikhail's face went pale. "What?"

She exited, pushing both men off the porch. "Let's not contaminate anything until we know what we have."

Wally made the call. "Chief's sending out their evidence tech, but they're not equipped for this. I'm calling Juneau for reinforcements."

Mikhail stood shaking. "What's happening? Is somebody dead?"

She touched his arm. "It's okay, Mikhail. There're no bodies, but it looks like we have blood on the couch. We need to check it out. We'll get some samples to see what we have."

The man wiped his long black hair from his forehead. "I knew that damn Parrish kid was a freak. I told my uncle he was trouble. I'll never sell this place now."

CJ strung crime scene tape around the porch, and the three of them waited. Finally, Freddie and the tech arrived, and they agreed this was beyond what they could handle. The FBI forensics team would arrive within a few hours, so they pulled the door closed. Two officers were assigned to stand guard.

She looked at Freddie and Wally. "Guys, I may be wrong, but I think we solved our puzzle. Bryan Parrish killed your two women here in Sitka before he came to Charleston."

Freddie nodded, his face solemn. "Okay, we'll keep it safe until we can collect our samples. Do you still need to talk to Seth?"

"Yes. Let's head back." *There's something else I need an answer to.*

The shaken Mikhail handed CJ a piece of paper with Sasha's number on it as she prepared to leave. "She lives in town."

As he walked away, she remembered one other question. "Mikhail, I'm sorry about your uncle. How did he pass away?"

He stopped and turned back. "He drowned. Apparently, he was drunk and fell off the dock."

CJ's eyes went to the dock. *A dock he'd walked a million times.*

Thursday, November 4
Sitka

Seth Burgess looked to be in his late fifties, but the years of hard drinking made it difficult to tell. His eyes were sunken. His graying black hair was greasy and needed to be cut. He stared at the officer standing in the corner. "Why in the hell am I still here? I need a damn drink. You guys can't hold me for no reason. I'm fucking suing your pants off."

He looked up at CJ when she walked into the room. "Hello, Seth. I'm CJ. It's my fault you're here. I wanted to meet you." She sat in a chair across from him.

"Why in the hell would you want to meet me?" He snorted.

She smiled. "You're important to one of my cases, and I need your help."

His bleary eyes fixed on her. "Ah, well, okay."

"How about we go somewhere where we can talk? I promise it won't be long." *Maybe a change of scenery will help, and this room smells like a brewery.*

Seth licked his lips. "Can we go to Mickey's? It's just across the street, and I need a drink."

They stood, and she took his arm and led him out the door. "I tell you what. We'll go to Mickey's, and once we talk, I'll buy you a beer. How does that sound?"

He stopped in his tracks, and his eyes went wide. "You'll buy me a beer?"

"Sure." CJ shrugged. "But only after we talk."

"Okay. As long as we don't talk long. I have a headache and need a drink bad."

Wally watched the two of them cross Lake Street and enter the dark space of Mickey's Tavern. He decided to walk over himself and sit at the bar.

CJ had her answers within thirty minutes, and Seth had his beer. She managed to get him to eat most of a burger before honoring their deal. He guzzled his prize as she walked over to Wally, and every eye at happy hour followed her. "We have another twist to the story." She motioned him outside and away from prying ears.

They walked to his truck and got in. Wally sat before putting the key in the ignition. "Okay, what's the twist?"

CJ gazed out the window, her eyes glued to a dark patch of clouds floating over the peak of Mount Edgecumbe. Night was falling. "Seth told me he saw two men. Well, to be accurate, he saw one man walk away from where the body was found and get into the passenger side of a black SUV. He's pretty sure the driver was male."

Wally joined her in staring at the dark clouds. "Do you believe him?"

"I do. I thought his prior statement didn't make sense."

He turned his puzzled face to her. "Why?"

"When I walked the area and studied the aerials, it occurred to me that if Seth saw a man walk away from the body and he was sitting at the bus stop where he said, he'd have to be able to see where he went. I mean, the guy couldn't just evaporate."

A low whistle escaped Wally's lips. "That would mean there were two perps, and if the evidence shows it was Bryan Parrish, we have a second person to track down."

A second person to track down. CJ leaned forward and rested her head on the dash. The murders of the eight women in Charleston rolled through her mind like some obscene slideshow. She blew out a big blast of air. "Okay, let's go back and see if the evidence crew has arrived."

Wally turned over the engine, and the two rode silently back to Popov's Seafood.

Thirty minutes after leaving Mickey's, Wally pulled the truck onto the grass alongside numerous other vehicles. CJ counted at least six FBI jackets scurrying around the property. Chief Richardson stood a few feet away from Bryan Parrish's shack while no less than four Sitka PD officers secured the perimeter. Temporary lights made the scene look like something out of a sci-fi movie.

Wally went to find the lead CSI as CJ eased up beside the chief. His glossy eyes met hers, then refocused on the shack. Finally, after a long pause, he spoke up. "Detective, I owe you an apology."

She tilted her head to the side. "Excuse me, Chief?"

"To be more accurate, I owe you multiple apologies. First, I was annoyed because I thought you were only second-guessing what was done and not adding value. I was wrong. Second, we should have already known about the evidence in this shack. I have no excuse. Ivan was dead, and once we heard about Parrish, we should have searched everywhere. We probably didn't even need a warrant. Hell, you got in no problem without one." He turned to face her. "Third, based on your text, we obviously did a piss-poor job getting Seth's statement. We should have already known two men were involved and the vehicle was a black SUV. Exactly what Parrish drove. It's what happens when you assume before you do your damn job."

Clearing her throat, CJ quietly said, "Chief, we are where we are. You're limited in what you can do with a small department. Serial killers are complex. Hell, I had a task force, one of the FBI's best agents, and the small army he brought with him to catch Parrish. Still, he damn near killed me." She reached out and touched his shoulder. "You asked for my help and pushed until you got it. That's worth something. Let's just focus on getting all of our evidence together, solving this one, and giving these women's parents some level of closure."

Unexpectedly, he put his arm around her and gave her a quick squeeze. "Thank you for not rubbing my nose in it and doing what I couldn't."

Wally joined them, and they stood for the next several hours watching the small FBI army cover every inch of the scene.

———

At 11:15 p.m., Wally approached CJ and Freddie with a petite man wearing black horn-rimmed glasses too big for his face. "Guys, this is CSI Rich Simmons. He'll give us a preliminary."

The tiny man with the big glasses focused on his notes. "We still have an hour or so left to make sure we get everything, but here's what we have so far. It's definitely blood on the underside of the couch cushion, and we'll be able to get DNA.

"We've collected numerous fingerprints, which we can assume belonged to the suspect since he lived here, and perhaps someone else. In addition, there was a partial fingerprint in the blood on the cushion. It appears too large to be from a female. This should prove who was involved in the murder of whoever's blood is present.

"Last, we found three pairs of women's panties in a box under the bed. It was attached to the bottom of the box spring with some wire. The box also contained three small jars of blood with fingerprints on their lids. We'll analyze these and should be able to ascertain the owners."

Light-headed, CJ swayed slightly. Wally grabbed her arm. "CJ, are you okay?"

Her face flushed. "Yeah, just a little dizzy. It's been a long day." An overturned bucket magically appeared, and Freddie eased her down. Then a bottle of water touched her lips. Within a couple of minutes, she had composed herself and stood up again. "Anything else?"

Rich turned toward the shack. "We'll complete our fieldwork, and we're gonna take the bed and couch back to Juneau. I want to analyze them more closely in the lab. I have no doubt, though, with what we already have, we'll be able to confirm who was killed here and who killed them."

"Excuse me, Detective," said a voice from behind. The group turned to find the gap-toothed Mikhail Popov. "I wanted to come to see this disaster and to bring Sasha to talk to you."

A plain-looking woman around CJ's age stepped forward. She reached out and shook CJ's hand. Her hands were rough, but her smile revealed perfect teeth under her short sandy-blond hair.

"Thank you for coming, Sasha, and thank you, Mikhail, for bringing her," CJ said. She motioned toward Wally's truck. "Let's go find a spot where we can talk."

After the two were seated, CJ asked, "So, Sasha, I understand you worked for Ivan Popov?"

"Yes," she replied. "I helped him during the peak fishing season, processing his catches. I helped a couple others, but I like to pick up all the work I can to carry me through the off-season."

"Did you also know Bryan Parrish?"

"Sort of. He was a mean son of a bitch, and Ivan didn't want me around him when he wasn't here. Especially after . . ." Sasha's eyes grew wet, and a single tear ran down her cheek.

"After what?" CJ softly asked.

Sasha wiped her nose with the back of her camouflage sleeve. "He raped me three years ago . . . It was my fault, though. Ivan was gone, and I thought I'd come get some work done and . . ." Her soft sobs increased.

"I'm so sorry. Being raped, though, is in no way your fault." She patted Sasha's leg. "Did you report it?"

She shook her head. "No. Well, I told Ivan. He told me to keep it quiet, and he'd deal with it."

CJ's face grew hot. "Did he?"

"I'm not sure, but I do know Bryan's face was black and blue afterward, and he didn't work for several days. He stayed in his room. I stopped working here after that."

Good! I hope Ivan beat the hell out of him. "Sasha, did you ever see any other women here?"

"No. Only Ivan and Bryan. No woman in her right mind would come here, which says a lot about me, I guess."

"Last question. Did you ever see anyone visit Bryan?"

"No. Oh, wait. I had already quit working here, so maybe a year ago, I came by to drop off some parts to Ivan. I don't know who the man was, but he was standing on Bryan's porch. Bryan saw me and started cussing, so I got the hell out."

"Did you get a good look at the man?"

"Not really. The guy was sorta tall like Bryan and had dark hair."

CJ sat quietly, then thanked her and opened the door.

"Detective?"

CJ turned to a photo in Sasha's hand of a beautiful little girl with dark brown hair and brown eyes. "This is my daughter. She just turned two."

Bryan Parrish fathered a daughter.

SIXTEEN

Friday, November 5
Sitka

CJ woke with a start—her ringing cell phone. She rubbed the sleep from her eyes as she answered. "Detective O'Hara."

"Hello, Detective. This is Senior Forensics Analyst Brett Phillips from Quantico. I hope I didn't wake you."

"No, no. I'm up. What can I do for you?"

"Special Agent Patterson assigned me some evidence for your cases. I was told to get it done ASAP. I have some results for you."

She fumbled with the light switch and found her note-pad buried under the files spilled across her bed. "Go ahead."

"I'll send you a written report by tomorrow, but Special Agent Patterson wanted me to give you a verbal. For the rape case fiber evidence, I have three key findings. First, the fiber is a thread manufactured by American Threads and Yarns in Spartanburg, South Carolina, from 1975 to 1980. The thread is cotton, which isn't notable, but the manufacturing process allows us to nail down the period.

"Second, the dye on the thread is a specialty dye. The formulation was manufactured from 1975 to 1978 under a particular order from the Gamecock Club. I assume the exact color is what they were after.

"Last, the thread was used on one of three unique patches. All for placement on various sweatshirts and jackets. I'll email you a picture of them."

She finished scribbling. "Do you know where the sweatshirts or jackets were sold?"

"They weren't sold to the public. They were given to athletes who lettered in a sport at the University of South Carolina or boosters for the athletic department who donated large sums. The public can buy these today as replicas, but they're not the same as the originals. What we have here is the real deal, not a replica."

She stared at her notes. "So, if this thread were left at a scene—"

"It had to come from one of the original patches on one of these gifted garments."

She underlined the dates. "If I understand correctly, then the years of interest are 1975 to 1978?"

"Correct. Ready for the murder case shoe impressions?"

"Fire away."

"We've confirmed what your lab found. The shoe impressions at the two scenes in question are a match. They are the same shoe—size, tread, and tread wear. It's difficult to be precise due to the different surfaces where the prints were found, but the impression depths point to a person of the same weight in both cases. I'd guess a hundred ten to a hundred thirty pounds."

She added to her notes. "Okay, I'm glad we have that confirmed. And the substance?"

He chuckled. "This was the most fun. It's a natural substance. A mixture of herbs or roots. I've got an expert working on nailing it down further, but her preliminary says peony, frankincense, and a third unknown. Sorry, but it's gonna take us a couple more days."

"Thanks, Brett. I appreciate the quick turnaround. I'll be on the alert for your report."

"No problem. You've clearly got allies in high places."

She rolled out of bed and opened the curtains. It was still dark, and the rain had returned—streaks ran down the windowpane. *Frankincense, like in the Bible.*

CJ crossed the deep brown hardwood floor of the hotel restaurant and found a table by the window and away from others. She looked for her eagle as the rain came down harder. *Flying out today will be fun.* She texted the pilot to confirm the departure time. The return text read, "Let's leave at ten this morning. Home by ten tonight, Charleston time."

She laid her cell phone on the table and smiled as the waitress approached. "Good morning, Cheyenne. You must work every day?"

The woman smiled. "It seems like it, but I usually only work Monday through Friday during the day. I worked a double on Wednesday to cover for a friend. I brought you a pot of coffee."

"Thanks. I have two more coming, so we'll order once they arrive."

Wally arrived around eight, followed by Freddie short- ly after that. Freddie told them more about Sitka and the surrounding areas as they ate. After Cheyenne cleared the table, CJ opened her notepad.

"I thought we'd make sure we had everything buttoned up before I leave. The pilot wants to leave at ten o'clock this morning. Fair?"

Both men nodded and reached for their pads, then glanced up at her. *Guess I'm in charge.*

"Assuming the results come back on the blood, panties, and fingerprints the way I believe they will, we can safely conclude Bryan Parrish killed the two women here in Sitka and the young woman in Ketchikan. Wally, I assume you're tracking this to a conclusion?"

"Yes. I'll stay on our forensics crew and lab and be sure to send you both reports."

She continued. "That leaves two more open items, ex- cluding my suspicion Ivan Popov didn't die from accidental drowning."

Freddie frowned. "Two?"

"Yes. Where was the Ketchikan woman murdered? I'd assume there, not here. I guess it's a minor issue if the DNA shows it was her, but it'd be nice to close that loop. Freddie, can you work with Ketchikan PD on that one?"

"Sure. What's the second item?"

She exhaled. "The mystery man Sasha told me she saw on Bryan's porch, and the driver Seth said he saw at the first drop site. I think they were the same person since Bryan was a loner, but it could be two different people. It's important since this person or persons could be accomplices at a minimum. Worst case, they commit similar crimes."

The chief rubbed his forehead. "How can we run this to ground?"

She sat with her fingers intertwined as she chewed on her thumbnail. "Honestly, it seems the only way is to interview the boat owners in the marina and rule them out one by one. Or, one of the fingerprints in Bryan's home tells us. Wally?"

Wally's eyes were fixed on rain dripping off the awning. "I think you're right. But we can always follow up with Sasha and Seth again to see if there's anything else they can remember."

Freddie spoke up. "I'll take those actions."

She circled the words *second man* in her notes. They were assuming this person lived in Sitka, but was this true? "I think that's it. Can you think of—" Her cell phone vibrated, and she glanced at the name. She stood. "Please give me a minute, guys."

She moved to the window. "Hello, Robert."

"Hey, CJ. How's Sitka?"

"Rainy and foggy at the moment. How's Roanoke?"

"This case is a royal pain. Every time I think we're close, we seem to slip further away, but we'll get this guy. Listen, I know you're leaving today, but I wanted to thank you for your work. Wally gave me a rundown earlier, and he's ecstatic with you. Told me you're the best non-FBI person he's ever worked with or seen work. I think he wanted to say the best period, but he and I have worked together, and he's being kind to me."

She smiled. "I'm just glad we made the progress we did. We can close the book on the three Alaska cold cases if everything goes as planned. I hope this helps the poor parents and communities find peace."

"Well done. Fly home safe. Brett has confirmed they'll have everything for you in the next couple of days. Herbs and roots, eh?"

Freddie shook CJ's hand in the airport lobby and handed her a box wrapped in shiny red paper. "It's a little something to remember us by." As they stepped onto the tarmac, he held the umbrella over her as she dropped the gift into her bag.

Wally flipped up his hood and grabbed her bag as the co-pilot ushered her onto the plane. He shook her hand in the galley as his eyes scanned the interior. "Wow, impressive ride. Be safe and have a great trip home. Come back and see us sometime."

SEVENTEEN

Saturday, November 6
Downtown Charleston

CJ spread the files across the conference room table and sorted them into piles. She was still groggy from her trip home the previous night, but she wanted to get reorganized. The room seemed dark even with the fluorescents, so she pulled the cords on the blinds and let the natural light enter. Unfortunately, the Charleston midmorning sun was blocked by low gray clouds. Her eyes shifted upward when the door latch clicked.

The bright smile of Sam met her. "Good morning. Welcome back."

"Morning. What are you doing here in the station today?"

Sam dropped her purse and a canary-yellow shopping bag on her desk. "I knew you'd be here, so I came to help. You can't stay here all day. You need a break. I'm taking you to lunch."

"Oh, really?"

"Yes. Really. Let's get to work so we can get out of here." Sam immediately started sorting through the files. "I'll get these back where they belong. What else do you need?"

CJ smiled and shook her head. She was happy to have Sam back. The young woman was a godsend. "I wanted to bring back the Alaska files and pick up the files for our rapist case. Unfortunately, I didn't take them all on my trip. At least I can review them at home instead of sitting here."

Sam snorted. "You need to take a break and do something fun. It's the weekend, and you've been at it really hard."

Both women turned to see Johnny come through the door. "Good morning."

CJ's head swung between her two coworkers. "Okay, what gives? Did you two plan this?" She was met with sly smiles.

He spread his hands. "All I know is Sam invited me to lunch, and I can't pass that up." He winked. "Besides, I was raised to believe you should work when your boss works."

CJ went back to the files. She was already fond of Johnny. She handed Sam the last of the Parrish case files. "Well, I suppose we can get a little work done before lunch. How about we review your progress while I was in Alaska and get ourselves ready for Monday? We have an officer's briefing on our rapes first thing."

They reviewed the facts they had on each of the four rapes. Sam captured notes, and the group worked together to put them into briefing format. This task completed, CJ reviewed the outstanding items and made assignments.

"Sam, can you find out all the USC athletes who lettered in a sport from 1975 to 1978? Let's assume they all got a gift that included the patch. Also, please see if you can find a list of donors from the same time period."

The younger woman nodded. "Sure. I have an old roommate who works with the USC Alumni Association. She'll help me."

"Next item. Sam, where are you on the background checks of the vics?"

"They're done. Nothing stands out for any of the four. But there is one odd thing."

CJ's eyes left the sheet. "Oh? What's that?"

Sam handed her a calendar with markings. "All four of the women were stopped for a traffic violation four to five weeks before their rape."

Turning the calendar, CJ and Johnny stared at it. Sam handed over four more sheets. "They were all given a ticket."

CJ's eyes went wide. "By the same officer. Whattaya think, Johnny?"

He exhaled. "It doesn't prove anything, but it certainly needs to be investigated. It'd be a great way to get their addresses." He pointed to the name on the tickets. "He's a new officer right out of the academy. I think he joined three or four months ago."

Without looking up from her notes, CJ pointed. "Sam, can you run any other women this officer has ticketed since he joined us?" She exhaled. *What if it's a cop?* "For now, this stays here as well. Got it?"

Sam and Johnny both nodded.

The group moved to the next case—the murder in Harleston Village. Johnny went through the interviews he'd conducted with the neighbors. So far, nothing appeared to help with who might have committed the crime.

———

A woman with red hair, a pale complexion, and a face full of freckles smiled as the group entered the Boathouse at Breach Inlet for lunch. "Hello, Sam. Great to see you again. We have your table with a view ready." She took them to a four-top and passed out menus. The afternoon sun made the water sparkle, and the marsh grasses swayed in the breeze.

Within minutes, a waiter put a plate of fried calamari and a basket of sweet corn hush puppies on the table. CJ immediately reached for one of the golden-brown balls. "I'm addicted to these."

Sam laughed. "Yep. It's hard to go wrong with hush puppies. I ordered our appetizers ahead so we wouldn't have to wait. You're on your own for your meal."

Johnny popped a piece of calamari into his mouth. "Holy crap, this is tasty. The sauce is delicious."

They were still working on their appetizers when the waiter dropped off the second round of drinks and their main course. They'd all decided to try the daily special, grilled swordfish with long-grain brown rice and asparagus.

Sam smiled at Johnny. "Tell us a little about yourself."

He finished chewing. "Well, let's see. I was born outside Beaufort and grew up on St. Helena Island. My mom still lives there."

"How about your dad?" Sam asked.

He cleared his throat. "He was killed by a drunk driver when I was ten."

She touched his arm. "I'm so sorry."

A lump rose in CJ's throat. *I know how that feels.* "I'm sorry too."

He continued. "After high school, I went to Charleston Southern. I was fortunate I got a scholarship to play defensive back. I wound up getting my degree in criminal justice and joined the force. Just finished my fifth year last month."

CJ grabbed another hush puppy. "Charleston Southern is the one above North Charleston, right?"

"Yep. Between Ladson and Goose Creek."

Sam added, "It's a Baptist school. Were you raised Baptist?"

He smiled. "I was."

CJ suddenly thought of her visit to St. Helena. "Did you ever go to the Brick Baptist Church?"

He swallowed a bite. "That was my church growing up."

He has to know Grannie.

He pointed to Sam. "Your turn."

"I'm pretty dull. Grew up on Daniel Island. My mom and dad still live there. I went to the College of Charleston, where I got my computer information systems degree with a minor in Southern studies. I played midfield on the soccer team, which was fun. I've been with the department for almost six years, and I love the research side of the job. I guess I'm just a big ole snoop."

CJ took her turn and gave them the highlights of her life in Boston. Johnny and Sam looked pained when she told them about the death of her parents and sister. "We have something in common, Johnny. A drunk driver destroyed our families." She clapped her hands and gave them a big smile. "Okay, enough history and sad stuff. Sam, tell us what the heck Southern studies entails. Sounds hokey!"

Johnny laughed as Sam's jaw dropped. "Yeah, me too. I wanted to ask, so I'm glad you did. Spill it, Sam."

The group passed on dessert and piled into CJ's truck. As they rode back to the station, CJ gave them a quick summary of her trip. After turning off Lockwood Drive, she put the truck in park. "There's one thing I keep coming back to. The woman who worked with Bryan said she saw him with a man on the porch where he lived. Then, a witness told me he saw someone driving the black SUV that someone, presumed to be Bryan, got into. The second man bugs me."

"You think Bryan had help?" Johnny asked.

She shrugged.

Sam frowned. "How could anyone help that bastard? Is Sitka PD gonna check it out?"

CJ nodded. "Yeah. They'll see if they can close things." *All we need is another Bryan Parrish.*

CJ peered through the peephole, removed the chain, and opened the door. A jet-black Labrador retriever's block head poked through the gap. She swore he smiled as he entered. She dropped to her knees and hugged him. "Hey, Jake. I missed you, boy." He slid his head onto her shoulder and nuzzled her ear.

"Can I come in too?" Ben leaned around the corner.

She laughed. "Hmm, I don't know. Whattaya think, boy? You wanna share?" A small bark erupted. "Jake says it's okay, but wipe your feet."

"Very funny. Traitor!"

She moved to a chair near the picture window, and Jake immediately stretched himself out by her feet. Ben shook his head as he dropped to the couch. "Wow. I house him, feed him, and this is what I get."

Jake rolled onto his back as she rubbed his belly with her foot. "He's just not seen me in a while."

Ben asked, "How was Alaska?"

"Interesting. I think we closed the three cold cases."

"Was it . . . my brother?"

"I'm afraid so. I'm so sorry." She exhaled. "How about we talk about something else?"

He quietly nodded.

"How's Bill?" she asked.

"He's doing fine. He and Will left early this morning to fish. They're planning on making it an overnight, so they won't be back until tomorrow."

"You didn't wanna go?"

"I did, but I'm helping Jackson on a case. We're hoping to interview a suspect tomorrow morning. We've been trying to catch up with him. We hope if we go to his house at daybreak on a Sunday, he'll be home." Ben checked his watch. "Listen, would you like to go grab some dinner?"

"I'm beat and had a late lunch with Sam at the Boathouse. How about we order pizza? Keep it easy. Plus, we have Jake." The dog's long black tail thumped the floor.

"Works for me."

She went to the kitchen and handed him the menu. "See what you want, and I'll call it in. I've got the stuff for salads, and I still have some of Jake's food from the last time I kept him." Jake was up in a flash. He sat patiently in the kitchen while she poured his kibble.

The two chatted about everything but their cases for the next thirty minutes. Ben told her what he knew about the Gullah culture and its influence on the Lowcountry. She made mental notes on places she hadn't seen yet and promised herself she'd take the time to go.

A low growl rose in Jake's throat at the sound of footsteps coming up the stairs. He immediately positioned himself between CJ and the door—tense, alert, and ready to pounce. She rubbed his ears. "It's okay. It's the pizza man."

Ben answered the door to a teenage boy whose eyes never left the dog. "He gonna bite me?"

"Not unless you mess with her." His thumb pointed back over his shoulder.

"No way, man." He quickly took the cash and his ten-dollar tip and hightailed it back down the stairs.

———

Ben leaned back and rubbed his stomach. "That hit the spot. I haven't had pizza in a while."

"Yeah, I've ordered from them a time or two," CJ replied. "They have great pasta too."

He stood and stretched. "I know you're tired, so Jake and I'll get going. I need to be up early anyway."

The big dog didn't move when Ben stood. She smiled up at Ben. "I think he wants to stay. Can I keep him?"

He rolled his eyes. "Sure. I'll pick him up tomorrow afternoon if that works."

"Perfect. I'll take him to the Battery for a long walk."

"He'll love that. Don't forget, he sleeps on the floor and not on the bed. When you kept him while I was in Florida, it took me a week to straighten him out."

"Sure. No problem."

———

CJ pulled a T-shirt over her head and slipped into bed. Jake sat on the floor, eyeing her. She unwrapped the box Freddie had given her. It was a colorful replica of a totem pole. She placed it on her nightstand and glanced down at Jake's head, resting on the edge of the bed. "Don't tell Daddy. Come on up, boy."

EIGHTEEN

Saturday, November 6
Downtown Charleston

Wendy Watts sat staring into the mirror in her hotel room. She was pissed she'd been banished to covering only fluff stories. She had been a News 4 reporter on the fast track to the big time when . . . "It's because of that bitch CJ O'Hara!"

She angrily finished removing her makeup and started the shower. She dropped her robe and stood assessing her naked body in the full-length mirror. She smiled at what she saw and knew it would get her what she wanted. He'd be here soon, and she'd be ready.

She showered, dried her hair, and wiggled into a short, low-cut red dress over the white lace underwear she'd bought especially for this night. She slipped on high-heeled shoes and dabbed on a hint of perfume. When the light tap on the door came, she set her glass of wine on the counter.

"Hey, baby. I've missed you so bad. I could hardly wait for you to get here." She pulled the sixty-year-old man through the door, wrapped herself around him, and gave him a long, deep kiss. The fact was she found him distasteful, but as always, she knew he was clueless about her true feelings.

Entwined, they fell to the couch and eventually made it to the king-size bed. She did all the things he liked and left him breathless. "I'll be back, sweetheart. I need to freshen up," she said as she untangled herself from him and got up. What she really needed was another long drink.

Congressman Randolph Lee Jr. lay there with a satisfied smile. She thought she was playing him, but he knew the skinny. He wasn't stupid, and he didn't care. He got what he wanted from her and gave her just enough of what she wanted to keep her around. After thirty years in politics, her games were no match for him.

Wendy returned and nuzzled up against him. "Baby, I need your help."

Randolph gently took her hand to show her how much he cared. *You're not the only one who can put on an act.* "What is it, sweetheart?"

"I need you to get me back on mainstream stories. Ever since that bitch O'Hara lied about me, the station manager has only assigned me the bullshit. I'm not allowed to do anything on my own." Wendy hadn't been able to sway the asshole even after she'd ridden him.

He stroked her back. "Sweetie, I'm not sure how I can help. I understand you had highly confidential information that was stolen from the department's files."

"That's a lie! I never stole anything. My informant gave me certain things, but how did I know where he got it? O'Hara only did it to discredit me because I was holding her incompetence out for all to see." She turned on the waterworks and threw herself on top of him.

"Darling, I just don't know how I can help you."

She raised her head. "I knew it. You don't love me at all, and after everything I've given you."

He gently caressed her cheek. "Honey, look at all I do for you. You know I care."

"You could at least talk to the station manager. Tell him he needs to reinstate my full investigative privileges."

"But what if he declines?"

"Tell him there'll be no more stories from you! You tell him you'll make sure News 4 never gets the first scoop again from anyone. You're powerful, darling. He'll listen to you." She threw her face back down on his shoulder.

Jesus, this girl is getting to be nothing but a pain in the ass. "Let me give it some thought. I need to make sure I handle it properly. We don't want anyone to think I have an agenda."

Her blue eyes gleamed. "You could tell him you've noticed how the press isn't ensuring transparency by

Charleston law enforcement. They have to be held accountable, and you always thought I did such a great job at that."

He ran his hand down to the small of her back. "Okay, tell you what. I'll give him a call and see what I can do."

"Really?"

He smiled. "Yes. Now, how about you focus on making me happy?"

***

After he'd showered and dressed, Randolph gave Wendy one last long kiss, cracked the door, and snuck down the hotel hallway. He had told her what she wanted to hear and gotten what he wanted. He had no intention of calling anyone on her behalf. She was guilty of everything she was accused of . . . actually, lots more.

He slid into the leather seat of his pearl-white Jaguar XF, glanced into the rearview mirror, and practiced his line. "Baby, I talked to him and pushed him hard, but he won't listen to me." Then he roared with laughter.

***

Wendy sat on the edge of the hotel bed staring at the small screen. She saw what she wanted on the video, and her lips curled into a big, evil smile. His face was crystal clear, and her naked back could have been anyone's. She popped open the recorder and put the memory card in its case. She knew he was lying to her. He wouldn't call anyone for her . . . unless, of course, he had no choice.

Randolph was whistling along with the radio as he crossed the Broad River and turned onto Highway 278 on the last leg of his drive to Hilton Head Island. He was rehearsing in his mind how to tell his wife he was so sorry he'd missed her fundraising dinner but the budget meeting had just run too long.

His cell phone buzzed, and he glanced at the message. He opened the video—a naked man lying on a bed with a woman on top appeared. The video and audio were pristine. His eyes went wide, and he fought to maintain control of his car. "That little bitch!"

Another chime, and he stared at the message. "Good luck, baby. Here's the cell phone number for the station manager. Love you."

NINETEEN

Monday, November 8
Downtown Charleston

The Monday morning briefing was standing room only. The chairs were full, and the back wall was lined. CJ squeezed through the door and found a spot by Johnny. He smiled at her. "Big crowd today."

She scanned the room. "Yeah. Not sure I've seen this many here before."

"Chief had the night shift hang around. With the holidays approaching, he wants to be sure we're prepared."

Ben wound his way through the bodies and joined CJ. Her eyes went wide. "Christ, Ben. What happened to your face?"

He laughed. "I got into a little tussle this morning. Caught an elbow."

She gently touched his red and bruised right eye. "It looks awful. Does it hurt much?"

"Not too bad. I'll just have a little black eye."

"What happened?"

"Remember yesterday when I picked up Jake? I told you our guy wasn't home when Jackson and I went by. His wife said he stayed out all night. I had an officer swing by there at four this morning, and his car was there, so we went back. I knocked on the front door, and he made a run for it. Jackson went after him, and I wound up cutting him off in the alley. Tackled him, and he elbowed me, trying to get away. We got him, though."

"Is he your guy?"

Ben sighed. "We think so. We'll get his DNA to confirm what we found at the scene, but he matches the witness description, and he had a knife that should match our murder weapon."

She nudged him. "Nice job."

A mocking voice on her right caught her attention. *Officer Jared Parker.* The man who had given her a nickname as soon as she arrived and seemed determined to irritate her at every turn. He motioned her over.

"City Girl. Come meet my new pup." He poked a young officer in the ribs and pointed at CJ. Reluctantly, she stepped forward and accepted the officer's hand under his leering eyes. "I'm Officer Jamie Turner. Should I call you City Girl too?"

"Detective O'Hara will work fine." *So, you're mister ticket writer.*

The chief entered, and CJ dropped back in between Johnny and Ben. The room was becoming a sauna, and she tugged at the neck of her blouse for air. The volume went to zero when the chief raised his hand.

The chief turned to Ben. "I'd like Investigator Ben Parrish and Detective Vincent Jackson to step forward. Congratulations to these two for apprehending a suspect we are confident is the murderer of a man who was killed in the Business District three months ago." He led the applause.

CJ covered the rape case near the end of the briefing and provided the general description of the suspect or suspects. She made it clear she thought it was one rapist, but it wasn't confirmed yet. She stayed silent on the fiber they had found and tickets that had been issued to each victim.

CJ was sitting at the conference room table thumbing through a file on the fourth rape case when Sam's voice interrupted her. "Don't forget your doctor's appointment."

CJ looked up from the file at Sam. "I may need to reschedule. This case—"

"Nope. No way, no how. If you don't go, I'm supposed to call Thomas, and he'll call the chief."

CJ exhaled loudly. "Damn it! I'm fine, and I have too much going on right now."

Sam handed her the keys to her truck. "Tough shit. You're going. I'll be here when you get back."

The chubby nurse escorted CJ to a small room and asked her to undress and put on the dreaded paper gown. "The doctor will be in soon. I'll get the order for your blood work, but you'll need to fast at least twelve hours beforehand, so I can't take it today."

She gave up trying to tie the gown up at the back. *I hate these damn things.* She did her best to cover herself as she climbed onto the edge of the exam table. There was a light tap on the door, and Dr. Charlene Willis entered. She was a small woman, maybe fifty, with high cheekbones and shoulder-length brown hair.

"Hello, CJ. Nice to meet you. Thomas speaks very highly of you. He's worried about you after the incident in his exam room, and that means I am too."

CJ gave her a weak smile. "I'm fine."

For the next twenty minutes, CJ went through the usual process of being poked and prodded—"How's this feel . . . Stick out your tongue . . . Does it hurt when I do this?" Then she had to address each of her scars.

She pointed to her right side. "A wife-beater stabbed me with a broken bottle here." She slid her finger up. "The Lowcountry Killer got me with his knife here in May. A drugged-out man in an alley got me with a piece of metal here on the left calf, and I caught another knife blade right here at a robbery gone bad." She touched her left shoulder when she mentioned the knife injury.

Dr. Willis added the information on the scars to her chart. "With your permission, I'll get your medical files sent down from Boston, so we have a complete history. The nurse will come give you an EKG and schedule your blood work. I don't see anything obvious, but your fainting spells aren't normal, so we have to rule out any underlying cardiovascular issues and diabetes.

"Your issues may be due to dehydration or anemia, which are easier to treat than anxiety. Your job doesn't help with anxiety, and that'll be a challenge for us to handle. I'll review your test results and give you a call to come back in for a follow-up. In the meantime, I want you to drink a gallon of water every day and take the multivitamins I'm prescribing for you. Will you do that?"

"Yes," CJ said, "I'll do my best."

Sam raced to the door when CJ entered the conference room at two o'clock. "What did the doctor say?"

"She told me I was totally fine. Healthy as a horse, and you and Thomas may need to be checked out as excessive worrywarts."

Sam grunted. "Wonderful. I guess you'll have no problem then giving Thomas permission to speak directly to the doctor and get her report."

She exhaled. "Sam, I'm touched you and Thomas are worried about me, but I'm fine. The doctor didn't seem too alarmed. She's gonna do my blood work to make sure I'm good, and she prescribed a multivitamin. I also need to drink more water."

"Get more sleep and eat better too," Sam said quickly. "I'm watching you."

"Yes, ma'am!" CJ slipped into a chair. "Where's Johnny?"

"He had a couple of interviews to do, but he'll be back soon."

"Okay. Any luck yet on finding out if Officer Turner has written any more tickets to women in the last two months?"

Sam grabbed a sheet and passed it to her. "He's written two more tickets to women. One was almost a month ago, and the other was last week. Here's their driver's license information and photos."

CJ looked at the photos. Two women, twenty-six and thirty-one, smiled back at her. Both were attractive. "What about the gift list for USC?"

"I spoke to my friend, and she'll have something for me by tomorrow. The athletic department keeps a complete list of those who lettered, so it should be easy to pull. They also keep a detailed donor list. She hopes to be able to tell us who was given gifts."

CJ ran her finger down the page. "It looks like one of our women is single. Can you see if she lives alone?"

TWENTY

Tuesday, November 9
Downtown Charleston

CJ's ringing cell phone broke the silence of the conference room. She grabbed it and answered. "O'Hara."

"Hello, Detective. This is Brett Phillips here in Quantico again. I have the last piece of information for you about the substance you sent us. The third item is a root called High John the Conqueror."

She jotted down the name. "I have no clue what that is or what it means."

"I'm not sure either. I'll send you our report."

She stared at her pad. *Peony, frankincense, and High John the Conqueror. What does that mean?* She stood and wrote the names on the board.

The door opened, and Sam entered with a smile. "Good morning," CJ said.

"Morning." Sam wiped her bottom lip. "Sorry. I just had a tooth filled, and my jaw feels like a balloon. I hope I'm not drooling."

CJ laughed. "Nope. You're good."

"I didn't think I'd be this late, but I hadn't planned on the filling. What's that?" Sam pointed at the board.

"That's what the FBI said was in the substance found at the crime scene of our Harleston Village murder. I'm not sure what it is."

Sam started writing down the names. "I'll see if I can research—"

Johnny had entered the room and said, "Peony is a typical garden flower. It's claimed the root can provide power against misfortune and help boost health. The frankincense comes from the sap of a particular tree, and it's believed to help strengthen the power of other herbs. I've heard it's often used when performing candle-burning spells. High John the Conqueror is a root. Some believe the root provides power and strength."

CJ's mouth hung open. "How do you know this?"

He smiled. "You hear things hanging around in St. Helena. But, of course, there're other things these are supposed to work for and different ways of using them."

"How do we tell what he's using them for from what we found at our crime scene?"

He shrugged. "I'm not sure. We'd need someone who knows roots and herbs to take a look."

CJ rubbed her chin. *Like Grannie.*

"I think it's safe to say whoever put the stuff on our vic's forehead is looking for power for some reason."

Sam frowned. "You mentioned health too."

He nodded. "Yeah. Peony supposedly helps with that, is all I know. Maybe our guy is sick and trying to cure himself."

Sam dropped in front of her computer. "I'll do some research and see what else I can find." She looked at Johnny. "Should I just start with the names of the items?"

"Yeah. But I'd add herbal medicines to the list, and maybe hoodoo herbs and roots."

Her fingers went to work, but CJ wondered what else Johnny knew. *Maybe Paul can help.*

———

Paul and his son sat in his office after they'd had lunch. "How's your mom?"

"She's fine." His son kept his eyes down and fidgeted with his cell phone, scrolling with his thumb.

"That's good. I'm glad—"

"Glad about what? You left us and moved up here to Charleston." Paul Jr.'s eyes bulged, and his face grew red. "That's why I have a stepfather now instead of a father."

A sharp pain went through Paul's chest. "Son, that's not what happened. It's more complicated than—"

"Save it, Dad. I don't wanna hear it."

There was a knock, and CJ stuck her head in. "You got a minute?"

Paul glanced at his son, who clearly didn't want to talk to him anymore right now. "Uh, sure. Come on in, CJ."

She saw a young man of high school age leaning on the credenza. "Oh, sorry. I didn't know you had a guest."

"This is my son, Paul Jr.," the lieutenant said. As she extended her hand, he added, "Son, this is Detective O'Hara."

The eighteen-year-old stood and took her hand. "Nice to meet you, ma'am."

He sat but never took his eyes off her—the tiny gold flecks against the emerald green of her eyes seemed to mesmerize him.

Paul spoke up. "I'm so proud of him. He's doing great in school and will graduate with honors this year. He also works part-time at a grocery store."

She smiled. "That's wonderful. What's your favorite subject?"

Paul Jr. shrugged. "I guess I like science the best. Biology was cool."

The proud dad added, "It looks like he'll get into USC. Right, son?"

Paul Jr. gave a feeble smile. "I hope so. They've told me things look good." His cell phone rang, and he hopped up. "I need to go. Mom's here." Before Paul could hug him, he was out the door.

Paul followed him down the hall with his eyes before returning to his chair. "It's been hard on the kid. His mom and I split up a few years back. He's having a tough time with it."

"I'm sure that's been an adjustment for him," CJ said softly.

"Yeah. I don't get to see him as much as I'd like. He lives with her on St. Helena, and you know how things are here." He sighed. "Okay, what do you have?"

She settled into the chair across from his desk. "I wanted to let you know what the FBI said was in the substance we found on our victim in Harleston Village. It's a mixture of peony, frankincense, and something called High John the Conqueror."

Paul pinched his bottom lip. "Hmm, interesting. A root for health, a root for power, and a tree resin to enhance both."

Am I the only person who doesn't know this off the top of their head? "That's what Johnny said and Sam's research shows so far. My question is, what does it mean?"

Paul nodded. "Johnny would know. To answer your question, I'm not sure. Maybe the guy is in bad health. It couldn't have been an accident these were left behind. Is it possible our victim would have had the mixture?"

She slowly shook her head. "I don't think so, but I'll check. Seems you'd have to know what goes with what, right?"

"Absolutely. In fact, some herbs and roots can be quite dangerous if not handled properly or mixed with the wrong stuff. It's why root doctors are held in such high regard. Think of it as being a natural pharmacist."

"Didn't you tell me Grannie is experienced in herbs and roots?"

"I did. She knows a ton about hoodoo medicine, but she focuses on the health side of things. She doesn't delve into the other aspects."

"So, an herbalist," she murmured.

He smiled. "Yep. Sounds like you've been studying."

"Actually, that came from Sam." She paused. "Do you think Grannie would talk to us again about what this means?"

He slowly exhaled. "I'm not sure. Grannie was clear she didn't want to get involved. She's spooked."

CJ pursed her lips.

Paul leaned forward. "I tell you what. I'll ask her and see. Who knows? Maybe she'll give us something."

TWENTY-ONE

Tuesday, November 9
St. Helena Island

A single tear fell on the faded, colorless photo. It was another one of Elias's most prized possessions and something he always carried with him. He stared at the woman who had left this earth as he entered it. *She would have protected and loved me.*

Tucking the photo away, he stood. He still didn't feel any more powerful, and his pain hadn't ceased. He opened his box and dug through the items inside. He stared at the sheet of paper and wished the old man were still alive to help him. The old man knew exactly what was needed and how to prepare it.

Is the timing right? Roots and herbs had different seasons when they were best harvested. There had been so much to learn. He had been a good student, but the time had been short. This needed to work and make him better.

Carefully, he removed the bark from the grayish root of the small sassafras tree he had been lucky to find. He cut the roots into small pieces and dropped them into a pot of boiling water. He wasn't sure how long to let it boil, but he assumed ten minutes would suffice.

He stirred the deep-red mixture, poured it into the white ceramic mug, and eased it to his lips. Inhaling the vapors, he slowly drank—vanilla, licorice, and root beer. After consuming about half the cup, he decided that was enough. Too much, like last time, and he'd be puking his guts out and seeing things.

Elias squeezed into the dark corner and waited to see if the tea would take the pain from his joints. His face flushed, and he felt moisture on his forehead, but it was not as bad as last time.

TWENTY-TWO

Wednesday, November 10
Downtown Charleston

CJ jerked herself awake. For a couple of minutes, she wasn't sure where she was. Her mind played a trick on her, and she saw the ceiling of the old fish-processing site where Bryan Parrish had trapped her. *Jesus, CJ, get a grip.*

Her bedside clock read 5:04 a.m. She climbed onto the punisher twenty minutes later and rode hard for half an hour. Then she showered, dressed, and headed to Sal's Coffee. Caffeine was in order.

She rounded the corner of her building and bumped right into her local red-haired paperboy. He stood smiling up at her. "Uh, good morning, miss. I'm sorry I ran into you."

"Good morning. How's your route going today?"

"Fine. I saw you riding your exercise machine." His face flushed, he gave a quick wave and hustled away before she could respond.

At a few minutes past seven o'clock, CJ raced up the stairs and into the station with her usual large black coffee in hand. Bodies parted as she hurried down the hall. She returned a few hellos but had too much to do to spend time on the usual chitchat. Her meeting with the brass was at two o'clock in the afternoon, and there was no time to waste.

She opened the door of the conference room to a sweet odor. Sam smiled and held up a plate of round baked dough discs covered with a cinnamon-sugar glaze. "Morning. I brought you and Johnny some homemade treats, and the coffeepot's full."

"These look yummy. I almost let Sal talk me into a pumpkinseed muffin. Glad I passed." She took one and went to work.

CJ spread the files from the four rapes across the honey-colored table. One by one, she went through them. *I should have these memorized by now.* Sam captured headlines on the board as she dictated.

As the two were finishing, Johnny joined them. He gobbled a cinnamon roll in four bites. "Oh, these are good. I need one more." A second roll soon disappeared.

CJ stood at the board, and they went through the headlines of each case one last time—the victims' info, locations, and dates. Johnny added vital notes from his interviews. Once they were satisfied they had everything properly captured, Sam's fingers went to work on the keyboard.

Sam glanced at her second screen and froze. "I got an email from my friend in Columbia. It should be the list of who got the sweatshirts and jackets with the patch." The printer whirred and whooshed as the sheets appeared.

Her eyes scanned the sheets. "I told her to only send us the list for 1975 to 1978. Looks like she organized it by year and sport. The athletes are broken down in alphabetical order by last name. Some of the first names are missing. Here's the first batch. I'll print the donors."

Johnny scooted over next to CJ. "So, if these athletes graduated during these years, they'd be early to midfifties today."

Her eyes stayed fixed on the names. "Yeah. I think that'd be about right. We'll need to group them by their year to be totally accurate. Let's at least see if anyone jumps out at us from a first pass."

He nodded. "Guess we can focus on the male athletes first. Our unsub can't be a woman, although I guess they could have given their sweatshirt or jacket away."

Her eyes stopped in the Ps of the 1975 football team. "What's Officer Parker's father's name?"

Sam dropped back into her chair. "Let me see if I can find it." Her fingers flew on the keyboard and ten minutes later, she announced, "Jerry Parker."

"Bingo." CJ circled the name. "He was a senior in 1975 and lettered in football. Assuming he was around twenty-one, he'd be fifty-six today. Sam, can you get us a team photo?"

The search continued, and nothing else jumped out until they looked over the donor list. Johnny pointed. "We have a Russell Turner who donated every year from 1975 to 1978." He closed his eyes. "Wait, though. If he's Officer Jamie Turner's father, he'd be kinda young to be a major donor."

"Yeah." She frowned. "You're probably right. Lots of Turners in the world."

Sam spoke up. "What about a grandfather?"

CJ turned. "Possible. Can you check it out?"

Sam's fingers worked the keyboard again. "Found him. Russell Turner is Jamie Turner's grandfather. He's retired now, but he was a USC alum and a bigwig attorney at a firm in Columbia. Do you want me to add this stuff to the board and briefing notes?" Sam asked.

CJ paused. "Hmm, not yet. I'll add this to my notes, but I'm not sure I want to put it on the board or in the briefing note just yet. We need to be more certain before adding two officers to a potential-suspects list. Remember Ben?"

Sam quietly answered, "Yeah. That was a disaster for all of us, not to mention devastating for Ben."

Digging through her notes, CJ found what she was after. "Okay. The next thing we need to look at is Turner's tickets to women over the last six weeks. We have Rosalie Ricketts on October 12 and Amelia Boozer on November

2. Wait a minute." Her head snapped around to the board. She jumped up, went to her desk, and grabbed a calendar. Her eyes went back and forth from the board to the calendar. "Son of a bitch. Three of our rapes occurred on a Wednesday. All were four to five weeks after they received a ticket."

Johnny stood and went to the board. "That means we might expect a fifth rape between now and the middle of next week if the pattern holds."

She whispered, "Yes. If the rapes are connected to the tickets and Officer Turner." She tapped on the table. "Sam, can you pull the schedule for Turner since our first rape?"

Sam printed the list. "He worked from eight in the morning to eight at night on each of the days the rapes occurred. All have been on a Wednesday except the last one. That was on a Sunday, but again, he worked the eight-to-eight shift."

CJ took the list and ran her finger down. "He's working the same shift today and next Wednesday. Wait, what does that mean?" She pointed to a strange mark and leaned over to Johnny.

"That means he was with a training officer. Looks like he rode with someone until the first of November. Sam, pull this badge number for us."

Sam's fingers worked the keyboard. "Officer Jared Parker for all four. Parker's working the eight-to-eight today too, but they're not riding together."

"Matches up with how Parker introduced him," CJ said. "Called him his 'puppy.' So, it means Turner wasn't working on the nights and times in question, and even if he had been, he'd have been with Parker."

Johnny spoke up. "You think it's Turner?"

She stared at the board. "My gut tells me it's him or Parker. Johnny, you up for a little night work?"

"I'm up for whatever you need. What are you thinking?"

"Stakeout."

Paul and Stan arrived at two o'clock and slid into the black high-back mesh chairs in the conference room. CJ stood at the board and covered the pertinent facts of the rape cases.

Stan exhaled. "Where are we on any suspects? Do we have anything?"

Her eyes connected with Johnny's. She cleared her throat. "It's early, but we have a theory."

Stan leaned forward.

Here goes. "We believe the rapes may have been committed by a police officer."

Paul dropped his head, and Stan's eyes went wide. "What? Why in the hell do you think that?"

She picked up her notepad and went over the reasons for her theory. Stan sat with his hands on top of his head. Paul rubbed at a knot in his neck. The room was silent.

Stan broke the silence. "I hope like hell you're wrong. Knowing their father and grandfather got some damn patch on a shirt and tickets were issued to the rape victims isn't much to go on. What do you think, Paul?"

Paul grunted. "I agree. It's probably circumstantial evidence." He looked at CJ. "However, you have to admit, the tickets and timing are suspicious. Without more, though, we can't accuse anyone yet."

Stan stared at CJ. "We need more than this. Until then, this stays with us. Understand? Last time you arrested a fellow officer, it didn't work out too well."

Her insides quivered and her chest tightened. "Yes, sir."

CJ sat in her Jeep at the back of the LEC parking lot. Her Jeep wouldn't be recognizable since she never drove it to the station. Johnny had an unmarked car way past its prime.

At 8:35 p.m., Turner emerged with Parker. The two men walked together to Parker's Ford pickup, got in, and pulled out onto Lockwood Drive.

CJ whispered to herself, "Where are they going?"

Her phone buzzed. *Johnny.* "I'm not sure why they're together. Let's follow them but stay well back," she told him.

The plan had been for her to follow Turner and Johnny to follow Parker. This was an unexpected twist, so they'd need to improvise.

Ten minutes later, Parker slowed and parked on Society Street. CJ managed to find a spot to park about thirty yards behind them, and Johnny turned onto East Bay Street to circle around.

She watched as both men got out of the truck and went into the Society Street Alehouse. She hit the number. "Johnny, where are you?"

"I'm parked on the corner of Anson Street just ahead of you."

"Good. I think there's a back exit, so we should be able to see both. Yell if you see them."

At 10:35 p.m., one of the men emerged. CJ leaned forward. "Where's your buddy?"

She was about to call Johnny when her cell phone buzzed. *Johnny.* She hit the green circle and listened. "Stay with him. I'll take this one."

TWENTY-THREE

Wednesday, November 10
Downtown Charleston

CJ sat in the darkness under the overhanging trees. Her eyes were glued to Jared Parker. *What's he doing?*

Parker pulled a hooded sweatshirt over his head and flipped the hood up. She leaned forward as he disappeared around the corner of a blush-pink house. The faint glow from her cell phone illuminated the address she'd written in her notes—Rosalie Ricketts's home.

The only sound breaking the silence was her breathing. As carefully as she could, she opened the car door, quickly stepped out, and eased the door closed to cut the inside light. She stood still. Watching. Listening. There were no signs of him. She squatted behind her truck and dialed.

"This is Detective O'Hara. I need backup at 1601 Fortress Court. I think we have an intruder."

She ended the call. She heard a faint noise that came from the back of the house. *Damn it!* As she stood, she pulled out her Glock, then moved forward in the dim moonlight. Her eyes had adjusted to the darkness, but she still couldn't see well—there were bushes and shadows everywhere. She got to the corner of the house, sucked in a deep breath, and rounded it. Nothing. *Where the hell is he?*

Creeping forward, she darted her eyes back and forth. She worked her way down the wall until she reached an open window—its screen sat on the ground. She held her breath and peered inside. No movement. *I need to wait on backup, but if he's inside . . .*

She raised her leg and pulled herself into the room. It was too dark to see, so she took the risk and switched on her Maglite. The beam made its way around the small living room. Still nothing. As lightly as she could, she moved forward. Her breath caught at the creak of the floor above her. She cocked her head, closed her eyes, and listened. Back to quiet.

Moving across the oak floor, she reached the bottom of the steps leading to the second floor. Glock raised, she moved quickly upward when she heard a muffled scream. Her light pierced the darkness in the room on the right. Nothing but an empty bedroom. The floor creaked underneath her—she froze and held her breath.

He hit her running fast, and she was tossed backward against the wall, losing her gun. CJ dodged his kick and returned a punch to his side. His arm came down, she ducked, and a knife just missed her. She grabbed his arm and tried to pin it behind him, but he was too strong. She heard the knife rattling down the steps as she took a fist to the right side of her face. CJ returned a stiff jab to his nose and knee to his groin.

"Bitch!"

She tried to grab him again but lost her grip, and he raced down the stairs.

She was up in a flash, grabbed her gun, and was off and running after him. As she rounded the bottom of the stairs, a voice yelled, "Charleston PD!" just before there was a loud crash ahead of her. She fumbled to find the light switch, and the room went bright. Johnny was straddling the intruder with the muzzle of his gun pressed to his head.

She moved over and yanked the mask off to see wild eyes. "Officer Jared Parker. You're under arrest."

Johnny cuffed Jared and sat him up. CJ finished reading his rights as two more officers arrived to take him away. "Fucking bitch. You can't arrest me."

She smiled at him. "I believe I just did." She waved her hand. "Get him the hell out of here."

Johnny reached up and gently touched her face. "You okay?"

"I'm fine. Let's go check on our girl."

Rosalie was curled into a ball on her bed, whimpering. She was facing the wall and didn't respond when CJ called to her. CJ softly sat on the edge of the bed. Finally, the woman rolled over, trying to cover herself with a sheet.

"Did he hurt you?"

The waterworks came faster. "I don't know. He had a knife and told me not to move. He tore my gown off and—" Her cries overcame her voice.

Johnny spoke up from the bedroom doorway. "I've got medical on their way."

CJ motioned him away and whispered, "Wait downstairs." She figured Rosalie wanted whatever privacy they could provide.

With a thumbs-up, Johnny retreated to the bottom of the stairs.

CJ watched the ambulance pull away with Rosalie thirty minutes later. Johnny walked over to her. "You get your face checked out?"

"Yep. The paramedic said I'll have a nasty bruise, but that's all." Her fingers touched her cheek. "It was worth the punch to get that asshole off the streets."

He rubbed the back of his neck. "Yeah, it sucks for all of us he's a cop. I'm sure the press will have a field day."

"I'm sure you're right."

"My money was on the new guy," he said. "Parker's an arrogant ass, but I didn't think he was this depraved."

She nodded. "You'd think. Key now is to tie him to the other rapes and see if we can determine why he did it."

"You mean other than being a sicko? At least I got a good shot in on him." He chuckled. "Reminded me of my football days."

"You mind finishing up here? I'd like to go to MUSC and check on Rosalie."

He shook his head. "Not at all. We shouldn't be long. The CSI techs told me they haven't found any fingerprints except for one spot. The knife. I guess he handled it before he put on his gloves and didn't wipe it."

"At least he'll have a hard time denying it's his," CJ said firmly. "Make sure they cover every inch of his truck. By the way, how'd you get here so quick?"

"Right after you left, Turner came out the back door hand in hand with a woman, who I assume was his wife or girlfriend, and two other couples. I watched them load up and was driving around the zone when I heard your call for backup. Luckily, I was close."

"I'm glad you got here when you did," she said. "We'd have gotten Parker, but better to catch him at the scene."

Johnny grinned. "Plus, I got to knock the shit out of the asshole."

———

All in all, Rosalie was doing pretty well when CJ arrived at the hospital. Thankfully, CJ had disrupted Parker before he could rape her. She was emotionally damaged, but physically, she was fine. CJ left her room and was headed out when the double doors whooshed open and Paul entered.

"How's the young woman?" he asked.

"She's still shaken up, but physically the doc says she's fine."

He nodded. "I was about to chew your ass out for going in before backup arrived, but you saved the girl from being raped. How's your face?"

She gently rubbed her cheek just under her eye. "A little sore, but it'll only bruise."

"Looks painful. Put some ice on it." He flipped open his pad. "I hate to ask you to do this tonight, but Parker's lawyer is raising hell about, let's see—police misconduct, police brutality, and violation of his rights."

"What?"

He shook his head. "He's reaching for anything. Says he was working undercover to get the rapist when you showed up. Officer Jones assaulted him."

She shook her head. "Unbelievable!"

"Don't worry about it. As usual, Parker's being a blowhard. I'd like to get your report, though, to have a clear statement for the press. Parker will undoubtedly reach out to friends in high places and stir things up." He sighed. "I wanna get ahead of the bullshit. The chief will hold a press conference at eight o'clock in the morning."

"No problem. I'll head back to the station now and get you my report within an hour."

He patted her shoulder. "Thanks. Copy the chief on it so he can have the details. After that, go home and ice your face. Get some rest."

She was buckling her seatbelt when her cell phone buzzed. "Hey, Johnny. What's going on?"

"We found a USC sweatshirt in Jared's truck," he answered excitedly. "It has the emblem we're looking for on it."

Her lips curled into a smile. "Great work. Let's see if the thread matches." She turned the key and started her truck. *Maybe now my nickname, City Girl, will be retired.*

TWENTY-FOUR

Thursday, November 11
Downtown Charleston

"Are the women of Charleston safe in their homes? When is the Charleston PD going to do its job and catch the rapists?" Wendy Watts was back and full-throated. She was fake as ever—hair dyed blond, eyes an unnatural shade of blue from her contacts, and a chest twice the size God gave her. She was front and center as the chief approached the podium in the station's press room for the 8:00 a.m. conference.

CJ whispered to Johnny, "I see the princess of the press is back. I had hoped she'd moved."

Johnny shook his head. "Jeez, she's obnoxious. Does she think screeching at the chief is gonna get her questions answered?"

"Not the point. She just wants attention. She could not care less what the chief has to say."

"Wait until she finds out it's one of our own."

She nodded. "And it's actually someone she knows well."

Johnny glanced at her, puzzled. "Huh?"

She leaned close and whispered, "Jared Parker was her informant on the Lowcountry Killer case. Leaked her files. I imagine he was well rewarded physically."

His eyebrows rose. "Oh. I see."

The chief provided an overview of the rape cases and advised the press that a suspect was in custody but left out the name. The room exploded as he finished, and Wendy was red faced. "No further comments at this time. We'll provide more later."

CJ slipped out the side door. As she came down the hallway, Sam handed her a sheet of paper. "Here's the search warrant for Parker's home."

Her eyes ran down the page. "Perfect. Can you let Paul know we're on our way? I'll brief him and Cap when we get back. Johnny should be downstairs with the search team ready."

"Excuse me, Detective."

She turned to see Wendy's rebuilt pearly whites. *Damn it!* "Hello, Ms. Watts. You're not supposed to be here."

Wendy's shark eyes glistened. "An officer told me it was fine. I have a few questions."

Before CJ could respond, a cameraman stepped forward. Wendy shook her hair. "Okay, we're live. I'm here with—"

"No comments at this time. The chief was clear more will be forthcoming."

"Is it true you've arrested a Charleston PD officer for the rapes of four poor women? Have you been protecting him? Is he your boyfriend?"

CJ clenched her jaw. *Stay calm.* "No comments at this time."

"Can you give me his name? The public has a right to know."

CJ glared at her and fought not to respond. Instead, she turned and headed toward the stairs. In the background, she heard, "As you can see, the Charleston PD is circling its wagons to hide the truth. This is Wendy Watts, and I'll get the public answers."

Thirty minutes later, CJ's tires crunched along the gravel driveway as she pulled up in front of the gray two-story home of Jared Parker on James Island. Two other police vehicles pulled in behind her along with the forensics van. Cheryl Parker read over the warrant with puffy red eyes. She stepped back out of the doorway and retreated to the couch in the living room.

The officers and forensics techs scoured the house for the next two hours. Cheryl sobbed and rocked throughout. As the search team was completing their work, CJ sat down beside her. "Mrs. Parker, is there anyone who can come to be with you?"

The mousy woman with soft, almond-brown eyes shook her head. "No. My mama lives in Louisville, and I don't have many friends. Jared doesn't like it when I leave the house. He wants me here to take care of things."

Jared's an even bigger ass than I thought. "Mrs. Parker, I'm sorry about all of this."

Cheryl sniffed. "Jared's going to be so mad at me when he gets home, and the place is a mess. He's already furious at me."

"Why is he mad at you?"

"He told me it was my fault he was in jail. I told him I tried to bail him out, but the judge set the bail so high and I don't have enough money."

CJ took her hand. "It's not your fault. This is on Jared."

The woman's head hung down. "He's going to make me pay."

Her anger rose. "Does Jared ever hit you?"

A loud sniff, then silence.

CJ asked again. "Mrs. Parker, does he?"

Her voice was a soft squeak. "Please call me Cheryl. Yes. It's my fault, though."

"Why is that?"

She stared out the window, her eyes glassy. "I don't do the things he likes right. I try, but I don't like it. If I were a better wife . . ."

CJ cleared her throat. "Do you mean in the bedroom?"

Cheryl nodded, and the tears came again. "He likes to be really rough when we . . ."

"Have sex?"

The mousy woman squeezed her eyes shut. "It hurts, and if I cry, Jared hits me."

CJ fought to control her anger.

"It's my fault. A wife is supposed to please her husband. Jared says—"

"Cheryl, that's bullshit. It's not your fault if you don't like what Jared does, and it's certainly no reason to abuse you. Marriage is a two-way street."

The woman mumbled, "I guess."

CJ looked at her notepad. "I have a question I hope you can answer. Did you notice if Jared had any scratches around October thirteen? About a month ago."

"What kind of scratches?"

"Say from fingernails. They would have been in the neck area."

Cheryl fidgeted with her fingers. "Uh, yeah. I saw scratch marks on the bottom part of his neck when he got out of the shower. So I asked him what happened."

That matches what Marcy Willis told us. "What did he say?"

"Jared told me he didn't know. Then he slapped me and told me to shut the hell up."

One of the techs approached. "We've finished covering the house. Haven't found much of interest. However, he has some porn on his computer. We'll take his system back to the lab so we can look at it more closely." Cheryl flinched.

CJ waited until the tech left. "Cheryl, did you know about the porn?"

"Yes. Jared makes me watch it with him sometimes. He says it'll help me learn how to make him happy."

"I take it you're not a fan of watching it."

Her head shook. "No. I don't like to watch. It's not that I don't like sex, but not the stuff Jared does. I didn't like . . ."

CJ pressed. "What else didn't you like?"

"I . . . I didn't like it when he made me have sex with two of his friends. They were all drunk, and he promised me he wouldn't ever do that again."

Oh, Jesus. "Is there anything else you'd like to tell me before we leave?"

Her almond-brown eyes met CJ's. "You need to look in his man cave."

"Where is that?"

"It's out in the back." Cheryl turned and pointed. "You have to go through the woods. He keeps it locked, and I'm not allowed to go in unless I'm with him. Since his friends . . ." She suddenly stood, and her soft eyes turned defiant. "I can show you, and you have my permission to break down the door."

Cheryl led CJ and two techs along the path to a shed of about twenty feet by twenty feet. There was only one window, and the heavy blinds prohibited anyone from seeing inside. The only door was padlocked and had a dead bolt. It was nothing a battering ram couldn't open. An officer stepped forward and with one blow, CJ stood in the center of the room.

There was a small television in the corner, a DVD player, and a library of hard-core porn videos. In addition, there were several photos of nude women pinned to the wall. A double bed sat along one wall opposite a wooden table and four chairs.

CJ pulled a small trunk from under the bed. "Open this please," she said to a tech, who used bolt cutters to remove its padlock. She opened the lid. "All of this needs to be collected." Carefully, she held up a pair of women's panties. "There are several pairs in here. Send me photos of each, and let's get these to the lab. This needs to go as well." She pointed to a black gym bag.

She exited to find Cheryl standing with her arms folded. Her face was wet, and she shivered. CJ put her arm around her and led her away.

When the search wrapped up around three o'clock, CJ returned to the LEC to interview Parker. CJ opened the door to the interrogation room—now a hot box. Officer Jared Parker sat at the table, his handcuffed wrists flat. He sneered at her. "Well, well. City Girl is coming to interrogate me. Save your breath, honey. Ain't done shit, and I ain't talking to you."

She leaned in and closed the gap. "No problem. With what I have, I don't need your statement."

He was defiant. "Honey, you're grasping at straws. It's a damn shame the only way you can solve a case is to railroad a fellow officer. Last time, you arrested Ben, and look how that turned out. Go to hell!"

She pulled the chair out and propped her foot on the seat. "Let's see. I caught you attempting to rape Rosalie Ricketts. You attacked me, an officer. This is irrefutable. But, of course, the biggest evidence is what we just found in your shack. It ties you to four other rapes."

His eyes went wide, and he blinked wildly. "I don't know what you're talking about. I don't have a shack. More bullshit!"

She slid a photo across the table. "Here's a photo of it. Your wife and I are standing right by the front door. And here are photos of women's underwear in your lockbox. Wanna bet whether our rape victims will claim them? Or maybe we bet on whether the thread we found at the fourth scene matches the one from your dad's USC sweatshirt we found in your truck?"

Parker mumbled, "It'll never stick."

She shrugged. "Yeah, right. By the time I put all of this together, my money says a jury will return a guilty verdict in record time. Hell, they may not even need to deliberate."

The toughness faded, and his eyes grew wet. "You . . . you can't do this. I'm a cop."

She grunted and turned for the door. "That makes it ten times worse in my book. Good luck in prison, ex-officer Parker."

TWENTY-FIVE

Friday, November 12
Downtown Charleston

CJ stood after everyone was settled in the conference room at the LEC for a briefing about the Parker case. She approached the board. In addition to the brass, Assistant Solicitor Tim Drummond had appeared—he was slightly taller than her, with blond curly hair and bluish-green eyes that were too close together. She guessed he was in his late thirties, and he sat quietly, circling items on the evidence reports. *Not much of a talker.*

She eyed the group. "Ready?"

"It's all yours," replied Chief Williams.

She covered the details of the four rape cases, the attempted rape, and Parker's treatment of his wife for the next hour.

For each, she pointed out the pieces of evidence that led her to believe Officer Jared Parker was the perpetrator for all five. Then, finally, she wrapped up her summary and waited.

Tim spoke up. "So, for the first two rapes, all we have is the underwear you found at the suspect's home, correct?"

She nodded. "Yes. The first two victims have confirmed it's their underwear, and we're waiting on the DNA to give us confirmation as well."

He jotted on his pad. "For the third rape, we have the same underwear evidence and the scratch?"

"Yes. Marcy Willis has confirmed it's her underwear and the suspect's wife corroborates the scratch. Both are willing to testify." She watched him jot more notes. *May as well be proactive.* "For our fourth victim, we have the underwear plus the thread from the patch on the sweatshirt found at the crime scene. The FBI lab is analyzing the thread and patch to confirm they match."

He was straight faced. "The attempted rape is easiest to prove. Our suspect was caught in the act, attacked you, and tried to attack another officer."

"Correct. And don't forget the knife with his fingerprints. He reportedly used a knife in the prior four rapes."

Stan spoke up. "Did we get anything from Turner?"

She shook her head. "He says he doesn't know anything about the rapes. He knew Parker wrote down the addresses of the women, but that's all."

"Do you believe him?" Stan asked.

"I do. There's nothing to tie him to anything. He voluntarily took and passed a polygraph."

Stan motioned to Paul. "Anything from your end?"

He exhaled. "No. CJ's covered it all nicely. Some of what we have is circumstantial, but put all together, it's solid. If we find DNA on the underwear, that'll be the final nail."

Chief Williams stood. "Tim, it's your call how we proceed." He walked over and refilled his coffee mug.

Tim drummed his fingers on the table as he stared at his pad. Finally, he stood and walked over to the window with a sweeping view out across the Ashley River, which was lost in the heavy gray clouds about to burst. He turned. "I'm charging Officer Parker with four counts of rape and one count of attempted rape. In addition, I'm adding aggravating circumstances for the use of a knife, two counts of assault on a police officer, and resisting arrest."

His bluish-green eyes caught CJ's. "I may even change the attack on you to attempted murder, and I'm also considering throwing in criminal sexual conduct for the forced rape of his wife. Sick bastard made her have sex with his friends against her will." He faced the other three men. "You guys okay with that?"

Chief Williams answered for the group. "Yes. This kind of thing can't happen on this force, and I want a crystal-clear message sent. What chances do you give us for a full conviction?"

He sighed. "Well, it's hard to say how a jury might handle this, and a good defense attorney will cast doubt on some of what we have. Paul's right—some of the pieces alone could be refuted but together they're solid."

He looked at CJ. "It helps our case that you've got all five women and the wife set to testify. I'll put them on the stand with you, Officer Jones, and Officer Turner. Hell, I may subpoena a few of his sicko friends to testify on his character." He exhaled. "In the end, I bet he'll take a plea and avoid a trial. Of course, his ego will make him want to fight it, but he won't want the negative publicity."

She slowly nodded. "How long do you think Parker gets if he's convicted or pleads?"

"Hard to tell. Each count of first-degree rape would carry up to thirty years. Ten years for the second-degree and another ten for third. I'd probably accept thirty years without the possibility of parole if he pleaded. I'll go over the files again and pull a case together. Can we go over it once I have it drafted?"

"Yes," she replied. "That'd be fine."

CJ sat alone in the conference room after everyone left. She wasn't sure how she felt about a possible pleaded-down sentence, but she had to admit the solicitor was being aggressive, and that was all she could ask. She rubbed her temples—it had been a long week. She'd sent Sam home early, and Johnny was out interviewing potential witnesses in their Harleston Village murder case.

She glanced up at the round clock over the window—4:10 p.m. *I think I'll bug out.* She called and made a date with Harry for coconut shrimp. She was dropping the last of the manila folders into her bag as her cell phone buzzed. *Uh-oh.*

"Hey, Wally. How's Alaska?"

"Going fine. Listen, I wanted to let you know we're opening a case into Ivan Popov's death. The ME will take another look."

"Really? I see. Keep me posted."

She hung up and gazed out the window, watching the seagulls floating. The buzzing of her cell phone broke her trance—5:52 p.m. *Oh shit!* "Hey, Unc. Sorry, I got hung up, but I'm on my way."

"No problem," Harry replied. "How about a table with a view?"

"A table on the deck overlooking the ocean would be fabulous."

CJ steered onto the ramp leading to the Arthur Ravenel Jr. Bridge and dropped into Mount Pleasant. Traffic slowed along Highway 17 until she made the right onto the Isle of Palms Connector. The tension in her neck eased as she looked out across the sparkling water.

The white building with plum-and-turquoise trim was a feast of colors—bright and cheery. There was a friendly pelican on its sign, and an oversize red Adirondack chair beckoned everyone to sit and relax. She heard Harry call to her from the rooftop. He raised two drinks, and she climbed up to meet him.

"Hello, sweetheart. I was worried you'd forgotten our date."

She flushed. "Sorry. I got hung up on a last-minute project." *Staring out the damn window.*

He motioned to the covered patio. "We have a four-top on the porch in case it rains. The view is perfect, and we'll have a nice sunset."

She slipped into the red plastic chair and sipped her piña colada—a blend of pineapple and coconut. A bright-eyed young woman, college age, left them menus and a basket of hush puppies.

CJ reached for a golden ball. "Yes! My favorite."

He grinned. "I told our waitress to get these out as soon as you got here. Do you still want coconut shrimp tonight?"

"Absolutely. I'm starved. It just hit me I didn't eat lunch."

His smile faded. "You're working too much and not taking care of yourself."

She shot him a *Don't mess with me* look.

He raised his hands in surrender. "Okay, okay. I'll drop it. Oh, here's our girl. We'll take two orders of the coconut shrimp, please."

CJ looked past Harry at a small television hanging above the bar. She bolted out of her chair. "Can you turn that up, please?"

The brown-haired bartender handed her the remote.

"This is Wendy Watts reporting from the Charleston PD headquarters. I had a chance to speak with the lead detective who is responsible for the horrific rapes of numerous young women here in our beloved city . . ."

Her jaw dropped when the next shot was of her standing in the station's hallway saying "No comment" to every twisted question. She looked like an idiot. Sam was captured in the background, her eyebrows pulled together and lips tight. She was numb. *What an ambush.*

Harry touched her arm. He guided her back to the table while all eyes in Coconut Joe's remained fixed on her. Her appetite went down with the sun as she stood to take the chief's call.

His voice was angry. "Damn it, CJ! You made the department look like a bunch of fools in Watts's interview. Your face looked guilty as hell. Next time, you better be more professional. Understand?"

"Yes, sir. I understand." She whispered, "I'm sorry. It's my fault."

"It damn well better not happen again."

"No, sir. It won't happen again." She hit the end button on her cell phone and stood with her head hung.

Harry approached with a bag. "Everything okay?"

She shook her head as tears dripped to the wooden planks. "No. That was the chief. He saw the interview, and . . . let's just say he's pissed."

He put his arm around her.

"I should have told him. I just didn't think." She sniffed and wiped her nose with the back of her hand. "I need to go, Uncle Harry. I'm so sorry, but I need to go home."

"You could come home with me." He held up the bag. "I have our dinner."

"Thanks, but I need to go back to my apartment. I'm not good company."

He handed her the bag. "Here. Take this with you. You need to eat."

CJ drove back the way she came. Before she climbed the ramp onto the Arthur Ravenel Jr. Bridge, she steered her truck into the parking lot of a liquor store.

TWENTY-SIX

Friday, November 12
St. Helena Island

Excitement pulsed through Elias. He wished the volume had been higher, but he'd heard enough. The three women on the screen excited him. He could tell they were power-ful . . . and their beauty aroused him. He wrote the names from the screen down.

"Get your ass back to work! I want that stock put up, and the room better be spotless."

Elias cowered, but the old man who owned the place didn't hit him. He hustled back to the storeroom and con-tinued opening boxes and putting the stock on the shelves. He knew he was lucky to have this job, even if it was only part-time and involved shitty tasks after-hours.

"Aren't you done yet, freak? I need to get home."

"Yes . . . yes, sir. I just need to dump the dirty mop water." He opened the back door and dragged the mop bucket to the edge of the woods, where he dumped the water. He put the bucket back and hung the mop to dry.

"Okay, sir. I'm finished."

The old man scoffed. "The floor still looks like shit. You're too fucking weak to get it clean. I can't wait for you to redo it. Here's your money, so get!"

He bent down and picked up the money—eighty dollars. "Sir, I worked twenty hours this week." He held up the four twenties.

"Yeah. What's the problem?"

He cleared his throat. "I get five dollars an hour. I should get twenty more dollars."

The old man glared at him. "That's all I'm paying you. You spent at least four hours screwing around. I ain't paying for that. Now get!"

Elias opened his mouth, but nothing came out. The old man grabbed him and shoved him out the door onto the ground. He balled himself up, expecting more. Instead, he heard the door slam. The old man was right. He was weak—for now.

Soon I'll show them all.

TWENTY-SEVEN

Saturday, November 13
Downtown Charleston

CJ's mouth was dry as a desert, and her head pounded. Her stomach flip-flopped, and beads of sweat clung to her forehead. She finally eased her feet off the bed and wobbled up, taking a long, deep breath. *I feel like death. How much did I drink? Oh, shit!*

She raced to the bathroom but came up short as she vomited on the floor. She finally got to the toilet, barely avoiding losing everything on the tiles again. Then, after dry heaving, she lowered herself to the cold surface.

CJ raised her head and peered at the clock on her bed-side table—8:10 a.m. She wished she hadn't made plans that day. Her bed was where she belonged. The four aspirin and cold shower helped her head, and the dry bagel calmed her stomach—a little. She pulled on her jeans and a light sweatshirt, tied her hair into a ponytail, and added her Boston Red Sox cap. Not professional, but it was all she had in her today.

She answered a knock on the door to find the smiling face of her landlord, George Watkins. She joined him on the landing of her second-floor apartment over his dress shop.

"Good morning, CJ. Hope I'm not disturbing you."

"No. Not at all." *Just hope I don't puke on you.*

"Wonderful. I wanted to come up and let you know we'll be doing inventory today, and I didn't want to scare you since we don't usually work on Saturdays." He handed her a plastic container. "My wife sent you some lasagna. I think she put some homemade sourdough bread in there too."

She smiled past her queasy stomach. "Thank you, and be sure to thank her for me. I'll have this for dinner." *Boy, I sure lucked out with my landlord.*

As George was headed down the stairs, Johnny came up. "You ready?"

———

Johnny parked in a lot just off Market Street. "We're meeting our guide over on the corner at ten o'clock. We have a few minutes if you wanna grab a coffee."

"I think I'll stick with my water for now. My stomach's a little upset this morning."

"No worries. I see our guy, so let's head over. He's got a tour this afternoon."

They got out of the car and approached a Black man about CJ's height. He had gray hair and bright, dark brown eyes. He beamed. "Good morning, Johnny, and good morning to you, young lady."

Johnny extended his hand. "This is my friend CJ. We work together. CJ, this is Marcus Williams."

Marcus took her hand and stared into her eyes. "Nice to meet you. Johnny tells me you want to learn more about the Gullah."

She nodded. "I do."

Johnny patted Marcus on the shoulder. "He's the man to teach you. Marcus has been leading Gullah tours in Charleston for twenty years and knows the Gullah language and culture. He also knows a thing or two about hexes, fixes, and roots."

Marcus motioned to a small van. "How about we get moving? I'd like to show you as much as I can before my one o'clock tour."

For the next hour and a half, he provided background and details for the places he used for his tours—Old Slave Mart, now a museum, and Sweetgrass Market—and the history of the Gullah people. He told them about Edward DeReef, a freed Black man who had once been one of the richest men in Charleston and a slave owner.

"Let's stop here. Johnny mentioned you're not feeling well today. I may have something that'll help."

They left the van and entered an old drugstore. Marcus led them to the back, where the wall was lined with various candles, books, pamphlets, and herbs. The fragrances of burning candles and incense filled their noses.

CJ watched him put leaves into a small electric pot of boiling water. Then, after several minutes, he poured the mixture through a strainer into a thick ceramic mug.

"Here, try this. Of course, I could use pine tar, pokeroot, and Epsom salt, but this is easier, and it'll work."

She put the mug to her lips, blew, and sipped. "Tastes minty."

He chuckled. "That's 'cause it's wild mint. You use the leaves to make tea, and it helps relieve stomach distress. Certain herbs or roots are simple to use, others are more complex. Tell you what, it's not as much fun, but let's pour your tea into a Styrofoam cup, and we'll keep going on our tour."

For the next hour, Marcus talked about how roots and herbs were used. CJ was surprised at how many different remedies there were for a wide range of medical ailments. For the first time, she understood how complicated it was and why so many held root doctors in such high regard.

He pulled his van into the parking lot across from Market Street. "You have to know what you're doing to get what you're after. Do it wrong and you can find yourself in a world of trouble. I'd argue a root doctor is comparable to any doctor today.

"Take nightshade as an example. The root can be boiled to make a tea and used to treat a fever. Unfortunately, deadly nightshade, which isn't native to the US but can be found here, is highly poisonous. Its black berries are appealing, and some have used it as a medicine, but I wouldn't want to risk it."

"How about magical purposes?"

He smiled at her. "Well, some claim certain herbs and roots have magical powers. But root doctors or conjurers are the ones with the skill around this."

"What do you know about a root called High John the Conqueror?"

Marcus exhaled. "Lots of ways to use it. A root doctor might prepare a mojo bag, which one carries for success and personal power. Hoodoo actually picked the use of this root up from the Native Americans."

"How would that work?"

"I'm no root doctor, but I've heard you place the whole root in a red flannel bag along with master root and Sampson snakeroot and carry it with you. It is said to provide you with great strength."

CJ added to her notes. "Jeez, all this sounds really complicated."

Marcus smiled. "Yes. Very. One must know what and when to harvest, what parts to use, and what goes with what. Done correctly, you can have success. Done improperly—well, you can wind up dead."

She stared at her notes. "Last question before you head to your tour. How does someone learn all this?"

"There are a few books out there, but it's mostly passed down from person to person." He took her hand and squeezed. "By the way, how's your tummy?"

Oh, wow. "Uh, actually, it's totally fine now."

Marcus winked at her. "Told you hoodoo is real."

TWENTY-EIGHT

Saturday, November 13
Folly Beach, South Carolina

The day was perfect. The light breeze caused the tops of the sawgrass to sway, dance, and rustle under the crystal-clear blue sky. The faint smell of salt mingled with odors coming from the grill. Typically, the temperature was slightly lower this time of year, but not today—shorts, a T-shirt, and flip-flops were in order.

The tall man with dark brown hair watched the people moving up and down the beach. The day had brought out families, young and old, and numerous women. Tight, toned bodies glistened in the sun. His eyes were fixed on a group of four college age women stretched out on their stomachs in a row across the sand—*College of Charleston coeds?*

Hungry. He stood from his folding chair, stretched his six-foot-four frame, and cruised to the snack bar. The smell from the grill had overtaken him. He grabbed a burger with lettuce, tomatoes, pickles, onions, mustard, and ketchup—the perfect combination.

He sat at the edge of the sand and licked his fingers. His hunger for food was satisfied, but he was still hungry. Would he satisfy that as well? He knew it was risky. He had been lucky before. *Control yourself. Walk away and go home.*

His legs refused to work when the blond-haired young woman on the end of the row turned over and sat up. He held his breath as she smeared oil over her chest, then down the rest of her body. Finally, she stood, adjusted her white bikini, and laid flat. He exhaled slowly and ran his fingers through his dark brown hair. *Just leave.*

———

The sun eased toward its nightly resting place, and the glow of the day began to fade. He knew he should have left hours ago, but he'd stayed. His group of four was now two, and his favorite, the blond-haired girl on the end, remained.

He watched a young man in board shorts approach. He squatted down, leaned in, and kissed the black-haired woman. She laughed and threw her arms around him. His pulse rate increased as they packed up and left—the blond-haired girl was alone. *You need to go!*

After several minutes of watching and fantasizing, he finally found the determination to listen to himself. He folded his chair, grabbed his towel, and headed for his SUV. He tossed the chair in the back.

"Excuse me."

He turned to find her smiling up at him—the blond-haired woman. Her bright blue eyes twinkled in the late afternoon sun, and her face was a work of art. "Hey. Everything okay?"

"My friends have all left, and I'm such an idiot. My car keys and phone were in my friend's bag. I'm stranded." She pointed. "My car's over there on the other side of the bushes. I hate to ask, but could I borrow your phone?"

He was frozen—at first, no words came. "Uh . . . Sure. Here you go."

She smiled sweetly at him as she dialed and then spoke to someone. "Thanks a bunch." Her hand brushed his when she handed him back the phone. "She and her boyfriend are coming back. You saved me. By the way, I'm Kerri Ann." She extended her hand.

He slowly reached out and took her dainty hand. His heart raced as their skin touched. "Happy to help. I'm Joe." He lied about his name.

She thanked him again and walked to her red Toyota Celica. He moved close enough to see her through the vanilla sweetgrass. She leaned against the trunk, and he watched as she pulled her hair into a ponytail. She caught him looking and gave him a flirty smile. *Fuck it!*

"Do you want me to wait with you?" he yelled. "It's getting late."

"I'm okay. My friend should be here in about twenty minutes."

"Okay. I don't mind waiting, though. I could at least leave you a bottle of water. I hate to leave a damsel in distress." He gave her his best smile.

"Ah, that's sweet. Thanks. I'll be fine."

Good. Now leave before you—

"Tell you what, a bottle of water would be nice." He turned, and Kerri Ann was within three feet of him, smiling—a mixture of perfume and suntan oil tickled his nose.

"Ah, okay. I have a cooler in the trunk. Let's grab you one."

He walked behind her to the back of his black SUV. He flipped the trunk lid up, and she leaned in. Within seconds, she was tucked away, and he was pulling onto East Arctic Avenue. *Oh, shit! What have I done?*

Joe's mind raced as he pulled onto the dirt road and drove through the thick foliage. Kerri Ann had calmed down in the back, except for an occasional whimper. His heart pounded, and his hands trembled on the wheel. *All this time, and I finally get myself caught!*

He jumped out of the truck, opened the swinging doors, and pulled into the building. He walked around to the back of the truck and opened the trunk lid. Kerri Ann's eyes were wide. She squirmed and did her best to scream.

The rope held, and all she could manage was a muffled groan. Her weak kicks missed their mark.

She lost her breath when she landed on the wooden table with a thud. She almost broke free when he untied her—almost. In the end, she was tied to the table, and struggling only caused the ropes to cut into her wrists and ankles. He made her world go dark when he pulled a burlap bag over her head.

He sat for hours, watching her chest rise and fall. He took another sip of whiskey and let the warmth fill his body. Then, finally, he took one last long drink of liquid courage and stood. His panic had subsided, and the hunger for her had returned with a vengeance.

Kerri Ann had no idea where the man who called himself Joe had taken her. The tape over her mouth kept her from screaming for help. Her thoughts raced, and she fought not to panic. *What's he planning?*

She lay on the dirty, sticky table. The rancid odor of fish stung her nostrils. Her hands and feet were tied tight, and no matter how hard she tried, she couldn't free herself. She could only wait in the darkness for him to return. Wetness covered her face, and her sobs broke the silence.

Creaking—footsteps from behind her. Panic engulfed her when he jerked the bag off her head, and she frantically fought to get free. His face appeared, he squinted, and a wicked smile crossed his lips. "Did you get some rest?" He leaned in close. "I hope so." Her eyes pleaded. *Please, no, please.*

A sharp edge touched her neck. Joe ripped off her bikini top and pawed at her breasts. She squeezed her eyes shut tight as her shorts and bikini bottoms tore. She felt his weight as he moved on top of her and smelled the alcohol on his ragged breath. The searing pain spread through her until dizziness faded to black.

———

Cold and wet—a cloth caressed her face. Kerri Ann opened her eyes from her horrific nightmare, until she realized it wasn't a nightmare. Joe stood over her with the same sick smile. "Welcome back, sweetheart. I was so worried about you after our little workout." She yanked her face away when he leaned down and tried to kiss her cheek.

The early glow of the sun peeked through the crusty windowpane. He went to the workbench. She couldn't see what the monster was doing until he turned. The metal blade glowed in the morning light as he crept toward her.

A hot line crossed her throat, a stinging sensation escalated, and a coppery odor was the last thing Kerri Ann knew of this world.

TWENTY-NINE

Monday, November 15
Mount Pleasant, South Carolina

Ringing startled CJ awake—5:24 a.m. She fumbled to flip on her bedside lamp and retrieve her cell phone from where it had landed when she knocked it off the table. *Damn it!*

Hoarsely, she answered. "Detective O'Hara."

"Hey, CJ. It's Helen. I'm sorry to call so early, but you need to get to Shem Creek. We have a body."

"Location?"

"It's hard to find," Helen said. "A Mount Pleasant officer will meet you just past the bridge over the creek."

"On my way. Has CSU been called?"

"That's my next call."

CJ passed on the shower. She threw on her jeans, blouse, and boots then bolted down the stairs for her truck.

The Arthur Ravenel Jr. Bridge sparkled with lights against the dark sky. Traffic was sparse as CJ roared down the incline onto Highway 17. Flashing lights appeared on the right as she neared the bridge over Shem Creek. A female officer waved to her as she slowed and rolled down her window.

"Thanks for coming so quickly," the officer said. "How about you follow me back?"

Limbs tugged at CJ's truck as she bounced her way along the dirt path. Calling this a road would have been a stretch. The clearing produced a small gray metal shed, about sixty by sixty feet.

She pushed the truck into park. A man who was at least seventy years old, with a haggard face, rested on a rusty five-gallon bucket by the shed. He struggled to his feet and stepped forward, limping on his right leg. He waved at her—his ring finger and pinky were gone from his right hand. "Are you in charge?" he asked.

CJ glanced at the officer, who stood there, silent. *Okay, not my jurisdiction, but—here we go.* "I'm Detective O'Hara, and I'm here to help however I can."

"Good. Nobody's telling me much. I'm Butch, and I own the place."

"Tell you what, Butch." She gently took his arm. "Why don't you sit in my truck here and let me take a look, then we can talk? My truck will be more comfortable than your can."

He worked to pull himself into the seat. "Hey, wait. I know you. You're that detective who caught the serial guy a few months back."

"Yes, sir. That was me."

"Holy shit! I thought that was awful, but this may be worse."

After getting the old man settled, she turned to the officer. "Okay, let's see what we have." Her eyes caught the badge. "You're Officer Jenny Morton."

"Yes, ma'am. I went to one of your briefings on the Parrish case. Jenny's good."

"I thought you looked familiar," CJ replied. "Sorry I didn't recognize you earlier."

Jenny shook her head. "Not a problem. Just happy we could get you here. My chief said to ask for you specifically. You're quite popular here in the Lowcountry, and as you know, we're a small department."

"I remember meeting one of your detectives," CJ said.

"Detective Metcalf. Jack's still with us, but he's out of commission for a while. He was cleaning gutters, fell off his roof, and cracked some ribs."

As they approached the open double doors, Jenny motioned to two other officers. "This is Officer Sampson and Officer Carlyle. I've had them securing the place."

The larger of the two men, Officer Carlyle, stepped forward.

CJ quickly lifted both palms to stop him and yelled, "Wait, wait! Back up!"

The officer hotfooted it backward. "What? What is it?"

She squatted. "Tire tracks. They could be from our unsub's vehicle. Let's not disturb them."

"Oh, shit. Sorry. I hadn't noticed them." His face turned red.

"Let's get some more tape and secure this area. I'd like to have the CSU mold these and see if we can determine what type of vehicle it matches."

Sheepishly, the officer went to his cruiser and retrieved more crime scene tape. "I've got these stakes. Tell me where you want them." She used her foot to show him where to drive the stakes. He muttered, "Can't believe I didn't pay attention."

She answered her ringing cell phone and let Eddie know the place was hard to find. She'd send someone out to meet him. "You'll need to be careful driving in. It'll be a tight squeeze for the van."

Before she could ask, Officer Carlyle responded, "I'll go get 'em."

———

CJ's flashlight beam led her to a table in the back of the building. The space only had two small windows and one set of double doors. Two overhead lights buzzed and flickered. It was full of various pieces of equipment, some junk, and several fishing nets. She approached carefully, her eyes scanning. "Oh, man."

The young woman was face up on the table. Her wrists and ankles were secured with ropes, and tape covered her mouth. Her naked body looked bleached and her face bloodless. CJ held her breath, doing her best to handle the odor—rotten eggs, garbage left in the sun, and feces.

She leaned in closer to get a look at the cut across her throat—black, dark purple, and deep red. Blood had run from the victim's wound to the table and then dripped to the concrete floor. Her milky eyes stared blankly at the ceiling as flies swarmed.

"CJ?" Eddie stood in the doorway.

She exhaled. "A woman, early twenties. She's been dead awhile. Throat's been slashed, and this looks like the kill spot. Blood is everywhere."

He looked past her. "Okay, we're on it."

"I'll look around some more, but we have some tire tracks near the front." She joined Eddie and pointed them out. "Let's process those as well. They're fresh, and the owner said his truck is at the dock. He walked here. Who's the ME today?"

"That'd be me," Thomas said as he approached.

She shook her head. "It's all yours."

Jenny spoke up. "What do you need from us, Detective?"

"You stay here with me. I wanna walk the perimeter more closely." CJ looked at the other two officers. "If you can get your cruiser by the van, go back and block the entrance. Last thing we need is the fucking press back here."

"You got it. If we can't get by, we'll hoof it out."

CJ walked the area, and other than the tire tracks, there was no sign of anyone's being here. She watched a tech photograph, measure, and mold the tracks.

She opened the door to her truck and joined Butch, and he told her he'd walked over from the dock where he kept his boat to pick up an extra net. He was a shrimper and it was the middle of white shrimp season.

"I don't come over here too often. I wouldn't have today, but I tore a couple of nets yesterday. I noticed someone had cut the lock off when I got here, and the door was cracked open. I figured it was some damn kids looking for stuff to steal, but when I flipped on the lights and went in . . ." He started to cry.

At ten, Eddie motioned for CJ to join him by the body. "We found a partial fingerprint," he said. CJ peered at the piece of tape at the end of his fingertip. "It's not perfect, but we can pull it. To make sure we get the best print we can, we're gonna leave it for now and remove it at the lab."

"Has to be his, right?" Her pulse skyrocketed.

"I'd think so," he said. "Can't imagine it's hers. Our witness said he didn't touch anything." He motioned to the two techs. "Okay, guys. Let's load her up."

Thomas and Eddie joined CJ and gave her the preliminary. The blond-haired, blue-eyed woman was believed to be in her early twenties and, most likely, had been killed early Sunday morning. The cause of death was the laceration to her throat, and she had been raped—there were no signs of fluids or semen. The only unique marking on her body was a belly-button piercing—a small diamond with a silver ring.

CJ's favorite ME eyed his notes. "She also had some abrasions on her face. We found this burlap bag by the table. I think he had it over her head at some point." He held it up.

"Had to be removed before he killed her," she mumbled. "There's no blood on it. The only question is if it was on while he raped her or if he wanted her to see him."

The two men left, and Jenny joined CJ. The two women watched the body being loaded into the coroner's van until a noise on their left startled them. "Detective O'Hara, can we get a statement?" Wendy Watts's nasty smile gleamed at them.

"No comment, Ms. Watts," CJ said. "This area is off limits, so please go back the way you came."

Wendy motioned for the cameraman to film the body being loaded. Jenny stepped forward and sent the cameraman and camera crashing back into the bushes with a huge push. "This is a crime scene."

"You can't do that! The public has a right—"

Wendy stopped short as Jenny grabbed her and spun her around. "Out now!"

Wendy helped the cameraman gather the equipment, and they disappeared. She whispered to him, "I hope you got that."

"Officer Jenny, who knew you were such a brute?" CJ chuckled.

"Sorry. I'll probably get suspended, but I can't stand that bitch. She's not a legit journalist, just a tabloid gossiper."

It was almost noon when CJ got in her truck and headed back to the LEC. She called Sam and let her know that she had another dead woman and she was on her way back to the station. She asked her to search missing persons and see if there was a White twentysomething on the list and call her back.

Answering her cell phone as she pulled off Lockwood Drive, CJ asked, "Did you find anything, Sam?"

"A woman, twenty-one, was reported missing Saturday night. Her roommate said she went to pick her up at Folly Beach, and she wasn't there. Folly Beach PD responded, but the missing person report wasn't officially filed until yesterday."

"What's she look like?"

"Blond hair, blue eyes, slim build . . . oh, she had a belly-button ring."

CJ turned off the engine. "Name?"

"Kerri Ann Russell. She's a junior in business school over at the College of Charleston."

"We can close the report," CJ whispered. "We found her."

THIRTY

Tuesday, November 16
Downtown Charleston

Jeez . . . I stink.

CJ had gowned up for the early morning autopsy, but the fragrance of death followed her from the morgue. She trudged up the stairs and into the station. The bullpen was alive as her shoes squeaked down the hallway from the morning rain shower.

Sam was engrossed in the display on the computer screen. Without looking up, she said, "Good morning. How was the autopsy?"

CJ gave a long exhale. "Always the same . . . shitty. Whenever I think about how bad my job is, I think of poor

Thomas. Dealing with the dead day in and day out must be the worst. Where's Johnny?"

"He's off today."

"Oh, yeah. I forgot." She dropped into a chair. "I need to get myself organized to brief Stan and Paul. You get them scheduled?"

"Yep. They're coming by at eleven o'clock. I'm gonna pick up lunch for y'all. What's your fancy?"

The last thing CJ could think of was food. "You can surprise us."

She spread her file out and opened her pad to the autopsy notes. The blank face of Kerri Ann stared at her. She flipped the photo over. *Enough of that.*

Stan and Paul entered the conference room a few minutes before eleven. They told CJ they were ready to get started. She pulled out her notes and stepped to the board.

"Okay, guys. I'll go over what we have so far, including what Thomas provided me this morning. He's not gonna join us, but we can call him if needed."

For the next hour, she covered Kerri Ann's murder findings. Paul and Stan sat quietly until she finished.

Paul rubbed his chin. "Wait. How did she call her friend if she didn't have a phone?"

"Excellent question. She must have borrowed a phone to call. We traced the number . . . a burner."

"Dead end," Paul said.

Stan shifted in his chair. "Is the guy who found the body a possible suspect?"

She shook her head. "I don't think so. He's seventy-two and not in good health. I'm not sure he'd be capable of subduing anyone."

"Does Thomas have any ideas on what hand was used for the cut?" Stan squinted as his eyes scanned the image of the corpse.

"He thinks the perp is left-handed based on the pattern of the cut. He also said Kerri Ann had some bruising around her neck, so maybe he strangled her or held her down," CJ explained.

Paul's eyes lifted. "Held her down?"

"As he raped her. Thomas reported bruising and tearing consistent with forced intercourse. No fluids or semen, so he wore a condom."

As he pointed to a photo, Stan spoke up. "How about the tape on her mouth?"

CJ pointed back to the board. "There's nothing unique about the tape. It can be found in any hardware store. However, the circled area on this photo shows where we found a partial fingerprint. The forensics crew was gonna pull it in the lab and run it through CODIS." The Combined DNA Index System was a nationwide database that contained DNA profiles for a wide range of criminal offenders, evidence from crime scenes, and information about missing persons. Law enforcement found it invaluable.

Stan walked around the table and stood next to her. "Do we think it's from our guy?"

"Hmm . . . not sure, but Eddie says it looked too big to be hers. Plus, he's not sure how she would have touched the tape. Her hands were tied down over her head. So, in summary, the only solid evidence we have so far is the fingerprint. It'll be our best lead if we have a good print and match. If not, lots to do to get this guy."

"Excuse me." Sam had returned and placed containers on the table. "Here's lunch. Baked chicken, mashed potatoes with gravy, green beans, and corn bread muffins from Sully's. I'll grab you some sodas and water." She passed a bottle to CJ. "Here's yours."

"What?" CJ laughed. "I get this gallon of water?"

Sam nodded. "Yes. Water for you, and it's not a gallon, although that's what you're supposed to drink every day."

CJ glared at her.

Paul swallowed a bite of chicken. "CJ, do you think there's any connection to the Harleston Village murder?"

"No. The MOs are different. In Harleston Village, there was no rape, and he took her heart, not to mention the hoodoo connection. Here we have an abduction, rape, no signs of taking a trophy or ritual." *This actually reminds me of—*

"This is more consistent with the Parrish case, but of course, he's dead," Paul said, interrupting her thoughts as if he'd read her mind. "We also don't have a signature cut down her midsection. Were her clothes left at the scene?"

CJ dug through the file. "We found a pair of shorts . . . hmm, no bikini bottoms. I'd assume she had on the bottom to her bikini. I'll check with Eddie again." *I should have caught that.*

"Okay. What's next?" Stan asked her as he stood.

"Well, we wait on the fingerprint to come back, and I'm set to talk to Kerri Ann's boyfriend this afternoon. He reportedly worked on Saturday until midnight. Folly Beach PD is looking to see if any cameras caught anything or anyone who might have seen her. I'm going to meet with her parents later today at the morgue. They're flying in from Dayton." CJ struggled with a bite of her lunch.

Paul looked at her. "What time?"

"Four o'clock."

"I'll go with you for moral support." He excused himself and joined Stan as they headed out the door.

Tyler Gannt waited. The tiny interrogation room was hot and humid, and he struggled to breathe. He rested his forehead on the edge of the table. CJ entered at 1:45 p.m., and he didn't move.

"Mr. Gannt?"

His bloodshot hazel eyes caught hers, and he gave her a slow nod. She slid into a metal chair across from him. "Sorry we're meeting this way. I appreciate you coming in. Promise I won't keep you long." She opened her notebook. "How long had you and Kerri Ann been dating?"

He sniffed. "Almost two years. We met our freshman year and have been together ever since."

"Would you say you two had a good relationship?"

"No. I'd say we have a great relationship. We are—were—" Tears streamed down his cheeks.

She waited while he composed himself. They spent another fifteen minutes going through her questions. He confirmed he was working all day on Saturday, and she didn't uncover any reason he would have hurt Kerri Ann. He volunteered his fingerprints, and she left him in the stuffy room to wait on a tech.

———

CJ and Paul stood in their gowns at the morgue just before four o'clock, their hands folded. She whispered to him, "Thanks for joining me."

"No problem. These things suck, but having numbers helps."

Thomas opened the door, stepped back, and motioned for Kerri Ann's parents to enter. A tall, gangly man escorted a sickly-thin woman. Both looked to be in their late forties. They stood silent while Thomas stepped past them, then slow, uneasy steps carried them to the edge of the shiny silver table. Their eyes glistened under the bright light.

Thomas introduced CJ and Paul, but neither parent acknowledged them. CJ held her breath as Thomas lifted the sheet and flinched as the woman howled and fell onto her husband. CJ wiped her eyes, stepped forward, put her arm around the mother, and whispered, "I'm so sorry." The pain of their loss stabbed at her chest.

THIRTY-ONE

Tuesday, November 16
Downtown Charleston

Elias opened the bag—a box of saltines, sardines, tuna, and a bag of oranges. He'd been shorted on his pay, but at least he'd gotten enough food for several days. After all, he was accustomed to only eating once a day.

He carefully opened a can of tuna and spread it on crackers. He was hungry, but he ate as slowly as possible. He decided to allow himself one orange and stretch the bag for six days. His stomach rumbled.

He stood on his sore leg and hobbled over to his special box. His eyes searched until he found it. Reading the scribbles, he pulled what he needed from his burlap bag—pieces of wild black cherry bark. He ignited a match and started the propane stove. He poured water into a pot and set it on the grate.

Once the water was warm, he dropped in the bark and soaked it. He was careful to not let the water get too hot. The old man had told him hot water would ruin the tea. His lips touched the mug, and he sipped the mildly sweet cherry liquid.

It was pitch-black under the Spanish moss hanging from the oak. From his hiding spot outside the window of the one-story lavender blush house, Elias could see her, but she had no idea he was out there—watching. She rinsed the last dish, and she absentmindedly dried it and put it away. She switched off the kitchen light and headed to her bedroom. Elias crept along the wall to the next window; his lips parted, and his pale blue eyes flared.

He eased closer as she washed her face and swapped her jeans and pink blouse for a simple midthigh, sheer mint-green nightgown. His breathing escalated as he watched her body silhouetted by the bathroom light's glow. She was beautiful, but most importantly, she was petite. "She's perfect," he whispered.

THIRTY-TWO

Wednesday, November 17
Downtown Charleston

CJ grabbed a towel as she ran soaking wet for her ringing cell phone. "Hello—uh—Detective O'Hara," she answered breathlessly.

"Hello, CJ. It's Wally. Did I catch you at a bad time?"

"Not at all." *I'm just standing here in a towel.* "Wait! Isn't it like three o'clock in the morning in Alaska?"

Wally laughed. "It is, but I'm at Quantico for some training, so it's only seven o'clock for me. Same as you. Listen, I wanted to follow up on a couple of things."

She fumbled with the knob to turn off the shower. "Sure."

"I got a report from the lab for the Popov scene finger-prints. With one exception, the prints in the shed, on the jars we found under the bed, and on the couch were all Bryan Parrish's. We found one print that's different on one of the jars. We've run it through the system . . . no matches."

She scribbled. "But the lab is sure it's from a different person?"

"Yes. They're certain."

"So, this confirms what Seth told us. There was a second man with Parrish, and it appears he was involved in the murder of the first victim. Any luck on finding possible leads?"

Wally sighed. "Not yet. Freddie's run down all the boat owners, and none appear reasonable suspects."

"Anything else?"

"Actually, yes. I had another ME review the autopsy report for Ivan Popov. Your hunch was correct. It looks like he was murdered."

So he didn't just drown. "What's the ME basing this on?"

Papers rustled before he spoke. "Let's see. His report said there was a small abrasion on the right side of the back of his skull. The original ME had passed it off as the result of the fall from the dock, but if you look at the location, it would be difficult for it to occur from a fall."

"He was hit from behind then?"

"Seems so."

She pressed at the knot in her neck. "Well, there's no way we can prove Bryan Parrish did it, but it's reasonable to assume he did."

"Yeah, I agree. That's all I have for now, but I'll keep you posted— Oh, wait. Sasha, the girl who worked for Ivan, wants you to call her when you get the chance."

"Okay, I'll call her." CJ hung up and sat on the edge of the bed. A second man had been with Bryan Parrish when he killed the first Sitka victim. The question was, who was he?

Hair dried, dressed in jeans and a navy blue blouse, she locked her door and headed for her truck. She jumped in, pulled onto Broad Street, and made the quick drive to the station. It was too early to call Sasha—only 3:50 a.m. in Sitka. *Why does she need to talk to me?*

———

CJ flipped the folder closed after spending the morning reviewing files in the conference room. "Sam, Wally gave me the name and contact info for the analyst who has the mystery fingerprint in Juneau. Can you email her and see if we can get a copy of the information?"

"Sure. I'll shoot her an email and give her a call once she's in the office. What do you want me to do with it?"

"I'm not sure." She approached the evidence board. "Let's get it and then decide. Hopefully, they'll find the owner there in Sitka."

She wanted to believe that, but something bothered her. Perhaps Sasha had the answer. She made a note to call her later as she took a bite of the breakfast sandwich Sam had brought her. Sam had clearly decided to make sure she ate better, and somehow the water bottle never seemed to get empty no matter how much she drank.

Her cell phone vibrated along the table, and she ran over and grabbed it. "Detective O'Hara."

"Hello, Detective. Do you have a few minutes right now?" Assistant Solicitor Tim Drummond asked.

CJ glanced at the clock—10:05 a.m. "Sure, Tim, now is fine."

Fifteen minutes later, Sam opened the conference room door to Solicitor Drummond, who wore a charcoal suit, starched white shirt, and maroon power tie. He smiled as he took a seat across the table from CJ. "Thanks for meeting me on short notice. I want to bring you up to speed on the Parker case." He cleared his throat. "We have a tentative plea agreement."

She tried to read his face—nothing. "Okay. What's up?"

"Well, after going round and round with his attorneys, we have a tentative agreement—Parker will plead guilty to four counts of rape and one count of attempted rape. We would drop the other allegations."

Like him trying to kill me. Her gaze remained fixed on his eyes. "What does this mean?"

He fidgeted with his notebook. "He would get fifteen years with no possibility of parole."

"Only fifteen years!" She slammed her fist on the table. "He brutally raped four women at knifepoint and was close to a fifth. What happened to the minimum of thirty years you talked about?"

"It's, well . . . complicated."

Her chair slammed against the wall as she jumped up. "Unbelievable." She rubbed her face with both hands. "Wait—you said 'tentative agreement.' So, what's this hinge on?"

He folded his hands. "On you and the women. I agreed to bring this to you so you can talk to the victims before anything goes final."

She turned and walked to the window. The sky was a weird mixture of sun and black clouds—whitecaps rolled across the Ashley River. Her back stayed to him. "So, you want me to sell it to the victims?"

He joined her as they both stared at the horizon. "Not really . . . well, I guess. I'm struggling with it, but I also know how difficult a trial would be on the victims. His attorneys will definitely want to make it as painful as possible."

She turned to him. "How about using their affidavits?"

"I have them, and they were quite useful in negotiations, but his attorneys will push for subpoenas and do their best to force them to take the stand. I know you've said they'd do it, but let's be honest, it'll be horrific for them."

CJ pursed her lips and asked, "Are you sure Parker will agree to this?"

"He will. He's lost his bravado. The victims identified the panties we found in his shed, and DNA came back as a match as well. So he's tied to all four of them."

CJ dropped back into her chair. It wouldn't be fair for this situation since consent wasn't in question but, in her mind, she saw the victims on the stand being crucified for their sexual relationships, every sordid detail of their lives exposed, and a defense attorney holding up their panties. Sadly, they'd be raped all over again. "Okay, I'll talk to them, but I won't sway them either way. It needs to be their decision."

He held up his hands. "Agreed. That's all I'm asking you to do. I'm happy to meet with them—"

"No. I'll do it alone. The last thing these poor women need right now is a male face. When do you need an answer?"

"I've agreed to provide our answer to Parker's attorneys and the judge by noon Friday."

She pinched the bridge of her nose. "I guess this wouldn't be first-degree rape?"

"No. Third degree."

"What does that mean?"

"Legally, Parker would plead guilty to five counts of criminal sexual misconduct through the use of force without aggravating circumstances."

"What the hell! Why is it without aggravating circumstances? The bastard broke into their homes, held a knife to their throats and threatened their lives, ripped off their clothes, and forced himself on them. Some fucking laws we have."

He sighed. "I know it doesn't make sense, but it's how pleas work."

She stormed out of the room. "Plea deals suck then."

CJ walked out of the building and sat on the edge of the concrete wall, watching the cars go by on Lockwood Drive. That piece of scum Parker would get off with less than a third of what he deserved. He'd be free in fifteen years and going on his merry way. Yukking it up with his buddies while five young women were sentenced to a life of torment. She made her plan . . . and wandered back into the station.

At four o'clock, CJ sat across the conference room table from six sets of eyes that belonged to the women victimized by Jared Parker. All waited nervously. Sam watched them from her desk.

"I appreciate all of you coming in on such short notice," CJ said. "I realize it's late in the day, but time is of the essence. Each of you has your own pain, but as a group, you're connected."

For the next several minutes, she brought them up to speed on the case of *South Carolina v. Jared Parker*. As they listened, sniffles and light sobs echoed off the walls. Finally, she finished with the proposed plea deal, which would replace a trial by jury.

"Do you understand what's on the table?"

Cindy Evans spoke up first. "So, he pleads guilty to raping us and goes to jail for fifteen years?"

"That's correct."

More sniffles and sobs.

Cindy asked, "Do we have a say—like do we vote?"

CJ nodded. "You do have a say. I'm not sure we vote, but I asked you to meet me as a group because I think it's best to all agree on what happens. If we turn down the plea deal, we'll all need to go to court together—a unified front. That way, we can support each other. Does this make sense?"

All five women nodded. The mousy wife of Jared Parker sat eerily still, holding her breath. *What's she thinking?* Suddenly, Cheryl spoke up. "I don't agree with the deal." *Oh, shit! I made a mistake inviting her.*

CJ's head slowly bobbed. "Okay. Why is that, Cheryl?"

"The bastard deserves to pay more for what he did to these women. As for me, well, I had a chance to leave him, and that's on me." Cheryl motioned to the others. "But, unfortunately, they didn't have a choice." CJ's eyes went wide.

The other five women turned to face Cheryl. Marcy Willis asked her, "Do you think we should go to court then?"

Cheryl chewed her lip. "I don't know, but I'll go if you girls want. He needs to pay for his sins. He needs to confess what he did."

All six women's gazes rested back on CJ. "There could be another way," she said. "I can't speak for the solicitor, but what if we gave him an option?"

Silence.

"What if we asked for a confession to a higher degree charge and added time?" CJ asked. "Parker agrees to six counts of second-degree rape and thirty years without parole? That way, all of you are included, and he has to admit it and serve twice the time."

More silence. CJ stood. "Tell you what. I'm going to let you discuss it and decide. Sam and I will give you some time to talk about it. Let us know when you've reached a decision. Remember, if we turn down the current deal on the table, going to court may be our only path forward."

CJ and Sam left the room and stood in the hallway. "Sam, do you think I made a mistake having them meet as a group?" CJ asked her.

Sam grasped CJ's arm. "No. I think the way you're handling it is perfect. Besides, they all need each other to lean on. That'll be critically important if we go to trial. Listen, I had a friend who was raped in college, and it nearly caused her to take her own life. But when she finally joined a support group, she found others who had the same experience. She moved forward with her life and still has several of those women as her friends."

They sat silently on a bench, and the minutes seemed to pass like hours. Then, finally, the door rattled open, and Cheryl motioned for them to come back.

CJ whispered to Sam, "Here we go."

CJ settled back in the chair across from the six women. "What did you decide?"

The five young women's eyes all shifted to Cheryl. She cleared her throat. "We've decided to turn down the offer.

We like your idea . . . second-degree rape and thirty years. Nothing less. If we don't get this, we'll all go to court and sit in the front row together. Let his attorney do whatever he does to us. We'll take it and put my soon-to-be-ex-husband away." She leaned forward, and her eyes were fire. "But please tell the solicitor, if we don't get our offer, we want first-degree rape and life in prison without parole when we go to trial."

All the women nodded in unison.

CJ watched the group leave and dialed Tim's number to deliver the news. She thought of Cheryl and smiled. The mouse had become a lion.

———

CJ glanced at the conference room clock—it was 7:10 p.m. She punched in Sasha's number and moved to the window, gazing at the headlights moving across the Ashley River bridges. A night mist made everything fuzzy.

Sasha answered on the second ring. "Hello."

"Sasha. This is Detective O'Hara in Charleston."

"Oh. Hello, Detective."

"I hope things are going well with you. Listen, Wally said I needed to call you. Is there something I can do for you?" CJ moved back to the table and lowered herself into a chair. She thumbed through the files as she pressed the phone to her ear with her shoulder.

"I found out something that might be helpful," Sasha replied. "I'm not sure. Remember I told you I sometimes deliver equipment for a marine supplier? Well, I was talking to the man I work for—his name is Guy—and he mentioned something."

"Go ahead," CJ said.

"Guy told me he went by to drop some stuff off to Ivan and saw a man there. He asked Ivan about him, and he said something like he was a friend of Bryan's from out of town."

"A friend?" CJ stopped shuffling files.

"That's what he remembered. Not sure if that helps you, but I wanted you to know."

"Okay, thanks. Did Guy happen to tell you when he saw this man?"

"Hmm, he didn't say, but I'll see if I can find out for you. He might have some paperwork for the delivery."

"Okay. If you find out anything else, please let me know. Hug your little girl for me. Thanks so much."

CJ flipped open her notebook and jotted down some notes.

Friend from out of town.

THIRTY-THREE

Friday, November 19
St. Helena Island

Elias stood in front of the gas station and rubbed his eyes. *What's the damn problem?*

He raised the hood on the only thing his father had ever given him—a car on its last leg. He'd done his best to take care of it, but no one had ever taught him how. It was dead, and he was stranded. He climbed back in and turned the key—nothing. Dead as a doornail.

Thumbing through his wallet, he knew he didn't have enough money to get it fixed. He wiped the tears streaking his cheeks. *What am I gonna do now?* His eyes widened, and his mind scrambled. *My plan is gonna be ruined.*

He climbed out and went back to the front of the car, leaned in under the hood, and surveyed the engine again. It was all foreign to him, and he had no idea what he should do to get it running. He cursed under his breath when a voice behind him caused him to flinch. "Car problems?"

A man in jeans, a white T-shirt, and boots stood staring at him, his arms loaded with a case of water. Elias wasn't sure how old he was but guessed he was older than his forty-year-old father. He threw up his hands and tried not to cry. "My car won't start. I stopped for gas, and it was fine, but now—nothing."

The man lifted his purchase slightly and smiled. "Hang on." Elias's eyes followed the man to his truck. He put the water in the back of his pickup, grabbed a toolbox, and returned.

"Perhaps I can help. I'm pretty good with cars. What's this . . . an '89 Crown Vic?"

Elias nodded slowly. "Yes, sir. It's old, but it usually runs fine."

"Let me take a look."

He watched the man tug at wires and run his fingers along hoses. He worked his way around the engine, wiping grime and mumbling as he went. When he'd finished, he grinned. "I think I see the problem."

The man leaned down and picked up a screwdriver and a pair of pliers. "Your connectors on your battery are corroded. Let me clean them up, and we'll give her a try."

Elias was dumbfounded. *Why is this stranger helping me?* "Uh, okay. Thank you."

The man chuckled. "Don't thank me yet. I could be wrong."

It took some work, but the cables gave way to the man. "How 'bout you hand me that steel brush there?"

"This?"

"Yep. I'm gonna clean the corrosion off the couplings. That should give you a better connection. The battery's old, but it seems okay." Whitish-green dust fell as he scrubbed each connector. Once he was satisfied, he leaned down and blew the particles away. The man stood up and wiped his forehead with the back of his wrist. "All right, hop in and give her a crank."

Elias dropped onto the cloth bench, held his breath, and gripped the key. *Please, please, please.*

The man smiled proudly as the engine roared to life. "Ha-ha. There she goes." His eyes appeared around the hood. "Shut it down so we can check it again."

Elias did as he was told—as always.

"Let's check the plug wires one last time, and we might as well make sure the oil is okay." He held up the dipstick and showed Elias the faint mark of the oil level. "I'll be right back." Elias's eyes followed the man as he went back into the service station.

Within five minutes, the man had added another quart of oil. "Try her again."

On the roar, the man closed the hood. "You're all good to go now, son."

Elias wiped his eyes on his sleeve. "I don't know how to thank you. I have some money—"

The man's palms went upward. "No, no. You don't owe me a thing. Happy to help."

"But—the oil costs money."

"My gift to you," the man said.

Elias extended his hand and the two shook. "Thank you, sir. You saved my life."

He smiled as the truck pulled away. The Good Samaritan had no idea his deed had just doomed another young woman.

My plan can continue.

THIRTY-FOUR

Friday, November 19
St. Helena Island

Grannie sat under a patchwork quilt on the white porch in the midmorning sun, rocking, slowly rocking. Her eyes followed them up the red brick walkway.

"Hello, Grannie." Johnny leaned in and hugged her. Her arms remained wrapped around him, then gave a final squeeze. "Do you remember CJ?"

CJ smiled at the old woman's solemn face. "Hello, Grannie. It's nice to see you again."

Grannie pulled Johnny's ear to her lips and whispered.

"Grannie, she's here and needs your help," Johnny said.

The old woman stood and wobbled her way into the house.

Johnny took CJ's arm and led her to the swing at the end of the porch. "Let's have a seat."

"Where did she go?"

He shrugged.

"More importantly, is she coming back?"

"Who knows?" Johnny replied. "We'll wait here and find out. Do you have the list?"

She handed him a white sheet of paper with three items scrawled on it. Ten minutes later, he popped up from the swing. "Wait here."

She heard voices inside the house, but they were too low for her to make out the conversation. She fidgeted, opening and closing her fingers on the swing's metal chain. Her eyes rose at the squeak of the door, and she saw Johnny. "She's agreed to look at the list, but she won't talk to you. Only me."

She gritted her teeth. *This is fucking crazy.*

Grannie returned to her rocking chair. Her green cat eyes scanned the words on the paper Johnny handed her, then slowly closed. Then, after what seemed like forever, her eyes opened and cut to Johnny on the stool. She mumbled words CJ didn't understand—the language of the Gullah. Johnny squinted as she continued, raising and lowering the volume of her voice.

He squeezed Grannie's wrinkled fingers, and CJ heard him respond in Gullah. The two went back and forth while

CJ struggled to understand. As before, she'd pick up a word or two, only to be lost. She wasn't sure why, but Grannie's agitation led her back through the door.

"What's going on, Johnny?"

He exhaled. "Grannie will give me some information, but she's not willing to tell me who's doing this."

Her eyes went wide. *Holy shit!* "She knows who it is?"

His head shook. "Not exactly. At least, not now. Uh, how do I say this? She has a gift of being able to—uh—see things. Under the right circumstances, she may be able to . . ." His voice trailed off, and he sucked in a deep breath.

Another squeak, and the old woman ambled back to her rocker. She squinted at the swing and waggled a finger, beckoning Johnny back to the stool at her side. He again handed her the paper, and she spoke—still no English.

For the next fifteen minutes, CJ listened to more back-and-forth between the two of them. Then she watched Johnny stand and hug Grannie. "Okay, you ready to go?" Johnny asked.

"What? Wait! What did she say?"

As he ushered her down the steps, he said, "I'll fill you in on the ride back."

"Bye, CJ. Be careful of those close to you."

CJ's head snapped around. Grannie's eyes were closed, and she was rocking, slowly rocking.

When they got into the car and shut the door, she grabbed Johnny's arm, eyes wild. "What the hell does she mean? Be careful of those close to me? Am I in danger from someone close, or is someone close to me in danger?"

Gravel crunched as Johnny backed up and pulled away. "Let me tell you what she said. First, nothing new, but she confirmed the herb-and-root combination means whoever's killed Naomi is after power. This person believes the combination, along with a heart, will help him."

"Power for what?"

He sighed. "Grannie believes he's been hurt or is being hurt by someone."

"Is it normal to use human sacrifices in hoodoo?"

"No. Grannie's not sure why he thinks this. Her sense is whoever he learned from taught him an impure version of hoodoo, or he's simply confused. Even the herb-and-root combination puzzles her."

"Why?"

"She knows much better charms to seek power. It adds to her sense he really doesn't know what he's doing."

She stared at the marsh out the side window. "What else?"

"Grannie believes he will kill again. He won't gain power after one ritual, especially since what he's doing won't work. He'll see no choice."

Her eyes narrowed. "And the part about those close to me?"

He cleared his throat. "She didn't tell me anything about that."

"Damn it, Johnny! She throws this out and gives me no fucking details."

"I'm sorry. Grannie is being cagey. Something is scaring her, and she won't open up about it . . . yet. Paul and I will keep prodding her, and hopefully, she'll tell us what she knows."

Tears formed in her eyes. *Those close to me?*

"Oh!" He reached into his pocket and handed CJ a small red flannel bag with gold drawstrings. "Grannie said to give you this."

Her fingers caressed the soft cloth. "Is this a mojo bag?"

"Yep. She didn't tell me what she put in it, only that it would help you."

CJ stared at it. "Should I look in it?"

Johnny shook his head. "I wouldn't. You're supposed to keep it with you, or it won't work." He pointed to the service station up ahead on their left. "I'm gonna swing in for some gas."

She shoved the gift from Grannie into her jacket pocket. *Great. No information, but she gives me a damn souvenir bag.* She barely glanced at the '89 Ford Crown Victoria that passed.

THIRTY-FIVE

Friday, November 19
Downtown Charleston

At a little past six o'clock, CJ peeked through the peephole, then twisted the knob and opened her apartment door.

Sam stepped over the threshold. "Wow! You look unbelievable. What a dress."

CJ flushed. "Thanks. So do you. Love that shade of blue on you." She ran her hands down her long-sleeve, emerald-green cocktail dress. "To be honest, I'm not much of a charity ball kind of girl. Give me jeans, a sweater, and boots, and I'm happy."

Sam's fingers reached for the emerald stone CJ wore. "This necklace is stunning. It and the dress match the color of your eyes perfectly."

"It was my mom's. I hardly ever wear it except for special occasions. I guess I'm afraid of losing it." She tugged at her dress again. "Are you sure this isn't too short? I feel—well—exposed."

"No. Don't be silly. It's to your knees, and it's perfect. The lace on the sleeves and at the bottom are spectacular. Every guy will notice you."

CJ looked at herself in the mirror. "Great. Not sure that's a good thing."

Sam laughed. "You'll be fine. You're enchanting with those eyes and auburn hair. The dress is merely a bonus."

"Okay." She groaned. "I guess we might as well head over. How chilly is it?"

"It's not too bad, but grab a jacket. It'll be cold by the time we leave."

CJ peered up at the banner above the door in front of them. *Charleston Preservation Society Annual Gala.*

Two handsome young men in tuxedos greeted them as the double doors opened.

She whispered, "Jeez, Sam. This is fancy, and we're definitely not overdressed." Expensive designer dresses floated around the room, and every guy was a penguin.

Sam smiled. "The beautiful people love an excuse to be gaudy."

A wave of intense nervousness hit CJ, and she grasped Sam's hand. "Remember, I don't know anyone, so don't leave me." *I can chase down serial killers, but a room full of strangers freaks me out.*

"No worries. I'll know a few people, and I'll introduce you."

The two meandered around the spacious room filled with flowers, its walls adorned with expensive tapestries. Sam introduced her as they went and seemed to know everyone. A gray-haired man smiled as they got to the bar. His eyes locked on her.

"You look absolutely mesmerizing. What can I get you?"

She wanted a beer but said, "A glass of white wine would be nice. How about you, Sam?"

"Yes, white wine, please."

As he handed them crystal glasses, he said, "I'm Congressman Randolph Lee Jr. So nice to meet you." He took CJ's hand and gently kissed it. "You smell wonderful."

Her skin crawled. "I'm CJ, and this is Sam."

He leered at CJ and leaned closer. "Too bad there's no dancing. I'd love to give you a whirl—"

"Honey, aren't you going to introduce me?"

Randolph turned to the pear-shaped woman behind him. She pushed past him. "I'm Beatrice Lee. Randolph's wife."

CJ and Sam introduced themselves, and for a few awkward minutes, the group engaged in small talk before CJ and Sam were able to escape.

Sam giggled. "I think Congressman Lee has a thing for you."

CJ blew out a breath. "Yeah, great. Not sure he'd have let go of my hand if his wife hadn't arrived. Did you see her daggers?"

"Yeah," Sam said. "Mrs. Lee wasn't too happy. I'm sure it's not the first time she's found her husband lusting after some young woman. Rumor has it he's got a thing for your buddy."

Puzzled, CJ asked, "Who's that?"

Sam smirked. "None other than Wendy Watts. And speak of the devil, there she is." She tipped her head to where Wendy was standing.

CJ turned to look. Wendy's skintight white dress barely covered her. She was wrapped around a swaying man with glossy eyes twice her age.

CJ rolled her eyes. "Figures. God, I hope she doesn't see me and make a scene. Could her dress get any skimpier? I've seen more clothes on people at the beach." They quickly wound through the crowd to the other side of the room.

The hour seemed like ten, and CJ was miserable. She loved Sam and had agreed to come, but a charity ball wasn't her thing. She sipped her wine as she caught a familiar pair of eyes—Ben. At six feet four, he stood above most of the crowd. He winked at her, and her heart bumped.

"Sam, I see Ben," she whispered.

"Where?"

She tipped her head toward him. "Over there."

"Let's go say hi." Before she could respond, Sam dragged her through the masses.

Oh, shit! "Sam, I don't think this is a good idea."

"Why? Oh."

A twentysomething woman with long, silky blond hair and ocean-blue eyes had her hand around Ben's arm. CJ had to admit the girl was stunning in her pale pink gown tailored to every curve.

"It'll be fine, CJ. We're just gonna say hello, and he's looking right at us."

Sam smiled up at him when they reached him. "Hey, Ben. Fancy meeting you here."

He chuckled. "Yeah. I'm not much for these things, but they're fun every so often." He greeted CJ and then turned to his date. "Kelsey, do you remember Sam and CJ?"

Her perfect white teeth flashed as she tightened her grip on his arm. "I do. From the oyster roast at Harry's. Great to see you again." She pulled Ben's face to her, kissed him, and eyed CJ.

They chatted for several minutes while CJ looked for a hole to crawl into. She did her best to fake it as she twisted and pulled at her dress. Then, finally, relief came as Sam whisked her away. "Great to see you guys," Sam said to Ben and Kelsey. "I see someone I need to introduce to CJ. Have fun!"

After another two hours of discomfort, CJ hid in the women's bathroom away from the crowd. She had managed to excuse herself while Sam chatted with a friend of her parents. She stood staring in the mirror. *Why did I agree to come to this stupid party?*

She was trying to come up with a reason to go home. She hated to leave her friend, but this wasn't her element. The long hallway was dark, so she hid out, letting the time pass. Finally, she decided she'd find Sam and tell her she'd catch a cab home.

As she walked down the hallway, there was a muffled noise on her right. There was someone behind the cracked door around the corner—people whispering. Through the sliver of the open door, she saw Wendy Watts, her dress pushed up above her waist, straddling Congressman Randolph Lee. "You need a special reward for getting me back on the air, baby," Wendy purred at him.

Wonder what Beatrice would think of this?

CJ wandered back toward the noise and found her friend. "Sam, I'm going to go home. These shoes are killing my feet, and it's been a long week."

She waited for Sam to try to talk her into staying, but instead she just asked, "Are you sure?"

CJ bit her lip and slowly nodded.

"Okay." Sam smiled. "Well then, I'll go with you."

"No. You should stay. You're having fun, and I'll feel terrible if you leave."

Sam took her arm. "Come on. Let's go to your place and order a pizza. I'm starved, and the finger foods here aren't cutting it."

CJ glimpsed Ben as they exited the way they came. Kelsey was still hanging on to him.

THIRTY-SIX

Saturday, November 20
Downtown Charleston

Elias stood under the same oak tree, hidden under the Spanish moss. The inside of the lavender blush house was pitch black. He knew it was too early for her to be in bed. *Where is she?* His pulse picked up, and his breathing got faster. *What if she's gone? My plan will be ruined.*

He pushed himself against the stone fence and leaned on the base of the tree. His mind was frantically searching for another option. *Wait . . . wait.* A car stopped in front of the house. He held his breath as his eyes strained. Then he saw her. She was home.

Anna stood talking to the driver—smiling. He heard her say goodbye, and his pale eyes followed her up the stone front path to her door. The motion light lit up the porch as she neared, and she unlocked the door and dropped out of sight. He slithered around the corner and positioned himself to see through the tiny crack in the blinds. There she was, following her nightly routine.

He pulled in a breath as her dress and underwear fell to the floor, exposing her petite frame. He fought his urges—*Concentrate on why you're here.* The nightgown slipped down over her head, she climbed into bed, and the house went pitch black again.

Elias let an hour go by as the stillness consumed the neighborhood. Then, finally, he slipped from his hiding spot and floated to the back door. Within seconds, the door eased inward, and he entered. He held his breath when the floor moaned and he listened—nothing.

She lay on her side, barely visible under the dim night-light from the bathroom. She seemed to materialize as his eyes became more accustomed to the darkness. He stood over her. Panic almost took him when she shifted and rolled onto her back.

Anna squirmed under his weight as the feather pillow stopped her breath. The jagged cut in her nightgown from the stone knife revealed her chest, and moments later, he had his still-warm prize.

Elias moved back secretly the way he came.

THIRTY-SEVEN

Monday, November 22
The Boroughs, Charleston, South Carolina

CJ checked the time—8:40 a.m. She slipped on her jacket, took a deep breath, and headed inside the courthouse. *Not sure why I'm invited to this.*

The clerk escorted her into the oak-paneled judge's chambers and to a black leather high-backed chair in the corner. She tugged at her black skirt and smoothed her white blouse. Her heels pinched her toes. Dressing for success was uncomfortable.

The judge entered through the opposite door. She was in her early fifties, with dark brown hair pulled into a bun. She overlooked CJ as she slipped on a long black robe over her dark blue suit. *Should I say hello?*

"Good morning, Your Honor."

The judge's light brown eyes flashed up. "Oh. I didn't see you back there. I was lost in thought. You must be—Detective O'Hara?"

"Yes, Your Honor."

The judge chuckled. "Outside of court and formal proceedings, you can call me Abigail. But, formally, I'm Judge Clowney." She winked. "You're here today to listen only. So, blend in with the woodwork. Understand?"

"I do."

Assistant Solicitor Tim Drummond entered the chambers ten minutes later, followed by the high-priced attorney for Jared Parker, hired by his wealthy father. Neither acknowledged CJ as they took seats across from Judge Clowney's walnut desk. She listened as the agreed plea bargain was described for the next ten minutes. Finally, Judge Clowney read over the plea agreement.

Glancing up, she asked, "The two of you and the defendant agree to this?"

Both men answered, "Yes."

She eyed Parker's attorney. "The defendant understands what this means. Thirty years with no possibility of parole."

"Yes, Your Honor. He does. He wants to avoid a trial."

The Honorable Judge Abigail Clowney smiled and stood. "I guess that settles it then. Y'all can leave, and I can get to court. I'm late."

CJ waited until she got to her truck before she let out a whoop. Then, one by one, she called and let each woman know their demands had been met.

CJ grabbed her bag with a change of clothes and scampered up the steps and into the station, keen to get out of what she'd worn to the judge's chambers. As she made her way down the hall past the bullpen, she got a few whistles. A couple of the officers clapped. She laughed, gave them the finger, and kept moving. As she passed Officer Turner, she got a respectful, "Good morning, Detective." *Hmm—no "City Girl."*

She pushed the door open and dropped her bag in a stall of the women's restroom. Quickly, she removed her business attire and replaced it with jeans, a mustard-yellow blouse, and boots. She folded and shoved what she had worn into the bag and hustled to the conference room.

Sam smiled. "Were the women happy when you called them?"

Her broad smile answered before her words. "They were. Probably more relieved than happy."

She glanced at the number when her cell phone vibrated. *Johnny.*

"Hey," she answered.

His voice was somber. "We have another body, in the Boroughs, just south of Morris Street. I'll text you the address."

She turned back for the door and said, "I'm on my way." Her smile was gone as she raced for her truck. *That happiness was short-lived.*

Johnny saw her running up the sidewalk to the crime scene fifteen minutes later. "It's our guy. It mirrors our Harleston Village scene."

She nodded to him as her eyes scanned the area. "Is the scene secured? Press will be crawling all over us any minute now."

"Yeah. I've got six officers in place. I told them no press and no statements."

As CJ slipped on a gown and booties, he let her know they only had one witness. A neighbor had seen the back door cracked and come over to investigate. After there was no answer when he yelled, he went in and saw the body. He ran home and called 911.

Bending down, she examined the hole in the back door glass. "Is this how our guy got in?"

"I think so. He cut the pane, reached in, and opened the dead bolt. They're not much use when it doesn't require a key inside and there's a window someone can break. Flip the latch, and you're in. She didn't have an alarm either."

She scanned along the eaves of the roof and those of the neighboring homes. "No cameras. Our guy's picking his victims carefully. He has to be planning ahead." She turned and stepped into the home. "I'm gonna go take a look. Don't let anyone else in until the CSU arrives."

"Not even me?"

The voice behind her caused her to turn back. "Hey, Lieutenant." She handed him a gown, pair of booties, and gloves.

They followed the odor in the direction of the first-floor bedroom. Like the home of Naomi Sims, this one was small but well kept—lots of bright colors and floral patterns. The pictures sprinkled along the shelves and walls indicated their victim was single and likely lived alone. Photos of Charleston adorned the hallway walls as they made their way to the bedroom.

CJ gazed at the stark white body with the grotesque dark patch running along the center. She flipped on the overhead light, and the sprayed blood made the buttercup-yellow walls look like some abstract painting gone wrong. To withstand the intense odor, she breathed through her mouth—rotten eggs mixed with stinky cheese and feces.

"Aw, shit." Paul groaned. "Poor girl. I can never get used to this."

Easing forward, CJ made sure to avoid the blood on the floor along the side of the bed. The woman was small and awkwardly positioned, arms flailed open and one leg bent under the other. Her eyes were glass.

"She fought to get away," Paul said. He leaned closer. "Does this look like the first victim?"

"Not really," CJ said. Our first victim almost looked like she was sleeping. Arms and legs were in a more natural position than this." She squatted near the head of the bed. "Hmm, she may have been smothered just like last time." She pointed at the woman's face. "Thomas will need to confirm, but look at the abrasions on her face. I also see what looks like the same black substance on her forehead. Her chest's been opened. I wonder if our guy took her heart."

Her eyes locked on the small red rose tattoo on the victim's right hip. Something so beautiful, surrounded by all this horror and ugliness.

Putting a hand on the floor, she scanned under the bed. "There's something under here. Take a look."

Paul joined her. "That looks like . . . a mojo bag."

Her brow furrowed. "Why is there a mojo bag here?"

"Unless the girl was into hoodoo, it's probably our perp's."

Using the tip of her finger, she flipped the small red bag over. "You think he left it by accident or on purpose?"

He rubbed his chin. "I'd think he dropped it by accident. One wants to keep one's mojo bag on them." Without picking it up, Paul carefully pulled the bag open and used his Maglite to peer inside. "Tell you what. Let's leave it for forensics. Maybe we can get some DNA or fingerprints."

The two worked their way out of the bedroom. Nothing else appeared disturbed or unnatural. Thomas, Eddie, and two forensics techs arrived and went to work, and CJ and Paul joined Johnny on the front porch. Johnny handed her a card. "The girl who lives here is named Anna Cato. She's single and lives alone. Works over at MUSC as a nurse. She's only twenty-four."

She stared at the name. "Can you pull her driver's license so we can confirm it's her?"

"I have it here." He held up his cell phone, and she and Paul both looked.

A vise gripped her chest. "It's her. Let's find out who her emergency contacts are . . . I'd assume her parents."

Johnny headed for his cruiser. She leaned against a post, drained and light headed.

Paul mumbled, "Why don't I go talk to our witness?" He turned and slowly walked away.

She pushed herself away from the post.

Johnny returned, his eyebrows raised. "You okay, CJ?" He gently touched her arm.

"Yeah, I'm fine."

He cleared his throat and handed her a sheet of paper. "I've got her parents' names. They live in Asheville. I can call them—"

"No. I'll handle it."

An out-of-breath officer rounded the corner. "Detective. That News 4 reporter, Watts, I think, is raising hell out front. I think maybe you better—"

Before she could respond, Paul flashed past her from out of nowhere. "I got this. You two stay here with the scene. I've had about all I'm gonna take from that bitch. She may need a night in jail for disturbing an active investigation."

CJ let out a strained laugh. She grew fonder of Paul every day.

———

Two hours later, Thomas and Eddie joined CJ, Paul, and Johnny as the body rolled past on the gurney. The CSIs' preliminary report mirrored that of the first murder. Anna had been smothered and crudely sliced open. There were no signs of fingerprints, and blood samples had been collected in case the assailant had cut himself. The only new item was the mojo bag, which was on its way to the lab.

Thomas confirmed the heart had been removed and there was no sign of rape. He indicated he'd perform the autopsy first thing in the morning. Based on his assessment, Anna was killed late Saturday night, early Sunday morning, and by the same person who had killed Naomi in Harleston Village.

CJ strapped into her truck and checked the time—7:05 p.m. Her thumb scrolled, and she punched the entry she wanted. "Hey, Robert," she said when he answered.

"Hey. How're things going down there?"

She grunted. "It's been better, but I'm hanging in there . . . at a murder scene. It looks like this is the second by the same perp."

"Ah, Jesus."

"Listen, I need another favor. If I send you the time frame and destinations, can your researcher pull some airline passenger manifests for me?"

THIRTY-EIGHT

Tuesday, November 23
Downtown Charleston

CJ despised starting her day with an autopsy—they were the worst. She walked into the morgue's changing room. She stripped down to her underwear and put on scrubs before she gowned up, hoping she wouldn't stink of death all day. The odor always permeated her gown, found her clothes, and clung to them. She pulled her hair up under the cap, took a deep breath, and went to meet Thomas. A slight tightness gripped her chest. *I hope I don't pass out again.*

Thomas glanced up as she entered the sterile white exam room. "Good morning. I'm a little behind here, but I'll bring you up to speed and give you the play-by-play on the finish."

Oh, wonderful. Play-by-play. "Works for me."

The door opened, and Byron appeared, the tech she'd met earlier. He smiled and gave her a little wave as he positioned himself at the foot of the exam table, only a couple of steps from her.

"Byron here will get the report ready for you, and you'll have it by day's end." *Sure. And he'll be here to catch me if I faint.*

Thomas spent the next fifteen minutes recapping what he'd found so far. Anna was a healthy twenty-four-year-old, with the only unique marking being the red rose tattoo. She had the same mysterious substance on her forehead and abrasions on the bridge of her nose, indicating a pillow was used to smother her. Thomas wasn't sure whether she was dead or passed out before the lacerations to her midsection occurred. *Just like last time.*

The lacerations were consistent with the first murder—crudely done with a dull knife. Her heart was missing. CJ's eyes were fixed on the tattoo as Thomas used his fingers to show the knife markings in Anna's midsection—stark-white skin ruined by dark purple, red, and yellow discolorations.

He stretched. "He surprised the woman, like he did Naomi Sims, and used his weight to hold her down while he smothered her. There's a bit of bruising on her right thigh. She must have struggled more than the first victim, so he roughed her up more. Once she was passed out, he started cutting and extracted her heart. Everything points to the same person who committed the Harleston Village murder."

She nodded as she wrote this down. *"Extracted her heart" is a nicer way to say "pulled her heart out."* "How about the weapon? The knife or whatever it is."

Thomas pinched a flap of Anna's skin in his right hand and ran his left pointer finger along the edge of the cut. "Whatever he used to make the lacerations is dull. Notice how the edges of the cuts are ragged."

She leaned in as he adjusted the overhead light with the magnification lens. "It's more like he rips the skin instead of cutting it."

"Exactly," Thomas said.

"Why in the hell would he do that? He could pick up a sharp knife anywhere. He obviously plans out his kills. So why not make it easy on himself?"

The ME exhaled. "I have no clue. Unless whatever he's using has some sort of meaning."

Wait! "What did you just say, Thomas?"

"Maybe whatever he's using to make the lacerations has some type of special meaning to him."

Byron's deep voice broke the silence. "Excuse me, miss. Could it be part of his ritual? He puts his special mixture on his victims. So maybe he also has a knife he made himself."

Thomas nodded. "That would make sense."

She scribbled, *Types of knives used in rituals.*

"How about the victim type? Anything consistent?"

He rubbed the bridge of his nose with the back of his hand. "Well, let's see. Both are White females who were healthy. Both were attractive, although he's shown no interest in sexual assault."

She pulled the photo of Naomi Sims out of her folder. Her eyes worked back and forth from it to the body on the cold steel table. "Our two victims are both petite, wouldn't you say?"

Thomas went to his computer and pulled up Naomi's file. "You're correct. His first victim weighed one hundred and eight, and Anna here weighed one hundred and five."

She added the weights to her notes. "You think that means anything? Maybe our guy's weak or not very big himself, so he has to choose victims he can control?"

"I hadn't thought of that, but it makes sense. Even with the element of surprise, he'd need control to asphyxiate them. Once they woke up, they'd fight like hell."

She added another note—*Perp is weak or smaller.*

***

Sam handed CJ a report as she entered the conference room at 10:40 a.m. "This came in from Columbia. It's the report on the tire tracks at the Shem Creek scene."

CJ flipped to the summary, which read, *Based on the tread blocks, voids, and pattern, the tire tracks are most likely from an eighteen-inch-diameter all-terrain tire used on an SUV.* Her guess had been correct. "Sam, it's a long shot, but can you see if you can pull a list of everyone in Charleston who is registered as owning an SUV?"

She answered, "Sure. It'll be a monster list."

CJ noticed a new addition to the room. "I see you got us another evidence board."

The younger woman smiled. "Yep. I figured it would be easier to manage the two open cases. At least we won't need a third with the rape case solved."

"Great idea. Let's split up our evidence and organize it on its own board."

Sam grabbed a file. "What do you want to call each case?"

Oh, jeez. "I'm not sure. The damn press will probably come up with some crazy name at some point. How about we just use case one and case two. Case one will be the murders in Harleston Village and the Boroughs. Two, the Shem Creek case."

Sam started pinning items to each board, leaving space for CJ to write critical points. "Oh. Before I forget, dinner on Thursday will be around two o'clock. You can come as early as you like, watch football, and hang out. Harry, Bill, and Will are coming at noon. Craig's on a fishing trip, so he'll miss it."

CJ had forgotten about Thanksgiving dinner. "Okay. Thanks. I'll probably just come for dinner. I need to work—"

"No work on Thanksgiving Day! That's a rule."

She held up her palms. "Okay. Okay. What can I bring?"

"Nothing," replied Sam. "My mom and I will fix everything. Well, except for the turkey. My dad handles that. They're both so excited you guys are coming."

"Thanks again for the invite. I look forward to it." *She didn't mention Ben.*

The ringing of her cell phone startled her. "C'Hara," she answered. She listened, rubbing the back of her neck. "I'm on my way."

She headed for the door. "That was Johnny. We found Anna's heart in the back of a warehouse over near the intersection of Laurens and Concord."

Sam scrambled for her phone. "I'll let Paul know."

CJ pulled her truck in behind the flashing blue lights at the crime scene. Two patrol officers pointed to the weathered backside of a metal warehouse. "You can go through the door around the corner, Detective. Officer Jones is inside, and he said to let you know the CSU is on their way," one of the officers told her.

"Do you guys know what's in the warehouse?"

"It's used for boat storage, but the crime scene is in a back storage room full of junk. The owner called it in."

"Okay. Thanks. No one besides the CSU comes in unless I say. Got it?"

They both nodded.

She stopped abruptly. "Let's turn off the flashers. Make it tougher for the press to find us."

"Yes, ma'am."

CJ made her way past various pieces of equipment and debris to the back of the storage room. She dropped to a knee as her Maglite showed the familiar scene—six white candles, chalk marks, and . . . She leaned close and used her gloved hand to gently nudge the blackish-red object. Anna's heart. She yanked her hand back when the maggots squirmed.

She looked up at Johnny. "The officers said the owner found it?"

He looked at his notes. "Yes. He told me he was looking for some parts and stumbled on it. Freaked him out when he saw the candles and—his words—'black piece of meat.' He called 911 at 1:43 p.m."

She stood and dug through the file she'd brought and found the Harleston Village photo. "This matches the first one."

"Yep. The same ritual."

She faced him. "Find anything else?"

"Nope. It looks like our guy jimmied the lock and came in through the side door. CSU will dust for prints, but my guess is he wore gloves."

She offered him the photo. "The only difference we have here is the candles are burned lower."

Johnny stared at the photo. "Maybe he let the ritual go longer this time."

Wonder why.

"Hey, guys," Eddie said as he approached. "I'll get the techs scouring the area. See if we find anything. I'll handle the heart."

They stood by as he meticulously gathered the evidence, making notes as he went.

CJ turned to Johnny. "Where's the owner?"

He pointed to the parking lot. "He's out back. I told him to wait in his truck so you could talk to him."

———

The heavyset man sat with his bald head resting on the steering wheel. CJ tapped on the window and slid into the passenger seat. His head rose. "This is awful. Who in the hell would do such a thing?"

The man told her what he knew, which wasn't much. He only had four employees and provided her with their names. She copied down the information as Eddie approached. He placed the cooler in the van, and she joined him at the back of the warehouse for his report.

"We didn't find any prints. I'll have the lab see if we have any on the candles. There were none at the first scene, but maybe he touched them with his bare hands this time. It's definitely a heart, but we'll need to confirm it's our vic's.

"On another item, we opened the mojo bag we found on Monday at the lab. It'll take us a couple more days to sort everything out. It has some type of herb or root in it, but what's most promising is we have a fingerprint."

Her head snapped up. "A fingerprint?"

"Yes. It's on a medallion of some kind. It's old and has some strange markings." He held up a photo on his cell phone. "The fingerprint is on one side, and I've got the guys analyzing it. We'll run it through the system to see if we can get a match."

She worked to quell her excitement. "Okay, thanks. Let me know ASAP on the print."

CJ had just pushed the truck into park at her apartment when her cell phone rang. She eyed the caller identification and hit the speaker button. "Hello, Robert."

"Did I catch you at a bad time?"

She rubbed her eyes. "I'm not having many good times right now. We found our second victim's heart. Whoever's doing this is performing some type of ritual with candles, chalk, and a mixture of herbs and roots."

"Sounds like Lowcountry voodoo. Combo of herbal medicines and witchcraft."

Her eyebrows rose. "You know about that stuff?"

"Not really. I've worked a couple of cases in New Orleans involving voodoo, and my research uncovered the Lowcountry version—hoodoo."

"Yeah. That's what we're thinking. I solved my serial-rapist case and replaced it with a double murderer."

"Do you think the other murder we talked about over by Shem Creek is connected?"

"I don't. The MO is totally different." She flipped through her notebook and peered at her notes.

"Well, good luck. Let me know if I can help. Unfortunately, I'm buried—still chasing my psycho—but I'll do my best to support you. Speaking of that, I have the airline info you asked about on Monday. I'll get it emailed to you, but during the time frame you gave me, four people flew on the same flight from Charleston to Sitka."

She flipped to a blank page. "Okay, I'm ready."

There was rustling paper on the other end of the line. "Let's see. The four were all men. Logan Bivens, Asher Copeland, Oliver Feaster, and . . ."

She stopped writing. "Sorry. I didn't get the last one."

He cleared his throat. "Will Parrish."

"Excuse me?" CJ asked as her heart raced.

"Will Parrish, as in the brother of Ben and Bryan," he said.

Her heart almost jumped out of her chest. "Are . . . are you sure?"

"According to my researcher, yes."

Numbness spread in her chest, and she shivered.

"You still there, CJ?"

"Yeah. I'm here."

"I'm not sure what this means," he said. "I know the Parrishes periodically go to Alaska to fish, so it may be nothing. I'll shoot you an email with what my researcher found."

"Okay. I appreciate your help."

She hung up and pressed her forehead with her palm. Will traveled to Sitka just before the first victim was killed.

Was Will the one Seth saw driving the truck with Bryan and the owner of the second fingerprint?

THIRTY-NINE

Wednesday, November 24
Downtown Charleston

Charleston slept as CJ cruised down the steps and jumped into her truck. The glow of streetlights illuminated the city. As she pulled out of her driveway, a pair of eyes watched her leave.

Traffic was scarce as she turned off Lockwood Drive into the LEC parking lot just before six. CJ slid her key card, opened the door, and hustled down the hallway. One of the officers at the scene yesterday was dumping sugar into a brown paper cup when she stopped at the break area. "Good morning, Detective. You're here super early."

CJ smiled. "Any coffee left?"

"Yes, ma'am. It's a little old, but it's hot."

She filled her travel mug while he fidgeted. "You worked yesterday. You're here early too."

"Yeah. I came in at midnight," he replied. "I picked up some overtime. My wife's pregnant, so I'm trying to make some extra cash."

She patted his shoulder. "Congratulations. When's she due?"

"Early March. It's our first one, so I'm kinda nervous."

"It'll be fine. Do you know what you're having?"

He smiled broadly. "A boy."

"Best of luck to you and your wife." Her quota of daily chitchat filled, she wheeled and hustled down the hall to the conference room.

The fluorescent lights gave the room the eeriness she hated. CJ paused. She'd be the only one in the room with Sam and Johnny taking the day off. She almost returned to the bullpen but forced herself to her desk, where she fired up the computer. She printed the attachments Robert had sent her. *What's this?* She opened an email and read a note from Dr. Willis. *Great, that's all I need.* She made a note to call her on a yellow sticky.

For the next two hours, she went through the files from Alaska. She pulled everything off the board and laid the pertinent pieces across the table. After shuffling the information until she was satisfied, she went to the board and pinned items back up. *Now what?*

She grabbed the erasable marker and wrote some notes on the board.

- *Witness (Seth) saw two men. Bryan Parrish + 1*
- *Unknown second fingerprint on a jar with blood of the first Sitka victim*
- *Witness (Sasha) saw a second tall man with dark hair with Bryan*
- *Will and three others flew to Sitka on the same plane six days before the first Sitka murder*
- *Young woman murdered here last week*
- *Victim fits the profile of the prior Lowcountry Killer victims (young, White, pretty, blond hair, blue eyes)*
- *Fingerprint on tape on Shem Creek victim. Match the Sitka print?*

She dropped into a chair and laced her hands behind her head. *What else am I missing?* She wrote "Will" on her pad. She stared at the name.

Out of nowhere, her heart started racing, her breathing became ragged, and she was sweating even though a chill went through her. Sliding out of the chair, she lay down on the cold tiles under the table, praying no one would come through the door.

Thirty minutes later, she felt better. She climbed back into her chair and glanced up at the clock. She couldn't put it off any longer. It was after eight o'clock. She rubbed her aching head, found the number, and dialed. A chipper woman answered.

"This is CJ O'Hara calling for Dr. Willis. I got a message—"

"Hang on. She's right here."

Her stomach suddenly got queasy, and she was a bit dizzy.

"Hello, CJ. Thanks for calling me."

Like I had a damn choice.

"I received your blood work back and had a chance to review everything."

Am I dying?

"On the positive side, we can correct things. You're dehydrated and severely anemic. My instructions for more liquids and daily vitamins should help you improve. Your iron levels are extremely deficient. Are you drinking more water and taking the vitamins I prescribed?"

She wasn't totally truthful. "Yes, Doc. I am."

"Good. You must continue to do both—religiously. Understand?"

"Yes, Doc."

"Now for the tricky part. You may also be suffering from stress and anxiety. I know your job is stressful, but you've got to learn to better cope with it. If not, your physical symptoms will only worsen, and your health will further decline. I'd need to have some more information to nail it down, but my guess is you could be suffering from a generalized anxiety disorder and perhaps a panic disorder."

"So, what are you recommending?"

"First, let's see how the increased liquids and vitamins work. Add making sure you get more rest and have better overall eating habits. How about we go this route and check in after the New Year? Unless, of course, your symptoms get worse."

"Okay, Doc."

"Have a great Thanksgiving, and we'll speak again soon."

CJ hung up the phone and stared at the files spread across the conference table. She glanced up at the clock—8:40 a.m. She grabbed her cell phone and dialed the number for the Forensic Services Division. "Yes. Hello. This is Detective CJ O'Hara, and I'm expecting results for some fingerprints from a crime scene at Shem Creek."

"Can you hold?" a woman asked.

"Sure. I'll hold."

A couple minutes later, a male voice answered. "Hello, Detective. This is Barry Carnes, and I'm the analyst assigned the two fingerprints you sent over." She heard him tapping on the computer. "I have two key findings for you. First, neither the Sitka nor Shem Creek fingerprint is in the system. I ran them through the state's system and through AFIS. Neither popped up with a match." AFIS was the federal Automated Fingerprint Identification System, which CJ frequently used to identify perpetrators. "Now for the interesting part. The two fingerprints have a ninety-nine percent probability of matching. So, in a nutshell, they both came from the same individual."

Oh, shit! "Okay, Barry. Let me ask one more question. In a recent case, I learned about the three basic types of fingerprint patterns: loops, whorls, and arches. What do we have here?"

"Both these prints are the arches pattern."

She made a note. "Remind me. That's uncommon, correct?" *Bryan Parrish had the same pattern.*

"Very good, Detective. You're correct. Only about five percent or so of the population has the arches pattern. Anything else?"

She chewed on her bottom lip. "I don't think so right now. Will you send me your report?"

"Absolutely. I'll email it to you today before I leave at noon for Thanksgiving. Happy Turkey Day!"

"Oh, wait! If I have another fingerprint I need to get processed, would you or someone be able to do that on Friday?"

"This Friday?"

"Yes."

He exhaled. "I'll be out until Monday, so I'm not sure. I'll check and let you know when I email you the report."

She wheeled the board back around and changed her last summary point.

- *Fingerprint on tape of Shem Creek victim matches the Sitka jar print*

She mumbled, "So, you were both places. Now, who in the hell are you?"

FORTY

Thursday, November 25
Daniel Island, South Carolina

CJ lay in the center of the spacious room, surrounded by white candles burning brightly. She was frozen—her wrists and ankles were bound. The small man approached her, mumbling words she didn't understand. He raised a crude knife—

She jerked herself awake, her heart racing, and her T-shirt clung to her. *Jesus, what a nightmare.* She sat on the edge of the bed, working to calm herself. She trudged to the window and opened the blinds to the morning rays and crystal-blue skies. A lone pigeon sat on the ledge and pecked at the glass.

A little after ten, CJ pulled on her jeans, slipped a pale green sweater over her head, and stepped into her boots.

She took one last glance in the mirror. *At least you can't tell I tossed and turned all night.* She grabbed a bottle of wine and swung the door open.

———

Mason and Savannah Ravenel lived on Daniel Island, and their house backed up to Beresford Creek. The white two-story home with black shutters reminded her of the plantation houses she and Harry had visited. Ferns hung in wire baskets all along the porch, which extended the length of the house. The palms littering the yard rustled. Two gargoyles guarded the front walkway.

The front door opened to an older version of Sam, a woman in her fifties with golden-brown hair and baby-blue eyes. Her perfect smile was as bright as the sun. "Hello! Welcome, CJ. It's great to see you again. We're so happy you came."

She accepted the woman's hug. "Thank you for inviting me." She passed her a bottle of wine. "I brought a cabernet. Hope that's okay."

Savannah patted her arm. "You weren't supposed to bring anything, but thank you. I love cab. Now come on in."

Mason Ravenel, also in his fifties, rounded the corner and gave her a hug and a kiss on the cheek. His brightly colored sweater reminded her of the patchwork quilts she'd seen in the market. His sharp azure eyes stood out from his silvery hair.

CJ heard a loud noise from another room—yelling and laughing. It was rowdy. Savannah smiled. "The boys are watching the football game. I'm not sure who's rooting for who, but as you can tell, it's highly competitive."

Crossing the light oak floor, CJ found Harry, Bill, and Will camped on a stuffed floral couch and matching side chairs, glued to the wide-screen TV. "Excuse me!" she called. Harry and Bill raced to hug her—individually, then as a group. "My, my. Seems you boys are already drinking," she said.

Harry pointed to the TV. "The Pats are killing the Lions." He turned to Bill and said, "I told you!"

Bill waved his hand. "It's all been on lucky plays. I'll get you the next game."

Mealtime came, and so did another two dozen people—more family and several friends, but no Ben. Tables and food filled the den and dining area—turkey, ham, crab, and every side dish imaginable had been set out. The slow-cooked green beans, cinnamon sweet potatoes, and corn bread stuffing were yummy. *Dr. Willis would be proud of me today.*

A couple hours later, there was another massive explosion of sound in the den, more yelling and cheering. CJ leaned around the corner to see grown boys high-fiving and poking at each other. "What's going on in here, guys?"

Harry was in his sock feet and had his arms in the air. "You missed it! Brees hit Moore for the go-ahead score with less than two minutes left. Cowboys are going down!"

"Not yet, Harry," Bill said. "There's plenty of time left."

She laughed. "You guys are gonna hurt yourself, and I hope you're not betting."

Harry roared, "I got twenty of Bill's cash coming!"

She rolled her eyes. "Who needs a beer?"

Arms went up around the room, and she turned for the kitchen. Sam grinned. "You'll make a hell of a waitress."

CJ, hands on hips, replied, "Who said I was bringing them beers?" She laughed. "Do you have a tray?"

Savannah passed a tray filled with beers to her. "Make sure they tip you." CJ climbed through the legs, dropping fresh beers. She picked up the empties, being especially careful with one particular bottle, and carried them to the kitchen. Then, before Sam could intercept her, she went to the opposite side of the island. "I'll take these to the recycling."

Sam pointed. "It's through the laundry room, right beside the back door. Just below Mom's storage shelves."

CJ put all the bottles in the blue can but one. She put it in a plastic bag and then put the bag in her purse. She hung her purse back on a coat hook and covered it with her jacket.

Will's voice startled her. "Why are you taking a beer bottle?"

Oh, shit! "Oh. Well, I wanted it so I could remember to get some of that kind of beer." *Jeez, that's weak.*

He leaned closer to her, and his eyes narrowed. "You could just take a picture of it with your phone or write down the name."

She smiled and shrugged. "But the bottle is kind of unique, and I thought I'd keep it." *Weak!* She reached for her purse. "I can throw it away if you want. A picture of it would do. By the way, do you need something?"

He blew a little puff of air and shook his head. "Naw. It's fine. Keep it." He chuckled and turned back to the den. "You're nuts, CJ." He stopped and turned back. "Oh, wait! I need another bag of corn chips. Your uncle has eaten 'em all." He reached above her head and grabbed a bag off the wire shelf.

CJ stood for a moment, letting her heart slow down before she headed back to the kitchen. "You guys need me to dry?"

Sam tossed her a dish towel. "Yes, ma'am."

Another roar erupted. "Pay up, Bill!" She caught a glimpse of Harry's victory dance. *I guess the Saints won.*

Savannah winked at her. "To think we haven't even fed the guys their pie yet. Wait until they get some sugar in 'em." She motioned to at least half a dozen assorted pies lining the island—pecan, pumpkin, apple, and blueberry.

———

The sun was dropping out of sight when CJ leaned over, hugged Harry, and kissed him on the cheek. "I'm heading out. Are you okay to drive?"

Harry unlocked his eyes from the Jets and Bengals game long enough to give her a squeeze. "I'm fine. I cut myself off a couple of hours ago."

She looked at Bill and Will. "How about you two?"

Will raised his hand. "I'm good. I stopped drinking after the last beer you brought me. Dad made me the designated driver."

She hugged Mason, Savannah, and Sam good night. "Thank you so much for including me."

Savannah patted her arm. *Mama Ravenel loves to pat.* "Come anytime, dear. We loved having you. You're Sam's big sister." She made sure CJ carried a plate of leftovers and a slice of pecan pie with her.

As CJ got in her truck, she carefully placed the plastic bag with the beer bottle on the passenger seat. She'd get it to the lab first thing in the morning. She hit the speed dial as she crossed the Arthur Ravenel Jr. Bridge, now sparkling with lights. She spoke to Eddie and they agreed to meet in the lab the next morning at nine o'clock.

Is Will the second man?

FORTY-ONE

Thursday, November 25
St. Helena Island

Elias sat alone in his dark corner. His tears dripped down his face. He hated holidays more than any other days. He'd never had a good one. Not once. The closest thing he'd had to an actual holiday was when his grandmother let him have his grandfather's leftovers on Thanksgiving when he was six. His happiness at getting the treat was short lived—it was the day he got the scar.

He rested his chin on his knees. He hurt all over. Colder weather meant more pain, bone-chilling and sharp. He had followed the steps, but still, nothing seemed any better. Not here, not at work . . . not anywhere. At least he didn't get the shit kicked out of him at school anymore. He was happy he'd quit.

He almost smiled when his mind found the memory of the stranger. The man who had helped him with his car. Was he someone's father? He'd be a great one—he was patient, loving, and kind. Who went out of their way to help a weak little freak like him? His stranger had.

Elias's own father was absent. Always absent. He barely said a word to him, and it was without feeling when he did. He came and went. Never a "Hey, how are you?" Never anything. When he had tried once to let him know what his grandfather was doing to him, his father had laughed and said he deserved it. Who tells their only child they deserve to be beaten, abused, or—raped?

He exhaled. Like most, this day had been terrible. He'd eaten a can of chicken noodle soup and consumed his daily ration of saltine crackers—six. That was his Thanksgiving breakfast, lunch, and dinner all rolled into one. At least he'd been able to wash his clothes and get the blood off. The washateria had been empty, so there was no one to stare at him. He guessed he could be thankful for that. No one washed their clothes on Thanksgiving morning.

His fingers ran through his yellow hair—more stubble than hair. It was the peril of cutting it himself, but it was all he could afford, and no one else would do it. The line on his cheek was a brighter red today. Cold weather did that.

Why did I lose my mojo bag? I really am worthless. He dug through his box. A minor stroke of luck. He had what he needed to make another. He'd loved the red bag the old man had given him. It was elegantly sewn and the golden drawstrings were exquisite. He'd loved the feel of it in his pocket. *You're a dumbass, Elias.*

His fingers worked to do the best job he could—he wasn't much good at sewing. Slowly, the thread went in and out of the piece of red T-shirt. *God, this is nothing like my old bag.* It would have to do. He had no other choice—his money was low, and he needed it for food and gas. He could steal one, but that'd be wrong.

One by one, he added the pieces to the bag, except— he'd lost his shiny silver medallion. It was his last gift from the old man.

He stood and stretched. *Wait!* For the first time he could remember, there was no pain in his right shoulder—a separated shoulder was a gift from his grandfather. Electricity went through him, and his lips curled. *My plan is starting to work.*

After their last time together and several tense phone calls, Paul hoped dinner with his son at Jill's Place, a restaurant known for its home-cooked menu, would go well.

"Dad, I've been thinking," Paul Jr. said when they'd ordered.

Paul smiled. "About what?"

"About how you broke up our family and abandoned Mom and me. It's all your fault that we're not together."

Paul chewed his lip and tried to control the anger building inside him. He didn't want to tell Paul Jr. the whole story. How his mom had an affair with a guy at work. Counseling had helped them, but it had been over for him when she did it a second time.

"Son, there are reasons your mom and I aren't together. Reasons that really aren't important now. The main thing is that we both love—"

Paul Jr. exploded and slammed his fist down on the table. The salt and pepper shakers crashed to the floor. "That's bullshit. You fucking broke up our family. You chose your career over us." He jumped up. "I'm out of here. I'll call Mom to pick me up." He slammed the door as he ran out.

Tears ran down Paul's face as the few onlookers in the restaurant turned away.

FORTY-TWO

Friday, November 26
Downtown Charleston

CJ opened the truck door when Eddie pulled up to the Forensic Services lab a few minutes before nine o'clock. "Thanks for coming, Eddie. I know you planned to be off today."

He smiled. "No problem. I need some exercise after yesterday's feast. Besides, it shouldn't take us long and we'll be out of here. How was it at the Ravenels'?"

"It was wonderful. We must have had thirty people for dinner, and the guys watched football all day." She laughed. "Harry may still be there."

He unlocked the lab door and motioned her in. "Let's see what you have."

She held up the bag with the bottle. "I made sure the bottle was clean before I handed it over and did my best not to smudge any prints when I picked it up."

Eddie chuckled. "This is a new one—undercover Thanksgiving."

CJ suddenly felt a bit guilty. *Jeez, I get invited to dinner and collect evidence.*

She watched him take the bottle out of the bag by the neck and set it on the stainless-steel table. He turned to a cabinet.

"So, how does this work?" CJ asked.

His hands kept moving. "Well, the first thing I'll do is examine the bottle with a light to see if we have a print. If we do, I'll get some photographs. After that, I'll probably dust and lift it as well and grab more photos. Then we can check the system for a match if we have a good print."

He set up the bottle and started the process with the light. "You see that?" He pointed to a spot on the bottle.

CJ leaned in with her eyes peeled. "I do."

"That's a print. In fact, we have two or three clear prints. Beer bottles provide nice nonporous surfaces."

CJ's heart rate picked up. "So, these prints are good enough to see if we have a match?"

"Yep. These are clear and intact." Eddie stopped and glanced at her sideways. "So, you gonna tell me whose prints these are?"

She sighed. "I'd rather not, but—between us, the prints are Will's."

His eyebrows rose. "Will Parrish? As in Ben's older brother?"

"Yeah. Believe me, I have mixed emotions over all this, but I have to check him out."

Eddie silently continued taking photos, dusting, and lifting the prints. "Okay, I think we have what we need. Of course, I'll want to have one of our techs double-check and verify things, but we can see what we find today." His eyes met hers. "I'll label these as 'unknown subject' for the records."

"Thanks. I'd appreciate it."

Shifting her weight side to side, back and forth, she continued to watch and wait.

Eddie finally glanced up. "I'm classing these as arches. Pretty rare type."

Less than five percent of the population.

He stretched his shoulders back. "Now for the Galton's details."

"The what?" She frowned.

"The individual characteristics of a person's prints. We're all different. I'm examining the image for ridges, bifurcations, and dots made from sweat pores. In simple terms, I'm identifying the unique design of the print. Once I have this, I'll compare it to the other prints and see if the patterns line up. It's easier to do this through AFIS, but the old-fashioned way is kinda fun. Been a while since I've done it."

Once again, she waited, trying not to pace. Finally, he leaned back. "Your print doesn't match the other print. I'll get it all double-checked, but it's clear Will's print isn't the same as the ones found in Sitka and at Shem Creek.

Come here, let me show you a couple of key differences." She leaned close to the sheet with the print. "First, Will's print has an independent ridge missing in the other prints. Second, the other prints have a lake; Will's print doesn't. Those are easy catches."

"I understand the ridge part, but what's a lake?"

He grabbed a pad and drew an oval. "It's basically as it sounds. A circular ridge that's all connected."

She was both happy and frustrated. She was glad it wasn't Will, but then who in the hell was it? He reached over and squeezed her hand. "I'll get all this verified. Sorry it wasn't what you were looking for."

She sighed. "I'm glad it's not Will. I'll keep looking, but at least I can take him off my radar."

CJ went back to her apartment after she left the lab, swapped her jeans and sweater for her favorite sweats, and curled up on the couch. She dug out the copy of the airline information—Logan Bivens, Asher Copeland, Oliver Feaster, and Will Parrish. A line went through Will's name. *Wait a minute!*

She wrote down the seat numbers. Bivens, Copeland, and Feaster didn't sit close together. *But this is interesting.* Will sat beside Asher Copeland on all three legs of the flight to Sitka. *That can't be a coincidence. How do they know each other?*

One more item jumped out at her. Three men returned on the same day—seven days after they arrived. Copeland stayed six more days before he returned. CJ grabbed a calendar for the previous year. *Oh, shit! It has to be him. He was the only one there.* She circled Asher Copeland's name.

She grabbed her cell phone and dialed. "Hey, Sam. I wanted to thank you again for yesterday. I had a blast. Please make sure your parents know how much I appreciated their invite."

"I'm glad you made it, and my parents loved having you," Sam said. "What are you doing tonight?"

"I just put on my comfy clothes and am gonna take it easy."

Sam laughed. "Really? I can't believe it."

"Well, I did bring a file or two home."

Sam's tone was sharp. "I knew it."

"Listen, I was looking over some information Robert sent me, and I have a person I'd like to know more about. I have the name and his address. I was thinking that I'd—"

Sam cut her off. "Not go to the station! You stay home, and I'll make you a deal. I'll go by the station, dig up what I can, and swing by later for a movie and popcorn."

"That's a lot of trouble, Sam. Why don't I—"

"Stay at home and wait for me." Sam laughed. "I'll see you soon. I'll be the one with your information, popcorn, and beer. I'm sure we can find a movie we can watch from your stack of DVDs. Text me the name and address."

———

An hour later, CJ heard a knock on her door. *That was quick.* CJ peered through the peephole. *Oh.* She opened the door but remained in the doorway. "Hey, Ben."

He stepped in as she finally moved back from the door. "Uh—I was downtown and thought I'd stop by. I wanted to see how you were."

"I'm fine. I thought you were Sam. She's coming over to watch a movie."

There was an uncomfortable silence as he fidgeted.

"What were you doing downtown?" CJ asked. "Out on a date?"

His face flushed. "Okay. I lied. I made a special trip since you hadn't returned my messages. No. I wasn't on a date. I felt bad about yesterday—"

"You mean Thanksgiving dinner with Kelsey and her parents?"

He ran his fingers through his dark brown hair. "Okay. I see you're pissed."

She shook her head. "Nope. It's none of my damn business who you're dating. Not sure why Sam even told me."

"Kelsey and I aren't dating. We've been to dinner a couple of times and to the fundraiser."

She huffed. "And Thanksgiving dinner with her parents. Sounds like dating to me." As he rubbed the knot in his neck, she grabbed her notes. "Since you've graced me with your presence, you might as well be helpful. Do you know any of these people?" She thrust the pad at him.

His eyes scanned the page. "Asher Copeland. He lived near us growing up. He still fishes with Dad and Will sometimes." Ben handed the pad back to her. "Are you happy now?"

Before he could ask her why she wanted to know, she said, "Yep," and stepped over and opened the door. "You should go before Sam gets here."

Sam finally left CJ's apartment a little after midnight. They'd laughed a lot, cried a little during *Steel Magnolias*, and finished a six-pack. As CJ slid into bed, she opened the file Sam had left her. There was not much to know about Asher Copeland—he'd never been married, was a fisherman by trade, and had no record. She stared at the photo of the man and his dark brown hair. He owned a black Chevy Blazer.

I'll need to pay him a visit. Is this the second man from Alaska?

FORTY-THREE

Monday, November 29
Johns Island, South Carolina

The single-story house was an odd shade of brown with black shutters. It needed new paint, and the yard needed an overhaul. CJ slipped the truck into park behind a black Chevy Blazer. "There's his truck. It's his only registered vehicle, and it's only 6:10 a.m., so he should be home."

"Hopefully," Johnny said.

CJ knocked on the storm door and called out, "Mr. Copeland. It's Charleston PD. We want to see if you can help us with something."

Silence, then a rattle.

CJ cocked her head. "You hear that?"

Johnny tilted his head, listening. "Came from the back."

She unsnapped her holster. "I'll go around the back. Stay here in case he answers."

Knocking on the back door didn't yield any response. As she stepped off the deck, she caught movement out of the corner of her eye. She yelled, "Mr. Copeland?"

She briskly crossed the thirty yards to a small shed backed up to the marsh. The door was cracked. "Mr. Cope—"

The wooden door flew open, hitting her and knocking her backward—she landed hard on her butt. A tall man with dark hair bolted past her, and she grabbed a leg, dragging him down. His arm swung downward, and she dodged a blade. A kick dislodged the knife, and the sole of her other boot slammed him backward to the ground.

He lunged and grabbed for her throat, but she twisted away. Then, in one smooth motion, she grabbed his wrist, yanked it behind his back, spun on top of him, and straddled him. Her weight and pressure on the arm left him facedown in the dirt.

"You're breaking my arm, bitch!" Copeland screamed.

"Stop struggling! I'm Detective O'Hara with Charleston PD."

Johnny flew across the yard and slid to her side. "You got him, CJ?"

"I got him. Cuff him for me."

"Fuck!" Copeland screeched. "That hurts. I didn't do anything."

She rolled off and jerked him to a sitting position. "Asher Copeland. You're under arrest for assaulting a police officer."

He spat, "Go to hell! You were trespassing."

She peered into the shed. "What are you trying to hide, Mr. Copeland?"

"Nothing. You can't go in there."

"What do you think, Johnny? Do we have probable cause?"

"Sounds like it to me." He leaned down and stared into Copeland's eyes. "He attacked you, so no warrant is needed."

She stepped into the shed and pulled the overhead chain—a light buzzed to life. Workbench and drawers full of tools, except for one unusual item . . .

"What's in this red box, Mr. Copeland?" she yelled, and touched the metal container with the toe of her boot.

"Nothing. Go fuck yourself."

"No, thank you, Mr. Copeland. I'm good."

She slipped on a pair of latex gloves, pulled the box from under the shelf, and squeezed the bolt cutters she found on the tool rack. The hinge creaked as the top fell back. "These bikini bottoms seem a little small for you."

"Those aren't mine. I've never seen them before."

She dialed her cell phone. "Yeah, this is CJ. I need a couple of officers to transport a prisoner and the CSU, please."

Minutes later, two officers dragged Asher Copeland to the cruiser. He screamed, cursed, and fought the whole way. A search of the house by the CSU revealed nothing except he was a slob. "Guys, let's make sure we see what prints we can collect."

The only valuable thing from their investigation in the shed was the red toolbox—with no tools. The CSU collected the pair of bikini bottoms that matched the top found at the crime scene at Shem Creek, two other pairs of women's panties, and a small jar of something dark red—blood. Fingerprints were all over the box and the jar.

***

At two o'clock, CJ pushed the door open to the interrogation room to find Copeland glaring at her. "You can't hold me like this! I have rights."

She took the metal chair opposite him and slid a photo across the table. "Do you recognize this woman?"

He never looked down. "Nope. Never seen her before."

She held it up in front of his eyes—a snapshot of Kerri Ann Russell. "Well, that's one lie. Do you wanna keep lying or tell me what you know and make it easier on yourself?"

He gritted his teeth.

She held up another photo—the first Sitka victim. "How about this woman?"

His eyes flashed, then he shook his head. "Nope. Never seen her." His tongue lapped at his lips.

"She's a pretty thing, isn't she? She sure has a great body." He squirmed. *Sick bastard's getting aroused.* "Whose bikini bottoms and panties were in your shed?"

"Don't know nothing 'bout them. Someone must have put them there when I wasn't looking. These fucking cuffs are too tight."

She sighed and leaned forward. "We got some great fingerprints on the inside and outside of the red box. We also got some off the jar. You know, the one with the blood in it. Wanna bet whether the blood is from our victim?"

His breathing ramped up, and his eyes darted wildly. "You're lying, bitch! I think I need an attorney."

She shrugged. "I guess we'll find out, won't we? We might even get lucky and find DNA on the underwear. You know, now that I think about it, I don't need your help. I have everything I need. I mean, if you helped us, we'd probably owe you something." She stood. "This way, we don't owe you a damn thing, and we can charge you with the maximum. Good luck with life in prison." She closed the door.

CJ left Copeland, went back to the Forensic Services lab, and stood watching Eddie, who was bent over the table. "How's it look?"

Eddie raised his head. "Remember the fingerprint on the tape at Shem Creek and on the jar in Sitka had a distinctive lake? Well, guess what? The prints on the box and jar from Johns Island have the same ridges and the lake." He smiled. "Congratulations. Asher Copeland is your second guy."

She sucked in a long breath. "You're sure?"

He nodded. "Yep. We'll verify it all, but I've studied the images, as has another print analyst, and we agree it's a match."

She exhaled. "Okay, let's triple-check everything. What's the story on the possible DNA from the blood and underwear?"

"I expect to have results within forty-eight hours. The chief made some calls and got us to the top of the pile in Columbia."

"Oh, wow. Really?"

"Yeah. Our Folly Beach vic is the niece of some bigwig developer, and he's been raising hell with the governor. I guess the guy donates a pile of cash."

CJ left Eddie and returned to her truck where she sat, numb. *Is the Lowcountry Killer case finally over?* She rubbed her forehead, took a deep breath, and dialed Robert's number. She gave him the news, then gave Wally an update. She should have felt more excited and happier, but the victims' faces were all she could see. She put the truck in drive and headed for Harry's.

FORTY-FOUR

Wednesday, December 1
Downtown Charleston

CJ and Johnny were sitting at the conference room table reviewing files when Sam handed her a lab report. CJ's eyes widened. She ran her finger down the page.

Johnny waited until her head rose. "Well?"

"There was DNA on the bikini bottoms, and it matches our Shem Creek victim. No doubt they were hers."

"How about the two pairs of panties?" he asked.

She grinned. "Both had DNA, and it matches two of our unsolved rape cases."

"So, Copeland is your second guy," Johnny said.

She stood and walked to the window and stared at a flock of seagulls drifting over the Ashley River. Finally, the

Lowcountry Killer case was closed. Johnny joined her, and they both watched the floating balls of white feathers.

"I tell you what, Johnny. I think I'll take one more crack at Copeland. We have what we need to nail his ass, but there are still a few items I'd like to know more about."

"You think he'll tell you anything? He's got a lawyer now."

"He might if he thinks he can get a deal. Won't hurt to try."

"Want me to go with you?"

"No. How about you stay on our double murder case. Keep looking for witnesses who may have seen something."

Johnny nodded. "Okay. I also thought I'd walk the two areas again. Maybe we missed a camera that caught something."

She called down to the holding cell and asked to have Copeland put in an interrogation room.

———

Two days. It was not long in most terms, but two days in a six-by-eight box wasn't most terms. CJ's nose almost touched the glass as she stared at Asher Copeland in the two-way mirror. *The guy's already aged ten years.* The heavy-set guard motioned that she was free to proceed.

The door squeaked as she entered the stark room. "Hello, Mr. Copeland."

He sat glassy-eyed—lost in space. The metal chair scraped as CJ sat across from him. His fingers caressed the bracelets on his wrists, which were locked to the table.

"First, I want to make sure you understand you don't have to talk to me. You can choose to have your lawyer present, or you can simply leave. Understand?"

Her pointer finger grazed his hand, and he jerked awake from his trance. His eyes flared at her.

"Do you understand, Mr. Copeland?"

He smirked. "Yeah. I understand. I can tell you to fuck off whenever I please. I like that rule."

She spent the next several minutes telling him about the latest cards stacked against him. His eyes seemed to glaze over. *Is he even hearing me?* She spread the glossy photos in a row—eleven young women and Mary Beth Parrish, Bryan's mother. She added the last picture, of Kerri Ann Russell, as her stomach turned over. His only response was a slight curl of his lips. *I think the bastard is enjoying this.*

Her pointer finger tapped the last photo. "We all know you are responsible for this victim. You raped and murdered her. We have DNA, fingerprints, clothing, and a witness who saw you at Folly Beach. Oh, yeah. We also have DNA tying you to two other rapes. However, you might be able to help yourself with the judge if you cooperate on the others."

He sneered. "I don't know nothing 'bout the others. You're a stupid bitch, ain't you?"

She pressed, and he remained silent, back in his trance. *Let's try something new.* "Well, it was worth a shot, I guess. You'll go down for three rapes and one murder." She slowly stacked the photos, saying each victim's name and physical features. "Lillie Ferguson, twenty-one, blond hair, blue eyes."

His eyes flickered down as she tipped the photos toward him, then placed them in the stack. He shifted and squeezed his legs together. *This sick bastard is actually getting aroused.* "Too bad you weren't as good as your mentor. All those lessons and all you could manage was one real victim. Your sorry ass—"

"That's a fucking lie!"

Bingo. She shrugged. "Ah, come on now. The evidence is clear. Bryan Parrish was much stronger than you. He was a serial killer. You . . . well . . . you're pitiful compared to him. He had great skill, but you—"

He erupted, slapping his palms on the table. "You're a stupid slut! Do you really think Bryan did all this by himself? I should have taken care of you a week ago. You've never even seen me watching you—not on the Fourth of July when you were with your uncles or the other morning at your apartment."

She listened as he bragged, his eyes flashing and sweat gathering on his flushed forehead. "Our last girl together, Lillie, was luscious. Bryan and I both—"

She held her rage as the door burst open. Copeland's appointed public defender raced in, screamed for him to shut his mouth, and ended the session. "That was a dirty trick, Detective. You talked to my client without me. I'll—"

"He chose to talk to me," she said calmly. "I was clear he was within his rights to remain silent or have you here. I'm happy to play the tape for you."

He stomped away.

She had the answers to her questions.

CJ crossed the parking lot, heading to her truck.

"Excuse me, Detective O'Hara. I'd like a word." Platinum-blond hair and cleavage exposed by a low-cut sweater greeted her when she turned—Wendy Watts.

"I don't have any comments at this time, Ms. Watts."

Shark teeth flashed. "Is it true you missed a major item in the Lowcountry Killer case? There were two ruthless killers, not one. How could you make—"

"Ms. Watts, Chief Williams plans to make a public statement soon. I'm sure he'll be happy to answer any questions." CJ slid her key into the lock and pulled the door open.

Wendy turned and smiled at her cameraman. "Did you get that?"

He nodded. "Yep."

"She looked guilty, don't you think? She knows she made a huge mistake. Wonder Girl's in big trouble now."

He shrugged. "I don't know. She looked really profess—"

"Shut up, asshole! Let's get back to the station to get this ready for the six o'clock news. How about we lead with 'Detective O'Hara and the Charleston PD's Major Blunder'?"

CJ got into the truck, slammed her door shut, and pulled away, leaving Wendy standing on the pavement. She glanced back in the rearview.

Time to put a stop to this.

FORTY-FIVE

Friday, December 3
Downtown Charleston

CJ jotted the last note on the board as the brass and Solicitor Drummond grabbed coffees in the corner of the conference room. Sam put a tray of coffee cake on the table and passed plates around. Once everyone was seated at the conference table, all eyes fixed on CJ.

"Well, now that you have your treats, we can get started." CJ glanced at Tim. "I'll cover the Asher Copeland case first so Tim can make his next meeting. After that, the rest of us can cover the progress on the double murders. Chief, I'm happy to help you with whatever you need for the press conference."

Walter, mouth full, gave her a thumbs-up.

For the next thirty minutes, she covered the critical aspects of the Copeland case, including his past and how he was connected to the Parrish family.

Tim stared at his notes, then asked, "Did any of them indicate any issues with him?"

She shook her head. "Not after he moved from Johns to James Island. Bill did say Asher seemed to gravitate more to Bryan when he was little, and there were a couple of weird incidents. He found Bryan and Asher with a dead cat on one occasion and with a bunch of dead birds on another."

Tim looked up from his scribbling. "They killed a cat?"

"Bill wasn't sure. They told him they found it on the road, but Bill was shocked because the two had gutted it and smeared blood all over themselves." CJ saw Sam flinch out of the corner of her eye.

The group went over a few more details before Tim excused himself. He indicated he would pursue a murder one charge plus seven counts of rape based on the evidence CJ had provided. He planned to leave it to Sitka about how they wanted to handle the rape and accessory to murder in their jurisdiction.

Walter stood in front of the board, eyes running down the list of pertinent facts. "Great work, CJ. I think we can finally close the book on the Lowcountry Killer case here and in Alaska."

"Thank you, sir." *I just wish the dead faces would go away.*

Walter went back to his chair. "Where are we on the other two murders?"

She went over the evidence they had to date. Then she had Paul add what he understood about the Gullah connection.

Stan asked her, "What's your profile on this guy?"

She went to the board, marker in hand. The group watched as she added bullet points.

- *Male, less than twenty-five years old*
- *Small body size*
- *Local, grew up here*
- *Likely a loner and lives alone*
- *Planner, organized*
- *Weapon—crude knife*
- *Seeking power (rituals), cure (herbs)—hoodoo*

Walter asked, "What's your sense of the race?"

She shifted. "My sense is he's Black, but only because of the Gullah connection. He could be any race, though, so we're staying unbiased at this point."

She answered the last questions about the profile. Paul added his insights based on his knowledge of hoodoo and what information Grannie had provided.

Walter stood. "Okay. Let's stay on top of this one, CJ. With the Parker and Copeland cases resolved, this is priority one. I'll see you at the press conference.

"Paul, can I see you a minute?" Walter asked. The two stepped out.

Two hours later, Chief Williams waited until the press room quieted.

"Good afternoon. Thank you for coming. I wanted to update you on the recent murder of Kerri Ann Russell. I'm pleased to announce the man responsible, Asher Copeland, has been arrested, and rape and murder charges will be filed. Additionally, we have evidence this individual was also responsible for two unsolved rapes. These charges will also be filed."

He pointed at his officers. "I'd like to thank Detective CJ O'Hara and Officer Johnny Jones for their tireless work in solving this case." He closed his notebook. "We'll have more later."

Wendy Watts's arm shot up from the center of the front row. "What about the connection between Copeland and Bryan Parrish? Are you intentionally leaving this out since it was a mistake—"

Chief Williams's voice was controlled but stern. "We do have evidence Copeland and Parrish were connected and will be investigating that further. At the appropriate time, we'll inform the public. The solicitor will include any appropriate charges in addition to what I've given you."

Wendy's lip curved upward in a smug smile.

FORTY-SIX

Sunday, December 5
St. Helena Island

Paul sipped black coffee and picked at the corner of the wooden kitchen table as he stared out at the dark clouds looming on the horizon. Then, sighing, he filled his travel mug, grabbed his keys, and headed for his pickup. He had an idea, and there was only one way to check it out.

The truck swayed over the Ashley River Memorial Bridge. Whitecaps kicked up on the water's face and seagulls scattered for cover. Traffic was sparse—people were sleeping in after a big Saturday night. He filled his tank and picked up another coffee and a stale Danish at the final turn to St. Helena Island.

Gravel crunched as he pulled into the driveway of a sunshine-yellow single-story home. The black shutters made him think about sunflowers. He smiled at the well-kept yard—trimmed grass, clipped bushes, and fresh pine straw in the beds. *My son's keeping up with his chores.*

Paul's foot had barely touched the ground when the front door swung open and he saw his ex-wife. She smiled, waved, and gave him the *Just a minute* sign. He nodded and leaned on his truck, waiting. He and his ex-wife had a good relationship, but she liked to keep him at a distance. At least she'd gotten Paul Jr. to agree to meet him.

"Hey, Dad."

"Hey, son." The two shared a brief, tense hug. "Whatcha hungry for?" Paul asked.

Paul Jr. shrugged. "Anything's fine. Gullah Grub would be okay."

When they pulled up to the restaurant, several cars were parked next to the white two-story building with black-trimmed windows. A simple brown sign let everyone know the name of the business—Gullah Grub Restaurant. They stepped onto the forest-green porch, and an older Black woman seated them. "Can I get you some drinks?" she asked.

"Yes, please. How about two swamp waters?" Paul and his son always got the half-sweet-tea, half-lemonade drink. "How's school, Junior?" Paul asked after the waitress had their orders.

"Good. We're almost to winter break. I should have straight As again."

"I'm so proud of you. Just think. You've got less than six months before you graduate. Any word from Columbia?"

"I had a second phone interview, and they scheduled me to come up over the break. They said my file was complete. So, if I do well in the face-to-face, I think I'm in."

"You'll do great when you see them. They'll love you."

After they gobbled down the barbecued chicken, red rice, green beans, and potato salad, Paul asked, "You want some dessert?"

Paul Jr. leaned back. "I'm stuffed, Pop. But, man, I love their chicken. Most places smother their chicken in sauce. The dry rub they use here is so much better. Would it be okay if we headed back home? I've gotta finish a paper."

"Sure. By the way, how's work?"

His son shrugged. "Fine. I've been getting about fifteen hours a week."

"Does that little guy still work there?"

"What little guy?"

"I'm not sure. About five four and . . . scrawny. He always looked sickly."

"Oh. You mean Ghost."

Paul's brow furrowed. "Ghost?"

His son laughed. "That's what we call him. His name is Elias."

"Doesn't he live with his grandfather, Henry Lewis?"

"Yeah. I think. Elias's dad lives there too, but he's always gone. I feel sorry for Elias. He has no one. I mean, he's kinda strange and all, but he doesn't deserve how old man

Moberley treats him. I've had to step in a couple of times to defend Elias from him."

"What does he do to the kid?" Paul asked.

"He yells at him, berates him—calls him a freak, worthless, and weak. I haven't seen him do it, but I think he's hit him a time or two."

"That's terrible. No one deserves that. You're a good man for trying to help. If you need my help, let me know." He paused, then asked, "Didn't you say Elias was into hoodoo?"

Paul Jr. smiled. "Yeah. He's always telling me about it." He stared at his father. "Why are you askin' about him?"

"Just curious." Paul shrugged. "I had a case he might be able to help me with."

Paul Jr. roared with laughter. "Ghost? No way he could help. Guy's afraid of his own shadow."

Paul paid, and they headed back to drop Paul Jr. off. The return ride was quiet, and Paul wasn't sure what his son had on his mind. He pulled into the driveway and turned off the engine.

"Hey, Dad? Can I talk to you about something?"

"Always, son."

Paul Jr. sat nibbling his lip. He sniffed. "I owe you an apology." His eyes grew wet, and he hung his head.

Paul put his hand on his shoulder. "Why?"

He suddenly lunged over and hugged him. He whispered, "Mom told me what really happened. She said it was her fault you guys got divorced and—"

"It's okay, son. It was years ago." He pushed the boy back, used his hand to lift his chin, and smiled. "The important thing is that your mom and I are on good terms now. We both love you more than anything in this world. Your mom was my one and only. It's why I've never remarried. I still love her and always will. But we just aren't good together."

They sat for several minutes, hugging. Both men cried.

The house was tattered—its blue paint was peeling, screens were missing, and weeds had overtaken the place. A beat-up Ford pickup was parked half on the driveway and half in the yard. Paul knocked on the doorframe, stepped back, and waited at the bottom of a short flight of steps.

Elias's grandfather, Henry Lewis, opened the door and staggered onto the top step. The smell of alcohol filled the air as he rubbed his temples, and his eyes were bright red and watery. He hissed, "Who are you, and what the hell do you want?"

"I'm Paul. A friend of Elias."

The old man snickered. "Freak ain't got no damn friends. You gay and lookin' for some action?"

Paul's eyes went wide. "No! He works with my son, and I just wanted to see how he was doing."

"You're just a regular do-gooder. Ain't seen the little shit, but when I do, there'll be hell to pay. Sneaky little bastard stole some of my food." He waved his hand. "Now get the fuck out of here! My head hurts, and I don't wanna be bothered with you or that worthless little freak of a grandson." The door slammed in Paul's face.

———

Moberley's Grocery stood at the end of a dirt road. The red brick building wasn't big, but it offered locals a nearby option. Unfortunately, the place was empty—closed on Sundays. Paul cupped his eyes against the window and tried to see inside. Nothing but a dim light in the back.

Paul tapped on the glass. *I swear I saw movement.* He tapped again—nothing. He exhaled and went around the side of the building to the back door.

———

Elias peeped at the man in the window from the shadows in the store. He recognized him—Paul Jr.'s father was a cop. Why was he here? He knew old man Moberley would kick his ass if he let anyone in. He'd be back soon, and if he found someone in the store, Elias would get fired. *Wait! Maybe he knows.*

Elias scrambled to the back storeroom and switched off the light. He went to hide in the corner—and stopped. He stared at his hands—they weren't trembling. He picked up his backpack and found what he needed.

I can't let him stop me.

———

Paul knocked on the metal back door and called out, "Anyone inside?" He heard the door click. He rapped on the door again and tried the handle. The door creaked open, and he stuck his head inside the dimly lit space. "Anyone here?" *That's weird. Why's the door unlocked?*

Paul felt for and flipped the light switch—it was still dark. He went to his truck, found a flashlight, and reentered the back door. He swore he heard footsteps along the back wall. "Anyone here? I'm a police officer. Identify yourself."

Searing-hot pain spread across his chest and he dropped to his knees. Pale blue eyes, almost pink, stared down at Paul as the darkness took him.

FORTY-SEVEN

Sunday, December 5
Wando

CJ and Sam found a table under an overhang on the roof of the bluish-gray building with red shutters—Henry's on the Market. It was 1:10 p.m., but the lunch crowd was still buzzing.

Sam peeped over the menu. "What are you getting?"

"I think a cup of the she-crab soup and house salad with shrimp," CJ said. "How about you?"

"The soup and a pimento cheese sandwich," Sam said, smiling.

CJ winked. "I'm gonna see if the waiter will sneak me a few hush puppies too."

The college-age waiter took their orders and hustled away. They weren't listed on the rooftop menu, but CJ's little wink convinced him to get her the golden-brown balls of cornmeal.

As they ate, the two women talked about everything but work. CJ was happy about the distraction. Then, after a lull, Sam asked her what she thought of Will.

"I think Will's great." *I got his fingerprints, and he's not a killer.* She grinned. "Why?"

Sam shrugged, and her face flushed. "I dunno. He seems nice, and—he asked me out."

CJ almost spit out her bite of soup. "Really? Good for you. Where's he taking you?"

"Uh, I'm not sure. Will's not fancy, so probably somewhere casual. I'd like to go to Vickery's and watch the sunset."

After eating, they headed out for one of CJ's least favorite activities—shopping.

"I don't know, Sam. I'm not sure it's me." CJ spun in the mirror. "It's kinda short."

Sam laughed. "It's not too short, and you look fabulous. Better than that. You look totally amazing." There was a slight pause as Sam tugged at the back of the dress. "Is this your size?"

"Yep. Why?"

"Well, it seems a little . . . baggy," Sam replied. "Have you lost weight? You're not eating like you should, and sometimes I worry, you're drink—"

"Jesus, Sam! I'm fine. Now drop it."

The younger woman whispered, "I'm sorry. I didn't mean to hurt your feelings." She hurried off to look for shoes to go with the dress. A couple minutes later, she returned empty handed. Her eyes were still damp. She sniffed. "So, are you buying it?"

CJ ran her hands down the black fabric and slid her fingers along the back. "Jeez, Sam. It feels low in the back and high at the bottom. I'm afraid to move. I'd rather not have everyone know what color underwear I'm wearing."

"You won't fall out," Sam replied. "Haven't you ever owned a black cocktail dress?"

"Nope. Never. I've never owned any dress this short." She ducked back into the dressing room and emerged, dress in hand. "It's settled. I'm passing."

"Noooo. It looks so good on you."

"My mind's made up. It's crazy to pay all that money for a dress I'd probably never wear."

Sam smiled at her ever-practical friend. "Okay, but let me go on record as saying you should get it. Next time you go to a formal event, you'll be sorry."

CJ rolled her eyes. "Oh yeah. All the formal events I attend." She checked her cell phone. "We need to go. Harry's expecting us soon for dinner."

Market Street was bustling—locals were shopping and tourists were out seeing the sights. CJ maneuvered her truck out of the slot without bashing the silver Cadillac parked way too close to her fender. She hit the speaker on her cell phone and let Harry know they were on their way.

——

The lights on the Arthur Ravenel Jr. Bridge flickered to life as they crawled up and over it. Traffic was slow on Highway 17 through Mount Pleasant, but it cleared once they took a left on Highway 41. CJ pointed to homes on her right as they passed. "Is Dunes West nice?"

"Yes," said Sam. "Most of the homes are on big lots and spaced out. It has an interesting golf course—lots of sand, sawgrass, and a few alligators."

"I never thought of golf and alligators going together," CJ said, amused. "Only in the Lowcountry."

CJ crunched to the front of Harry's house as the sun hid; orange, yellow, and a touch of red hung over the marsh. Panic pulled at her when she saw Bill's truck. *I wonder if Ben and Will are here.* Sam squeezed her hand.

"Uncle Craig!" The man, the spitting image of her father, bear-hugged her as she came up the walkway to the back deck, lifting her feet off the ground. "My favorite niece." Sam got a huge hug as well.

CJ nervously waved to Bill, Will, and Ben, who met them on the deck steps. *I was secretly collecting Will's fingerprints the last time I saw him, and I gave Ben a ton of shit.*

Coming onto the deck, his apron covered in batter, Harry kissed both women on the cheek. He was careful not to get the sticky white dough on them. CJ, hands on hips, asked, "Uncle Harry, did you leave any batter in the bowl?"

He sighed. "Well—let's just say the mixer and I had quite a battle. The damn thing has it out for me."

"Are my hush puppies safe?" she asked.

"Oh, yeah." He winked. "I managed to save them." He turned for the kitchen as he asked Will, "Do you mind cranking up the heaters? It may get a little chilly." Will turned the knobs, and the heaters sparked on with a red glow and hissing. Ben handed CJ and Sam Coronas with his usual ease. *Is Kelsey coming?* CJ wondered.

With Sam's help, Harry put platters and dishes on the table—baked whiting, red rice, fried okra, coleslaw, and hush puppies. Harry said a quick prayer, gave a toast, and then said, "Let's eat."

CJ immediately grabbed a hush puppy. "I'll start with these in case we run out."

She caught Sam smiling up at Will out of the corner of her eye. *I think she really does like him.* The two chatted throughout dinner and sat side by side on the deck, watching the stars afterward. *They are kinda cute together.*

Ben joined CJ at the rail. "Lots of stars tonight."

"Yep." There was an awkward silence before she cleared her throat. "Ben, I owe you an apology. I shouldn't have given you shit about Kelsey. We're not together, and she seems sweet. I guess I was . . . well, jealous. Stupid, right?"

He nudged her with his shoulder. "It's not stupid. Flattering, to be honest. Listen, I was attracted to you the first time I saw you. There's always been chemistry, but we both know it's complicated."

"Yes. It is. I don't know what I want, and I can't expect anything from you. It was nice to have you around, though, even if just as a friend."

He leaned over and gave her a quick hug. "Agreed. Let's not overthink it."

They stood quietly, staring at the night sky. Ben spoke up. "By the way, Kelsey and I aren't seeing each other anymore. She's great, but I'm not sure we fit together." He gave a low whistle. "Man, the sky's kinda dark tonight. Not bright like it was when we had a full moon a couple of weeks ago."

CJ's head snapped around. "What did you say?"

"Uh, Kelsey and I aren't dating."

"No. About the moon."

He shrugged. "The moon's not bright like it was."

She raced through the back door. "Uncle Harry. I need to use your computer?" A few minutes later, CJ was staring at the dates for the full moons the last three months.

FORTY-EIGHT

Monday, December 6
Downtown Charleston

CJ waved to the pear-shaped woman from her table in the corner of the coffee shop and stood. "Good morning, Mrs. Lee. Thanks for meeting me here."

"No problem. Please call me Beatrice." Congressman Randolph Lee Jr.'s wife sat and motioned to the waitress. "Can you bring me a latte? Double shot of espresso."

"Yes, ma'am."

Beatrice's eyes followed the waitress. "I hope their lattes are drinkable." She looked back at CJ. "So, what do you need to talk to me about? Let me guess, you're sleeping with my husband."

"Uh, no. I'm not involved with your husband. I only met him the other night at the fundraiser."

The older woman scoffed. "You're one of the lucky few the bastard hasn't bedded. At least you'd be a step up from all those Washington bimbos. He thinks I don't know, but he's stupid. If my dad's influence and money hadn't helped him, that dumbass would have never been elected."

CJ cleared her throat. The abrupt and candid nature of Beatrice made her head spin. Not exactly the high society language she'd expected, but she remembered Sam saying that Beatrice was "new money." Her father had made his wealth in shipping through the Port of Charleston. "You're aware of his infidelities?"

"I like that." Beatrice laughed. "*Infidelities.* Makes it sound all professional and proper. Yeah. I know all about my horndog husband."

"Oh. I guess I thought—"

"I was clueless. Well, I'm not."

"It's none of my business, but why do you stay with him?" CJ asked.

Her eyes narrowed. "You're right, it's none of your business, but I'll tell you anyway. I stay with Randolph to enjoy all the perks of being a congressman's wife. As long as he keeps his 'infidelities' in Washington, I couldn't give a shit what he does."

"I see," CJ said skeptically.

The waitress dropped the latte off, and Beatrice greedily took a sip. She frowned and then shrugged. "It's not good, but I can drink it. So, is that all there is to your bombshell?"

CJ shifted. "Well, I'm not sure. You told me you were okay as long as the affairs were kept in Washington."

"I actually said I don't give a shit as long as he keeps it in Washington."

"Okay." She exhaled and pulled the envelope from her notebook. "Maybe this is no big deal either, but I thought you deserved to know."

She watched as the older woman scanned the photos, her eyes squinting and lips pursing. "That son of a bitch. Where did you get these?"

"I took them," CJ answered.

Beatrice glared at her. "You took them? Where? When?"

CJ pointed to the date and time stamp. "At the fundraiser in a side room near the women's restroom."

The older woman burst out laughing. "You mean to tell me the bastard was dipping his wick right under my nose?"

"I suppose."

Beatrice leaned forward, eyes glistening. "Tell me the whole story. How'd you catch him?"

"I had gone to the restroom and was on my way back to the ballroom when I heard a noise. The door was cracked, and I—uh—I saw the two of them."

The older woman clapped her hands. "And you snapped some photos?"

"Yes, ma'am. On my cell."

"Damn, I wish you'd gotten a video. That'd have been perfect."

Eyes wide, CJ said, "You don't seem mad."

Beatrice shook her head, and her eyes narrowed again. "Oh, I'm mad as hell, but having this works for me. I've told him more than once to keep his shit out of Charleston or else." She pointed. "I'm gonna skewer his ass with this." She looked at the photos again. "Is this that little tart reporter?"

"Yes, ma'am. Wendy Watts."

"From what I hear, she spreads her legs for anyone who can give her what she wants."

"I can't speak to that," CJ said, shrugging.

Beatrice patted CJ's hand. "You're too sweet, Detective. Let's call it like it is. She's a two-bit slut. The kind my husband loves." She stared at CJ. "Why else did you tell me this?"

"I'm not sure. I thought you should know."

Beatrice leaned across the table, closing the distance between them. "We both know that's not all. This little bitch is a thorn in the Charleston PD's side with all her wild accusations and lies." She leaned back, motioned to the waitress, and held up her cup. "Honey, can you get me a big one of these to go?" She winked at CJ. "I'll handle this, Detective. Don't you worry. No one will know where these photos came from, and let's pretend we've never talked beyond briefly at the fundraiser. Hell, I'll only need to show two people to solve both our problems." She took the latte the waitress dropped off, tossed a twenty on the table, and waltzed out the door.

I hope I didn't just screw up.

The ever impeccably dressed solicitor, Tim Drummond, smiled at CJ as he sat across the conference room table from her. He wore a navy blue suit, pale yellow shirt, and colorful paisley tie. "Detective, I want to thank you for all of your hard work on the Copeland case. It's made my job easy." He opened his notebook. "Is Paul joining us?"

"I thought so, but I haven't heard from him this morning." She frowned. "I tried to call his cell but only got his voicemail. Let's go ahead, and I'll catch him up later."

He nodded and went over the charges filed against Asher Copeland, outlined the evidence supporting each, and explained the statutes. He told her he expected Copeland to want a plea. She disagreed, and he asked why.

"Because Copeland's an arrogant piece of shit," she replied. "It's why he copped to so many of the crimes. He's been in Bryan Parrish's shadow, and now he has a chance to grab the spotlight."

He stared at her. "You may be right. A trial would be a spectacle."

The door opened, and Sam appeared. "Excuse me. CJ, Paul hasn't been in this morning. I put a note on his office door."

That's strange. He's always here early. "Thanks. I'll try his cell again in a bit."

After her meeting with Tim was completed, CJ dialed Stan's cell phone. She exhaled and hung up. Stan hadn't seen Paul today and hadn't reached him. She glanced at the clock—3:10 p.m. "Sam, I'm gonna swing by Paul's house."

Sam nodded. "Okay. If he does come in, I'll call you ASAP."

———

CJ drove to Paul's house. She knocked on the front door of the steel-blue one-story home in West Ashley—nothing but quiet. She looked through the living room window. The house was dark. *No truck, no lights.* She peered through the back door's window into the kitchen. Same as the front. Dark and no signs of life. She tried Paul's cell again and listened to his message. *Where the hell are you, Paul?*

An elderly woman pushed her trash can from the curb. CJ crossed the yard. "Excuse me. I'm a friend of Paul's. Have you seen him?"

The woman's almond-brown eyes stared up at her. "Not today. I saw him yesterday morning before he left."

"Do you know where he went?"

The old woman looked puzzled. "No. I'm not sure. I saw him get in his truck early. I was in the kitchen, and we didn't talk. He's such a good neighbor. In fact, he always brings my cans in for me."

She started up her drive, then stopped. "Did you check with Paul Jr.? Paul goes down to see him as much as he can. He's a great kid."

"Thanks. I'll check with his son. I left a note on his door, but if you see him, can you ask him to call CJ?"

The old woman nodded. "Sure. You take care, honey."

CJ grabbed the last can and rolled it up the driveway. She called Sam and asked her to find Paul Jr.'s number. She sat in her truck with a bad feeling. Within minutes, Sam called her back and, as usual, had what she needed.

"Hello, Paul Jr., this is Detective O'Hara. I was hoping you could tell me where your dad is."

"Hello, Detective. He should be home. He came down yesterday, and we had lunch, then he left."

The knot in her stomach grew worse. "I'm here at his house and there is no sign of him. He didn't come into work today."

Paul Jr. exhaled. "That doesn't make sense. He never misses work. Let me go check with Mom and see if she knows anything."

CJ listened to the silence, then heard rustling. "Hello, Detective. Mom says she has no clue where he'd be."

"Do you know if he was stopping anywhere on the way home?"

"No, ma'am. I assume he drove back to Charleston."

CJ hung up and sat in the truck as her pulse escalated and her head pounded. She punched Stan's code on her cell phone. "Hey, Stan. Paul is nowhere to be found. I'm at his house and there's no sign of him. His neighbor hasn't seen him, and his son said he saw him yesterday in St. Helena, but he left for home after lunch."

Stan exhaled. "Okay. Let me know if you hear from him."

"Yes, sir. I'll keep you posted."

She turned onto Highway 17 for the hour-and-a-half drive to St. Helena. She called Sam. "I'm driving the route to St. Helena. Can you give the hospitals a call and text me a photo of Paul?"

CJ drove back to her apartment and trudged up the steps a little past ten o'clock. There had been no signs of

Paul's truck along her drive, and no one she'd asked re-membered seeing him. Hospitals had no record of him. He'd vanished.

The stars in the sky stared into her picture window as she sat on the couch in the dark.

Where are you, Paul?

FORTY-NINE

Tuesday, December 7
St. Helena Island

Elias stood at the marsh's edge. A late afternoon mist covered the ground. He inhaled the salty, faint odor of rotten eggs. The dark clouds hovered, and a flock of blackbirds squawked noisily in the trees. He felt different . . . alive.

He stretched his arms high over his head. There was no pain in his shoulder, and his joints didn't ache. His nausea had left him. His lips curled at the corners as he watched the truck sink further from sight as the tide rose.

Elias unwrapped his prize as he sat in the corner of his shack. He could only remember having steak once in his life—when he was twelve. His father had gotten a big bonus at work and celebrated by buying treats to cook on the grill. The meal had been savory and delicious until his grandfather had ruined it—drunk.

The charcoal flame burned orange and yellow, reflecting in Elias's eyes. It soothed and excited him. Once the coals glowed red, he placed the two sirloin steaks on the grate. The meat sizzled, and gray smoke twirled into the air. He mumbled a simple prayer of thanks to the man who had made this meal possible.

He enjoyed the best meal of his life. Grilled steak and fried potatoes. He even had chocolate ice cream for dessert. Then, belly full, he moved the lantern to his corner and pulled out the paper that contained the last words of his plan. Then he got in his car and headed for Charleston. He needed to drop something off.

Elias watched the last employee hustle out the back door and pull their car out of the lot. His '89 Ford Crown Victoria went unnoticed in the corner spot by the dumpster. The warehouse was now dark—safe. He turned the key and eased his car nearer. He ignored the odor as he struggled to lift his cargo out of the trunk.

Bolt cutters invited him into the black space, and the beam led him to an excellent spot. He wiped the sweat on his forehead with the back of his gloved hand and drew one last big breath. It hadn't been easy, but his wrapped gift was in place. He moved boxes on the shelves until he was content that it was positioned correctly. The body would be found, but not easily.

It was 10:35 p.m. when Elias parked his car just off Market Street. People moved along the sidewalks until only a few remained. He flipped up his hood and climbed out. Then, head down, he walked into the still night.

He cast his eyes downward if anyone passed nearby. He acknowledged no one, even if they spoke. Until now, Elias would have been too afraid to venture out this early, but not now.

He found his spot. His eyes flared as he watched the brush slip through her hair; she was unaware of his presence. His pulse ticked up when she moved to the window and drew the shades, and the room went dark. She was perfect for the final step of his plan. She would make him powerful and whole—the enchanting woman he'd seen on television.

Elias whispered, "See you soon."

Wednesday, December 8
Hilton Head, South Carolina

Congressman Randolph Lee Jr. turned between the plumes of pampas grass swaying like feathers in the ocean breeze. His irritation increased. *I don't know why she insisted I come down here in the middle of the damn week.* He parked his pearl-white Jaguar alongside her charcoal Range Rover, exhaled, and headed up the steps.

"Hello, sweetheart," he called to her. Nothing.

He checked the den, master bedroom, and kitchen. Finally, he noticed movement on the back deck, and the sliding door opened. She glanced at him. "Randolph. I didn't hear you arrive." Beatrice stood with hands on hips and a sly smile. "How was the drive?"

He smiled. "It was fine. Of course, I'm busy with work, so it was hard to take the day off." He hid his building anger. "I'm not sure why this couldn't wait until Saturday."

"Oh, it's important we talk sooner than later." She motioned to the mahogany bar. "You want a drink?"

"Please. Bourbon and water would hit the spot." He watched as she poured the brown liquid into a short glass and added an ice cube and a splash of water.

She passed him his drink and motioned at the sliding door. "How about we go sit on the deck?"

His uneasiness started to climb. He'd seen this before. She was up to something. "Uh, sure."

They talked for thirty minutes about nothing. His work. Her charities. *She made me come down here for this bullshit?*

"Sweetheart. I love to sit and talk with you, but I'm swamped—"

She flipped her hand. "Okay. Let's get to it then. I want a divorce."

Randolph's eyes widened. "What? You know how much I love—"

"Save it, you cheating bastard. We had a deal, and you broke it."

"Baby, I don't understand. All I do is think about you and how to—"

"Screw every woman in sight," Beatrice said, finishing his sentence. "You're a lying piece of shit. I'm sick of it and have had enough."

"I . . . I don't know where this is coming from, darling."

She popped up, grabbed her purse, and tossed the photos at him. "You brought your crap here to Charleston. I told you I didn't give a damn what you did in Washington, but don't throw it in my face here."

He flipped through the pictures. His face went white. "Honey, this isn't me."

"Don't fucking keep lying! That's clearly you and your slut reporter. Of all things, you sneak off at the Preservation Society fundraiser to get you some."

His face grew hot. "Where did you get these, anyway? Were you having me followed?"

She laughed. "No. Someone actually saw you by accident but had enough sense to snap these. They thought I should know you're a scum dog. Like that was some big revelation."

He downed his drink and began pacing. "Sweetheart, this was a one-time transgression. I promise I'll never—"

"Shut the hell up, Randolph. Your smooth talking isn't saving your ass this time. You're done." She leaned close, and her eyes narrowed to slits. "Now sit down so I can tell you how this is gonna go."

He spread his arms. "Darling, we need to—"

"Sit!"

Obediently, he dropped to the floral chair. Tears dripped off his cheeks onto the deck boards. "Pleeease, honey. Please."

She roared again. "Your whining won't work. Here are your options. We get divorced quietly, and I get the Charleston house and this one. I keep what I brought to this marriage. According to my accountant, that's about eighty percent of our cash and investments." She laughed and flipped her hand. "I'll waive alimony."

He shook his head. "But, sweetheart, that'll leave me with almost nothing. I can't—"

"Don't lie to me! You'll have your town house in Washington, more than two million dollars, and God knows what else you stole. I should probably have someone see what other accounts you have hidden away."

Randolph sobbed harder. "There has to be another way."

She smiled. "Well, option two is we fight it out. Make it public and as big a scene as possible. These photos get shown on all the news channels. Oh, by the way, I've got some other photos that'd play well too."

"That would ruin me! I'd never get reelected. The voters would—"

"Stop sniveling." She tossed a stack of papers in his lap. "Sign these, and you can quietly go on your way. Say we had irreconcilable differences. Keep your position." She smiled. "Just think. You'll be able to have all the whores you want in your bed."

"You know this isn't right," he quietly replied. "You're taking advantage of me when I'm down."

Beatrice patted his shoulder. "Yeah. Yeah. Poor old Randolph." Her eyes narrowed. "You gonna sign the papers, or should I release these photos? My attorney is ready to roll, and once I call Daddy, I'm sure he'll be more than happy to help me. Either way, I'm done with you."

"But, honey, what about the kids?"

"They're grown adults, they'll be fine," she laughed. "Besides they're not stupid. They know about your affairs like everyone else in Charleston. Quiet or noisy way. Up to you."

Randolph rocked back and forth, his face buried in his hands. *She has my balls in a vise.* "Can't we negotiate? I shouldn't have to—"

"Sure. We can do that. It's option two. We fight it out, and perhaps you'll get more money."

"But it would cost me everything else."

Her eyes gleamed. "Yep."

He thumbed through the papers. "I need to have my attorney review these."

She patted his shoulder again. "Sure, honey bunny. There'll be no changes, though. Tell you what. I'll give you until five, then my attorney hits the button on the no-holds-barred option." She winked. "The photos will hit the six o'clock news. Speaking of the news, I'll give you the option of calling the News 4 station manager."

His red, puffy eyes glared at her. "What? I don't want to tell them about my—"

"Not that, stupid," she hissed at him. "The Watts woman. She has to go."

"How can I make that happen? I have no control over—"

"God, you're a weak little bastard. Figure it out."

His eyes followed her as she walked away. She had one more dig. "You know, Randolph. I think option two is best. You're too stupid to represent the great people of South Carolina."

Randolph flipped to the last page, signed it, and didn't bother closing the front door when he left.

———

Wendy Watts threw her belongings into a cardboard box. She fumed and mumbled to herself. "How can they fire me? What the hell is 'failure to demonstrate journalistic integrity?' Such bullshit!"

She tossed the box in her trunk, squealed her tires as she left the parking lot, and shot onto Highway 17. She pulled over to the curb at the foot of the Arthur Ravenel Jr. Bridge. The reality of what had happened hit her like a ton of bricks. Her dreams of anchoring and landing a job in New York evaporated in the salty air.

FIFTY-ONE

Thursday, December 9
Wando

The pelican was perched on the post—a brown body, white head, and long orangish bill. CJ's eyes were fixed on him, and she was lost in thought.

"Here's your coffee." Harry handed her the steaming mug and joined her in an Adirondack chair.

"Thanks, Uncle Harry."

He pointed. "I see your friend is back this morning."

"He is." She grinned. "I love watching him find breakfast and gobble it down. He's such a funny-looking bird."

"You sure you're not hungry? I'm happy to rustle you up some eggs and bacon."

She shook her head. "No. I'm good."

Harry cleared his throat. "You're supposed to be eating better. Thomas told me—"

She reached over and squeezed his arm. "Uncle Harry, I'm good." Cocking her head, she asked, "Are you and Thomas teaming up on me?"

He raised his hands in surrender. "No. No. It just came up in passing."

"Yeah. Right."

"Any news on Paul?"

She exhaled. "No. Not yet. I'm beyond worried now. It's been four days since anyone's seen or heard from him."

He stared across the marsh for a couple of minutes before he spoke again. "Did you bring the files?"

"I did." She held up a manila folder. "Are you sure you don't mind looking and giving me your opinion?"

"Not at all." He stood. "Let's spread the files out on the table and go through them."

She took one last look at the pelican and joined Harry. "Thanks. I have a profile, but there's something new that may add to it."

Harry listened as she went through what she had so far. Finally, he looked at her summary. "So, you believe he's local based on his knowledge of the area and Gullah practices? That makes sense. Tell me again why you believe he's young and smaller."

She pointed to the victim's physical characteristics. "He's picking smaller women so he can control them. His inexperience with hoodoo makes me think he's young."

He sighed. "That's weak, CJ."

"What do you mean?"

"I'm not experienced with hoodoo, and I'm sixty."

"Fair enough. Do you agree he has some type of health issue?"

He nodded. "I do. Like you said, the type of hoodoo rituals leads me to this conclusion." Harry looked at her notes and rubbed his chin. "And you think he's most likely Black?"

"Yes. Again, based on the Gullah connection. There have been and are some White people who practice hoodoo, but they're much fewer in number." CJ handed him a calendar. "There's one last thing. I believe he's killing and completing his rituals during the full moon."

His eyes narrowed. "What?"

She pointed to the circled dates. "Our first victim was killed really late on Friday, October 22. The second was killed on Saturday, November 20. There was a full moon on both nights."

Harry leaned back. "So, we add a little witchcraft to the hoodoo."

She peered at him as she nibbled at her thumb. "What do you think? Does this make sense?"

His chin slowly dipped. "It's possible." He stared at the calendar. "When's the next full moon?"

"Tuesday, December 21, and there's something else." She pointed to the date and then pulled another sheet out of the file. "For the first time in nearly four hundred years, a lunar eclipse and winter solstice will happen together—a trifecta of a full moon, a total lunar eclipse, and the winter solstice. The longest night of the year.

"The eclipse will begin just after midnight on Monday, December 20, with the total eclipse around three o'clock that morning. Who knows, but I'd guess he'll perform his next ritual around that time, when he thinks the moon is most potent."

Harry exhaled. "That's twelve days away. Not much time to find and stop him. Many in the occult world don't believe in doing their rituals during an eclipse, but who knows with this guy?" He scanned the article she'd handed him and read aloud. "'During this type of eclipse, the moon will gradually get darker and take on a rusty or blood-red color.'" He looked at CJ, and she whispered, "A blood moon."

She jumped when her cell phone buzzed. *Shit!* "Detective O'Hara." She listened as Helen let her know there was a scene she needed to get to ASAP. Her eyes grew wet. "I'll be there in fifteen."

"What?" Harry asked.

"We have a body." Her breath caught. "They think it's Paul."

Harry raced into the kitchen. "Coffeepot's off. Let's go."

"There's no need for you to go, Uncle—"

He grabbed her hand. "I'm going."

They ran to her truck and headed for downtown Charleston.

———

CJ and Harry pulled into the drive that ran along the side of a gray metal building. Ben stood near a back entrance, staring at the ground and pushing gravel with his foot. She parked beside a row of blue dumpsters and jumped out. "Uncle Harry, how about you wait here while I check it out?"

He nodded. "Yell if you need me."

CJ briskly crossed the parking lot filled with flashing blue lights. "Ben, what do we have? Is it Paul?"

Ben glanced up at her, his face ashen. He sniffed and wiped his nose. "Yeah. I'm afraid so. Eddie and Thomas are inside now."

She swallowed hard as her chest tightened. "Okay. I'll go take a look."

He grabbed her arm. "CJ, it's horrific. He's been dead awhile, and . . . well, the body isn't in—"

"I understand." She rubbed her forehead. "I need to look, though. Who found him?"

"One of the workers smelled something and moved some boxes. Paul was hidden behind them. He freaked out and ran to the foreman, who called us. Johnny's got the employees in the break room."

CJ steeled herself and entered the dimly lit space. *This whole place smells rancid—fishy and salty.* Thomas stood about fifty feet ahead. His eyes glistened under the harsh lights. The man had seen it all, but this hit him especially hard. He tipped his head as she got close, stepped forward, and cut her off. "This is bad. Collect yourself."

Without a word, she slowly nodded and stepped forward. Eddie and two techs were scanning the area around Paul. The plastic had been pulled back to allow an examination of his body. Her heart fell when she saw his body—a bloated abdomen, swollen tongue, and glassy eyes. The marbled skin was blotchy with reddish-purple streaks and pale spots. The odor made her eyes water.

Eddie stood and ushered her back. "How about we chat over here?" Like Thomas's, Eddie's face was pained and his eyes were wet. "We haven't found anything so far, but we'll be able to examine the body much closer back at the morgue. The guys are taking the shelf and plastic as well. So basically, we're cutting the shelf and taking it all with us."

Thomas joined them, and CJ pointed at Paul. "There's a wound in his chest. Is that the cause of death?"

"That's my guess," Thomas answered. "I didn't find any other wounds, but I only opened his shirt. I'll need to perform the autopsy to confirm." The world swirled, and CJ blinked, trying to clear her head. Thomas squeezed her arm. "You okay?"

"Yeah. I'm just . . . devastated." She exhaled and fought to do her job. "How about the weapon?"

"A knife," Thomas said flatly. "My best estimate now is he's been dead about four days." He glanced at Eddie. "Do you agree he wasn't killed here?"

"He was dropped here." The CSI sniffed. "There's not much blood, and the indentations from the shelving on the body aren't four days old."

"I think whoever killed Paul did it elsewhere and put him here two, three days ago," Thomas added.

In frustration, CJ stretched her neck from side to side. She jotted notes in her notebook. "Okay, guys. Thanks. I'll let you work. I know I don't need to emphasize we need to cover every square inch of the scene."

"Detective?"

CJ turned to find the six-foot-six Chief Walter Williams in the doorway. Stan stood at his side with his head hung. She walked over and joined them. "Yes, sir."

"Is it . . . Paul?"

"Yes, sir. I'm sorry to say it's him."

CJ had seen men cry, but seeing the chief fighting tears tore her up. Stan simply stared at the ground, breathing hard. Finally, the chief composed himself and fixed his eyes on her. "CJ, make sure we do everything—and I mean everything—to find who did this. You'll have whatever you need."

"Yes, sir."

"Keep me posted." He turned and exited. Stan shook his head and followed.

Johnny stuck his head in the door. "CJ, I have the whole building locked down. Black-and-whites have closed the entrances, and I've instructed them there's to be no press within a hundred yards of the area. The foreman and ten other employees are ready to be interviewed."

"Thanks, Johnny."

"Do you want Ben and me to handle it? You could talk to the guy who found the body. We'd take the rest."

"Yes. That'd be great. I'd like to stay here and see what Eddie and the crew find." *And I don't want to leave Paul.*

Harry, who was standing by Ben, spoke up. "Let me know if you need my help."

CJ wiped at her eyes and sniffed. "You know what, Uncle Harry? I'd be happy if you interviewed the guy who found Paul for me." *It's not official, but I'm not leaving Paul.*

Harry took off with Ben and Johnny.

Thirty minutes later, CJ watched as Eddie and the techs lifted the shelf and body for transport. Thomas joined her. "Find anything else, Thomas?" she asked.

"Nothing other than what we've discussed. I'll start the autopsy early tomorrow morning. Eddie and his crew will work through the night to examine the shelf and plastic in the lab before I start my work." He cleared his throat. "I assume you'll want to be there."

"Yes. I want to be there."

Harry returned and joined them. He let CJ know the man who had found Paul didn't have any useful information. Her eyes were glued to the four men pushing the shelf and body to the van. A tidal wave of sadness washed over her. Her boss, and more importantly, her friend, rolled past her. As tears ran down her cheeks, Thomas and Harry put their arms around her.

The coroner's van pulled away, and her eyes followed.

Now I have two killers to hunt down.

PART THREE

COLD MOON

The full moon at the time of year when the cold winter air settles in and the nights become long and dark. Also known as the long nights moon.

FIFTY-TWO

Friday, December 10
Downtown Charleston

CJ pulled her hair up under the cap and slipped on latex gloves. She sucked in a deep breath and pushed open the shiny stainless-steel door to the exam room. Thomas and Byron glanced up at her. Thomas motioned for her to join them. "Good morning. I'm just finishing up. Give me a couple more minutes."

She stood just inside the door, trying to work up her courage. Autopsies were never pleasant, but when the body belonged to someone you cared about, it took it to another level.

Thomas cleared his throat. "I thought perhaps we'd use photos to show you what I've found and not the body. Spare you a bit."

"Thanks. Whatever works best."

He pointed to a monitor. "Byron, let's pop up the photos of the wound first, please." She moved next to him and gasped as the image of Paul's body came into view. Thomas paused to let her collect herself.

"The only wound I found on the body was the knife wound. This was the cause of death and consisted of a single thrust of the weapon." He pointed to a dark red area. "The edge is jagged, which indicates the knife was dull, and the perpetrator twisted it, causing tearing."

She leaned into the screen. "Wait. You said the knife was dull?"

"Yes. The cut isn't clean like one made by a sharper instrument. The depth of the wound tells me whatever our killer used had a blade about six inches long."

Her pulse ticked up. "We had a dull knife used in the murders of the two young women. Could this be the same guy?"

Thomas exhaled. "It's possible, but difficult to tell since our wounds are so different. Here we have a stab pattern while the others were long lacerations."

She wasn't sure she could stand the answer, but she had to ask. "Did . . . did Paul suffer?"

"Death wouldn't have been instant, but it would have been quick. The blade hit his heart."

She sniffed and blinked away tears.

"Let's look at something else I found," he said. A fuzzy yellowish object appeared on the screen. "I found this hair near the wound. It doesn't match Paul's hair. I'll send it to the lab for analysis."

"Do you think we can obtain DNA?"

"I'm not sure." He frowned. "We'll have to see if the lab can extract any. I can't tell if we have enough of the follicle."

"SLED has an excellent hair expert, so let's get the sample to Columbia," replied CJ.

He nodded. "I'll have it couriered up within the hour."

"Anything else?"

"No. Not really."

"Okay. Listen, is it possible for you to provide me with a set of the photos of the wounds for our two murdered women and Paul?"

He rubbed his chin. "Uh, sure. Byron, can you send those to the detective, please?"

CJ stripped off her protective gear, got dressed, and hustled to her truck. Eddie had left her a message, and she was interested in what he'd found. She called Robert as she left the parking lot.

She let him know about Paul and what information they had so far. Like everyone, he took the news of Paul's murder hard. She gave him her hunch about the knife, and he agreed to have his team analyze the photos ASAP. She ended the call. *Was it the same person?*

She met Eddie in a triple-garage-size room where he'd laid out the shelving and plastic that had been under Paul's body. He was on his hands and knees, scanning with a bright handheld light. Then, finally, he snapped off the light and stood.

"You said you found something interesting in your message?" CJ asked.

He nodded. "Come over here and take a look." He peered through the microscope's eyepiece and stepped back.

She stared. "What is that?"

"It's some type of fiber. I'm not a hundred percent sure, but I think it's from carpet. I'll ask the analyst to confirm. The warehouse where they found the body didn't have carpet. In fact, there was no carpet in the whole building. Someone had to introduce this to the scene."

"You think we can determine where it came from?"

Eddie shrugged. "I'm not sure, but we should be able to identify the source." Excitedly, he pointed to a steel table. "Here's something really good. We found a fingerprint on the plastic. It was on the inside corner. So, it can't be Paul's since he was . . ."

A vise gripped her chest, and she struggled to breathe. Eddie paused and took her hand. "You okay?"

She puffed a breath. "I'm fine. How soon until we can run it through the system?"

"Should be by later this afternoon. I've got a tech working on it now." He pointed to one other item. "I can't be sure what it is yet, but there's some type of stain on Paul's shirt near the neckline. It could be from him, but we'll analyze it for possible DNA."

CJ added to her notes.

- *Knife*
- *Hair*
- *Fiber*

- *Fingerprint*
- *Stain*

She called the chief and advised him on what they had so far. He agreed he'd make the calls to expedite things.

CJ found Sam in the conference room. Like everyone, she was devastated and doing her best to do her job. Wiping her eyes, she helped CJ add information to the evidence board.

CJ stepped back from the board. "Okay, Sam. We've summarized what we have so far. We're missing two huge pieces of information—where Paul was killed and what happened to his truck. Where are we on the alerts?"

Sam went to her desk and held up a list. "I've alerted every force in the state to be on the lookout for the truck."

"Okay, great. There are so many places Paul's vehicle could be hidden." *Needle in a haystack.* "I can't imagine that whoever killed him would be driving it. That would be stupid." She leaned closer to the board, her eyes scanning. "We have some good leads here. With any luck, we could have DNA and the fingerprint of whoever murdered Paul."

Sam rejoined her. "What does the note about the knife mean?"

CJ pushed a stray strand of hair off her cheek. "I'm not sure exactly. I'm hoping we can nail down what type of knife was used. I also have something else gnawing at me."

Sam's puzzled eyes met hers. "Huh?"

Her forehead wrinkled. "The wound patterns of our two murdered women look very similar to Paul's wound."

The younger woman's eyes went wide. "You think the killer is the same person?"

"Hmm . . . I'm not sure what I'm thinking. It doesn't seem like the three murders are connected, but I'm bugged by the similarities between the wounds made by the weapon." Rubbing the back of her neck, she added, "The methods aren't the same, but still . . . We need to find out where Paul was killed. We know he went to St. Helena to have lunch with Paul Jr., and his body was found here in Charleston. That gives us almost eighty miles of distance to cover." CJ dropped into a chair. "Let's set up a call with departments from St. Helena to North Charleston. I'd like to brief them all on what we have and make sure we've got everyone working together."

Sam rushed to her desk. "I'm on it. I'll aim for a three o'clock call."

"Let Stan and the chief know as well," CJ added. "I'd like to have them here for the call. I'll ask the chief to give a press conference, so the public is helping us find the truck." As Sam began making calls, CJ's dizziness returned, and she laid her forehead on the edge of the table. Her heart ached.

Every department was keen to help since an officer had lost his life, and Sam arranged the calls within minutes. Many knew Paul from his long service. Then, a few minutes before three, Walter and Stan entered the room and slid into chairs. Their eyes were glazed.

CJ provided a briefing, and everyone agreed to add patrols to their regular workload. She hit the end button on the speakerphone and glanced up at Walter. "Chief, are you okay with a press conference to get the public's help?"

"Absolutely." He stood and headed for the door. "I'll arrange it for five and make sure the news stations carry it at six o'clock."

CJ and Sam squeezed into the press room as the chief delivered the critical aspects of the case to the assembled media. He provided the details and a photo of Paul's truck and asked anyone with information to call. Afterward, he answered questions from a room full of reporters. CJ scanned the crowd. *Where's Wendy Watts? I can't believe she'd miss this.*

FIFTY-THREE

Friday, December 10
St. Helena Island

Elias's pale blue eyes flashed as the tall Black police chief pleaded for help. He took a break from mopping and stood rigid in front of the Zenith color television. The damn thing was old, and the colors were off, but it was better than nothing.

The tall man talked about a truck that was missing. Elias smiled. *I know where it is, but you'll never find it.* He held up a photo, and the screen displayed a larger image. *Yep, that's it.* He listened as the man gave a number to call if anyone saw the vehicle.

Elias reached for the switch. If old man Moberley caught him watching, he'd be in trouble. *Wait!* He saw her standing in the background and moved closer to the screen. His fingers caressed the glass. The last piece of his plan.

He stood mesmerized until the front door opened. Then, quickly, he turned the television off and went back to mopping. He was working his way into the corner when . . . *Oh, shit!* He kneeled and looked closely . . . blood.

"Where the hell are you?" Moberley shouted. "This place better be spotless, or I'm kicking your scrawny ass."

Rushing to the door of the back room, Elias called out, "I'm here, sir."

"Were you sleeping back there?" He stared at Elias's face. "Why the hell are you sweating?"

"No, sir. I wasn't asleep. I've been working hard, and I'm almost done. I want to be sure—"

"You should already be finished. Jesus, your ass is slow. What time did you get here, anyway?"

"At five, sir."

Moberley flipped his hand. "You should be done by now. How much longer are you going to take?"

Elias needed more time. He had to make sure he'd cleaned up the blood. "Maybe an hour."

Glancing at his watch, his boss replied, "So, midnight. Well, you better do a damn good job. When I come in the morning, I'm gonna inspect it, and if it's not done right, I'm not paying you one red cent. Got it?"

"Yes, sir. I'll be sure to make it spotless."

His nose almost touched Elias's. "And so you know, I'm only paying you for five hours of work. Make sure the door locks when you leave."

Elias went back to the corner after the door closed. The red stain was faint, but it was there. Fortunately, he did most of the stocking, and no one else went in the room that often.

Using a wire brush, he was able to remove the stains. He looked under the counter, grabbed a flashlight, and inspected to be sure. *That was close.* Elias propped the back door open and carried the bucket outside. The mop water soaked into the gravel. Water from the hose ensured any blood was gone.

He walked through the gravel, onto the grass, and up to the marsh's edge. Even with the flashlight, it was too dark to see, but he was sure the truck wasn't visible. He smiled. *I know where it is, but you'll never find it.*

His heart fluttered, and he whispered, "Maybe I should have put the body in there with the truck." *That would have been bad luck, though.*

———

Grannie jerked herself awake and sat up. Her breath was ragged. Moonlight had found the crack in the curtains and run across the foot of her bed. Her frail fingers fumbled with the lamp knob, and the room went bright.

After slipping her feet into pink house shoes, she pulled herself up. The house was silent except for the night noises—occasional creaks. She found her way to the refrigerator and poured a glass of milk. She opened the front door and eased herself into the rocker. She listened—nothing.

The air was heavy and cold. A shiver ran through her, and she wrapped her blanket tighter. She was warm, but the cold chill refused to leave. She rocked, slow and steady. An owl broke the night's silence with a screech like the scream of a woman. Her lids closed and she saw him.

Skin, black but bleached, eyes pale blue—no eyebrows. His hair was close cropped and golden, almost yellow. His nose was broad, almost flat, with large nostrils. As he stared at her, his eyes flashed pink.

She squeezed her eyes tighter and rocked faster.

The man stood gazing at the marsh . . . there was a truck underwater. The blood of an honorable man ran underneath the ground at his feet. He clutched something in his pocket. It was small and precious to him, gave him power, and eased his pain.

Grannie's head twitched as she looked through his eyes at a woman she recognized.

She was vital to him. She was beautiful, with feminine features. His hand rose, and the knife came down, and the woman screamed her last scream. He took her heart, raised it skyward, and placed it in the circle of six white candles. The moon turned to blood.

FIFTY-FOUR

Monday, December 13
St. Helena Island

When CJ pulled out and drove the route to St. Helena, the streetlights illuminated the city. Along the way, she stopped at service stations, convenience marts, and restaurants. No one remembered seeing Paul or recognized his truck.

After getting gas just past the Marine Corps air station, CJ climbed into the seat and turned the key. Her cell phone started buzzing, and she glanced at the number before answering. "Hey, Eddie. What's up?"

"We have a match. The prints are the same."

"Wait. What match?"

"Oh, jeez. Sorry. The print on the plastic under Paul's body matches the one we found on the medallion in the mojo bag left at the second murder scene."

The vise gripped CJ's chest. "Are you sure?"

"Yes. We've triple-checked. The prints are identical."

CJ exhaled. "So, we know the same person murdered two women and killed Paul. We just don't know who. Still nothing in the system?"

"No. Sorry."

Why would he kill Paul?

CJ scribbled some notes. "Anything else?"

"We have also confirmed the fiber is from a carpet. Specifically, the type installed in Ford automobiles in the late eighties, early nineties. It appears it was transferred when the body was moved."

"What type of vehicle?"

"We're still running that to ground. A fiber expert in Columbia has promised to call me if she has more."

CJ rubbed her eyes. "Okay. If she needs help or a second opinion, I'll call Robert for the FBI's support. Any news on the hair or stain?"

Eddie sighed. "No. Sorry. The lab wasn't able to pull DNA."

Robert was in Quantico, wrapping up the loose ends of his latest case, when CJ called him. His serial killer in Virginia had been caught and stowed away in a cell. He told her he was happy to process more evidence and help her catch Paul's killer in any way he could.

CJ was quiet a moment, then asked, "Robert, can you help me with something else?"

"Sure," he said.

"Do you know anything about clairvoyance? Remember I told you about Grannie and how many believe she can see things?"

"Hmm. I know a little. Are you asking me if I believe clairvoyance is real?"

CJ's finger tapped on the wheel. "I guess, and how it supposedly works."

He paused and then spoke. "I do believe in clairvoyance. Not everything, but I've seen enough to know it's real."

"So, how does it work?" CJ asked.

"Well, I'm no expert, and I can find out more for you, but some possess perception abilities. Some can visualize the past and fill in the blanks. That's called retrocognition. Others perceive the future—precognition. I've witnessed both. A third type is referred to as remote viewing, which I don't understand, to be honest. I've not experienced this."

She shook her head. *This sounds too weird.* "I have a hard time believing in this."

"Yeah," Robert chuckled. "It's hard to imagine someone can see the past or future without being there." He cleared his throat. "Let's try this. I'll use you as an example."

Okay . . .

"When you go to a crime scene, you observe what's there, correct? But do you ever visualize how the crime was committed? You know, do you see it in your mind?"

She frowned. "Yes, but that's different."

"Not really," he said. "The best detectives tend to have a sixth sense and the ability to get in the criminal's head. See through their eyes, visualizing the crime. They are also able to perceive future events."

CJ wasn't convinced, and Robert must have sensed it. "Think of it this way. We do profiles based on hard data and an assessment of what we believe the perp's behaviors are, right? Extraordinary profilers go beyond what's taught in the classroom."

She still hadn't connected those dots. "I suppose that's similar, but I'm still struggling to understand."

Robert laughed. "I agree it's not exact, but you actually have this ability. Some call it instinct. Your instincts are one of the reasons I hold you in such high regard as a detective."

"Do you think people could be right about Grannie?"

He sighed. "Hard to tell. You said Paul believed she has this ability. Did he say why he thought she was clairvoyant?"

"He did." A sharp pain ran through her chest. "I don't really remember how he described it. Paul believed it, though."

"Will she talk to you?"

"I'm not sure. She hasn't been willing to so far."

"Keep trying. It can't hurt, and if Grannie does have abilities, she could help you solve your case. Listen, I need to run, but please keep me posted."

CJ sat fixated on the rain trickling down her windshield. A sudden chill ran through her.

———

Sheets of water covered Charleston as CJ pulled in behind her apartment. The light of day had left. She slipped as she raced up the steps, nearly losing her notebook and files. *Damn it!* She fought the lock and found dryness. Her apartment was dark and lonely.

She decided to exchange her wet clothes for a pair of sweats. Her eyes scanned through her cabinets and fridge—sparse. A trip to the grocery store was past due. But instead, she poured green tea in a mug, grabbed some crackers and cheese, and settled on the couch—a sad dinner after no lunch. A sudden bright flash lit up her picture window, followed by a low rumble.

Her cell phone rang, and she smiled at the number. "Hey, Sam."

"You make it back okay?"

"Yeah, I made it back before the hard stuff started coming down," CJ replied.

"Any more news on Paul?"

"Nope, not yet. No one's seen the truck. We're still trying to figure out where he was killed."

"If you haven't had dinner, I made a chicken casserole and can bring you some."

"That's sweet, but I just ate dinner." *Stale crackers and hard cheese.* "Plus, you don't need to be out in this storm. I'm gonna go over a few files and turn in."

"Okay. I'm happy to swing over if you change your mind."

CJ hung up and stretched out on the couch as the flashes and rumbles continued. Then, finally, exhaustion took her, and she slept.

A short, frail man with no face waited until the lights went out, then approached. He knew which window he could open and climbed into the house without a sound. As he stood looking down, her chest rose and fell until he struck. CJ couldn't breathe, and her world went dark. A crude knife cut deep, and the hotness spread. Her heart was warm in his hands before he placed it in a plastic bag and left the way he had come.

A loud crash of lightning rattled her awake. "Holy shit!"

She staggered for more tea and waited for the morning light.

FIFTY-FIVE

Wednesday, December 15
The Business District

Funerals were the worst, and CJ hated them—they gave her flashbacks of her parents and sister. She crawled out of her warm bed. She massaged her neck, and her temples throbbed. *You can do this. You gotta pay your respects to Paul.* She wiped her tears, stood, and drifted to the kitchen.

She sipped her black coffee. A lone seagull sat on the rooftop across the street—she swore he was looking straight at her. At least the rain had stopped, and with any luck, the weather would cooperate. She checked the time and headed for the shower.

Standing in her robe, she ran her fingers down the navy blue uniform hanging on the door. The only time she'd worn it had been for her department photo—a happy occasion. She dropped her robe and started the task of getting dressed. For her last step, she added her badge and Glock. She sniffed at herself in the mirror and pulled her hair into a ponytail. *Hold it together.* Hat in hand, she locked the door.

The crowd was massive. Formally dressed members of law enforcement from every nearby department were out in full force. Typically, with so many officers gathered, there would be a buzz, laughing, joking, but not today. Instead, there were only stern, tight faces and sad eyes everywhere CJ looked. Strong, grown men and women doing their best to remain composed.

It was customary for law enforcement personnel to attend a funeral for a fallen comrade. CJ had participated in several police funerals in Boston, but she hadn't seen anything like this. In addition to law enforcement, it appeared the whole city had turned out. In their Sunday best, men, women, and even some children had lined the sidewalks to see Paul off.

The church was spectacular. The towering white columns and white paint were broken by only the honey-brown doors and windows elegantly adorned with stained glass. Trees of various shades of green—magnolia, oak, and palm—wrapped around the building.

Ben was regal in his formal attire, with a flat hat trimmed in gold. He worked his way to where she stood and hugged her. "Shitty day, CJ."

She bit her lip. "Yep." They stood shoulder to shoulder in silence as Sam, Harry, Thomas, and Eddie joined them—even Bill, Will, and Craig joined the group.

A man in his late fifties with close-cropped black hair and onyx-brown eyes crossed the street—FBI special agent Robert Patterson. He smiled at CJ, though his heart wasn't in it. "I'm so sorry, CJ. Paul was a great cop and a better person."

"Thanks, Robert. I'm glad you came, but—"

"I wouldn't miss this one. Unfortunately, I have to head back to Quantico after the service and can't go to the cemetery, but I wanted to pay my respects to Paul." He offered Ben his hand. "Ben, thanks for letting me know where you guys would be . . . so many people are here. Is this normal for a police funeral here in Charleston?"

Ben nodded. "Yeah. Pretty much. We do have more civilians here than I've seen in the past. Makes sense since Paul did a lot for the community outside of work."

It was silent again until bagpipes faintly sounded in the distance. CJ's chest tightened, and breathing was difficult. She hated bagpipes—they only played during sad times.

The humming tone whined louder as it led the long black hearse up Market Street. Law enforcement officers saluted as Paul's final ride through Charleston passed them. Other heads were bowed, and the only other sound was sniffles and sobs. Finally, the procession came to a halt in front of the church steps, and the pallbearers did their duty.

As they removed their hats, Ben led CJ and Sam to the row assigned to CID personnel, and the rest of the group squeezed into the standing-room-only back area. Over the next hour, CJ was numb—and lost. People spoke, but she didn't hear the words of the mayor, the chief, the councilman, and the union representative.

The last speaker, and the most difficult to watch, was Paul Jr., who would have made his father proud. Paul's only son stood tall and spoke of how his father had raised him, taught him right from wrong, and how much he would miss him. He broke down at the end and the chief had to escort him off the podium. No one had dry eyes.

As the six men lifted the casket again, the bagpipes played Paul's favorite song, "Amazing Grace." Ben leaned close to CJ and whispered, "Let's go. We're part of the last call." They exited the side door and joined a small group of officers around a cruiser. CJ's legs struggled to carry her.

The cruiser's radio crackled to life, and Helen's voice came in. She made a call for Lieutenant Paul Grimes to respond. Silence. She made a second call—no response. Finally, with a shaky voice, she made the announcement, "The officer hasn't responded." CJ's shoulders shook, and she lost it.

The hour-and-a-half-long ride to St. Helena had very little conversation. Ben drove with Harry in the passenger seat and CJ and Sam in the back. The sun sparkled on the water, and the clouds lightened over the long line of vehicles to the small cemetery, which would be Paul's final home.

CJ endured "Amazing Grace" one more time as the casket was lowered. Grannie stepped forward after the twenty-one bells and the chief's flag presentation to Paul Jr. She wore a black dress and hat with a petite red rose. Her voice quivered as she spoke in the Gullah language with her eyes shut. Her green cat eyes flashed at CJ when she finished. A sudden chill went through CJ. *She knows who did this.*

Charleston appeared as they crossed the Ashley River Memorial Bridge, and Ben asked if anyone wanted something to eat. No one was hungry. "Harry, I'll drop you off at your car and take the ladies home," he said.

Ben grasped CJ's hand as they sat in his truck in front of her apartment. "Are you sure you don't want to grab something to eat? I'm sure you've had nothing—"

"No. I'm fine. I just need to be alone right now."

"Okay. But you need to eat—"

"No, Ben!"

"Okay. Okay."

CJ entered her dark apartment. She stripped off her uniform and put on a pair of jeans and a sweatshirt. She sat staring at the fog over the harbor as the rain returned, and she sipped a beer. Then, after she'd finished the last of the six-pack, she slipped on her rain jacket and splashed down the steps.

FIFTY-SIX

Friday, December 17
The French Quarter, Charleston

Sam tried again. Voicemail. *Where is she?* She'd called Ben and Johnny, and neither had seen nor heard from CJ. She exhaled and paced around the conference room. The rain pelted the window, and the Ashley River was hidden by dreariness. She punched at the numbers, and a hoarse voice greeted her.

"Hello, Harry. Have you seen CJ?"

"Uh . . . no. Not since the funeral on Wednesday. She's not at work?"

"No. I haven't seen her, and I can't reach her on her cell. She was supposed to go to St. Helena yesterday to search for Paul's car. I didn't talk to her, but I figured she was busy or out of range."

Harry sensed her panic. "How about Ben or—"

"No. She's not spoken to Ben or Johnny. I walked down, and dispatch hadn't talked to her. Stan told me he hadn't seen her. It's not like her not to be here and . . ." Tears overtook her.

"No. It's not like CJ at all," Harry replied. "I'll try her and call you back. I'm headed to her apartment."

"I'll meet you there."

———

Harry and Sam knocked on CJ's door again. Nothing. There was no noise from inside, and the picture window was dark. The curtains in the bedroom were drawn. CJ's truck was parked under the carport in the back—locked. Harry ran his hand across the hood. "She's not been out anywhere recently."

"Let's check if Sal has seen her. She loves his coffee," Sam said. They took off for the coffee shop.

No luck. Sal hadn't seen her for the last two days. They walked back to her apartment and knocked again—still nothing.

"Hey, guys. Can I help with something?"

George Watkins, CJ's landlord, stood at the bottom of the stairs.

Sam blurted, "We can't find CJ. Have you seen her?"

George grimaced. "I think I saw her on Tuesday." He glanced over his shoulder. "Her truck's here. Could someone have picked her up?"

Harry's heart went into his throat. "I'm not sure who. We've called everyone we can think of, and no one's seen her."

"Wait a minute. I'll be right back." George raced around the corner and was back within minutes. "I have a spare key to her apartment."

"Did you find her?" Ben appeared, taking two steps at a time.

Sam shook her head. "Not yet. George has a key, so we're gonna—"

Ben pushed past her. "Let me go in first. In case . . ."

George turned the key and stepped back. Ben crossed the threshold to darkness, except for a sliver of light under the bedroom door. He drew his weapon, flipped on his Maglite, and eased forward. Sam clung to Harry in the doorway.

"CJ? This is Ben. Are you here?" He twisted the knob and opened the door to the dim cave. His breath caught when he saw her sprawled across the bed wearing nothing but a T-shirt. Her still body was tangled in the sheets, and her hair was matted and wet. "Oh my God."

He crossed the room and leaned close. Suddenly her chest rose, and there was a low moan. He gently touched her cheek. "CJ, are you okay?"

Her bloodshot, puffy eyes opened. "I'm fine," she slurred. "Leave me alone."

"Damn it, CJ. You're drunk." He reached for her. "What in the hell—"

"Get the fuck out!"

Harry flipped the switch to light up the room and stepped to the bed. "What's going on?"

"I'm sick," CJ moaned.

Harry grabbed her arm. "You're not sick. How much have you had to drink? This whole room stinks of vomit." He pulled her upright. "You scared the shit out of us." He pulled the hair off her face, hugged her, and his eyes grew wet. "I love you."

She groaned and put her head on his chest. "I'm sorry."

Sam touched Ben's arm. "Let's give them a minute." They went and stood just outside the bedroom door.

Harry controlled his frustration, and CJ admitted she'd been drinking since she'd gotten back from the funeral. She needed to escape from the pain—too many people she cared about were lost. The room was messy, with clothes all over the floor, empty liquor bottles, and puke. He rocked her as she cried.

"Hey, Sam," Harry called.

Sam raced into the room. "I'm right here."

Harry smiled at her. "I think our girl is ready for a shower. You think you can help her?"

She hustled to the bathroom. "I'll start the water." The shower hissed moments later.

Ben stuck his head in. "You need me to do anything?"

Harry shook his head. "I don't think so. I'll have Sam help her shower and dress. We'll need to change the sheets and clean up in here. I'll help Sam with that."

"Okay. How about I go to Sal's and grab her a coffee and something to eat? I'll make sure it's something to cure a hangover."

Harry winked at him, and Ben took off. George said his goodbyes and offered his and his wife's help. "Let me know if she needs anything. We absolutely adore her."

<hr>

Sam took over from Harry and carefully helped CJ to the bathroom. She undressed her and made sure CJ didn't slip as she stepped into the warm spray. "Okay. Put your head under so we can wet your hair. I'll wash it for you."

"I can do it," CJ complained. She pushed Sam's hands away. "I can wash my own hair."

Sam had had all she could take, and she exploded. "Damn it, CJ, you can't do it yourself," she replied. "You're still drunk. I'm sick and tired of you not taking care of yourself. You don't listen to anyone. You don't eat right, don't get enough sleep, and drink too much. Get your damn shit together!"

CJ's eyes were wide. Mild-mannered Sam, the girl who mothered everyone and never seemed to have a cross word, was pissed. "I . . . I'm sorry, Sam."

Sam pulled her out of the shower, wrapped the towel around her and hugged her. "You scared the shit out of me and so many others who love you. Please, please listen to those who are trying to help you."

"Okay. I promise I'll do better." CJ wiped her eyes.

"Now, let's get you back in the shower so I can wash your hair."

CJ feebly smiled. "Yes, ma'am."

Once she was showered, Sam dried her hair and took her back to the bedroom. She found clean clothes and put them on CJ. The apartment was back in order in a couple of hours, trash was collected, and CJ wore her fluffiest sweats. Sam insisted on putting cushy socks on her.

Ben had dropped off a thermos of coffee and a dozen fresh-baked bagels. Sal had sent a box of spreads—cream cheese, butter, and jelly. CJ choked down half a bagel and a couple of cups of coffee.

Harry tucked CJ in and kissed her forehead. He and Sam had agreed someone should stay with her, and Sam insisted it be her. "I'll take good care of her. I'll have Ben bring some stuff, and I'll whip her up some dinner."

CJ's eyes fluttered open around six in the evening. Her head was a drum and her mouth a desert. She heard Ben and Sam whispering outside the door. How could she have been so stupid? How could she have let everyone find her at her worst? *May as well get this over with.*

"Hey, guys."

Sam rocketed to her. "How are you feeling? Any better?"

CJ pinched her temples. "My head's throbbing and my tongue's sticky, but I feel better."

She washed the aspirin Sam handed her down with a tumbler of water and sat on the couch between Sam and Ben. "I don't know what to say. I'm so disgusted with myself and embarrassed." Four arms wrapped around her.

Ben's lips found her cheek. "It's okay, CJ. We're here for you, and you'd be there for us." He gave a quick squeeze and whispered in her ear, "Just don't let it happen again." She caught him grinning at her.

The room smelled terrific. The aroma of spices and freshly baked bread filled the air. Ben had gone by Sully's and picked up spaghetti, Caesar salad, and garlic bread—with hush puppies as an appetizer. After they ate, Ben headed home, and Sam went to her apartment to pick up some clothes. CJ surrendered the thought of staying by herself for the night. Sam wouldn't have it.

Elias pulled his car close to the bushes in an alley by her apartment. He was hidden. This was an important night—the final step in his plan. His heartbeat grew faster, and his fingers caressed his mojo bag.

FIFTY-SEVEN

Friday, December 17
The Business District

Sam crossed King Street and turned into the narrow drive-way to her town home. *Why is my motion light not working?* She gingerly made her way up the dark back steps with her keys in hand.

Dropping her clothes in a pile, she hopped into the shower. She planned to be quick, so she could get back to CJ. After drying her hair, she pulled on a pair of pink sweats and laced up her white tennis shoes. *I need a change of clothes for tomorrow.*

Sam grabbed a small overnight bag from under the bed and tossed in what she needed. A change of underwear, a pair of jeans, and a canary-yellow sweater. *Where's my rain-coat, just in case? Oh, yeah. The hall closet.*

Bag in hand, she made a stop in the kitchen. Leftover lasagna would work for lunch tomorrow. She wrapped the dish in aluminum foil and placed it into a brown bag with red Piggly Wiggly lettering. She smiled at the pig in the butcher's hat.

Carefully, Sam made the trip back down the dark steps. *I can't believe that damn motion light is out again!* She un-locked the passenger-side door and bent over.

She'd just put her bag and leftovers in the passenger seat when someone grabbed her from behind. Sam strug-gled to free herself, but the grip around her neck was tight. She pitched forward, slamming into her silver Honda Civic as her world went pitch black.

Her eyes began to focus as she began to wake up. Her an-kles, wrists, and mouth were taped, and her skin stung as if she'd been dragged. He pushed her body over the edge and into the trunk, and she landed hard on the cold trunk floor. She kicked as the lid closed, and her world went dark again. The engine sounded, and she rocked as he pulled away.

Sam gave up trying to break free of the tape, and her kicking the lid was a waste of energy. She wasn't sure where she was going, but the tires' humming on the as-phalt seemed to last forever. She was tossed against the hard metal of the trunk as the humming turned to bumps, and the noise changed to gravel crunching and limbs scratching the sides of the car.

Elias's heart raced as he covered the last thirty yards to the shack. He was grateful he had been able to ambush her outside and not in her bedroom. The distance from there to his car was shorter, and she'd fought harder than he'd expected. Elias exhaled as he turned off the ignition and listened to the banging in the back before he got out and went into the shack.

He stood in the center of the room and scanned it. He'd turned on the lanterns and made sure the chain was ready. All he needed was to move her.

Elias returned to the car and tied a lantern to a tree limb. He popped open the trunk and lifted it to see wild, wide eyes. Sam kicked at him, narrowly missing. She would fight, and there was no way he could choke her again.

The dim light reflected from the white stone knife. He waved it in front of her eyes. "I don't want to hurt you. Please don't make me."

Sam stopped struggling and stared at the man with strange eyes and uneven, close-cropped yellow hair. His eyes were an odd shade of pale blue, seeming transparent in the lantern's glow. She kicked hard again, throwing her lower half over the edge of the trunk. He yanked her by her feet onto the muddy ground. He threw himself on top of her, and a knife touched her throat.

"Please stop fighting me. I don't want to hurt you."

She lay still, breathing hard, and stopped her muffled screaming. She squirmed under him but stopped at the added pressure on the blade. "Please don't fight," he whispered, almost begging.

Her head spun as he yanked her up to a sitting position. "I'm sorry if riding in the trunk was uncomfortable. I need to take you inside. The house will be warmer. We can do it one of two ways."

He leaned closer, being careful of her feet. She'd already landed two kicks, and she knew it had hurt him. "If you don't try to run—and there's nowhere to run to—I'll cut the tape off your ankles. After that, you can walk in. Or I can drag you, but that'll be bad for both of us. Either way, you won't get away." He pressed harder on the knife against her neck. "I'll use my knife if you make me. Do you wanna walk and promise not to run?"

Her arms ached from being behind her back, and the tape cut into her wrists. Her ankles were taped and even if she was able to run, she wouldn't get far. She also had no idea where she was. She slowly nodded.

He gave her one last warning and cut the tape on her ankles loose. She wobbled to her feet as he pulled on her arm. She thought about running, but she thought better of it as the knife pressed to her throat again. "Please walk slowly, so you don't fall."

The building was no more than a damp, musty, cold shack. The only light was from four lanterns, one in each of the room's corners. A small wooden table and two chairs were the only visible furniture—except for a mattress with stained blankets on the floor in the corner.

A push propelled her through a side door and into a smaller room no larger than a jail cell. The room only had one window, and it was boarded up. She tripped over a piece of metal and fell facedown into the dirt and grime. His weight pressed down on her. "Please be still."

Elias quickly taped her calves together so she couldn't kick, and then carefully secured a chain to her right ankle. Sam moaned as he jerked it tight and clicked the lock shut. He whispered in her ear, "I'm sorry."

Sam managed to roll herself over. He stood staring at her, silhouetted by the lantern in the other room. He motioned to the ring with a chain connected to it. "You're chained to the floor, so you can't go far. I'll leave the tape on your mouth and wrists for now, but if you're good, I'll take them off for you to eat. I have this foam pad for you to sleep on. I'll give you some blankets later. Night brings the cold."

Her eyes followed him as he left and returned with a five-gallon bucket. "I don't have a bathroom, so this will have to do. I can help when you need to go." The door shut, and she was left in the darkness, broken only by the slices of light between the planks.

Tears ran down her cheeks as her shoulders shook.

FIFTY-EIGHT

Saturday, December 18
Downtown Charleston

CJ woke up on the couch with a stiff neck. At least her head had stopped throbbing and her nausea was gone. She flipped off the blanket, stretched, and slipped into her dark bedroom. *Sam must still be asleep in my bed.* She leaned closer to the bed in the dim light. There was no Sam.

She turned on the shower, climbed in, and let the hot water pound her neck. Sam was probably out grabbing breakfast and coffee. Dressed in jeans and a Boston Red Sox sweatshirt, she scanned the sidewalks from her picture window. Lots of people were hustling along, but there was no sign of Sam.

CJ tried Sam's cell phone and got her voicemail. "Good morning, Sam. You weren't here when I woke up. Are you getting food? Call me."

An hour later, an uneasiness crept in. *Where are you?* CJ punched Ben's number. He said he hadn't seen her since last night when she left to grab some clothes. Like CJ, Ben was uneasy. Sam wouldn't have left her alone. She grabbed the keys to her truck and raced down the stairs.

CJ pulled her truck onto East Bay Street and wound her way to Sam's town home. Her car was there, but looking in her windows, there was no sign of life inside. *That doesn't look right.* The door of Sam's Honda Civic was cracked open. She peered through the window to see an overnight bag and Piggly Wiggly sack.

She backed away and pulled out her cell phone. "Ben. It's me again. Are you busy? I'm at Sam's, and something doesn't look right. She's not here, but I found her car door partially open."

"I'm on my way," he said. "Be there in ten. I've got Jake with me."

While she waited, she called everyone she could think of who might know where Sam was—her parents, Harry, Will, and Johnny. But, unfortunately, no one had seen or talked to her. CJ fought not to cry as fear gripped her. Then, finally, Ben arrived, and Jake nuzzled against her leg. She rubbed his baby-soft ears and tried to calm herself.

Ben rubbed his neck and shifted his weight. "This doesn't look right at all. I'm calling Eddie to see if he's on today. There's a smudge on the window, and we need to check it out."

Eddie was off but arrived within twenty minutes, along with two techs. CJ and Ben stood silently as he dusted the window. "There're definitely prints," Eddie said. "They're small and probably Sam's."

One of the techs spoke up. "We have footprints over here by these hedges." He squatted. "There are broken limbs, and it looks like someone dragged something. Someone went through here recently."

"What's on the other side?" CJ asked.

"Looks like an alley," the tech said. "I'll go round and check it out." He jogged down the driveway. Moments later, he yelled, "Tire tracks. Someone was parked here."

CJ's eyes went wide at Ben. "Oh, shit! Someone took her."

Ben held up his hands. "We don't know that. Let's let these guys do their thing and keep calling around. I'm sure it's fine." His face didn't match his words.

Sam's father, Mason Ravenel, rounded the corner. "I have a spare key to her place." He bolted up the steps and opened the door.

"Hang on, Mr. Ravenel. Let us go in first . . ." Ben's voice trailed off.

Ben, CJ, and Eddie moved slowly around Sam's apartment. Nothing appeared out of place—everything was in perfect order and spotless. Eddie leaned close to the bathroom counter. "I'm gonna see if we have any prints. They'll probably be Sam's, but that'd help me eliminate what I found on her car."

Eddie finished collecting what evidence he could find, grabbed his case, and headed to the lab. He told them he'd call as soon as he had anything. CJ, Ben, and Mason tried to convince each other everything was fine. But CJ's stomach was in knots. *Something's badly wrong here.*

Eddie's early afternoon call to CJ caused all hell to break loose. The print on Sam's car was not hers. Instead, it matched the prints of whoever had killed the two women and Paul. CJ, Ben, and Johnny met at the station. News traveled fast, and the chief and Stan joined them. Jake greeted each arrival and settled under the table by CJ's feet.

The group spent an hour going over everything. A Lowcountry-wide all-points bulletin had gone out for Sam, and the chief arranged a five thirty press conference. It was CJ's job to deliver a profile. CJ and Ben sat alone in the conference room after everyone broke up.

"How are you feeling?" Ben asked.

CJ swallowed. Her determined eyes met his. "I'm fine. Embarrassed but fine."

"You up for this?"

"Hell yeah, I'm up for this," she replied. "This bastard better not have hurt Sam."

He stood. "All right then. I'll go help the crew find Sam. We've got two hours before the press conference, so you've got time to be ready to give the profile."

"Okay. Harry's coming in to help."

She watched him leave with Jake hot on his tail.

———

The chief kicked off the press conference and covered the issue at hand. A member of the Charleston Police Department had been abducted. Sam's smiling face appeared on the screen, and CJ's breath caught. He turned and introduced CJ. She provided the profile of the suspect.

"Based on the evidence so far, we believe our suspect is a Black male in his early twenties. He's of small stature and may have health issues. He's a local and knows the area. We believe he's driving a late eighties/early nineties Ford car. Indications are he's practicing a form of hoodoo. If anyone knows of someone that fits this general profile, please call the number on the screen day or night."

As she stepped back, hands shot up, and the yelling started. "What evidence do you have? Do you think the girl is dead?"

The chief addressed a few questions before ending the conference.

———

Grannie squinted at the TV as the pretty detective with emerald-green eyes and auburn hair spoke—she had circles under her eyes, and strain was evident in her face. Grannie got up, moved to the porch, and eased into her rocker. She slowly rocked. *He's taken someone close to her.* Grannie closed her eyes and rocked faster. *She'll be coming to me soon.*

FIFTY-NINE

Monday, December 20
St. Helena Island

At 4:47 a.m., CJ's cell phone rang, and she lunged to grab it off her kitchen counter. "Detective O'Hara."

"Detective, this is Officer Phillips with the Beaufort PD. We found Lieutenant Paul Grimes's truck."

Her heart raced. "Where?"

"In a marsh behind Moberley's Grocery on St. Helena Island. We're pulling it out of the marsh. So, it'll be ready for you to look if you want."

"I'm on my way."

"I'll text you the address."

CJ was already half-dressed. She buttoned her jeans; slid a black, long-sleeve T-shirt over her head; and yanked on her boots. She opened her closet, grabbed a jacket, and slipped it on. Then, her hair pulled into a ponytail, she crammed on a Charleston PD baseball hat and flew down the steps.

The blue flashing lights cut through the darkness as she roared across the Arthur Ravenel Jr. Bridge, doing more than eighty miles per hour. She called Ben, and he agreed to meet her and said he would call Johnny.

After two days of agony and no Sam, CJ hoped for some progress. Perhaps the truck could lead them to their suspect and Sam. She fought the gnawing in her stomach. This could mean the search area was more extensive than they thought—and Sam was already dead. *Stop it!*

December 20. *Tonight's the blood moon.* Her fingers squeezed the wheel, and she accelerated.

———

As CJ skidded to a stop, she saw no less than six Beaufort PD cruisers in front of the one-story red brick building. The sun was rising, and rays reached up above the marsh. CJ flashed her badge, and an officer directed her to the back of the store. Beyond the parking lot, Paul's muddy truck sat attached to a tow truck.

An officer about her age approached and introduced himself—Officer Phillips. "Have you looked inside yet?" she asked.

He shook his head. "No. We wanted to wait on you."

CJ exhaled, pulled on latex gloves, and stepped forward. Water, brownish yellow and cold, covered her feet as she opened the driver's-side door. She leaned in, her eyes scanning. Nothing stood out. No blood or signs of a struggle.

Using her Maglite, she checked under and behind the seat. No trash. No junk. She inspected every inch of the interior. There were no signs of foul play. She turned to Officer Phillips. "Did you walk the area along the marsh?"

"Yes, ma'am. Didn't see nothing."

She walked to the water's edge. "How deep is this?"

He shrugged. "I'm not sure. I'd guess five to ten feet. It all depends on the tides. We found it because the tide was out."

"Who found it?"

"One of our officers was patrolling the area and caught a reflection off the truck's mirror with his headlights. Didn't know what it was, so she checked and called it in. We've all been lookin' for the vehicle."

CJ nodded. "You have forensics?"

"Yeah. Not like Charleston, but we have a couple of damn good techs here. They're waiting until you give 'em the go-ahead."

"Okay. They can proceed." She handed him her card. "Ask them to give me a call at this number if they find anything."

A scream broke the morning calm. Paul Jr. was running across the parking lot toward the truck. CJ raced and intercepted him. He tried to pull away until he surrendered, crying on her shoulder.

"I heard on the scanner. It's Dad's," he sobbed.

She managed to talk him into waiting in her truck. As the door closed, Ben jogged up. "Paul's?" he asked.

She nodded. "Forensics is inspecting it now, but I didn't find anything."

Ben sighed. "I guess Paul wasn't killed in his truck."

CJ's head snapped up to the brown sign with white letters—Moberley's Grocery. "What if he was inside there?" She pointed at the store.

"I'm on it," Ben responded.

CJ was peering into the front window of the dark store when he returned. "They're calling the owner and getting him over here. He doesn't usually open until ten o'clock."

They turned to find Paul Jr. standing behind them. "I have a key. Well, I know where one is kept." He wiped his eyes. "This is where I work part-time."

"Whattaya think, CJ?" Ben asked. "Wait on the owner or go in?"

"Let's go in. The owner can kiss my ass if he gets pissed off." She started toward the building. "We gotta find something to lead us to this guy. He has Sam."

Paul Jr. led them to the back door, dropped to a knee, and reached under the siding. Key in hand, he unlocked the door and flipped on the lights. The back room came to life. "Old man Moberley will probably fire me, but I don't give a shit."

CJ stepped past him. "We'll say we were going to break down the door, but you saved it by letting us in."

The floors, walls, and shelves showed no signs of a crime. CJ crawled along on her knees, moving the beam. "This looks like a grate." She stood and grabbed the posts of the shelves. "Let's move this rack back."

She and Ben pulled the metal rack away. She shined her Maglite on the wire mesh covering the grate. "Ben, I think we have blood. Let's get a tech in here."

A red-faced man of about sixty barreled through the back door. "How in the fuck did you get in here? You guys have no right to enter my—"

CJ jumped up, her eyes blazing. "We have a crime scene and a missing woman. Unless you want to be arrested, you'll haul your ass back outside."

Paul Jr. spoke up. "Mr. Moberley, I let them in."

Moberley huffed and glared at CJ. "Fine. I expect you to pay for anything you break, and no freebies."

CJ and Ben waited until the forensics crew finished. There was nothing in the truck, but there was blood inside the store. They'd send the sample to the lab for DNA analysis. Everyone packed up and headed out. It was now late afternoon. CJ stood with Ben in the parking lot, her eyes fixed on Paul Jr., who sat in her truck, his head bowed. "Ben, I have something I need to do. You head back. I'll catch up later," she said to him.

He looked puzzled as he slowly nodded.

CJ opened her truck door and joined Paul Jr. "You up for a short ride?"

His eyes lifted. "Yeah. Sure. I got no place to be. Where are we going?"

CJ put the truck into drive and whipped it out of the parking lot. "You'll see."

———

Paul Jr.'s jaw dropped. "Why are we going here?"

CJ steered onto the dirt driveway that led to the single-story white house with black shutters as the light of day dimmed. "I need information to find my friend, and this is the last place I can get it. My time is running out."

"I'm not sure she'll talk to you. She's not much for strangers."

"We'll see. Wait here." CJ stepped out of the truck.

Grannie's green cat eyes were fixed on her as she came up the stone path. She slowly rocked and waited.

CJ smiled. "Hello, Grannie. It's good to see you again. I wonder if we could talk. I need your help."

The old woman didn't speak. She rocked back and forth as her eyes closed.

CJ waited, cleared her throat, and tried again. "Grannie, please. Paul's been killed, and my friend is in trouble, and I need your help." She waited several minutes—no response. Finally, she turned back for her truck. She motioned to Paul Jr. "Come with me."

He followed her back to the porch. "Grannie, I can understand it if you don't want to talk to me. If you don't like me, fine. But I need your help to catch the man who murdered his dad, your friend, Paul, and who will kill my friend. So, if you won't do it for me, do it for him." She pushed Paul Jr. forward.

The chair stopped, and Grannie's eyes opened. Paul Jr. stepped to her and took her hand. "Please help her, Grannie. Please. He killed my dad." His tears dripped onto her lap.

Grannie hugged him tight and finally smiled. "Okay, baby. You go back to the truck now, ya hear?" She leaned around him, and her bony finger pointed at CJ. "You come with me," she said in perfect English.

The old woman shuffled into a small living room and waved her hand. "Sit there." CJ obeyed and dropped to the couch, upholstered with a print of bright yellow and red flowers. Grannie pulled a wicker chair over within two feet of CJ and pushed up the sleeves of her white sweater. She extended her hands. CJ was confused but reached and took them.

"Don't let go of my hands and keep your eyes closed." CJ did as she was told.

Mumbling in Gullah, Grannie squeezed her fingers.

The darkness faded into light. A boy, about eight, sat alone at a table eating cereal. There was a sudden crash, and an old man entered the room. The boy recoiled as the old man drew back his hand. The boy hit the floor hard.

The old woman moaned, and CJ opened her eyes. "Grannie. Are you okay?"

"Hush, child. Close your eyes."

The boy was older now, maybe ten. He climbed in the small, dark window. The door burst open, and the old man staggered across the room, grabbing the boy and throwing him against the wall. He unbuckled his pants.

CJ jerked her hands away. "God, no. Please no. Grannie, why are you doing this?"

Grannie reached and retook her hands. "Quiet, child. Keep your eyes closed. Hold my hands tight. You'll see what you need . . . to save Sam."

How does she know her name? Did she hear it on TV? CJ wondered as the connection grew again.

The boy reappeared. The little corner where he sat was dark. His eyes were glued to a different old man with milky eyes sitting in the center of the room. The old man mumbled—Gullah words—and lit six white candles. He cut something up—some kind of . . . root. He motioned to the boy, who approached him.

Grannie moaned again, but CJ squeezed her fingers and kept her eyes shut tight.

The boy was around eighteen. He watched someone from the shadows—a faceless woman in her nightgown. He crawled through the window, slipped down the hall—the woman was asleep. The knife rose and—there was a red spray.

CJ flinched, but she held on and kept her eyes shut. Grannie whispered, "Last one, child."

There was a road through a devastated forest. The trees were snapped off halfway up. The car turned onto a dirt road leading into the ruined forest and moved through heavy brush. A building appeared out of the mist—more of a weathered shack.

The door opened, then another. A woman was chained, lying on the cold floor. Sam! She was still until her eyes popped open.

CJ jerked her hands away and fell backward. Grannie's breathing was ragged, sweat poured from her forehead, and her eyes were closed. CJ kneeled in front of her. "Grannie? Grannie? Are you okay?"

The old woman's eyes remained closed as she patted CJ's hand. "I need to rest, child. Go. Go find Sam and—be careful."

"Grannie, I don't know where the building is." She shook her head. "I didn't see any signs. How can I find it?"

The old woman's eyes fluttered open. "Leave Paul Jr. here. You go. I'll guide you as best I can. The man you're looking for is named Elias. Goodbye, CJ O'Hara."

CJ stared, shocked, for a long minute. Then she raced to the truck with no clue where she was going. She told Paul Jr. to stay with Grannie and take care of her.

At the end of the driveway, she glanced right, then left. *Which way? I think it's right.* She jammed the gas pedal and spun onto the road. *Where are the trees I saw?*

At a crossroads, she sat, confused. *Right or left? Damn it! I need Grannie's help. Wait!* She closed her eyes and whispered, "Help me, Grannie." She saw it. Right again!

CJ was flying, and gravel bounced off the truck, but she couldn't slow down. The sun was gone. The moon was taking over. She saw it in the dim light—the ruined forest and the pathway through the heavy brush. CJ swerved through the path's entrance, slammed on her brakes, and closed her eyes.

She floated along the path, through the brush, and it appeared—the shack where she would find Sam.

She eased her foot onto the gas pedal and moved forward.

SIXTY

Monday, December 20
St. Helena Island

The truck lights off, CJ eased ahead until she was within fifty yards of the odd-looking shack. She cut the engine, checked her weapon, and stepped out. The air was still and crisp. Eeriness surrounded her in the growing moonlight.

She paused, looking for movement. How much noise had she made, and did he know she was coming? Her mind flashed back to the last time she had been in this situation—ambushed, captured, and almost killed. She kneeled and pulled out her cell phone. There was only a weak signal.

After three tries, she was connected. "Helen, this is CJ. I need backup, but I'm in St. Helena. I've found the man who killed Paul and the two women. Get Beaufort PD over here ASAP. Whoever's closest."

"Will do. Are you alone?"

"Yes. I'll wait on backup before proceeding."

CJ gave Helen the best directions she could, describing the broken trees. When she hung up, she slipped along the path to within twenty feet of the shack. The building was tattered, a faded brown, and the wood-shingle roof sagged. One window was visible, but a heavy curtain blocked her from looking inside. There was a dim light. She waited.

The moon hung above, peering down at her—full and tangerine orange with faint gray-shaded dimples. Then, as she waited for what seemed like forever, the orange started turning dark red . . . the color of blood.

The dead silence was broken by a muffled scream.

Fuck it. I can't wait.

She drew her Glock and crept forward in the moonlight almost as bright as day. At the door, she listened. No sounds at first, then a chain rattled. She pressed her eye against a tiny crack between the door and the frame. *Sam! She's alive.*

Her head snapped back when the body of a man blocked her view. She moved to the side of the door, crouched, and held her breath, finger on the side of the trigger. *Where the hell is backup?*

She peeked through the crack again. Sam stood in the center of the room with her hands tied to a pole. She was naked except for her panties. Tears ran down her cheeks, and she was pleading with the man who she suspected was

Elias. He was on one knee, doing something—cutting a root of some type with a crude knife. He was mumbling strange words—*Gullah*.

CJ inhaled, stepped back, and splintered the door open with a kick. Elias jumped to his feet, knife in hand, and got behind Sam. The knife went tight against her neck as he stared at the barrel of CJ's gun.

"Charleston PD! Drop the knife, Elias."

The scarred face emerged from behind Sam—pale ice-blue eyes more pinkish in the dim light, close-cropped dark yellow hair, bleached-looking skin, and a flat nose. His enormous nostrils flared as he took deep breaths. *He's an albino.*

Elias stood no more than five feet four and couldn't have weighed more than one hundred twenty pounds. His voice trembled. "Leave me alone."

CJ closed the distance and stood her ground fifteen feet away. "You okay, Sam?"

"I'm not hurt."

"You're safe now. Elias, drop the damn knife. Now!"

His eyes grew wet, and tears trickled as his shoulders shook with his sobs. "I can't. I have to finish."

CJ shifted her weight into a better shooting position. "Finish what, Elias?"

"My plan. I have to do the last step." His sobs turned to anger. "You're fucking everything up." His fingers on the knife twitched.

Sam whispered, "Please let me go. I'll make sure someone helps you. I understand—"

"You don't understand! No one does!" he screamed. His eyes fixed on CJ. "Get out so I can finish. I need her heart."

Hoping to de-escalate things, CJ softly said, "Elias, you know I can't leave . . . I'll have to kill you if you don't put down the knife. Please don't make me."

The sound of sirens grew louder in the distance, and his eyes grew wider and wilder. CJ knew he was at his breaking point. He'd hurt Sam if she didn't stop him, and that meant killing him.

Officers rushed up behind CJ, guns drawn. "Beaufort PD!"

CJ yelled over her shoulder, "Hang back, guys." She knew Elias was staring down multiple gun barrels by the look in his eyes. The young man was terrified. His face was in plain sight, and she had a clean shot. *Is this on purpose, or is he just inexperienced? Okay. Let's try one more time.*

Her finger gently touched the face of the trigger. "Elias, last chance. Drop the knife and surrender. Make it easy for both of us. Please. I don't want to kill you."

His tongue went back and forth across his lips, his eyes darted, and he trembled.

Please, Elias.

He suddenly went calm. His body was rigid as his eyes bored through her. His fingers tightened on the knife, and he smirked. "Fuck you!" The blade flashed up.

The explosion of the Glock broke the night's silence. Elias staggered backward in a red spray. CJ rushed to Sam, wrapped her arms around her, and kissed her forehead. "Can someone bring me a blanket? Anything to cover her."

She pushed the tangled hair out of the younger woman's face. "Did he hurt you?"

Sam leaned on her. "No."

CJ stared into her eyes. "Did he . . . he—"

Sam shook her head and rested it on CJ's shoulder. "No. He didn't rape me. In a weird way, he was nice to me."

CJ squeezed her. "Okay. No more talking for now. We can go over the details later. You're safe." An officer carefully cut the ropes and freed Sam.

A female officer found Sam's clothes and helped her dress before loading her into an ambulance. Flashing blue and red lights helped the moon, now blood red, light up the night sky. CJ rounded the corner of the shack and stopped to catch her breath. A strange sensation came over her, and she closed her eyes.

Grannie sat in her favorite chair on the porch, a patchwork quilt draped over her. She was slowly rocking with her eyes closed. Then her eyes fluttered open, and she smiled.

CJ's eyes popped open, and she put her hand in the pocket of her jacket. She pulled out the small red object—the mojo bag Grannie had given her. She'd forgotten about it. *Grannie protected me.*

───

Ben skidded his truck to a stop alongside flashing lights, followed closely by Johnny. Both men ran to the shack. "Where's Detective O'Hara?" Ben asked.

An officer pointed. "She's over there somewhere in the woods."

CJ sat alone on a stump at the edge of the flawed forest, her emerald-green eyes skyward. The moon was spectacularly beautiful and terrifying at the same time. She wiped her tears and headed to the two men as they raced toward her.

He made me kill him.

Saturday, April 17
Wando

Charleston was awash in colors. The trees and flowers were blooming, and the grass was a deep green. Three full moons had passed since the blood moon in December—wolf, snow, and worm. The pink moon would rise later that night.

CJ sat alone on a bench. Her eyes were fixed on her pelican, grooming himself on a post in the marsh—such a funny-looking bird. She was lost in thoughts of her time in Charleston and three major cases that had nearly killed her and Sam. She'd lost her boss and friend, Paul.

Former officer Jared Parker had taken his own life in a jail cell. Prison had proved to be too much for him. Cops who were serial rapists never fared well behind bars. But, try as she might, she had no sympathy for him. She was happy his wife had moved on and found love.

The capture of Asher Copeland had closed the book on the Lowcountry Killer case once and for all. He'd spend what was left of his miserable life in prison after a jury of his peers convicted him on all counts. Her heart still ached for the twelve victims he and Bryan Parrish had taken. She felt responsible for their deaths, though everyone reminded her about how many she had saved. *Really?*

Paul Jr. had gotten good news. He'd been accepted into USC, and she knew Paul would be proud. CJ planned to help him move in his dorm.

Elias's death still woke her up at night. A young man who never had a chance—no mother, an absent father, and a grandfather who'd abused him. Perhaps God had delivered justice when his bastard of a grandfather choked to death on his own vomit after a three-day drinking binge.

How could I have saved Elias? Second-guessing was an everyday occurrence. Only three people had attended his funeral the day after Christmas—ironically, Sam, Grannie, and CJ . . . a woman he'd tried to kill, one instrumental in catching him, and the one who'd ended his life. She hadn't seen Grannie since. *I should go visit her.*

CJ stood and wiped her eyes. *At least I made sure he got a proper burial.* The Brick Baptist Church cemetery was a beautiful resting place. She walked across the grass to join the others. "Come on, boy." The black Lab wagged his tail and followed.

Ben stood at the edge of the yard, grinning. "Come on, you two. We can't have a party without the guest of honor."

CJ spread her arms. "We're coming. Jake wanted to meet my pelican." He took her hand and led her up the path.

———

The fish fry at Harry's was reaching full swing. Everyone gathered around the makeshift plywood tables with red-and-white checkered tablecloths. Harry laughed as he placed trays on the tables—fried grouper fingers, potato salad, coleslaw, and hush puppies. CJ immediately grabbed one of the golden-brown balls.

CJ smiled as she watched Sam and Will. She was happy Sam had found someone who adored her. She and Will had been dating and had even said the L-word to each other. They made a cute couple—Will at six three, Sam at only five six.

"Did you hear about Wendy Watts?" Johnny asked her.

"No," she replied. "What about her?"

"Well, it seems our lovable Wendy Watts is now tormenting the Charlotte PD. She landed a coanchor gig."

I wonder if this is the work of Congressman Lee.

When everyone's bellies were full, Harry and Sam went to work clearing the tables. Harry was anxious to bring out the desserts he'd bought at the Wreck—key lime pie and banana pudding.

Thomas sidled up to CJ. "So, young lady, you look like you're feeling much better. I understand your latest blood work came back with better numbers."

"Yes. I do feel better. I guess the doctor was right." *And maybe the mojo bag Grannie gave me is helping too.*

"Keep taking those vitamins and supplements—and eat."

She smiled. *Laying off the liquor works too.* "Yes, boss. By the way, I understand you're retiring."

Thomas exhaled. "Yeah. Well, not until the end of the year. Wife and I are gonna travel and spend more time with the grandkids."

"I'm happy for you. It's certainly well deserved." *I'm going to miss you more than you know.*

Bill approached CJ carrying a little girl with dark brown hair and brown eyes in his arms. His granddaughter, Alina. Sasha, the little girl's mother smiled brightly. She had agreed to move from Sitka to Charleston so Alina could be close to her grandfather and uncles.

"Isn't my granddaughter the prettiest thing you've ever seen, CJ?"

"She's darling," she replied. "Try not to spoil her too much."

The crowd quieted when Chief Williams rapped on a beer bottle. He stood halfway up the steps to the deck and motioned to CJ and Stan. "Come on up here, guys."

They joined him. "First, thanks to Harry for hosting a great party." Everyone clapped, and Harry took a small bow. "We'll have the formal ceremony in a couple of days, but I'd like to congratulate CJ on her promotion to lieutenant." More clapping, catcalls, and whistles. "We'll redo this, but, Stan, can you do the honors?"

Harry beamed as Stan pinned the *Lieutenant O'Hara* name tag on her chest. She smiled on the outside. But inside, she could only think of Paul. *This isn't the way I wanted to make lieutenant.*

After everyone had left, Ben took CJ's hand and led her to the edge of the marsh. The moon, now full and bright white, was high in the night sky. They stood staring out at the moonlight on the water until he spoke. "You know, CJ, I've been doing a lot of thinking." He cleared his throat and turned to her, gently using his hand to lift her chin. "I thought I'd lost you and it scared me. It's been four months but I can't seem to shake it—I can't lose you. I'm not sure what I want exactly but . . . would you let me take you to dinner?"

CJ smiled at him. "On two conditions."

"What's that?"

"You kiss me—and we bring Jake." She grinned.

He leaned down and softly kissed her. He wrapped his arms around her and they stood silently until her cell phone buzzed and broke the stillness. She looked at the text. "Sorry, Ben. I gotta go. We have a body."

Here we go again.

THE END

ACKNOWLEDGMENTS

First and foremost, I'd like to thank my readers. Writing has always been one of my dreams and I'm honored that so many have taken the time to take this journey with me.

Since I wrote this book for you, the reader, I hope you enjoyed it. I would be grateful if you could write a review if you did. Reviews are your way of introducing others to a book that intrigued and perhaps even caused you to read with the lights on. I'd love to hear what you think.

I also love to hear from my readers. You can reach me on my Facebook page, through my website, on Instagram, Twitter, or Goodreads. Please see the About the Author page for details.

This book would not have been possible without the inspiration from the people and places that make up the Lowcountry. The locations, most of the streets, and the restaurants are authentic.

I'm incredibly grateful to those restaurants who granted me permission to include them in my novels: Poogan's Porch, the Boathouse at Breach Inlet, Vickery's, The Wreck of the Richard and Charlene, Coconut Joe's, Henry's on the Market, and Dunleavy's Pub. If you make it to Charleston, I highly recommend you give any or all of them a visit.

It takes a village to publish a book, and I owe a giant thank you to all those who helped with beta reading, editing, and designing: Janet Carbone, Nancy Caudell Wesley, Destyn Hera, James Osborne, R. Ramey Guerrero, Aja Pollock, Michael Schuler, and Danna Mathias Steele.

Finally, I thank my wife, Lisa, for her continued support.

ALL THE NATURAL BEAUTIES

A cop starting over. A murderer on the loose. Will she prove she belongs, or is this her final case?

Boston. CJ O'Hara is drowning in guilt. Still struggling with her family's deaths, her emotions boil over when the driven policewoman fatally dispatches a culprit holding a gun to her colleague's head. So when she's denied a well-deserved promotion, she takes a job offer in Charleston, South Carolina, to track down a serial killer scattering the Lowcountry with corpses.

Though glad to be closer to the man who raised her, CJ attracts the wrong kind of attention as the city's first female detective. And while clues remain scarce, the haunted cop battles local prejudice, an escalating body count, and a handsome new partner who may not be what he seems.

In a twisted race against time, is the transplanted Northerner the hunter or the prey?

All the Natural Beauties is the riveting first book in the CJ O'Hara crime thriller series. If you like complex characters, nail-biting page-turners, and surprise endings, then you'll love this dark mystery.

ABOUT THE AUTHOR

John grew up in the South and currently lives with his wife in the California Bay Area. He lived and worked in Charleston for ten years and fell in love with the Lowcountry. Connect with John on his website, www.johndealbks.com, or via social media:

www.facebook.com/JohnDealBooks

www.instagram.com/johndealbks

www.twitter.com/JohnDealBks

www.ingramcontent.com/pod-product-compliance
Lightning Source LLC
Chambersburg PA
CBHW061052210726
48294CB00001B/122